Also by Sandra L Rostirolla

YA/Fantasy

The Cecilia Series

Cecilia—The Last Croilar Tier
Cecilia—The Order of Terefellian
Cecilia—The Caladium

YA/Coming of Age

Making Friends With Monsters

BOOK
3

CECILIA

THE CALADIUM

SANDRA L ROSTIROLLA

Pinkus Books

www.pinkusbooks.com

Sandra L Rostirolla

www.slrostirolla.com

Cecilia - The Caladium
The Cecilia Series - Book 3

Library of Congress Control Number: 2020925747

ISBN 978-0-9991891-4-6
ISBN 978-0-9991891-5-3 (eBook)

Cover Design by Ivan Cakic
Map by Matthew R. Hinshaw
Interior Text Design by Phillip Gessert

Printed in the United States of America

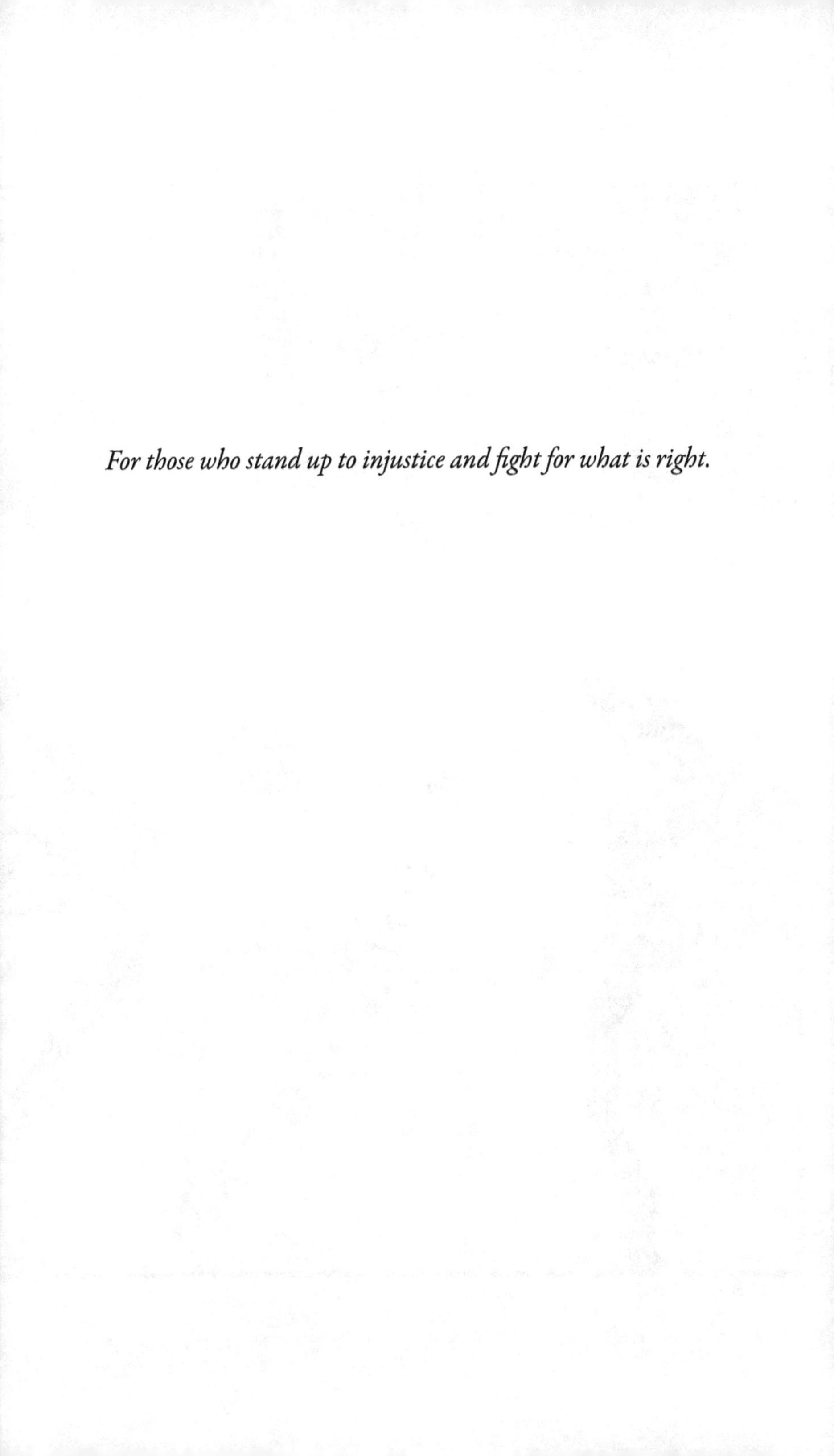

For those who stand up to injustice and fight for what is right.

N
BODWIN MOUNTAINS
Wym Forest
Braan River
Rabbit Cove
VITUS
EZEKIAN ISLA
EPONA OCEAN
Terefellian Valley

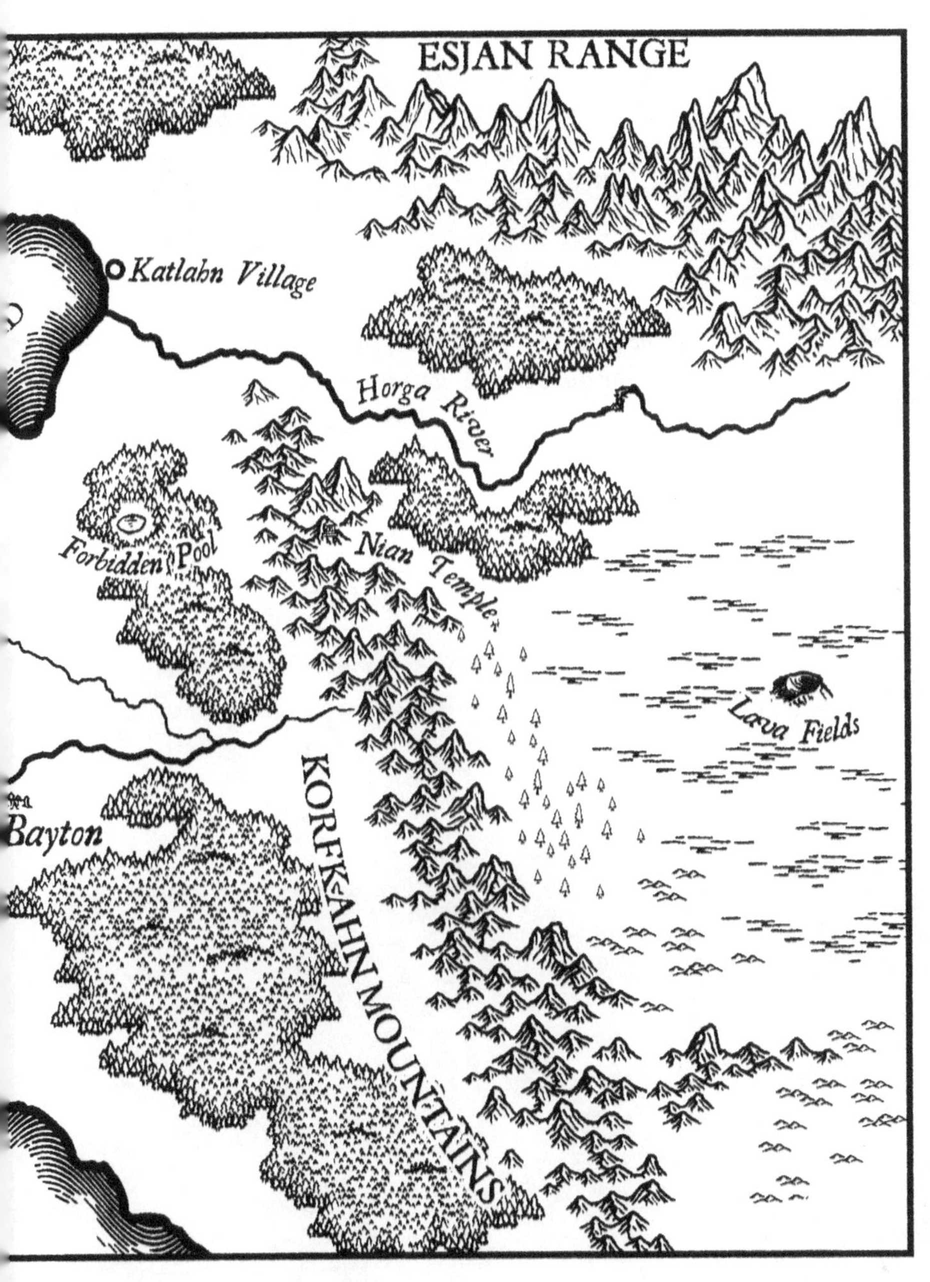

ESJAN RANGE
Katlahn Village
Horga River
Forbidden Pool
Nian Temple
Lava Fields
Bayton
KORFKAHN MOUNTAINS

*"In the absence of good, there can be no evil.
For there can be nothing at all."*

St. Augustine (354-430 AD)

A PAIR OF dark-skinned feet wearing leather sandals strode down a flight of stone stairs. The muscular calves connected to the feet disappeared under flowing, three-quarter-length trousers. The owner of these legs held Cecilia over his shoulder. Where was she? What was happening? The last thing she remembered was waking up in a small white room and talking with a dark-skinned woman, who had introduced herself as Countess Kosima of Bayton.

"Who am I?" Cecilia had asked.

"Your name is Cecilia," the Countess had replied. "As for who you are, you're just a girl who once had a dreadful nightmare. But you're safe now."

Cuddled under a lilac blanket, Cecilia had felt safe. Right now, she didn't. She tried to call for help, but no words came. Even if she could move, would she have been able to fight her way free from this hulking man's grasp?

Moss growing between the steps and an earthy scent suggested Cecilia was outside. Darkness confirmed that whoever carried her did so under the cover of night.

The sandaled feet stopped at a river where a rope moored a dinghy to a pebbly shore. The man laid her inside the rickety vessel next to another body—a white male with excessively short, dark brown hair, dressed in light blue clothing that matched Cecilia's wide-legged cotton pants and short-sleeved pullover. Was this person alive? Warmth radiating from his body suggested he was.

Her captor scanned the direction they'd come, perhaps worried someone was following him. *Please! Anyone! Help me!* she tried to yell, but the words remained locked in her mind.

The man's muscular arms rippled as he covered her and the unconscious person with a canvas blanket. Her heart thumped into her throat. Where was he taking them? Was he going to kill them?

The boat wobbled as he pushed it from the shore. He stepped aboard and a ray of moonlight illuminated a gold ring on his toe. Why did this ring seem familiar? Had Cecilia seen it before? Straining hard against the heaviness of her brain, she fought for answers, but her mind remained blank.

The man sat at the dinghy's back end. After a series of abrupt, mechanical-sounding splutters, a harsh throttling noise rang out, sending the boat lurching forward. The sound settled into a continuous whir that sent pleasant vibrations down her spine. Combined with the repetitive slap of water against the hull, a hypnotic effect took hold. Unable to fight the heaviness pooling in her eyelids, they fluttered closed.

The canvas cover lifted and chilly air clawed at Cecilia's skin. The whirring sound and vibrations had stopped, as had the forward movement. She blinked up at the dark-skinned man. Where was she? How long had she been asleep?

The boat rocked as he stepped into the water and dragged the dinghy to a muddy shore.

Moonlight silhouetted a dark canopy of trees.

The man flung a long canvas bag over his shoulder. "Eideard, my man," he said, patting the young man's cheek. "Wake up." His tone was soft. If he'd planned to harm them, wouldn't he be gruff and short-tempered?

The person next to her—Eideard was his name—opened his eyes. His brow furrowed at her and the dark-skinned man. Everything seemed as strange to him as it did to Cecilia.

"I know you don't remember me," the man said. "My name is Malek. You're both probably scared and confused, but I need you to trust me. You're safe now, okay?"

The Countess had told Cecilia the same thing. Who was telling the truth? Cecilia had certainly felt safer—and warmer—back in her bed.

After helping Eideard out of the boat, Malek offered his broad hand to her. "Do you think you can stand?"

She wiggled her toes. Earlier, her limbs had been entirely numb. With the return of some sensation, maybe her legs could hold her weight. Maybe she could run away. She reached for his hand, but her floppy arm dropped. Still a prisoner to her useless body, she remained at Malek's mercy.

"It's okay," he said. "Your strength will return." Picking her up, he waved for Eideard to follow. "Come on, my man. This way."

As Malek carried Cecilia along a muddy trail, Eideard obediently trudged behind. Stopping at a tree several feet from the shoreline, Malek leaned Cecilia against the trunk. "Do you think you can stand here? It's too wet to sit down."

She pressed her feet into the ground. They felt firmly planted. Unable to tell him, "I'll be fine," she nodded.

"Make sure she doesn't fall," Malek said to Eideard. "I'll be back in a minute." He let her go and trotted back to the boat.

With her chance to flee at hand, Cecilia leaned forward. She had expected her feet to follow, but they remained planted.

SPLAT! She landed face first in the rich soil. Something about the scent of decaying vegetation seemed familiar. Comforting. She eased onto her side. Her floppy hand slapped her cheek as she attempted to wipe the mud from her face.

Malek pulled the dinghy out of the water and covered it with camouflage netting. Spotting Cecilia on the ground, he sighed. He seemed genuinely grieved as he rushed back along the mushy ground. "It's all right," he said, sitting her up. "I got you."

Pulling a clean cloth from his pocket, he wiped her face and hands. For a man his size, he had a surprisingly gentle touch. He glanced at Eideard, who stared in the direction of nothing. "I thought you were looking after your sister."

Sister? What?

Malek gently shook Eideard by the shoulder. "Hey. Are you in there?"

Eideard blinked at him.

"There you go," Malek said. He smiled, exposing glistening white teeth. "I want you to follow me. Okay?" Eideard's unresponsiveness didn't seem to hinder Malek's enthusiasm. "You got this. Just keep your eyes on my feet."

Eideard's gaze dropped to Malek's sandals, as did Cecilia's. She narrowed in on the golden toe ring. What was so curious about it? Had she met Malek before? He seemed to know her and Eideard. Why didn't she remember him? Or Eideard? If the young man was her brother, surely she should know him.

"All right," Malek said to her. "For now, it looks like you're coming with me." He hoisted her up and over his shoulder.

Unable to see much, Cecilia focused on the schlip-schlop sound of Malek's sandals as they trudged along the damp undergrowth. He carried her across streams, up and down rocky embankments, over felled trees, and through veils of tangled vines. The deeper they went into the forest, the more at peace Cecilia felt.

"Nearly there," Malek said.

She craned her neck around his side to see what "nearly there" meant. Malek walked toward a grass-covered mound about ten feet high and just as wide. This couldn't be their destination, could it? Perhaps he was lost and was going to climb up to look around. Not that he'd see much. The thick canopy above snuffed out much of the moonlight.

Standing at the mound's base, Malek felt around the grassy slope. His searching hand stopped. He must have found what he needed. He pulled and a rectangular section of the small hill swung open. The mound wasn't a mound at all, but some kind of rudimentary hut covered with dirt and grass. Whoever built this place seemed intent on extreme privacy.

Floating amongst the cool, stale air came the mild stink of rotten eggs.

"Take a seat," Malek said, motioning to a woven mat.

Eideard lowered himself into a cross-legged position.

Seating Cecilia on a separate rug, Malek then closed the door. The small space went black. An urge to reach for Eideard's hand gripped Cecilia. If she felt this way, maybe he truly was her brother?

A sizzling sound of an igniting match cut through the silence. The flame illuminated Malek lighting a lantern. He dialed up the glow, allowing a clearer view of the cramped space. Strips of arched sticks bound with twine formed the foundation of the mud hut's cone shape. On the compacted ground to Cecilia's right sat four wooden buckets. Two appeared empty. One looked filled with water, and the other . . . her face crumpled. What was that black stuff?

Scooping a ladleful of the dark liquid into two cups, Malek handed one to Cecilia and the other to Eideard. "This will help," he said.

As though he hadn't had water in days, Eideard downed his drink in a single gulp.

Unable to hold the mug with one hand, Cecilia cupped it with both, brought it to her nose, and sniffed. Ugh. This was where the rancid egg stink came from. Malek couldn't seriously want her to drink this gunk, could he?

"What is this?" she tried to ask, but her words remained mumbled. She studied Eideard. He seemed okay. She took a small sip and gagged at the foul taste. She went to put the mug down, but Malek insisted she finish it.

Drips escaped the side of her mouth as she reluctantly gulped. *Yuck.* She needed to wash the horrid taste away. She reached for the water bucket, but her arm flopped. "Wa-wa," she mumbled.

"No," said Malek.

Eideard's breath labored. His face contorted as he cried out.

Cecilia tensed. What was happening to him? She glared at Malek. "W-what . . . are . . ."

Ignoring her, Malek held an empty bucket under Eideard's chin.

Eideard gagged, then vomited. Sweat glistened on his brow as he flopped to his side and moaned.

Cecilia's insides cramped. Oh no! Was the same thing happening to her? Doubling over in agony, she cried out. What was this nightmare? Had Malek poisoned her? Her belly twisted as its contents flew out and into the bucket Malek held for her. Feverish, she flopped down and began shivering.

Setting the puke bucket to the ground, Malek pressed his lips to his clamped hands and watched Cecilia and Eideard's torment play out. Was this all part of some sick plan? Did he enjoy seeing life struggle against death? As her insides ripped apart, Cecilia focused on the lantern's yellow beam. She had a strange sense that at the time of death, a light would come for her. Everything about this excruciating moment convinced her she was dying. She closed her eyes and prayed for the brightness to take her. But in the darkness, no light came.

WHEN SAFFRON HAD first stepped into this burned landscape, she had allowed the death and destruction of the surrounding trees and wildlife to strangle her soul. As she and Rabbie continued their journey northward to Vitus, she no longer saw the ugliness. Instead, she noticed the beauty of life as it burst through the blackness. Tiny green buds formed on stumps that otherwise seemed dead. Miniature green leaves sprouted from charcoal trunks, and grass tufts patterned the ashen surface with emerald dots.

The fire-ravaged panorama gave way to bushes and sporadic pines. Rusted cars and trucks littered the cracked road that she and Rabbie followed. Through their interspersed chatter, Saffron sensed Rabbie's worry. Had they done the right thing in letting Cecilia and Eideard fly away in the airship? Had his siblings made it across the ocean safely? Abandoning his brother and sister during this dangerous time surely weighed heavily. She took in his contemplative profile and was glad Rabbie had stayed with her.

Breaking the long silence, he began speaking of his life, growing up in a faraway village nestled deep in the Plockton Forest, and wistfulness engulfed her. Compared to Terefellia's unforgiving caves and biting dust, Rabbie's childhood sounded like a dream. Saffron listened intently as he told her all that had happened to him and his family, from the decimation of his village by the Soldiers of Vitus to Cecilia inspiring a rebellion against the then-Senators in what became known as the Battle for Freedom, and how the Prophecy had connected everything.

Saffron knew a little about this "prophecy." Those who worshipped Siersha, the goddess who her father considered a false god, believed in this tale. Saffron knew for certain the Terefellian queen—Eifa—existed. But Siersha—the supposed Goddess of Light? She could see the goodness of such an entity reflected in someone like Rabbie and the world he'd awoken her to, like glorious sunrises and twinkling nighttime skies. But as for the Goddess of Light being real, Saffron didn't know. She'd seen something within Cecilia repel Wirador Wosrah death-globs, but never felt what Rabbie described as "Siersha's glow" in herself. And part of her didn't want to. If not for Eifa's darkness, she wouldn't be able to maintain her hatred of her father—her people's leader. Saffron needed her anger. Without it, how would she ever exact revenge?

Some Soldiers who had massacred Rabbie's village remained alive, living side-by-side with Rabbie in the newly governed Vitus. When Saffron asked how he could forgive these men and not desire to slit their throats for what they'd done, he replied, "Under Siersha's philosophy, one doesn't have to be cold and callous in order to be tough and strong."

While Saffron could appreciate the intent of this mindset, Eifa still seemed a more powerful entity. Rabbie's people's way—Siersha's way—was to forgive. The Terefellian way—Eifa's way—was to seek revenge. Eifa, the Terefellian queen, had built her army on pain and suffering, which was why the Wirador Wosrah were so strong. Hatred was a greater force than kindness.

Saffron and Rabbie were trekking to Vitus to warn his people of Eifa's army, but to what end? How could Vitus possibly win against an army of five thousand near-indestructible Wirador Wosrah?

Over the next few days, whenever Rabbie and Saffron came across a tall pole, a high tree, or a still-standing tower, they took turns climbing the object and checking south for approaching Wirador

Wosrah, but no black warriors had come into sight. After several more miles, they hit upon a fifty-foot water tower. Saffron grabbed the lower rails.

"Uh-uh," said Rabbie. "You climbed the tree. It's my turn."

Begrudgingly, she let him go.

He clambered to the top and searched south for advancing warriors. "Clear as a whistle," he said.

"How much further to your city?"

"Probably still another couple of weeks." Turning north, Rabbie shaded his eyes with his hand. His head poked forward, as if not believing what he saw.

"What's wrong?" Saffron asked.

"If you were a Wirador Wosrah, and you were chasing an escaped Terefellian who had befriended the enemy, what would you do when you finally made it to Vitus?"

"What are you talking about?"

"Just humor me on this one."

Saffron pondered the bizarre question. "As a Wirador Wosrah, if I thought I was on the correct trail, I would expect to come upon the escapee and her companion before I reached Vitus because I know I'm faster than those I hunt. If I hadn't caught up to them, I wouldn't breach the city wall. Why expose my presence needlessly to the enemy when there was no possible way the people I chased would be there? If I'd headed to Vitus along the coastal path, I'd turn around and head back to Terefellia on the inland trail."

"That's what I was worried you'd say."

Saffron scaled the corroded ladder and joined Rabbie on the high platform. Her blood chilled at a massive dust cloud speeding their way. To spew up that much debris, at least a hundred Wirador Wosrah had to be on the hunt. Her father had sent that many?

"We have to go," Rabbie said.

Descending the water tower as quickly as they could, they ran.

The desolate surroundings offered little protection: a crumpled building here, an overturned car there.

As the sound of thunderous hooves closed in, Saffron faltered. What was the point of running? Every step only dragged out the inevitable. Her reckoning had come. She had failed her mother. And now, she had failed Rabbie. She'd been too spineless to do what she should've done before escaping Terefellia with her mother—kill her father and dispose of his tribal ring. The artifact had allowed the queen to birth the Maddowshin and build the Wirador Wosrah from the thousands of souls the Terefellians had collected over the centuries.

A deafening noise as trail bikes roared out from behind a ramshackle structure cut her despair. From the books Saffron had found inside her hideout house, she recognized the vehicles. Apparently, Rabbie wasn't the only one possessing the skill to wake up machinery from before the time of the Great War. The bikes slid to a dusty stop. With their faces covered by goggles and scarves, Saffron couldn't be certain of the riders' ages. Maybe mid-teens? Unlike Terefellians, who wore carbon-copy, neutral-colored tunics, these two dressed in a mishmash of colorful, pre-Great War clothing.

"Get on!" one of them yelled. She sounded female and wore a black T-shirt with a faded yellow smiley face. Bolting over, Saffron climbed aboard.

Rabbie hopped on behind the other rider, who wore denim trousers and a long-sleeve blue shirt with a white number "3" painted on the front.

"Hold on tight," Saffron's rider said.

As her bike sped forward, Saffron clung to the rider's waist.

Her eyes watered as biting dust stung her face.

Sneaking a peak over her shoulder, Saffron's tension eased. The distance between the bikes and the Wirador Wosrah herd was growing. Escape seemed possible.

Her joy plummeted as her bike slowed. What was happening? Why were the riders stopping? The bike engines continued rumbling as the two strangers bickered back and forth. Saffron's rider wanted to take "the pass." The other one, who sounded like a boy, insisted their "cargo" made the pass too dangerous. With the horde of Wirador Wosrah closing in, how much more dangerous could things get?

"I don't have enough fuel for the long way," Saffron's rider said. "I have no choice."

"Lyrik! You're crazy," said the boy.

While keeping the front wheel locked, Lyrik—Saffron's rider—powered the back wheel, forcing the bike to turn on itself. Saffron's gripped tightened. Why were they facing the galloping horde?

The front wheel momentarily popped into the air as the bike sped forward. Rabbie's rider was right. This girl was crazy. She raced directly toward the Wirador Wosrah. Moments before impact, Lyrik locked the brake and spun the bike into a dusty U-turn.

"Hold on," she said.

If Saffron squeezed any harder, she'd crush Lyrik's ribs.

The engine squealed as the bike burst forward. To Saffron's left, Rabbie and his rider disappeared behind a cluster of rocks.

Her eyes teared up from the sharp wind. She wiped them dry on her shoulder and looked ahead. Her breath froze at a looming ravine about twenty feet wide. Wait. What? This couldn't be "the pass," could it?

CHAPTER

3

THWUD!

The death Amalardh thought he was falling to didn't happen. Had he read the Prophecy signs wrong? The images clearly implied that before Alistair reached about eighteen months of age, Amalardh would die. He shouldn't have woken up after his mother—Senator Akantha—had stabbed him during the Battle for Freedom, and he shouldn't have survived this fall. How many times would Amalardh have to "almost" die before fulfilling the Prophecy's plan? Were these near-death experiences penance for the years he'd spent as an assassin killing mostly innocent people?

Rubbing his aching head, he opened his eyes and furrowed at a patch of blue sky. Where was he? As his foggy brain cleared, realization seeped in. He lay inside a six-foot-deep, vertical tunnel of snow that his plummeting body had created. He tried to free himself, but the layer of fresh powder that had saved his life was impossible to maneuver through.

From his pack, he unclipped the wooden snow paddles Forbillian had woven and slipped them on. Jamming their tips into the icey walls, he scaled up and out.

A few feet away, Sister Darna emerged from another hole with a pair of her own foot paddles strapped to her feet. Darna hailed from the Eifa-worshipping Terefellians. She was an elite Wrethun Lof—a Croilar Tier hunter—and Amalardh was her target. At least, he had been. Instead, she'd killed her partner and defected from her group. Amalardh had let her join him, Forbillian, and Oisin on their journey to find answers to the missing pieces of the

13

Prophecy because he couldn't very well leave her all alone in the dead Prophet's icy home.

Before Darna had dragged Amalardh over the snowy cliff, his trust in her had been thin at best. Now, he didn't trust her at all. She did, however, have his respect. Deliberately falling one hundred feet with no certainty that the snow was deep enough to cushion the landing took a level of bravery that not even Amalardh possessed. Then again, maybe her actions reflected stupidity more than courage. Amalardh took calculated risks. Luck drove the results of Darna's action, which meant she either had nothing to lose or everything to gain. Amalardh understood having nothing to lose. He'd been that way before meeting Cecilia. Nothing to lose meant not caring about dying. The flicker of uncertainty that had shot through Darna's eyes as she fell suggested she feared death. If Darna didn't have "nothing to lose" then what did she gain by separating Amalardh from Forbillian and Oisin?

He narrowed his eyes at her. "What are you playing at?"

She flicked the snow from her short brown hair and tawny tunic. "Nothing. It was an accident. How was I to know the edge would give out?" Her lying eyes held his stare.

"You pulled me with you. That was an accident, too?"

The muscles around her jaw flickered. She looked ready to tackle him.

Because of the intense heat emitted from her body, the snow under her paddles melted, causing her to sink. "We have to keep moving," she said. "Unless you're okay with my being buried here."

Amalardh remained planted. If she melted into the snow, so be it. This was her game, not his.

She squeezed her fist as if pumping an unseen ball. The act seemed to settle whatever brewed inside. "I'm sorry," she said. "It all happened so fast. I got scared." As she shuffled sideways out of her deepening snow hollow, she mumbled something about not being the right person for this.

"The right person for what?" Amalardh asked.

Her eyes widened as though she'd not intended for him to hear her. "Nothing," she said.

"Ahoy down there," called Forbillian. "Are you okay?"

In their respective animal capes, Forbillian and Oisin looked like a bear and a lynx perched on the high-up cliff edge.

"We're alive," Amalardh replied.

"Well, this is a darn mess," said Forbillian. "I told you not to trust that woman. What do we do now?"

"We could jump down to you," said Oisin.

Forbillian waved his hands. "Now, now. Let's not be hasty."

Amalardh agreed. While Oisin's light frame would easily withstand the fall, Forbillian's dense mass might not fare as well. Whatever Darna's end game, her current plan to split Amalardh from his companions seemed successful. He pulled out his map. The dotted path from the Prophet's ice home directed the journey to the topside of a waterfall along the Horga River. "Keep going south," he said to Forbillian. "We both should hit the river in about two days. Wait at the top of the waterfall. I'll walk upstream to you."

"You lay one hand on my nephew and I'll make it my life's mission to make sure you don't live long enough to talk about it," Forbillian said to Darna.

She didn't react. Forbillian's threats hadn't bothered her when he'd stood an inch from her face. Intimidation from one hundred feet away would hardly raise her concern.

"I'll be fine," said Amalardh. "I'll see you both in two days."

"At night time, you'd best tie that thing up," said Forbillian, "because she either wants your life, your flesh, or both."

CHAPTER

4

THWUD!

Blackness filled Wyndom's mind. He'd been receiving an experiential feed from Sister Darna—seeing, hearing, and feeling the world from her viewpoint—as she trekked a snowy mountain range thousands of miles away when she'd fallen from a cliff. As Wyndom felt himself plummet through the chilly air, he'd hoped the fall would kill him. The mess he was in with the Terefellian queen was too much for him to handle. Right now, a horde of Wirador Wosrah hunted his daughter, Saffron. Once they caught her, they'd return to Terefellia, where he'd either have to prove his love to his queen by killing Saffron or face his own death. But Sister Darna's fall hadn't killed Wyndom. Why would it? He'd once received a feed from a Wirador Wosrah while an explosion had blown the beast to bits and Wyndom had survived. As the Maddowshin had pointed out, a connection to the Terefellian collective conscious felt real, but it wasn't.

The fall must have had killed Sister Darna, though. Why else would the feed go black? Lying on his resting mat under the comfort of his palm tree, Wyndom rubbed his bearded face. When Sister Darna had fallen, she'd pulled Amalardh with her. Wyndom had always known the enigmatic man with the gripping blue eyes would one day have to die. For the past week, instead of killing Amalardh, Sister Darna had pretended she'd tracked him through the snowy range to protect him from her people. Why had she lied? And why had she chosen such a strange way to kill not only Amalardh, but herself?

17

He closed his eyes and sighed. Meeting Amalardh and spending time with him through Sister Darna's viewpoint had been a living dream. And now . . . Wyndom's dream was gone.

The feel of Sister Darna's chest expanding and contracting gripped him. He sat bolt upright. Darna was alive! Her feed had gone black because the fall had knocked her out. Could this mean Amalardh might also be alive?

Blue sky and compact snow filled Wyndom's vision. As Darna climbed out of her icy hole, his heart leaped. Rugged in his wolf cape stood Amalardh. Alive. And angry. Even though Sister Darna was at the receiving end, Wyndom felt as though Amalardh directed his rage at him. *Please don't be mad at me,* he wanted to tell him. *I had nothing to do with all of this. I'm just as confused as you. I have no idea why Darna separated you from your companions.*

While Wyndom couldn't control the stop and start of a visual feed (only the Maddowshin possessed that power), with enough concentration, he could diminish the visuals and focus on his own world. He glanced around the Terefellian encampment and spotted the Maddowshin's hulking frame standing by the fire.

You've kept me in the dark long enough, he said to the beast through his mind. *I am the leader of Terefellia and deserve to know what's going on. Sister Darna is our most skilled Wrethun Lof, yet has delayed killing the Croilar Tier. Why does she continue to complain about not being the right person for the job?*

The Maddowshin ordered a group of Terefellians to gather more wood, then turned Wyndom's way. *Killing Amalardh is not Sister Darna's issue. She's been wanting to slice him from the moment she saw him.*

She had? *Then what exactly is the problem?*

The beast trotted its cloven feet toward him. *Our glorious queen wishes for a child and has chosen Amalardh as the father. As you can see, Sister Darna lacks the temperament to bed him. Her forceful approach will never provide results. A man like Amalardh needs finesse and indisputable sincerity.* The Maddowshin's shadow loomed over Wyndom as it stepped up to him. "I know of only one person capable of such deception," it said in its gravelly voice.

Wyndom scanned from the beast's hooves, up its black, muscular torso, to its abominable goat-like head. He'd studied the creature a thousand times and still quivered when he met its human eyes—Rudella. His wife's soul inhabited the beast. When the Terefellians summoned Eifa—the Terefellian queen—to earth, Rudella had stolen Wyndom's ring, leaped into their queen's blackness, and re-birthed as the Maddowshin—the Shadow Mind. The beast's power created a collective conscious with the Terefellians, the Wirador Wosrah, and the queen. Through this connection, it saw all, knew all, and could communicate telepathically.

Wyndom scoffed lightly to himself. The Maddowshin needed someone to manipulate Amalardh into not only betraying his love for Cecilia but to sleep with, of all people, a Terefellian assassin? Good luck. The only person skilled enough to accomplish such manipulation was—

His mouth went round as he locked eyes with the Maddowshin. The beast had been referring to Wyndom. If anyone understood Wyndom's ability to deceive, Rudella did. She'd spent thirty years helping him hide his inadequacies from his people. In return, he'd done nothing for her. Well, now he would. "If you need me to coach Sister Darna on how to deal with a situation such as this, I would be honored."

The Maddowshin stared down its snout at him. "You will not be coaching our Sister on how to feign attraction to the Croilar Tier. You will be controlling her. And from the way your blood pumps when you look at Amalardh, I doubt much duplicity will be required at your end."

Wyndom went numb. The Maddowshin wanted him to be in control of Sister Darna while manipulating Amalardh into bedding her body? But that would mean feeling, seeing, experiencing . . . everything. The beast couldn't be serious.

"I am deadly serious," the Maddowshin said. "I warned you the day would come when you would need to control a vessel to precision perfection. This is the day."

Wyndom fanned the excessive heat rising from his neck. He'd assumed he'd been practicing controlling a Wirador Wosrah to prepare for the battle, where the queen would need his critical thinking skills.

The Maddowshin snorted. "You assumed wrong."

Wyndom scowled. The beast's ability to invade his private thoughts infuriated him.

"Table your anger," said the Maddowshin. "It's an emotion our Sister already possesses, and as you've seen, has been of little use. You have five minutes to settle yourself, then her body will be yours."

Sister Darna's shiver had to be in response to Wyndom's trepidation and not the endless snow, because the glut of Terefellians warming various body parts around the blazing campfire sent plenty of warmth to the Wrethun Lof's distant flesh. *Stay calm. You can do this*, Wyndom told himself. After piloting an eight-legged Wirador Wosrah, he should have no problems steering a two-legged human.

Does Darna know I'm controlling her? he asked the Maddowshin.

She does.

Sister Darna, Wyndom whispered in his mind. *Can you hear me?*

She can hear you, but she cannot respond. Think of it like a dream. She is aware, but also not.

Wyndom wiggled Sister Darna's fingers and toes. Everything seemed to move fine. In fact, better than fine. Her strong, coordinated body had no problem negotiating the soft snow while wearing the ridiculous paddles on her feet. Maybe Wyndom really could do this. The tip of Darna's snow shoe caught on a rock, sending her flat on her face.

Amalardh stepped over and offered his hand.

Wyndom's gaze went straight to Amalardh's dazzling blue eyes. His heart skipped. Why did this man affect him so? Flustered, Wyndom lost his concentration. Sister Darna's arms and legs flailed as he overcompensated with the movements.

Relax, ordered the Maddowshin. *If you keep the Croilar Tier on edge, you'll never get what the queen needs.*

The Maddowshin was right. Sister Darna would never be this clumsy.

"Is everything all right?" Amalardh asked.

Wyndom exhaled a shaky breath and nodded.

He took hold of Amalardh's outstretched hand and a tingle shot through to his toes. Never had he experienced this level of attraction to someone. As he brushed the snow from Sister Darna's tunic, his confidence faltered. Amalardh held grace, poise, and endless layers of complexity. How in all that was good in Terefellia was Wyndom supposed to manipulate this man into bedding Darna?

"Are you sure you're okay?" Amalardh asked.

His genuine concern mesmerized Wyndom. What bliss it must be to live a life amongst people who truly cared for others. "I'm fine," Wyndom replied. Hearing his words vocalized through Sister Darna felt strange.

Nodding, Amalardh continued the hike.

Wyndom pressed Darna's hands to her head. *You need to stop acting like an overcome teenager*, he told himself.

Indeed, said the Maddowshin.

Wyndom bristled. Knowing that the Maddowshin—Rudella—watched, judged, his every move stoked his ire. *You can't expect me to master this immediately*, he said. *I'll need a few days to settle into this body and get comfortable with our target.* Defining Amalardh as a "mission" helped settle Wyndom's anxiety.

You do not have a few days, said the Maddowshin. *You have one night to charm him.*

One night? Amalardh's assessment of the hike to the Horga River taking about two days came flooding back. From there, the time needed for Amalardh to reunite with his two companions might be as little as a few hours. *This is an insane amount of pressure.*

You've had half a century to perfect the art of deception, the Maddowshin said. *I'm sure you'll be fine.*

Following Amalardh's lead, Wyndom sat on a rock and removed the floppy paddles from Darna's feet. Maybe he could use this moment to strike up a conversation. "That's a relief," he said, smiling widely.

Without so much as a glance Darna's way, Amalardh smacked the snow from his paddles, attached them to his bag, and continued on.

Wyndom dropped Darna's head into her hands and bemoaned his idiocy. *That's a relief*, he repeated mockingly to himself. *And what's with the ridiculous smile? Sister Darna would never act like that.* Whacking his paddles together harder than necessary to clear them of snow, he attached them to Darna's pack and continued along Amalardh's trail.

As the sun fell in the western sky, Amalardh found a cave and prepared a fire. Wyndom had spent his life living in a rocky hollow, so the space didn't feel foreign. The person he shared it with did. He settled as far away from Amalardh as possible. He wanted to sit closer, but his nerves wouldn't let him. *This is it*, he told himself. Tonight was Wyndom's only chance.

When Sister Darna had controlled her own body, Wyndom had silently chastised her for staring anywhere other than at Amalardh's intoxicating features: his angular jawline, defiant neck, intimidating eyes. Now that Wyndom directed her gaze, his shyness kept her focus on her toes. *Say something*, he told himself. But his mind drew a blank.

Expelling his nervous energy, he brushed the back of his hands down Darna's front, sending tingles to unexpected erogenous zones. He blinked. Flesh to flesh contact anywhere on Wyndom's chest felt no more or less erotic than rubbing his elbow. When he had told Rudella that he wished he'd been a better husband, her response of "I would've preferred a better lover" suddenly made sense. Wyndom had not understood the female body's intricate connections and had put little effort into discovering them.

He glanced up and his cheeks grew hot. Amalardh was staring at Darna. Even though Amalardh wouldn't know Wyndom drove her looking at her own breasts, Wyndom still couldn't help feeling caught. He pretended to scratch a non-existent stain from the front of Darna's tunic as the reason for her downward gaze. He snuck a peek back at Amalardh. The ruse had worked. Amalardh had turned his interest back to the rabbit he'd earlier caught and was now prepping for dinner.

"You were right," Wyndom said. Darna's voice no longer sounded weird. In fact, it felt freeing to be someone other than himself. Amalardh's focus remained on making various knicks and cuts in the rabbit's fur. His disinterest made the confession Wyndom was about to make far easier. "When I fell, I pulled you with me. I wanted to get you away from those other two, so I could be alone with you." If Sister Darna's admission had any effect on Amalardh, Wyndom couldn't see it. The man skinned the rabbit without a flinch.

Wyndom sat in silence, staring at the fire's hypnotizing flame. He would need to dig deeper, offer more vulnerability. But how? He knew little about Darna's interests and had even fewer of his own. He mindlessly rubbed her thickened palm. Her intense Wrethun Lof training had resulted in callouses twice as hard as his own.

Because of his hideous hands, Wyndom had never learned the art of affection. No Terefellian had. How could they? Before they could walk, they were climbing ropes, hardening their grip. Numbing their souls. Terefellians didn't stroke each other's bodies because they couldn't. What right-minded person wanted their tender flesh hacked at with a course rock? Wyndom needed his thickened skin to survive. But at what cost? He had traded living for life. For how could he truly know what it was to live if he couldn't experience the touch of someone he loved?

The sound of fat crackling as it dripped from the roasting rabbit onto glowing embers pulled Wyndom from his thoughts. His hunger must have read on Sister Darna's face because Amalardh separated a hind leg from the lightly charred carcass, placed it on a strip of bark, and put it in front of her.

Although Wyndom had eaten rabbit many times before, this one tasted especially delicious. Was this because he experienced it through Darna's taste buds or did the sheer delight of eating food cooked by Amalardh heighten his senses?

When he finished, he tossed the bones in the fire and wiped Sister Darna's greasy hands on her tunic.

Frowning, Amalardh wet a cloth and gave it to her. Were Darna's cheeks glowing as red as the burn Wyndom sensed on his own for his poor manners?

Amalardh's high level of dignity, even in the wilderness, made Wyndom adore him even more. He wiped Darna's sticky fingers and handed back the cloth.

Amalardh's stare locked to Darna's palm. "May I?" he asked.

Wyndom gulped. The Croilar Tier wanted to inspect Darna's callouses? *Of course. Yes. Please do.* He nodded Darna's head. The touch of Amalardh's fingers on the tips of her knuckles sent a jolt to Wyndom's chest. Overwhelmed, he withdrew the extremity. How was he ever going to fulfill his vessel's duty when he couldn't endure the heightened sensation of Amalardh's touch?

"I didn't mean to hurt you," Amalardh said.

"You didn't hurt me. It's just . . . I'm not used to being touched. At least, not by hands as soft as yours." Maybe because hiding behind Darna's facade offered protection, or maybe because Amalardh seemed so balanced, Wyndom felt comfortable exposing his truth. "I have a daughter . . ." He cleared his throat, allowing time to set his story. To maintain believability, he would need to speak from the heart about Saffron. He would change her age, of course. Twenty-something Darna could hardly be a mother to a teenager. "She's four years old," he said. "When she was a baby, I used to adore running the back of my hand over her satin soft cheeks. I'd study her tiny, undamaged fingers and wish I could give her a better life. One without ropes . . ." He paused at the rawness of his own honesty. He'd never admitted this much to himself, let alone a stranger.

"You cannot imagine a fa—" He corrected himself. "A mother's heartache watching her child's delicate hands blister and bleed. My agony as I listened to my baby girl's sobs as she begged, 'Mommy, no. Please, I don't want to climb the yucky rope.' My anger and bitterness stung like a swarm of hornets as I made her climb, anyway. 'Mommy, it hurts,' she told me. 'Can I wrap them?' My heart bled at the sight of her angry blisters. But tears are for the weak, and Terefellians need to be tough. Only when she slipped and ripped the skin from her hands, did I offer her a protective cloth."

A tickle itched Darna's cheek. Wyndom wiped the spot. It was wet. Sitting under his palm tree, thousands of miles away, did he also shed a tear? He swallowed past the lump in Darna's throat. "The more I forced my little girl to climb, the more my heart closed to her pain, the more her hostility toward me grew. In the end, I stopped cuddling her, because the first time I did, my sharp skin sliced through the tender flesh of her chubby leg." He rubbed the jagged edge of Darna's palm. "As my daughter's skin hardened, so did my soul. The friend I thought I'd have my entire life morphed into a stranger. I became an outsider, an alien to those I loved." He looked up and his heart swelled at the genuine interest plastered on Amalardh's face. For the first time in his life, Wyndom felt heard.

"Why did you want to be alone with me?" Amalardh asked.

Wyndom cuddled Darna's legs to her chest. "The moment I saw you, I—" Because he'd never perceived this level of attraction to another, Wyndom had a hard time understanding his own emotions. "I saw you. And I immediately felt something inside." He dropped his forehead onto Darna's knees. "I sound so stupid."

Amalardh remained quiet. Non-judgmental. Wyndom could probably blurt "I love you" and Amalardh would accept the confession the same way he would if Sister Darna told him she hated him. Wyndom did not think Amalardh cold. Quite the contrary. As he suspected, Amalardh accepted and appreciated the truth. Getting close to him required little more than not telling any lies.

"I saw you," Wyndom said, "and I couldn't stop wondering what it might be like to feel the touch of unblemished hands on my skin; what it would be like to feel . . . normal."

Darna's heart—and his own—thumped as Wyndom held Amalardh's stare. He wanted to throw Darna's body at him, but he couldn't. Her aggressiveness might cause Amalardh to shut down. Wyndom had to play the situation carefully and in a way that would entice Amalardh to give himself over to Darna of his own volition.

THE TEREFELLIAN WOMAN put Amalardh on edge. Anyone too in touch with their emotions terrified him. Cecilia had terrified him when he first met her. She still did.

Locked in his dark prison during his childhood, young Amalardh had held tight to a statement made by Jacob, the Blind Prisoner who had brought him his meals. "Young boy," Jacob had whispered, "whatever becomes of you, remember one thing. The fabric of life is what holds us together. No matter how hard others may pull, don't let them make you a loose thread." Over the years, Amalardh had learned that in order to fulfill his job as an assassin, not only must he become a loose thread, he needed to actively pluck himself from life's cloth. Cecilia had threaded him back. But since the birth of their son, Amalardh had once again loosened himself. He needed the separation in order to cope. The problem was, since leaving Vitus, he'd increasingly craved Cecilia's warmth.

Beyond Cecilia, Amalardh had never been with another woman. Because of his sheltered existence, he'd not experienced the concept of a "come-on." He took Darna's earnest talk of her daughter at face value and understood her words of "what it would be like to feel . . . normal" to mean "what it would be like to feel . . . human." Amalardh's own murderous past made him feel inhuman and unworthy of Cecilia's—anyone's—love. He could live with his agony. But maybe, for the shortest moment, Darna—an assassin in her own right—would not have to live with hers. If touch from non-calloused skin could help ease her suffering, he would oblige. He offered her his hand. "Take it," he said.

Her eyes seemed wary. Or maybe Amalardh saw disbelief.

She placed the palm of his hand to her cheek. Her extreme warmth and unexpected softness sent a jolt to Amalardh's belly. He longed for Cecilia and missed her embrace. He should withdraw his hand. He would pull back, but not just yet. He wanted to savor the moment a second longer.

A tear rolled from the corner of Darna's eye. Amalardh wiped it with his thumb.

"I'm embarrassed," she said.

"Don't be."

Her lips pressed together as if trying to hold back unwanted emotions. "In Terefellia, we tell our children it's wrong to cry. I once did something to my baby girl. I destroyed something she loved. And I just stood there as she shed endless tears. What kind of fa—" She sucked in her breath. "What kind of parent throws a child's favorite toy into a fire?"

Amalardh's throat tightened. The same kind that runs from a son. He had not expected such a deep affinity with this woman. They were both damaged goods.

Her mouth parted the slightest bit as she guided his fingertips to her lips. He should withdraw his hand from her velvety touch. He would pull back, but not just yet. He needed to feel her breath a moment longer.

She guided his hand down her slender neck. The throb of her artery matched the beat of his heart. He could control his arousal. Senator Akantha's treacherous methods for blunting his attraction to the female form had numbed Amalardh's ability to experience internal desire. Even though Cecilia had broken through his steely shell and awoken his willingness to accept pleasure, he'd given in to his passion because he loved her. Because he had no such bond with Darna, he could offer his touch without succumbing to his body's growing lust.

She pressed his hand to her upper chest. For a woman who

could kill with her bare hands, Darna's slender collar bone felt so delicate. He needed to stop. He went to pull away, but she pressed his hand back to her. Breathing slowly, he settled his resistance. He would end whatever was going on between him and the Terefellian. But not just yet. He needed to feel her warmth.

She guided his hand over her breast.

Her gasp took him off guard.

"I had no idea touch could ever make me feel this way," she whispered.

"What way?" he asked.

"Like for the first time in my life, I'm actually living."

Amalardh knew that sensation. He'd once had it with Cecilia and had foolishly thrown it away. He wanted—needed—to feel connected with life again.

She pressed her satin lips to his.

He stiffened as guilt and desire tore through his veins.

Sensing his hesitance, she pulled back and apologized. "I shouldn't have done that," she said.

No. She shouldn't have. Then again, Amalardh shouldn't have been doing what he was doing, either. Since he couldn't explain why he was allowing this encounter to go on far longer than it should've, he threw his unanswered internal question back at her. "Why did you do it?" he asked flatly.

Most people inched back from his stony demeanor. Not Darna. Her expression held a strange mix of exposure and self-assuredness as she silently studied him.

"What?" he asked.

"I thought you hated games."

"I do," he replied.

With an air of seduction, she moved her lips close to his ear and whispered, "Then why are you asking questions that you already know the answer to?" Warmth from her cheek radiated to his skin. "You know why I kissed you. I did it for the same reason I did this." She sucked on his earlobe and desire shot to his toes. "I kissed you because I want to stop being afraid."

Her moist tongue caressed his lobe. "I kissed you for the same reason you let me. We both don't want to be the people we are anymore."

She pushed her firm curves against his body and ravished his lips with hers.

He should stop her; only he no longer wanted to.

Consumed with passion, he returned her kiss.

Shoving him onto his back, she untied his robe. He liked her aggression.

As if savoring the moment, she slowly, meticulously untied his trousers and pulled them down. Her wanton desire as she scanned his body fueled his lust. As she kissed along his lower abdomen, she seemed to know exactly what he wanted and when.

After teasing his arousal, she lifted her tunic over her head, unveiling surprising curves. Two nights ago, Darna had barely batted an eyelid Amalardh's way. Now, she kneeled motionless by his side, her mouth slightly gaped as though staring at her most prized possession.

He went to sit forward, but she forced him back and climbed on top. Her fight excited him. She knew what she wanted, and he was only too willing to let her take it.

At the height of their passion, she stopped. Horror gripped her.

Amalardh tensed. What was wrong?

She turned her hands upward. Blood from where her sharp grip had torn through his upper arms and chest covered her palms.

"I'm so sorry," she said.

"For what?"

The cuts barely registered. He pulled her back to his lips.

When the raw, primal, and deeply affectionate moment climaxed, the murderous Terefellian, who could kill a man with the flick of her wrist, dropped to Amalardh's chest and wept. Her tight grip drew more blood. Amalardh's wounds would heal. By the way Darna clutched him, as though she never wanted to let him go, he wasn't sure hers would.

He stared at the cave's rocky ceiling and an icy chill settled deep within. Who was Amalardh kidding? After what he'd just done, his wounds would never heal either.

CECILIA CUDDLED HER wooden bucket like a teddy bear. Even though the abdominal spasms from drinking the black liquid made her long for death, she no longer suspected Malek of wicked intentions. The more she drank and threw up, the quicker her numb body came back to life. Her lips began cooperating with her tongue, and she could move her arm without it flopping around. She still didn't know why Malek had brought her to this mound-hut, but at least she felt better. Unlike Eideard—her supposed brother. He remained curled in a ball, groaning.

"I had to give him more drugs than you," Malek said.

"You did this to us? Why?"

"Let me start from the beginning. Maybe something I say will jog your memory. I'd been in my room watching a storm travel out to sea when a bright light filled the sky, illuminating an object falling into the ocean. Because of my understanding of the Prophecy, I knew the sign came from Siersha, the Goddess of Light. I ran to the beach and happened across Davian. Do you remember a bald, light-skinned man similar in build to me?"

Cecilia shook her head. She still didn't know who Malek was.

"Some people are best left forgotten. If not for your leg wound, I would've slit Davian's throat and fled with you and your brother. Do you recall the shark bite?"

Cecilia massaged the large divot in her right thigh. "No. But a woman with your color skin told me about it. I asked her who I was. She said my name was Cecilia, that I was just a girl who once had a dreadful nightmare, and that I was safe. Then you brought me here."

Eideard moaned.

Malek wrung out a cloth and, with tenderness, wiped the sweat from Eideard's brow. "Her name is Countess Kosima of Bayton and you were far from safe. She is the reason you don't remember anything. When I found you on the beach, I tried to warn you not to mention the Goddess of Light to the Countess. You passed out before I had the chance."

"Who is the Goddess of Light?" Cecilia asked.

"Her name is Siersha. You truly don't remember her?"

"What does she look like?"

"She's a feeling." He pressed his hand just below his chest bone. "Deep. Inside. The Countess wiped your memory of the Goddess, but she cannot strip away Siersha's light. She is in you. You must try to find her."

Cecilia placed her hand on the soft spot between her rib cage. The area burned from stomach acid. She supposed this wasn't the sensation Malek meant.

Eideard convulsed and threw up. His lungs rasped for air.

"Give him some water, please," Cecilia said.

Instead, Malek scooped another cup of the ghastly stuff and fed it to Eideard.

Cradling his belly, Eideard curled into a ball and groaned.

Cecilia placed her hand on his soft, spiky hair. Was he truly her brother? If so, might this explain her desire to comfort him? She nodded to the wet cloth Malek had used. "May I?" she asked. He handed it to her, and she gently mopped Eideard's face.

"Your shark bite required twelve hours of surgery," Malek said. "During recovery, you developed a severe infection that kept you bedridden and incoherent for close to three weeks. Most people would not have survived. This is why I know you are the one I have been waiting for."

"I am nobody," Cecilia said.

"You are the Caladium. The poison flower that will kill Eifa."

She glared at him. Kill? Cecilia couldn't slay anyone. "Please don't say such things. You must have me mixed up with someone else." She held Eideard close. *If you are my brother, please wake up and take me home,* she said to him in her mind. Not that she knew where home was. "What did this Countess do to us?" she asked Malek.

"In order for you and your brother to end your belief in the Goddess of Light, the Countess reprogrammed both of you. Essentially, she wiped your brains using a combination of drugs and electric shock. Unlike you, your brother denied Siersha's existence at a relatively low dose of treatment. The problem was, he lied. I overheard him praying to the Goddess for your safety. If the Countess discovered his deception, she would've killed him. She has no tolerance for those who feel they can outwit her. Until your infection cleared, I had no other choice than to drug your brother and pretend the treatment had caused unintended side effects. Because of this, he has far more drugs coursing through his veins. The process to detoxify him will take longer."

Eideard convulsed. Cecilia thrust his wooden bucket under his chin in time to catch the retch.

"When you finally stabilized," Malek said, "I had planned to break you and your brother out and finally escape. Unfortunately, the Countess got to you before I could."

Cecilia poured fresh water onto the cloth, wrung it out, and pressed it to Eideard's heated forehead. He cuddled his arms around her. The contact felt normal. Comfortable. "If Eideard still remembered this Goddess, might he still remember everything else?" she asked.

"Once the drugs are out of his system, he should be fine. You, on the other hand, told the Countess you would rather die than deny your Goddess. And you almost did. Your loyalty to Siersha forced the Countess to increase your treatment to dangerous levels."

"Water," whispered Eideard.

His voice sent goosebumps across Cecilia's skin. Something

within her sensed familiarity. She went to dip a mug into the water bucket when Malek gripped her arm, stopping her. "No water," he said.

She yanked free and an awareness of how much she despised being controlled struck her. Was she absolutely certain she hadn't killed?

"I see your rage," Malek said. "Don't let go of it. Anger is your friend."

Anger is your friend? Why did that phrase seem familiar?

Malek studied her. "Did you remember something?"

"What you just said . . . I don't know. It just felt like I'd heard it before."

He seemed pleased, as though her statement had somehow confirmed his ridiculous belief in who she was. Eideard's groan broke the unsettling moment. "I gather the water slows the cleansing process," she said.

"It does," Malek replied.

Giving in, she filled the mug with the inky liquid. "Here you go, Eideard," she said. Speaking his name felt right. Insinuating the cup held water did not.

He chugged the contents and his face contorted. Dropping the cup, he gripped his belly. "Make it stop. Please make it stop." He flopped his head onto her lap and sobbed.

Malek wrung out a fresh cloth and handed it to her.

A desperate want to remember this young man swirled in her chest as she mopped Eideard's sweaty brow. "Why did the Countess want us to forget this Goddess?" she asked.

"In order for you to understand, you need to know what you have done."

Malek told her a wild tale about how she inspired an uprising in a city called Vitus, unseated the cruel Senators, and led her army to victory. As she listened, broken images flashed into her mind, only nothing stayed long enough to paint a clear picture.

"Before their downfall, we traded spices with the Senators," Malek said. "We had a smooth relationship until spoiled grain from Vitus killed many of our people, including the Countess's husband. Believing the Senators deliberately tainted the shipment, the Countess swore revenge. She was preparing her attack, when you turned up at Vitus's doorstep. A young woman with no battle training had accomplished overnight what the Countess had spent a year planning. You had something more fearful than an army of thousands. You had a voice. And a belief. You inspired the uninspired. You must see the threat someone like you is to the Countess."

"If I am such a threat, why go to all these lengths to save my life? Why not let me die?"

"People win wars. Words win people. Control the words and you have total authority. The Countess by nature is not a violent person. If a way exists to acquire Vitus without bloodshed, she would prefer such a path. Of all people to land on her beach, you did. You cannot imagine her thrill. You were the perfect vessel to test her reprogramming methods. If she could control the voice of the one who inspired the unimaginable, she could control anyone."

Eideard convulsed and threw up.

Cecilia wiped the spittle from his mouth. "If this Goddess of Light represents goodness, why should the Countess care if someone believes this god to be real?" she asked.

"Baytonites are a people of science. We only believe what we can see, what we can prove. Fact over fiction. Faith in our world is synonymous with fear because, in an argument between a person of science and one of faith, science will always lose. Science cannot prove the Goddess of Light doesn't exist, and the faithful cannot prove she does. Science loses because the faithful do not need proof. The problem with faith is that in the wrong hands, the deceitful can warp a belief and use the tainted version to control others. Rather than ferreting out which belief system offers good and which imposes danger, the Countess prefers to eradicate them all. Her rationale is that you cannot trust people not to take advantage of an honorable belief and corrupt it for their own benefit."

Cecilia sat with Malek's words. "You are saying that because humanity cannot be trusted with beliefs they cannot prove, we should not have any unverifiable beliefs?"

"That is the Countess's theory."

She studied two angry red patches on either side of Eideard's temples. Marks from the Countess's treatment, no doubt. "You believe in this Goddess of Light, but I don't see any scars on your face. Why hasn't the Countess tried to reprogram you?"

"When you live in a society like Bayton, you learn quickly to keep your beliefs to yourself." He moved the lantern close to Eideard's face. "His color is returning. Hopefully, he'll pull through soon, as we cannot stay here much longer."

From the long canvas bag Malek had carried from the boat, he removed two pairs of boots and two piles of clothes, neatly folded, and wrapped with string. Handing the larger bundle to Cecilia, he told her to put them on.

"But I'm already dressed."

"Not in your own clothing. The Countess ordered these to be burned. I managed to intercept. Personal items hold a strong link to memory, something the Countess didn't want."

Cecilia unwrapped her bundle and studied the various pieces: a long skirt made of taupe-colored hessian; a loose-fitting white cotton top; a buckled black leather corset; and a cropped fur jacket. She pressed the jacket to her nose and sniffed. It smelled of nothing in particular. She waited. No memories came. She studied a stitched section of her skirt.

"My needle work isn't the best," Malek said. "That's from where the shark bit through."

She folded the skirt over, covering the repair. A shark attack was a memory she didn't care to recall. A tree-shaped broach attached to the corset shimmered under the lamp light. She ran her finger over its twirling canopy and embellished roots.

"Do you recognize that image?" Malek asked.

"Not really."

"What about this?"

He pulled up his right sleeve. A garish tattoo of a wolf with red eyes wearing a swirled mask shaped like her tree broach jolted her. She'd seen this symbol before. But where? "What is it?" she asked.

"This symbol is a much longer discussion. Right now, you need to get dressed." Rolling down his sleeve, Malek stepped out of the hut, allowing her privacy.

In the dim lamp light, Cecilia swapped outfits. As she slipped her socked feet into her durable boots, Eideard groaned. She dropped to his side and held his bucket close. He retched, then flopped back.

"Hey, sis," he said weakly. "What happened to your hair?"

Cecilia froze. He knew her as his sister. Why couldn't she remember him?

His eyes widened as though realizing something. Sitting bolt upright, he flung his arms around her. "Oh my gosh, Cecilia. You're safe."

Unsure what to do, she hugged him back. Her body relaxed. This young man felt like home.

The sound of pulsing crickets and croaking frogs grew louder as the hut's door opened.

Malek stepped in. "Good," he said to Eideard. "You're back."

Eideard held Cecilia protectively. "You touch my sister and I'll break your neck."

"It's okay," Cecilia said, grabbing his rigid arm. "Malek's a friend. He saved us."

Eideard remained guarded. "I remember him from the hospital. That awful treatment. He was part of it." He scanned the cramped space. "Where are we? What happened?"

Malek handed Eideard a mug of water. "Drink this, and I will explain."

Although wary, Eideard complied. As Malek told him what he had told Cecilia, Eideard's face morphed from shock, to surprise, to disbelief, and finally, to despair. He pressed his warm palm to Cecilia's cheek. "You really don't remember me?"

She shook her head. She wanted to. Desperately.

"What about Plockton? Where we grew up? You must remember our forest."

"I don't recall anything beyond waking up in a strange, white room, where I spoke to a woman I'd never seen before—"

"The Countess," Malek clarified to Eideard.

"The next thing I knew, Malek put me on a canoe with you and brought us here."

Seemingly unconvinced, Eideard bombarded her with a bunch of "What about this?" "What about that?" questions.

Malek pulled him aside. "You must not overwhelm her. Now, get dressed." He handed Eideard a bundle of clothes, then whispered something to him. Whatever Malek said seemed to cut to Eideard's core. His despondent expression returned as he changed into beige linen trousers and a white, long-sleeved shirt with toggle buttons. As Malek stepped out to empty the buckets, Cecilia turned to Eideard.

"What did he say to you?" she asked.

"You don't remember anything? Any . . . one?"

"Is there someone I'm supposed to remember?"

Eideard seemed ready to say something when Malek stepped back in. Dropping to his haunches, Eideard fiddled with his shoelaces. Instead of making a bow, he'd formed a knot he couldn't get undone.

Kneeling, Cecilia brushed his hand away. Realizing her brusqueness, she glanced up to check if she'd offended him. "What?" she asked in response to his smile.

"It's just . . . you still feel like you."

Yearning gripped her. "Have I done this before?"

"Multiple times. I'm a klutz when it comes to shoelaces."

As she tied a bow, an image of sandaled feet jumped into her mind. She stopped.

"What's wrong?" he asked.

"I got this strange sense. You hate boots, right? You always wear sandals."

"Yes! You remember me."

His bright expression dulled as Cecilia shook her head. She didn't remember Eideard, only the vague concept of someone always choosing sandals over boots.

"That's enough questions for today," said Malek. He turned to the long canvas bag and pulled out a bow, a quiver full of arrows, and two swords stowed in their leather sashes.

"Our weapons!" said Eideard. "How is this possible? They went down with our airship out in the ocean."

"A few days after I found you, a container floated ashore," Malek replied. He tapped a tree emblem of similar style to Cecilia's broach embossed in the quiver's brown leather. "I recognized this image and knew the items were yours."

Eideard ran his fingers along the bow's string as though greeting an old friend. "I'm so glad I listened to you," he said to Cecilia. "During the storm, our air balloon ran low on fuel. We started tossing things to help lessen our weight. I went to throw this stuff overboard, when you stopped me."

Cecilia couldn't imagine why. The bottom of the ocean seemed an especially fitting place for such deadly instruments.

Eideard removed a long, shiny sword from its sash and handed it to her. "This is yours," he said.

Her skin chilled. She owned this heavy blade? She was about to give it back when ornate swirls on its handle caught her attention. For such a grim weapon, the patterning was striking.

"That's the finest sword I've ever seen," said Malek.

"Because it once belonged to Amalardh," Eideard replied.

Amalardh? The name rang familiar as the man from Malek's story who supposedly helped Cecilia win the battle against the Army of Vitus.

Malek admired her weapon with renewed appreciation. "A sword once owned by the last Croilar Tier. Its finesse should not surprise me."

"I really know how to use this thing?" Cecilia asked.

"Better than most," Eideard replied.

"Better than you?"

He grinned. "This is the one time I can lie and you would never know. Sadly, for me, you are far better. But don't go getting a big head. I'm way better than you at almost everything else."

His playfulness warmed Cecilia. Even though she didn't remember him, she liked the idea of him being her brother.

"All right, family reunion over," Malek said. "It's time to go."

Cecilia stepped out from the grass-mound hut and flung her arm over her eyes. She needed a moment to adjust to the bright morning light. Dressed in her new clothes, with a sword draped across her back, she felt like an imposter. As she followed Malek through the woods, Eideard spoke of their childhood and growing up in the Plockton Forest. The life he described sounded like a dream. Apparently, she had a talent for braiding her hair with flowers and creating fantastical designs. She touched her cropped head. She used to have long hair? He described their village's horrific massacre, and a deep ache gripped her. "I don't want to hear this," she said. "Don't tell me any more bad stuff."

"Of course," he replied. "I'm sorry."

They walked in silence, and Cecilia bristled. Why had Eideard stopped talking? She'd told him she didn't want to hear the bad stuff. Did his lack of chatter mean there were no good things to talk about? "Was that it?" she asked. "You say it's been two years since our village's destruction. During that time, I was happy, wasn't I?"

"Yes. Absolutely. You were more than happy. You were . . . I mean, you are in love."

She stopped in her tracks. "I have a boyfriend?"

"I think Amalardh is a little more than that."

Amalardh? Cecilia was supposedly in love with this man? Malek's abridged version of her and Amalardh defeating the

Army of Vitus mentioned nothing of this. Maybe because he didn't know the full details of her life, whereas her brother did. "Tell me more about . . . this Amalardh," she said.

After their village's raid, Cecilia learned that she'd set off from Plockton in search of Eideard and their other brother, Rabbie. Along the way, she happened upon Amalardh, an assassin sent by the Senators of Vitus to kill her. Only, he hadn't followed through with his order.

"The strange thing about you two meeting each other was that our family pendant, which looks just like this"—Eideard pointed to the tree broach on Cecilia's leather corset—"actually belonged to Amalardh's wolf knife. It's a mask that sits on the wolf's face."

"You mean like the drawing on Malek's arm?"

"What drawing?"

Malek pulled up his sleeve.

Eideard's mouth fell open. "You're a Croilar Tier?"

"No. My great grandmother was."

Eideard looked perplexed. "Women can hold the title?" he asked.

"Of the eight original Croilar Tier, two were women," Malek replied. "A Terefellian assassin murdered my grandmother in her fortieth year. Along with taking her life, the Wrethun Lof stole her knife. Without a symbolic blade, a Croilar Tier is no more. Even so, my mother led her life accordingly, and so have I."

Eideard smirked at Cecilia. "It would seem the Treoir Solas is never without her protector."

Her face tensed and she was certain she'd scowled. "You both talk of me being this Treoir Solas, but Malek also called me the Caladium. Which one is it?"

"The Caladium?" Eideard repeated. "What is that?"

"See? Even he doesn't know."

"You are both," Malek said. "The Treoir Solas, the Light Guide, was what you were. You brought Siersha's light to the darkest places, inspired the Citizens of Vitus to see their Senators' evil truth, and rid Vitus of Eifa's dark shadow. But because of the

Terefellians, the Dark Goddess has returned, stronger than ever. A world controlled by her evil is like living in the depths of an abyss. A place no light can ever illuminate. This time, we are not just fighting a society corrupted by her shadow. We are fighting her. You cannot eliminate her darkness with your light, but you can poison her with it, which makes you the Caladium—the Poison Flower."

"Poison a goddess? How am I supposed to do such a thing?"

He nodded ahead. "That's what I plan to find out."

In the distance, a set of wooden stairs clung to the side of a steep mountain. They wound upward, disappearing into low-hung clouds that obscured the lofty peak. Cecilia pressed her hand to her churning belly. Something about embarking on a dangerous road in search of answers to questions she didn't understand seemed all too familiar.

FOR SAFFRON, BRAVERY and fearlessness had gone hand in hand. She considered herself brave. But fearless? Not anymore. Her body numbed as Lyrik—the crazy girl controlling the motor bike—sped toward the cliff. The front wheel hit a short wooden ramp, and the bike flew through the air.

The canyon's far edge seemed way out of reach. *We're not going to make it. We're not going to make it. We're not going to make it.*

THUD! Saffron's spine jerked as the bike's wheels bit dirt. *Holy crap! We made it.*

The bike slid to a stop. Lyrik flicked down the kickstand and dismounted. Saffron followed. On the other side of the ravine, a handful of beasts broke away from the herd and galloped after Rabbie and his rider. The rest barreled toward the cliff.

"Aren't they going to stop?" Lyrik asked.

Saffron doubted it. The creatures mirrored what they saw others do. If she could fly, then they could, too. The front line of Wirador Wosrah sprung like a row of black cats from a tabletop. Surely those things couldn't jump this far.

Relief washed through her as they fell short and splattered on the rocky ground below.

But then—a beast's black claws gripped the ravine's edge. Hauling itself up, the warrior roared, sending a powerful billow of foul, wet breath across Saffron's face. She grabbed her bow. *Damn it.* Her rushing fingers fumbled as she tried to nock her arrow.

The beast sprang.

She froze. She was too late.

BANG! The Wirador Wosrah's goat head exploded. The rest of it dropped into a pool of black slush.

Turning, Saffron gaped at a smoking double-barreled gun in Lyrik's hands. She'd found a similar weapon in her hideout-house, along with a box labeled *shotgun shells*. She didn't know exactly how the long, tubular piece of machinery functioned, but the mechanisms seemed easy enough to figure out. She had aimed it at a tree and pulled the trigger. A powerful force sent her to the ground. Even though the shell's metal pellets had left an impressive hollow in the trunk, the noise had echoed far too loudly. Hunting with it would've exposed her location to prying ears, so she made do with her bow and arrow. What a fool she'd been for not realizing the weapon's worth against Wirador Wosrah. Any kind of damage to a warrior's eyes—including the force of a dozen metal pellets—seemed to render the creature into liquid slush.

Like mindless sheep, the remaining Wirador Wosrah herd made the leap.

Two more caught hold of the cliff's edge.

BOOM! BOOM! Lyrik's sharp shooting annihilated them. The color drained from her face as she stared at Saffron. "What are those things?"

"Your worst nightmare," Saffron replied.

Lyrik's wide eyes trailed to the canyon's edge. "What the . . .? What is happening down there?"

Mist rising from evaporating black puddles on jagged rocks below suggested several beasts had landed face down, and sharp outcroppings had skewered their eyes. Elsewhere, fleshy bits of black gunk from where beasts, whose eyes had remained intact but whose bodies had exploded on the rocks, rolled around, searching for each other.

"Damaging their eyes is the only way to kill them," Saffron said. "We've blown them up, burned them, and still they survive. A splattered beast can literally pull itself together and re-form."

In the shadows directly below stood two black pillars, twice the size of a regular Wirador Wosrah reformation pillar.

"What the heck are they?" Lyrik asked.

When Saffron and Rabbie had bid farewell to Cecilia and Eideard's airship, two beasts had collided at high speed, creating an eight-legged spider beast with four horns, two snouts, and four eerily human eyes. Bushy shrubs fed by the ravine's shallow stream must have cushioned one set of warriors, preventing their implosion. A second set must have landed directly on top of the first, resulting in a merge. "Those two columns will form into the most hideous creatures you've ever seen," Saffron said. "We have to leave. Now."

Jumping onto the motor bike, she and Lyrik sped off. Several minutes later, a massive concrete door built into the side of a mountain came into view. The door slowly slid sideways, exposing a wide tunnel and a sign: *Welcome to Rabbit Cove.*

A skinny guy with curly red hair and a big smile waved at Lyrik's arrival. White lettering on his green shirt read: *DUDE.*

Lyrik crossed the threshold and screeched to a smokey stop.

The red-headed guy jogged over. "Hey, Lyrik. Where's Zack?"

Lyrik leaped off the bike. "Code red!" she said.

He tilted his head at Saffron. "You were supposed to get supplies, not bring back a cutie." He stretched out his hand. "Hey, my name's Yoyo."

"Code red!" Lyrik yelled at him. She ran to the opposite wall and pounded a red button.

A strange alarm rang. Lights in the long tunnel blinked.

Yoyo stood motionless, as if trying to process what was happening.

"This isn't a drill," Lyrik yelled. Sliding open a metal door, she grabbed a shotgun from a row of them and pumped a round of ammunition into the chamber. The firm expression on her face as she glared at Yoyo screamed, "Do you understand me now!?"

Yoyo turned ashen. He snatched a black device from his hip and spoke into it with heightened energy. "Attention all able and willing personnel. We have a Code Red. This is not a drill. Repeat. This is not a drill. So, get your butts to the main gate, now!"

Lyrik thrust the shotgun at Saffron. "Do you know how to use one of these?"

Saffron hesitated. Should she lie and say yes? What if the kick-back sent her to the ground again? She'd look like a fool.

"Hello. Earth to . . . what's your name?" Lyrik asked.

"Saffron."

"Earth to Saffron. Can you use one of these?"

Saffron nodded. If petite Lyrik could remain upright, then so could she. She would just need to mirror her when firing the damn thing.

From the other end of the tunnel came an orange vehicle, its engine buzzing quietly. A dozen men and women dressed as uniquely as Lyrik and Yoyo sat on the machine's flat, metallic bed. It pulled to a stop, and the passengers jumped off and grabbed weapons.

The driver of the vehicle stepped over. Since running away, Saffron's hair had grown long enough to scoop into a ponytail, but nothing like this man's. His singular braid reached his mid-back. "What's happening?" he asked Lyrik. His authoritative demeanor suggested a status high in command. Unlike Saffron's father, who preferred to linger in the background whenever trouble presented, this man held his weapon with assured confidence.

Lyrik made quick introductions. Jensen was his name. As she explained the situation, his expression held disbelief. Understandable. Saffron had witnessed the creatures, and she still had trouble believing they were real.

"If we are in danger, why is this door still open?" Jensen asked.

"Zack's still out there," Lyrik said.

"And my friend," Saffron added.

Jensen turned to her. Unlike her father's perpetual state of distrust, his eyes held kindness and concern. He seemed ready to speak when Lyrik's words of "They're coming!" cut in.

Saffron's belly twisted at the sight of an eight-legged spider beast scuttling around a corner several yards away.

Lyrik fired.

The beast roared as black globs from its exploding horn flew in the air.

"Only the eyes!" Saffron said.

"Where do you think I was aiming?"

Thankfully, the beast's elongated body provided plenty of surface area for the globs to land and blend back into their original host. Within seconds, another horn sprouted.

The Rabbit Cove fighters began firing.

"No!" yelled Saffron. But her warning came too late.

The force of the fighters' bullets shredded the spider beast's legs, sending it to the ground.

"Everyone. Hold your fire!" Saffron yelled.

The fighters silenced and turned to her.

"Stay still. Don't move." She motioned to the newly formed black balls from the severed legs. "If they sense you, they'll come for you. Otherwise, they'll return to their original host. If we kill that beast before those separated bits latch back on, they will remain alive until they find a new entity to merge with. Be warned. They like human flesh."

The balls rolled back and forth, as if looking for something more preferable than the legless spider beast. Finding nothing, they zipped back into its rubbery substance.

Saffron set her stance, stabilized her core, and lifted her gun. "Aim only for the eyes," she said. "If any of that black stuff comes for you, get to high ground. If it touches you, you'll become one of them." Her focus narrowed onto the beast's upper set of eyes.

Saffron hailed from a long line of Wrethun Lof—elite Croilar Tier hunters. Her grandfather, and his father, and so on had held the title. All of them had, except Saffron and her father. Saffron could've been a Wrethun Lof, but she had fled Terefellia before completing her training. Her father had no such excuse. Not only did he lack the physicality and requisite disposition, he didn't possess a Wrethun Lof's natural ability to learn a skill simply by visualizing what they needed to. As the beast's shattered legs reformed, Saffron pictured her bullet connecting with its upper set of eyes. The last black ball connected. She fired. The gun kicked back hard, but her feet remained planted.

Black liquid dripped to the ground as the creature melted into a single Wirador Wosrah. One set of eyes down, one more to go.

Dropping to all fours, the beast roared. The guttural sound cut short as Jensen fired. The perfect hit sent the warrior splashing to the ground. Seconds later, the liquid evaporated.

Zack's engine squealed as his bike sped from around a rocky enclave. From the other side, another spider beast and a group of newly formed beasts from the ravine appeared. Turning sharply, Zack lost control. The bike skidded sideways.

Saffron's breath sucked in as the spider beast sprang on top of Zack and Rabbie. With its back to her, she couldn't get a clear shot at its eyes.

Two bullet blasts rang out. The eight-legged warrior liquified, revealing Zack, flat on his back, holding a shotgun. Coughing and spluttering next to him lay Rabbie.

As the other beasts bolted to the tunnel, another cartload of Lyrik's people arrived.

"Close the tunnel! Now!" yelled Jensen to Yoyo. He turned to his people. "Fighters, make your choice, you are either in or out."

"But everyone will be safer inside," said Yoyo.

"Zack is still out there and we cannot risk one of those things getting into our home. Now close this door."

Setting the tone, Jensen stepped across the threshold. Saffron followed, as did Lyrik and most of the others.

As the massive door slowly closed in front of Yoyo's terrified eyes, the Rabbit Cove fighters let loose their bullets. Because of these people's sharp aim, several of the approaching warriors dropped, marring the dusty ground with pools of black sludge that evaporated seconds later.

Pounding hooves from the left suggested the Wirador Wosrah chasing Zack and Rabbie drew near. The young men were sandwiched between the smaller group already under fire and those coming. As Saffron, Lyrik, and a splinter group of fighters rushed to their aid, more resurrected beasts from the ravine joined the attack.

Someone's ill-fated shot sent a warrior's arm flying. The lone limb formed a ball and sped toward Saffron. Holding her gun's barrel tip, she swung the weapon like a club and batted the muck at the nearest beast. As the mass dissolved into its new host, the Wirador Wosrah's horns grew longer.

Turning, a fighter came face-to-face with a beast. Panicked, he placed his gun's muzzle to the beast's belly and fired. Deadly bits of Eifa muck flew everywhere. The belly hole closed, and the beast shrank a few inches.

Although annoyed, Saffron couldn't fault the fighter's mistake. Few could mentally prepare for an encounter like this. The poor man had reacted reflexively. She aimed at the beast's face and fired. The empty click took her by surprise. Damn it. She'd forgotten to prime the chamber. The beast's curled horns straightened into spears and rammed through the fighter's chest. Displaying its skewered kill, it rose on its hind legs and roared. Flinging its head, it sent the bloodied fighter crashing against a rocky wall. Saffron pumped her gun and fired. Her round obliterated the Wirador Wosrah's face. The ensuing pool of black liquid offered no comfort. Her failing had cost another his life.

Screams, cries, and roars blended into a singular, overbearing discord. Even with the group's powerful weapons, Rabbit Cove fighters fell to the Wirador Wosrah's mighty grip and speared horns. Saffron sucked back her grief. Did her father truly understand the destruction five thousand of these things would cause? When the Terefellian queen—Eifa—marched her army on Vitus, the loss of life would be immeasurable.

Despite the carnage, the brave fighters didn't give up. The Wirador Wosrah that had survived the ravine fall and the ones that had chased Rabbie and Zack dwindled to a final, unrelenting beast.

BANG! Lyrik's skillful shot converted the creature into sludge.

Amongst the victory cheers, a scream rang out. A death glob had latched onto a young female fighter.

Jensen ran to her. Saffron followed. As he reached for the black stuff, she pulled back his hand. "Don't touch it!" she said. "Once it gets on your skin, it starts eating you alive."

"Daddy! Help me!" the young woman cried.

Saffron's insides knotted. This girl was Jensen's daughter. She couldn't let him live through the same horror she'd experienced when a chunk of Eifa's muck had devoured her mother. The glob clung to the back of the young woman's black leather boot. Slicing through the front laces, Saffron pulled the boot off. The thick sock came also, dragging smears of blood along the young woman's lower calf. As if aware the boot no longer provided access to a viable host, the glob peeled itself off.

"Everyone! Get to high ground," Saffron yelled.

The surviving fighters jumped onto boulders and sturdy ledges.

Seemingly frustrated, the black ball bounced along the rocky periphery in search of a host.

"We need to contain it," Saffron said.

Zack suggested capturing it in one of the heavy-duty cases attached to either side of his bike.

Rabbie had built the airship that Cecilia and Eideard used to fly across the Epona Ocean and was the smartest person Saffron had ever known. If anyone knew of a substance that could contain this stuff, he would. "What do you think?" she asked. "Will Zack's case hold that muck?"

Rabbie's expression held doubt as he eyed the object. "It's plastic, right?" he asked.

"Yeah, but, it's thick," Zack replied.

"I'd feel better with metal. Or glass."

"We have a hermetically sealed glass chamber in our lab," said Jensen. "Will Zack's case hold long enough to get it there?"

While Saffron didn't know what "hermetically sealed" meant, the idea sounded good to her. She flung a hopeful gaze at Rabbie.

"It should hold," he said.

"All right. This is what we'll do," said Saffron.

After laying out her plan, she turned to Zack and Lyrik. "You ready?"

They both nodded.

"Okay, Lyrik. Go!"

Jumping to the ground, Lyrik began stomping her feet and stirring up a fuss. The vibrations attracted the ball. As she ran to a set of rocks at the far side, the ball took chase.

"Now," said Saffron.

Zack dashed to his bike.

The black ball closed in on Lyrik. "Get off the ground!" Saffron yelled.

Lyrik leaped onto a rock seconds before the black glob reached her.

As Zack struggled to unclip the container, the commotion attracted the ball's attention. It turned his way.

Saffron needed to do something, and fast. She dropped from her rock and stomped around. Rabbie and others joined in. This time, the stuff didn't fall for the ploy.

"Zack! Watch out! It's coming!" Lyrik yelled.

In his panic to escape, Zack's shoe snagged on the bike's handle bars, sending him to the dusty ground. The ball sped at his face.

"Meco ymquene oivigeyu hebtare," yelled Saffron. The glob stopped. Saffron blinked. The stuff had understood. She'd taken a chance that if the substance came from Eifa, a host willingly offering themselves to the Terefellian queen would draw its attention. What better way to attract Eifa's essence to a sacrifice than to spout the praise given to the Dark Goddess during the queen's birthing ceremony? *Come, my Queen, I give you breath.*

"What are you doing?" said Rabbie.

"Buying time. Go help Zack." Turning to the glob, she repeated the phrase.

It started rolling her way.

"Let me know when you're ready," she called out, and she bolted.

The black ball gave chase as Saffron darted around the open area.

"Ready!" Rabbie yelled.

"I'm coming," she said.

As she ran past Zack's bike, Rabbie slapped the container over the black glob. The makeshift prison kicked up dust as the substrate pounded around inside like a caged animal.

Flinging himself on top, Rabbie steadied the container's movement with his weight.

Unsettled by the notion of the stuff eating through the plastic and into Rabbie's chest, Saffron found a flat rock and slid it between him and the case.

Nodding his thanks, Rabbie maintained his strain. Eifa's muck certainly had some fight.

Zack stepped over with the container's lid. "How do we get this on?"

"Very carefully," said Rabbie. "I'll lift a corner and we can slide it under."

The container stopped jiggling.

"Wait," Saffron said.

A dark, furry substance, like stringy mold, appeared on a side wall. Saffron dropped to her knees. Unbelievable. The glob had eaten through the container.

"Damn it," said Rabbie.

"It's not all bad," Saffron said. "At least now, we can do this." She shooed him away, flipped the rigid box right side up, and snapped Zack's lid on top. With the sludge adhered to the side wall, it had no chance of escape during the maneuver.

Jensen retrieved a black device from his hip, similar to Yoyo's, and ordered "entry and transportation to the lab." He clipped the device away and turned to Saffron. "Are more of those things out there?" he asked.

"There are," she replied.

"How many?"

She exchanged a quick look with Rabbie. "Close to five thousand."

Jensen's face drained.

Until meeting the Rabbit Cove people, Saffron had all but given up surviving the Wirador Wosrah army and had accepted the limited time she had left with Rabbie. Jensen and his guns offered hope. "Your weapons are very effective," she said. "We can fight those beasts."

"Not with our limited ammunition we can't," Jensen replied.

Burying his face in his blanket, Wyndom relived the magical encounter with Amalardh. A harsh jab to his hip pulled him from his sleepy thoughts. He opened his eyes and yawned. The hour was far too early to rise.

"Our queen is pleased with your work last night," said the Maddowshin. "Such a pity it took inhabiting a female for you to realize their bodies crave pleasure, too."

Wyndom's cheeks burned. Rudella experiencing his intimate night violated him. "I am pleased that our queen is pleased. Now I would appreciate time to rest. As you are well aware, I had an extremely long night."

"Sister Darna is up and ready to leave. I thought you might like to be there when she says goodbye."

Wyndom clenched his blanket. Sister Darna saying "goodbye" meant killing Amalardh. The Maddowshin—Rudella—certainly had a right to be angry about her years of neglect. But to suggest Wyndom watch as Sister Darna slit Amalardh's throat? That rose to an undignified level of savagery. "You are heartless," he uttered.

He covered his head with his blanket. Not that this would help. Regardless of Wyndom's wishes, the Maddowshin would send the feed, complete with all senses so Wyndom would *feel* Sister Darna's knife piercing Amalardh's flesh. He would be forced to watch the life drain from Amalardh's dying eyes and live with the image for a literal eternity.

"You are correct," the Maddowshin said. "Regardless of your

wishes, I will send you the full feed, because maybe I'm not as heartless as you think."

Amalardh's smooth, muscled chest, expansive shoulders, and defined arms filled Wyndom's mind. Sister Darna seemed to appreciate studying the sleeping Croilar Tier's polished physique more than before. The Maddowshin had described Darna's awareness of Wyndom's presence controlling her body as similar to experiencing a dream. Had she woken from this "dream" feeling a deeper connection to Amalardh? Was she doubting taking his life? Or did she simply find the image of his golden torso, half-covered with his tawny cloak and backdropped by his gray wolf cape, attractive to the eye like a masterful piece of art?

She pulled a knife from Amalardh's waist belt and held the shiny tip to his throat.

Wyndom tensed. Whatever "dream" Darna had woken from, she remained a Wrethun Lof, bent on completing her duty.

Amalardh's blue eyes opened. Sister Darna may as well have held a kitten to his neck, for he seemed undaunted by her threat.

"You know I must kill you," she said. "That is my purpose."

"I would be disappointed if you didn't try."

She pressed the blade more firmly to his skin. A drop of blood escaped.

Far from developing any new feelings for Amalardh, Darna's earlier scanning of his physique had been her savoring the moment of a defenseless prey lying ready for an easy kill. The steady beat of Amalardh's pulse reverberated through the knife and into Wyndom's heart.

Cut the feed, he begged the Maddowshin, but the beastly creature didn't.

Resolved to complete the task at hand, Sister Darna's jaw clenched. *This one is for you, Brother Wyndom*, she said. Instead of thrusting the knife into Amalardh's neck, she leaned forward and kissed him. Long and soft. A flurry of tingles shot to Wyndom's toes.

Breaking from the embrace, Darna stowed the blade. "I'm taking your knife," she said to Amalardh, "and this." She waved a rolled scroll at him.

"As you wish," he replied.

She flung her bag over her shoulder. "I hope I never see you again," she said and sped off into the snowy forest.

Wyndom choked back tears. *Why are you not stopping her and forcing her to complete her task?* he said to the Maddowshin.

You would have our queen's child grow up without a father? Our queen believes the time will come where Amalardh will join our fold. For now, we have what we need from him.

Wyndom's spirits soared. Amalardh joining the Terefellians? What a glorious idea. Sitting up, he wiped the tears from his cheeks. "Thank you, Rudella," he said.

"For what? It was not my choice to let the man live."

"Yes. But you knew what Sister Darna had planned with her goodbye. You could've denied me the experience of that one last kiss. You are right. You are not as heartless as you should be to me."

The Maddowshin tensed. The flicker through its eyes seemed uncharacteristic. Was Rudella's soul struggling to maintain its humanity inside the beast's savage shell?

"You will stop doing that," the Maddowshin said.

"Doing what?"

"Analyzing me." It snorted and marched off.

"Wait," said Wyndom. "What's so important about the knife and the scroll?"

The image of Sister Darna's fingers opening the scroll flashed into Wyndom's mind. Her vision trailed over a map showing lands beyond the Epona Ocean and narrowed in on a circular icon and the words: *The Forbidden Pool.*

"The waters in that pool are what you seek," said the Maddowshin. "One sip will deliver the queen's promise of everlasting life."

Wyndom pressed his hand to his gaping mouth. His glorious queen truly *did* plan to uphold her end of the bargain. Not that he ever doubted she would. Okay, maybe he'd had some doubts. Maintaining unconditional faith challenged him.

Lying back down on his resting mat, he breathed in the dewy air. What a wonderful morning. He'd returned to the queen's good graces for completing a job that was literally his pleasure to complete; Amalardh was alive; and the Terefellians possessed directions to the waters of everlasting life.

"Enjoy your rest, Brother Wyndom. You have . . . earned it," said the Maddowshin.

As Wyndom rolled onto his side and snuggled into his blanket, the image of the knife Sister Darna had taken from Amalardh flashed into his mind. The vision came from his memory, not from a feed sent by the Maddowshin. "One last thing," he said. "You still didn't explain why Darna took that knife."

The Maddowshin stopped. Its fist pumped as though annoyed that Wyndom was revisiting this issue. Without turning around, it spoke to him through its mind. *A Croilar Tier knife has a far greater purpose than just a trophy. Dead or alive, our queen requires Amalardh's weapon.*

"Yes. This much I understand," Wyndom said. Abhorring talking to the beast's back, he stood and walked over to it. "Dearest Rudella, I may not have been the best steward with learning the Terefellian scriptures, but I can assure you, the blade in Sister Darna's possession is not Amalardh's ancestral knife."

The Maddowshin's nostrils flared. "Perhaps you should keep this information to yourself. Perhaps you should go back to bed and let this day remain glorious. Our queen has just received news of her child. Would you have this joyous moment superseded by inconsequential information? She has greater things to worry about than an eighth Croilar Tier knife when we already have seven of them. Agreed?"

Wyndom nodded. Of course, Rudella was right. His silence on the matter would not reflect deception, but an act of protection. The queen did not need the additional trouble. He went to walk off when the queen's voice boomed in his head. *Are my Terefellian leader and celebrated Maddowshin keeping secrets from me?*

Wyndom recoiled from the Maddowshin's glare. The contempt in Rudella's eyes at his inability to leave well enough alone ran deep.

Come hither. Both of you, the queen said.

Smoke ribbons shot from the temple door and dragged Wyndom and the Maddowshin across the sandy ground and into the enormous chamber.

When the queen had first arrived, five thousand souls that the Terefellians had captured over the centuries flew into her, creating an enormous black mass that had filled the vast temple. Since birthing close to four thousand Wirador Wosrah, the mass had shrunk to a fifth of its former size. The undulating lumps and bumps from the warriors forming inside stilled. The queen had stopped her birthing process. A tubular striation arched out from the mass and suctioned to the temple floor. The other end broke free, and the arch straightened into a column. Ripples at the base shot upward, forming Eifa—the Terefellian queen. Her liquid skin shimmered as though the surface of her eight-foot-tall body remained in constant motion.

The Maddowshin bowed its head. "My Queen—"

"Do not 'my Queen' me! I will be the one who decides which news is troublesome and which is not."

The Maddowshin cowered. "Yes, my Queen."

"Show me these seven knives we have."

"I can assure you; they are safe—"

As if aided by an unseen force gripping its throat, the Maddowshin lifted into the air. Its face contorted as its cloven legs dangled freely above the ground.

Terrified that he, too, would suffer the same fate, Wyndom dropped to his knees. "My Queen. Your wish is always my command. I will open our lock box so you may see our work for you has been honorable."

The force holding the Maddowshin must have released because the beast collapsed to the ground with a harsh thud.

"Show me," the queen said.

Bolted to the back corner of the temple sat a chest that housed the captured Croilar Tier knives. Tarnished infinity snakes mottled the metal surface. Along the front, four goat skulls acted as turn locks. Sweat prickled over Wyndom's skin as he stepped up to the chest. He'd blurted the offer to present the knives without considering his ability to deliver. His father had taught him a rhyme to help remember the lock's combination, but the words escaped him.

He glanced at the Maddowshin, hopeful for Rudella's help, but she'd not been there when his father had opened the chest. Was this why the Maddowshin didn't want to discuss Darna's failure to take the Croilar Tier knife? Had Rudella feared the news would lead to this very moment, of the queen wanting to see the other knives, and because Rudella knew Wyndom better than he knew himself, she'd suspected he'd forgotten the combination? Oh. His dearest Rudella. She'd been trying to protect him.

"You are keeping your queen waiting," Eifa said. "I wait for no one."

"My deepest apologies," said Wyndom. "I just need a moment . . ." How did that silly poem go? His spine straightened as the first line popped into his head. "The first Terefellian takes three steps right," he said out loud. With each "step" reflecting a ninety-degree turn, and the words "left" or "right" signifying the directional twist, Wyndom dialed the first goat-head handle two-hundred and seventy degrees clockwise. "The second Terefellian is left with upside-down sight." He dialed the second goat handle ninety degrees counterclockwise. "The third Terefellian goes right back home." He rotated the next knob three-hundred and sixty degrees clockwise. "And the fourth Terefellian stays alone." He didn't touch the last handle.

He pointed to an indentation between the second and third dials, matching the size and shape of the Terefellian goat head ring. Since the Maddowshin wore the ancient artifact on its finger, Wyndom asked the beast to press the ring's top into the depression.

CLUNK! An internal lock released.

Hinges creaked as Wyndom lifted the heavy, wrought iron lid.

He gaped at the empty box. Oh no! Where were the knives?

CHAPTER

9

In the frigid morning air, Amalardh's naked torso should be cold. But the guilt tearing through him numbed his senses. What had he done? How could he have betrayed Cecilia, with a Terefellian no less? He stood and got dressed. Flinging his sword and bag over his shoulder, he trekked off. Hiking through the snow on an empty stomach probably wasn't the wisest thing, but right now, his belly couldn't handle food. He was correct in thinking he would never make a competent father to Alistair. No father should ever dishonor a child's mother the way Amalardh had. More than ever, he hoped the death he was facing would happen soon because he could never look Cecilia or his son in the eye ever again.

The warming southern air rendered the snow to slush. By late afternoon, green and muddy-brown dominated the once-white landscape. In the distance came the sound of running water. The Horga River. Amalardh stood on its pebbly bank as a gushing waterfall bellowed to his left.

"Ahoy down there!" called Forbillian. He stood at the waterfall's top, waving his arms.

When Amalardh reached the top of the thirty-foot climb, his uncle pulled him into an unexpected embrace. If he knew what Amalardh had done, instead of hugging him, Forbillian would have shoved him back over the edge.

"When you left with that woman, I thought I wouldn't see you

65

again," Forbillian said. "Since she's not here, I have to wonder, did the hunter become the hunted?"

"I didn't kill her, if that's what you're asking."

"That's a shame. So what happened? Where is she?"

"Nothing happened," snapped Amalardh. He marched to the campsite and dropped his gear on the ground.

"Steady on," Forbillian replied. "No need to get your knickers in a knot. While I would've preferred hearing you slit her throat, I take it she got what she needed from you and split."

She most definitely got what she needed from Amalardh. Riddled with shame, he strode off in search of firewood. Oisin joined him. Didn't the kid get the hint that Amalardh wanted his space? Apparently not, because Oisin lingered. "Is there something you want?" Amalardh asked.

Oisin's gaze dropped to Amalardh's empty sheath. "She stole your knife."

"No. She stole the one you switched with mine."

Oisin's cheeks turned bright red. He pulled Amalardh's Croilar Tier knife from his pocket and handed it to him.

Back in the Prophet's ice cave, when the normally sure-footed Oisin had "accidentally" knocked into him, Amalardh knew something was up. Since the Prophet seemed behind Oisin's actions, he didn't pursue the matter. The act's purpose would surface soon enough. The answer came just last night. While preparing the rabbit, Amalardh had pulled the knife from his sheath and felt the difference immediately.

"I'm sorry," said Oisin. "I did what the Prophet told me to. I figured he knew what Darna was up to."

Amalardh slotted his knife away. "You did good," he said.

"I guess it's lucky she didn't know what a real Croilar Tier knife looked like. Why do you think she wanted it?"

Amalardh didn't know. But he doubted the purpose was to use as a keepsake for their guilty night. "I'd say she needed proof that she'd completed her order and killed the last Croilar Tier," he replied.

*

After starting the campfire, Amalardh rummaged through his bag for his fishing twine. His fingers hit upon a crocheted red bear the size of his palm. Shoving it aside, he finished retrieving his gear. He closed his bag and a heaviness dragged on his chest. As much as he tried, he couldn't deny the ache tearing at his heart any longer. Pulling open his bag, he grabbed the red bear and headed upstream.

The rich soil provided plentiful bait. He threaded a worm onto his fishing hook and cast the line into the slow-flowing water. As he waited for a bite, he sat down and rubbed the bear's tattered ear from where Alistair had teethed. Before embarking on this journey, Cecilia had snuck the toy into Amalardh's bag. Until this moment, he had conveniently ignored it. Although he'd fought for the Goddess of Light, living life under Eifa's dark cloud as a cold, detached assassin had been an easier existence. Back then, he wasn't even aware of the Dark Goddess's presence. Now, every day was a struggle to resist her pull. Holding this bear helped Amalardh remember Siersha's light.

Footsteps crunched along the pebbly shore. Amalardh tucked the small piece of home into his pocket as Forbillian flopped onto a rock next to him.

"Before you get all crusty and start whining about, 'Can't you people take a hint for when someone wants to be left alone?' let me assure you, I can take a hint. I just choose not to." He scooped up a collection of pebbles. "I meant what I said earlier. I barely slept a wink, worrying about whether I'd see you again. And not just me. You know you mean everything to that kid."

Amalardh didn't deserve Oisin's or his uncle's worry. "You both think that little of my skill?" he asked dryly.

"No. Of course not. It's just . . ." He bounced the pebbles in his hand. "Let's just say, a man is more likely to let his guard down around a woman. So, with that in mind, she still could've harmed you."

Amalardh kept his focus on his fishing line. He didn't want to see the concern he knew would be etched in his uncle's eyes.

"Idiot me," Forbillian said. "I forgot who I was talking to. Here I am terrified that a Wrethun Lof had slaughtered my only nephew when I should've realized it's impossible to stab a heart made of stone." He tossed a pebble into the river.

Amalardh glared at him.

"What?" Forbillian asked, feigning innocence.

"If you'd rather not have fish for dinner, then keep that up."

Dropping the pebbles, Forbillian wiped his hands on his trousers. "The kid told me about what happened with the knife. I gather she took the map as well."

"She did."

Incapable of sitting still, Forbillian picked up a solitary pebble and fiddled with it.

"I wouldn't worry too much about the map. It was a decoy," Amalardh said.

Forbillian's fidgeting fingers stilled.

"At least, the directions to the Forbidden Pool were," he clarified. While not immediately apparent, Amalardh had noticed a slight variation in the ink used to draw the pool icon and write the *Forbidden Pool* text. Someone, the Prophet no doubt, had drawn it in after the fact.

"Those fools can have their eternal life," said Forbillian. "Me? Once I'm done with my years down here, I want out. The human soul is not made for eternity on earth. I saw as much on the Prophet's face."

So had Amalardh. The Prophet had seemed relieved to confront his death.

"Why do you figure the Terefellian chose not to kill you?" Forbillian asked.

Amalardh's jaw tensed. Couldn't his uncle just drop it? "Maybe my charm won her over," he replied.

Forbillian's chuckle turned into a full-blown belly laugh.

In another place, another time, Amalardh could see himself

becoming quite close to his uncle. But "another place and another time" wasn't Amalardh's destiny. His grave had been dug. And while he certainly wouldn't be as relieved as the Prophet to face his death, he would face it for, hopefully, the third and last time. "You should spend less time trying to figure out why I'm not dead and more time focused on the facts," he said.

Forbillian's laughter settled. "Which facts?"

"If a Croilar Tier knife is supposedly just a mere trinket, a trophy for the hunter to put on their wall, why did the Prophet not want my knife to fall into the Terefellians' hands?"

"The knife opens the Croilar Tier Archives," said Forbillian. "Maybe the Prophet wanted to ensure the Terefellians didn't get inside."

"The Terefellians supposedly possess seven other keys capable of unlocking the archive door. The knives have to hold an alternate importance."

Forbillian pondered the notion. "Well, I certainly have no answers. Hopefully, our next destination will. I dare say, it's not too far away. Do you remember a marking on the map of a building perched on top of a mountain peak? The Prophet told me that 'from where the waters fall, you will see my old home in the sky.'" He stood and motioned into the distance. "I can only imagine the Prophet intends that structure as our next destination."

Amalardh followed his uncle's pointing finger to a structure on a mountain top. Since the Prophet had wanted Forbillian on this journey because of Forbillian's navigational skills, Amalardh supposed his uncle was correct.

Studying the pebble in his hand, Forbillian grew quiet. "This Forbidden Pool—the one that gave the Prophet his eternal life; the same one the Terefellians seem so set on finding—can't be 'the' Forbidden Pool from Siersha's story, can it?"

A similar concern had crossed Amalardh's mind, only that would be impossible. The Forbidden Pool from Siersha's story lay in the gods' realm. According to the old scriptures, at the dawn of time, Eifa had not existed. One day, Siersha went against the orders of her father—the Great Creator—and swam in the Forbidden Pool. Moments before she drowned, the Great Creator pulled her out. Because of her disobedience, he commanded that henceforth the world would know what it was for the Goddess of Light to have a shadow. The water drained from Siersha's body, forming a black mirror image, whom the Great Creator named Eifa.

"I imagine the Prophet named the water hole with the power to give eternal life after the pool in the scriptures because they both contain evil," Amalardh said. "Not because they are the same."

The glowing red sun disappeared below the horizon and a chill set in. Amalardh pulled his empty line from the water. The three of them would have to go hungry. As he and Forbillian neared the campsite, an aromatic scent wafted through the air. By the fire sat Oisin, roasting a wild hen.

"You could've mentioned you'd already caught dinner," Amalardh said.

"You seemed so set on fishing. I figured it would be a nice opportunity for you and I to have some quality time," Forbillian replied. Snapping a leg from the bird, he bit into the juicy meat.

Surprisingly, Amalardh wasn't mad. The chat with his uncle had been a needed distraction.

"Hey, Forbs," said Oisin, "did you show Amalardh what the Prophet gave you?"

"Oh. Right. You're going to love this." He wiped his sticky hands on his shirt, retrieved the rolled scroll that the Prophet had given him, and handed it to Amalardh.

"This is the third section of the map, correct?" Amalardh said.

Forbillian made a dubious face. "Just open it."

Amalardh unraveled the paper. The parchment was blank. "What is this supposed to mean?"

Forbillian shrugged. "Your guess is as good as mine." He rolled it up, slipped it back into his pocket, and patted the area. "The Prophet told me to keep this on my person at all times."

As the flatbed buggy hummed along Rabbit Cove's long main corridor, Saffron hugged her arms to her chest. The smooth gray cement of the walls, ceiling, and floor made this underground world feel cold. The buggy turned into a smaller tunnel and stopped outside a metallic door marked *Laboratory*. The door opened of its own accord and out stepped two people covered head to toe in white, rubbery suits. They clamped long metal pincers to the container and carried it back through the open door.

Saffron, Rabbie, Zack, Lyrik, Jensen, and Jensen's daughter, who had introduced herself as Kayla, followed the rubbery individuals into a pristine white room furnished mostly with metal. At the back of the room stood a glass chamber the size of a large closet. The white-suited folk stepped inside and lowered their load. When they exited, the chamber's door made a whooshing sound as it closed.

"That enclosure is airtight," said Zack. "Nothing can get in or out."

"Well, unless that stuff can eat through glass," Lyrik added.

The two people, a man and woman of about forty years of age, peeled out of their rubber clothes and slipped white coats over their buttoned-down shirts. Jensen introduced them as Doctors Mike and Maureen and referred to them as Rabbit Cove's "resident scientists."

"They're our parents," Lyrik said.

Lyrik and Zack were brother and sister? Now that Saffron had time to study them, they did have similar button noses and heart-shaped faces, and they both had honey-colored eyes. Where Zack's seemed more reserved, Lyrik's had a wilder edge.

Several official-looking people piled into the room spouting, "What the hell just happened?" "What were those things?" "What is that stuff?"

Quieting them, Jensen suggested moving to the conference room, where they would have more space to talk.

About half of the black substance had oozed out of the plastic container. "I'm not leaving that unattended," Saffron said. "If it gets out, the only way to destroy it will be to let it eat someone and then stab the resulting beast in the eyes."

The room exploded with sharp chatter. One woman blasted Jensen for bringing "that stuff" inside "our home."

"If he hadn't," Saffron said, "it would sit outside and wait until someone left. You'd be prisoners."

"We would be as we've always been," the woman replied. "Safe and content in our home."

Jensen placated the room with his arms. "This substance is here now, so everyone, just settle down and get comfortable. It looks like we'll be continuing our discussion here." He turned to Saffron and Rabbie. "Tell us everything we need to know."

The group listened while Rabbie explained his connection to Vitus, the downfall of the Senators, and how his sister, Cecilia, and brother, Eideard, had crossed the Epona Ocean in search of a possible weapon to destroy the Dark Goddess. Saffron told her story, including her people's involvement in Eifa's rise and their creation of an all-powerful Wirador Wosrah army.

"We were on our way to warn my people of the threat brewing down south," said Rabbie, "When Lyrik and Zack saved us from those beasts."

Heads turned to a thudding noise coming from the glass chamber. The black blob had escaped the plastic container and was rolling around, looking for life.

Walking over, Saffron kneeled down and placed her palm to

the thick, clear wall. The ball sped at her and splatted against the glass. She flinched but kept her hand in place.

The male scientist—Dr. Mike—crouched next to her. "Nice work," he said. "Keep still. You have it in the perfect position." Saffron hadn't intended to do anything ingenious. She wanted to see if it could eat through its prison wall.

Dr. Mike placed a tubular object that he called a microscopy camera between her fingers and hit a button. A flat, rectangular object on the wall lit up.

"Unbelievable," Rabbie uttered. "It's television."

Twisting a small dial on the camera, Dr. Mike explained that with every turn, the image on the screen mapped a close-up of the foreign matter. What initially seemed like a flat, black surface morphed into tiny hairs, and then to—

"Geez," said Jensen. "What is that?"

Thousands of miniscule, sharp-fanged snakes opened and closed their mouths as they attempted to eat through the glass. Thankfully, they couldn't make traction with the smooth surface.

Since they now knew the substance wasn't going anywhere, Jensen suggested the group leave and allow the "more intelligent" amongst them space to do their work.

"I'm fine right here," Saffron said.

"Our parents are the best at what they do," said Lyrik. "Trust me. They'll figure out a way to destroy that stuff. Now, come on. We've got some cool things to show you."

Reluctantly, Saffron obliged.

As Saffron and Rabbie walked with Lyrik and Zack through several cement tunnels, Lyrik explained how Rabbit Cove was built before the time of the Great War in preparation for an apocalypse. When the first missiles hit, a thousand of the area's top scientists, military personnel, and various other specialists took shelter. "That's why you need to trust our parents," she said. "They're descendants of some of the smartest people ever born."

"Yes, but not everyone got the brain gene," quipped Zack.

Playfully, Lyrik whacked him over the back of the head. "And not everyone was lucky enough to develop common sense."

Saffron allowed herself a small grin. Considering everything that had happened, Lyrik and Zack's high spirits helped ease her tension.

They passed through an immense room filled with fish tanks to another area containing chickens roaming a cultivation of leafy plants. "As you can see, we are fully self-sufficient," Lyrik said.

In another room stood a massive metal cylinder that Zack called their power generator. Heat from within the earth's core, combined with water from an underground stream, produced steam to turn turbines and create electricity. As Saffron quietly took everything in, Rabbie asked a ton of questions, including how they rebuilt motorbikes from before the time of the Great War.

The siblings shared a smirk. "They're not rebuilt," Lyrik said.

She led them along another corridor and slid open a large door labeled *Garage*. Rabbie's eyes bugged at the dozens of shiny vehicles inside. And so did Saffron's. She'd only seen rusted versions of these magnificent machines.

Hoisting herself onto the hood of a mottled beige vehicle, Lyrik told Rabbie that Rabbit Cove knew of his people's "Battle for Freedom" fight. "When the dust settled, we sent up drones to investigate Vitus's new leaders."

"They're like flying cameras that let us see what's happening outside," Zack added.

"When central command determined Vitus was no longer a threat, Zack and I got special permission from Jensen to start using the bikes for our scavenger hunts."

"Your weapons and machinery are far greater than what the Soldiers of Vitus ever had," Rabbie said. "Your leaders could've ended the Senators' reign, and you would've been free to roam outside long ago."

"We have a saying here in Rabbit Cove," said Lyrik. "Don't

wake a sleeping dog. Vitus never really bothered us, so why stir up any trouble? Besides, how were we to know what weapons they did and didn't have?"

"Your people can't stay on the sidelines forever," Rabbie said. "When Eifa unleashes her army, everyone who doesn't submit will be a direct threat."

Lyrik slid off the vehicle's hood. "You guys are such doom and gloom. We've got a ton of fun things to show you. But first, I'm hungry. Come on."

She led the way into a large dining area filled with mumbled chatter, clanking cutlery, and wild smells. Saffron's stomach rumbled. She and Rabbie had lived on scant little over the past few days. As Lyrik guided them along a counter filled with food, various people side-glanced Saffron and Rabbie's way. Did their looks hold contempt? For years, Rabbit Cove had seemingly lived a trouble-free existence, and now two strangers had come along and upended their world.

"You'll have to forgive our busy bodies," said Jensen, who, tray in hand, had stepped up behind Saffron. "We haven't seen a new face in . . . well, never. How's the tour coming along?"

"You have a fascinating home," Saffron said. Which wasn't a lie. Although somewhat claustrophobic with its lack of windows, this place definitely drew her attention.

"Some spots have opened up, so you're welcome to stay as long as you wish," Jensen said.

Spots have opened up? What did that mean?

A young man, whom Saffron recognized as one of the earlier fighters, strode up to a young woman with brunette hair tied in a neat ponytail. His face beamed as he told her that he had good news. Six Rabbits had just died in a fight. The young woman bounced up and down. "I know," she said. She'd already heard the fantastic report. They flung their arms around each other and hugged.

Were these the spots that had opened up? How could these people express joy over such loss? While the Terefellians certainly didn't regard death with the same level of reverence as Rabbie's people, at least they didn't jump around with excitement.

"Rabbit Cove can only host a finite number of people," Jensen said. "Our rules stipulate that a couple cannot plan for a child until a resident passes away. Young Blake and Susan over there will receive a family planning pass."

Copying Jensen, Saffron scooped a pile of mushy stuff onto her plate. "With the fall of the Senators of Vitus, your people are safe to roam outside," she said. "If they want children, why not just leave?"

As they walked to where Rabbie, Lyrik, and Zack sat, Jensen explained that when the Rabbit Cove leaders determined Vitus no longer held danger, they told their people they were free to leave under the proviso they could only return if space became available. No one left. Given the choice to go and start a family with no restrictions, the Rabbit Cove people chose to stay and play what Jensen referred to as "the baby lottery."

Jensen and Saffron's chairs grated loudly on the cement floor as they pulled them out to sit. "We have to prepare for the worst-case scenario," Jensen said. "And by the looks of it, that scenario is just around the corner. When our front door is sealed, we have the resources to house a thousand people and not a single mouth more. If we grow to a population greater than our limits and we need to return to lockdown, what then? How do we determine who stays and who goes? If we cannot figure a way to beat these beasts, we will have to lock ourselves in—and stay sealed from the outside world forever if need be."

Lock themselves in? What did that mean? Before Saffron could ask, Kayla, Jensen's daughter, strode over and told her father he needed to come to the control room. Apparently, their sensors had picked up some strange activity. She glanced at Saffron and Rabbie. "You two should also come."

"You four, you mean," said Lyrik. "If this involves them, it involves us."

Jensen sighed as though he'd been up against Lyrik's determination before. Of the hundreds of people living in Rabbit Cove, Lyrik and Zack receiving sole permission to fire up the motor bikes for use outside was probably no accident. The persistent girl had probably worn Jensen to the nub.

The group followed Kayla along a corridor into a room with multiple screens on the wall showing different images of the outside world. On one screen, thick black smoke plumed into the air.

"It's coming from somewhere down south," Kayla said.

Saffron's stomach lurched. Terefellia.

Jensen must have caught her knowing stare. "What's going on?" he asked.

"That smoke is Eifa—the Dark Goddess."

The images on the other screens darkened.

"What is she doing?" Jensen asked.

Saffron shook her head. The act confounded her.

Rabbie grabbed the back of a chair. "She's blocking out the sun. Only in darkness can you see light." As the room shared a confused look, his fingertips dug into the chair's soft material. "The Dark Goddess is searching for my sister. Cecilia."

THE WOODEN STAIRCASE clinging to the mountain Malek had earlier pointed out looked far more dangerous up close. Its rotten beams and rusted bolts seemed barely capable of holding their own weight, let alone that of Cecilia, Malek, and Eideard. With every step since leaving the grass mound hut, Cecilia's damaged right thigh had felt ready to give out. How could she possibly climb such a steep ascent? Whoever built the precarious apparatus seemed to have been undecided on whether a ladder or a staircase best suited the trail, so they constructed something in between.

A rusted chain bolted to the mountain provided an anchor for Cecilia to haul herself with. Sweat dripped from her temples as she plodded one foot after the other. Several feet ahead, the steep stairs curved right. *Just to the corner, just to the corner, I just have to make it to the corner*, she said to herself. Something about the endless climb and telling herself "just to the whatever-it-was" felt familiar, like she'd said those words before during an equally exhausting hike. A few steps before reaching her target, Malek motioned for her and Eideard to rest on a small stone outcropping.

"I have to admit," Eideard said, "those mini-goals you set for yourself really do work on hikes like this."

She tilted her head at him. How did he know she'd been breaking the hike into bite-sized chunks? She'd spoken her mantra to herself.

Noting her confusion, he apologized. "I keep forgetting that you've forgotten everything you've told me. When you hiked the Bodwin Mountains with Amalardh, you said that setting mini-goals helped with the trudge. 'Just to the rock, just to the rock, I just have to make it to the rock.' I've been doing the same."

Comfort cloaked her. At least her inner self hadn't totally forgotten who she was. She reflected upon the person Eideard had mentioned—Amalardh—and her warm fuzzies dissipated. Even though she couldn't remember Eideard, she had felt a kinship with him right from the start. What if, upon reuniting with this man she supposedly loved, she felt nothing?

Malek stood, indicating that the rest break was over. "When we pass around the corner ahead, you must keep hold of the chain at all times. And don't look down."

His tone suggested the trail in front held more peril than the stairs they'd just climbed. How much worse could it get? Cecilia followed Malek around the curve and her stomach dropped. A series of long planks bolted three abreast ran parallel to the sheer cliff, forming a long, horizontal track barely a foot and a half wide. She glanced at the distant valley below and her legs went weak. *He warned you not to look down.*

The planks creaked as she stepped onto the first set. *This is insane. Who in their right mind would build such a dangerous path?*

Over the next few steps, Cecilia's nerves settled enough for her to appreciate the magnificent view. Shrubs and tall pines that somehow found life on the steep cliffs mottled the rocky surroundings. Even in such extreme conditions, they'd survived.

"Come on, sleepy," said Eideard from behind.

Her focus on the surrounding landscape had slowed her pace. She increased her stride. An anchor attaching the chain to the rock wall required her to let go in order to grab the links on the other side. Because of her widened step, her right knee buckled. She swiped for the lifeline, but missed. As she stumbled forward, the outer plank broke loose, sending her over the edge. Terror shot through her as she grabbed the remaining walkway.

"Help!" she yelled.

Eideard latched onto her wrist. "I've got you," he said. The days spent partially comatose had weakened his muscles and his effort to pull her up failed. Her hand began slipping in his sweaty grasp. She took in his terrified expression and a flash of recognition burst into her mind. She'd seen that look before.

Malek rushed back. Built like a brick tower, he hauled Cecilia to safety.

She plastered herself against the cliff wall. "I remember you," she said to Eideard. His drawn expression perked. "When I was little, I followed you up a tree, even though you told me not to. I slipped. You caught me before I fell." She recalled little else from her past, but she did know Eideard was her brother.

He wiped the sweat from his brow. "You couldn't have just remembered me from my winning personality?"

Cecilia smiled. Without a doubt, this sarcastic young man was family.

"I'm happy about this news," said Malek. "But this isn't the place for celebration. We must get moving."

Several hundred feet later, a place for celebration arrived. Cecilia stepped onto firm ground and threw her arms around Eideard. As she held him tight, her brother no longer *felt* like home. He *was* home.

She broke from the hug and her joy waned. Ahead lay another long stretch of steps. Made of stone, their pitch, at least, rose at a reasonable angle.

"They are the last of the climb," said Malek. He handed Cecilia and Eideard an apple. "After what just happened, I think we all deserve a rest."

Flopping to the rocky ground, Cecilia rubbed her right thigh. Eideard plopped next to her. Now that some of her memory had returned, he wanted to know if she also recalled this, that, and the other. Some moments he spoke about sounded familiar, like the time he and Rabbie had play-wrestled on their bunk bed and it collapsed. She had a sense of this other brother, Rabbie, but couldn't picture him.

Malek sliced a piece of apple with his knife and popped it into his mouth. "Right now, your mind is like a dam," he said, while chewing. "You've sprung a leak. Soon, you'll spring another and another until the dam collapses. Everything will come rushing back."

"How do I spring another leak?" Cecilia asked.

"The fastest way might be what just happened. Reliving a trauma from your past. But as you can see, it's not the safest. What you need is time. Let's hope we have enough on our side."

The ground darkened as though a cloud passed in front of the sun.

Black smoke filled the sky.

"That must be some intense fire," Eideard said.

The whites of Malek's eyes grew. He tossed his apple aside. "That's no fire. We need to hide your sister."

His sense of urgency rattled Cecilia.

"Eifa is looking for your light," Malek said to her. "Once that smoke fully suffocates the sun's rays, you'll be like a beacon in the night."

As the sky darkened, Malek's panic grew. Trapped on the mountainside, they had no cave or outcropping to shelter under. "Get on the ground, face down," he ordered of her.

Because Eideard seemed as worried as Malek, Cecilia dropped without question. Using their bodies as shields, the two men covered her. Until this moment, Malek's talk of goddesses, Croilar Tier, and a Prophecy had seemed more fantasy than fact. But with the rising smoke turning day to night, Cecilia sensed a reality behind Malek's tale. A knot formed in her belly. Malek had told her that as the Caladium, she possessed the power to poison Eifa. How was anyone supposed to poison something capable of turning itself into smoke?

"Are you okay?" Malek asked. "Let us know if we're squashing you."

"I'm fine," Cecilia replied. Based on the severity of the circumstances, the rock digging into her knee and the lumpy thing crushing her ribs hardly warranted complaint.

"It's been weeks since we left the western lands," said Eideard. "Why would Eifa wait until now to search for Cecilia?"

"I dare not say the Dark Goddess waited," Malek replied. "Until this point, I imagine she believed everything had been going to plan. Something must have made her think otherwise. As dire as this moment may seem, we must take it as a good sign. Whatever plan Eifa had in place has possibly gone awry."

Minutes later, the sky cleared. The weights rolled off Cecilia's back.

"Do you think she found us?" Eideard asked.

Malek couldn't be certain. Either way, they had to press forward.

As Cecilia rubbed out her knee and bruised ribs, a deep anger brewed. The idea of this entity—Eifa—hunting her inflamed her fury. While she wasn't sure why this Dark Goddess evoked such rage, she appreciated the drive it brought. Grabbing the rusty chain, she marched the last flight of stairs without so much as a flutter of weakness in her thigh.

She reached a grassy slope and marveled at a white, multi-level building with a burgundy roof and matching trim perched in the center of a series of circular, tiered levels of lawn. A pathway with stone steps cutting through the flattened sections led to the front porch.

"What is this place?" Cecilia asked.

"The Nian Temple," said Malek. "The last time I came here, I was just a boy. If anyone can help us figure out our next steps, the woman who lives here can."

When they reached the top plateau, one of the building's double doors opened. Out stepped a pale, elderly woman hunched over a cane made from a tree branch. Her gray hair, which she'd styled into a waist-length braid, retained strands of its former dark coloring.

"Malek," she said in a friendly, croaky voice. "You came."

Malek smiled.

A light-skinned, bald man built as broad as Malek stepped out. He wore dark clothing, thick boots, and a hard expression. A long, black gun hung from his shoulder. Two more similarly dressed individuals followed: a light-skinned male and a dark-skinned female, both carrying the same dangerous weapon.

"The Countess is extremely disappointed," the bald man said to Malek.

"I know that guy," whispered Eideard. "He was with Malek when we washed up on the beach. They work together in the hospital."

Malek's eyes thinned. "This doesn't concern you, Davian."

"Give me our two young friends and no one has to die," Davian said.

The old woman nodded at Malek, as if suggesting they'd lost. As Malek's head lowered, his eyes flitted from Cecilia to her sword. "Your mind may not remember," he whispered, "but let's hope your body does."

What did that mean—

Cecilia startled as the old woman smacked her cane across Davian's face.

Shoving Cecilia and Eideard onto the tiered surface below, Malek pulled a handgun from his belt and fired. Missing mortar between the retaining wall's upper row of stone slabs offered a filtered view of the fight above.

Davian's body jolted as a red dot marred his forehead. Behind him, a bloodied mess from where the back of his head exploded sprayed against the building's white wall. As his lifeless body crumpled to the ground, Cecilia's lungs stiffened. These weapons that could kill from a distance were far too dangerous.

As the other two fighters returned a stream of ear-ringing shots, Malek dropped to Cecilia and Eideard's level and pressed himself against the wall.

Although she had the body of a seventy-year-old, the old lady moved like a teenager as she scaled the building's outer wall to its roof, where she crouched low.

Pointing his gun over the wall, Malek blindly fired until the trigger made an empty click.

Like a flying fox, the old lady leaped from the roof onto the female fighter. The remaining combatant turned his gun on the struggle, but didn't shoot, possibly in fear that he would hit his own.

Reloading his weapon, Malek stood and fired. His bullet capped the male fighter's thigh. The gunman retaliated with another spray of bullets. Cecilia cradled her head from the biting shards flying from the retaining wall's ravaged top.

Malek returned fire, allowing Cecilia a moment to peer through the wall's crack. During the struggle with the old lady, the female assailant had dropped her gun, and the fight had morphed into an impressive bout of hand-to-hand combat. As they punched, kicked, and blocked, the fight progressively moved along the side of the building. Crouched low, Cecilia hugged the wall's periphery and followed.

"What are you doing? Come back," whispered Eideard.

Ignoring his plea, Cecilia continued tracking the fight.

A well-placed punch sent the old lady to the ground. Pulling a small pistol from her belt, the young fighter aimed at the woman's head. Without even thinking about it, Cecilia jumped onto the grassy tier and kicked the weapon from the fighter's hand. The shock on the young woman's face matched Cecilia's own. Where had this skill come from?

As if of their own accord, Cecilia's hands reached back and pulled her sword from its hilt. The weighted blade felt comfortable, like an extension of her arm. In this moment, she knew she had killed before and, right now, had every intention to kill again.

She swung the shiny blade at the fighter. Like a nimble cat, the young woman sprang back. As Cecilia swung again, the fighter dove out of the way, then dashed to the back of the building.

Grabbing a three-foot-long pipe from a pile of rubble, the

fighter blocked Cecilia's downward swing. The clang of metal rang familiar. Images of wielding this same sword at men dressed in fitted black leather, with articulated metal gloves sheathing their hands, flooded Cecilia's mind.

Her breath sucked in. *The Battle for Freedom!* With the memory causing a momentary falter, she failed to block the fighter's kicking boot. The painful blow sent Cecilia to her back.

Pinning Cecilia with her knees, the fighter pulled a dagger from her belt. As she swung down, the blade of a spinning knife lodged in her chest. Her eyes glazed as she collapsed sideways.

Pressing onto her elbows, Cecilia stared at the knife. The handle's silver tip had the same mask-wearing wolf as Malek's tattoo. Only, instead of two red eyes, the knife's wolf had only one red ruby and a dark hollow where the other jeweled piece had fallen out.

She looked over her shoulder. A man wearing a glorious wolf cape over a brown, hooded robe stood motionless, as if witnessing a sight that his familiar blue eyes didn't believe.

"Cecilia!" From behind the man ran a teenage boy draped in a spotted lynx coat. He threw his arms around her. Not knowing what to do, she tentatively hugged him back.

Another figure draped in a bear coat followed. His gray-flecked hair hung wild and woolly, like his beard. Thrusting his arms in the air, he joyously called out her name. These people seemed to know her, and Eideard seemed to know them. He greeted the strangers with a wide smile and warm hugs. Forbillian was the name of the woolly haired man, Oisin was the young boy, and . . . Cecilia's throat closed at the sound of the wolf-cape-wearing man's name. Amalardh. He didn't seem nearly as excited to see her as the other two. Not that Cecilia particularly cared. She had no memory of this man and no feelings either.

As Amalardh, Forbillian, and Oisin climbed the north side of the mountain housing the building spotted from the Horga River waterfall, gunfire rang out. Against Forbillian's advice to stay put, Amalardh sped to the top. He would rather face a threat than hide in fear of the unknown. At the building's rear, two young women fought: one light-skinned, the other dark, both equally matched in skill. Although the light-skinned woman's clothing and sword handling seemed familiar, Amalardh didn't recognize her shaved head and sunken pallor.

Knocking the light-skinned woman to the ground, the dark-skinned one straddled her. As she went to deliver a death blow, Amalardh's pulse spiked. Acting on instinct, he threw his knife, skewering the dark-skinned attacker's chest.

"Why in tarnation did you do that?" asked Forbillian in a labored voice.

Amalardh didn't know.

Pressing onto her elbow, the light-skinned fighter sat up and locked eyes with him.

When Cecilia had told Amalardh about the raid on her village and how the shock of the carnage froze her feet to the ground, he hadn't related. But now, staring at the last person on earth he expected to see this far east of the Epona Ocean, the shock turned him into a slab of stone. Even if he could make his legs move, he had no right to embrace Cecilia again. Her reaction compounded his angst. Far from excited to see him, her expression made him feel as though his betrayal with the Terefellian dripped brazenly for all to witness.

As Eideard's warm embrace broke Amalardh from his stupor, he took in Eideard's pale complexion. What had happened to them? Why were their heads shaven, and what were those red marks on Eideard's temples? Did Cecilia have the same?

Concerned for her safety, he rushed to her.

"Amalardh. Wait," Eideard said.

As Amalardh drew near, Cecilia inched behind Oisin.

He stopped in his tracks. What was wrong? Why did she fear him?

Eideard jogged up to his side. "She doesn't remember you," he said. "She barely remembers me."

As Amalardh narrowed in on Cecilia's temple welts, a flurry of anger, shock, and despair swirled within. "Who did this to you?" he asked. When she didn't respond, he went to reach out but immediately retracted at her guarded expression. She truly didn't remember him. The pain of standing so close to his only love yet feeling as though she stood a million miles away burned like hot coals through his heart. Was this how Cecilia had felt these past few months when he'd shut her out?

An elderly woman with a bloodied face and flowing clothing rushed around the building's corner. "I need help up here!" she said.

Pulling his knife from the dead fighter's chest, Amalardh followed the old woman to the front of the building where three men lay strewn, two of which wore clothing matching the person he'd just slain.

Cecilia ran to the one not dressed in black and dropped to his side. "Malek!" she said.

Her familiarity with this man jolted Amalardh. Who was he? How did Cecilia know him?

Malek had his bloodied hand pressed to his flank. Amalardh had studied dead prisoners who'd fallen victim to Senator Caratacus's callous target practice. A bullet lodged in a belly usually meant a slow death. A flank shot, which Malek appeared to have, was not always fatal. He kneeled down and asked permission to take a look. Upon Malek's nod, Amalardh rolled him sideways to check his back.

"There's another hole," Cecilia said. "Is that bad?"

For the shortest moment, the rift between Amalardh and her seemed erased. Then wariness flooded her as their eyes connected.

"It's just the exit wound," Amalardh said.

As if noting that the answer hadn't fully allayed Cecilia's concern, Malek added, "It's a good sign. It means your friend here doesn't have to cut me open to search for the bullet."

Although stung by jealousy for the bond this man had with Cecilia, Amalardh couldn't let it interfere with saving Malek's life. He grabbed a water pouch from Forbillian's belt and sniffed it. "Give me your other one," he said.

Forbillian seemed surprised as he handed over his other pouch.

The pungent aroma confirmed the container held what Amalardh needed. He gave his uncle a look. Did he seriously think Amalardh didn't know about the alcohol? "This is going to burn," he said to Malek. With everything Amalardh had faced during his training as an assassin, the excruciating scorch from when Soldiers poured distilled liquor on his torn flesh after a whipping ranked the worst.

Malek's silent nod held an understanding that pain was a matter of course. As Amalardh poured the alcohol on the weeping wound, Malek barely winced. Either Forbillian's stash contained more water than alcohol, or Malek possessed an iron tolerance. Amalardh supposed the latter. "I need some clean cloth and bandages," he said to the old woman. "And more alcohol, if you have it."

As she hurried to the building, Amalardh motioned for Oisin to help. He then regarded Malek's bloodied shirt. "That needs to come off."

Sitting up, Malek pulled the stained top up and over his head.

"Well, I'll be a pig's boiled trotter," said Forbillian.

Amalardh followed his uncle's gaze to a Croilar Tier tattoo on Malek's right upper arm.

"I do not have one of those," said Malek in regards to Amalardh's stowed knife. "But if I did, we'd be alike. My name is Malek. It is an honor to meet the one called Amalardh. The last Croilar Tier."

Honored? Malek's respect was certainly misplaced.

Right at that moment, Oisin returned with the supplies, including a flagon of distilled spirits. Irritated by his own misgivings, Amalardh poured an overabundance of the flagon's liquid onto Malek's wound.

This time, Malek's face registered pain.

Grabbing the flagon from Amalardh, Malek took a swig. "If I don't drink now, I fear there won't be any left by the time you're done."

As Malek smiled and handed it back, Amalardh sensed an immediate brotherhood, which made Cecilia's concern for this man harder to take. He finished packing the wounds and told him to change the dressing every hour until the bleeding stopped.

Hauling himself to his feet, Malek placed his hand on Amalardh's shoulder and thanked him. Uncomfortable with the praise, Amalardh nodded. Right now, all he wanted was to know what had happened to Cecilia and Eideard. Seeming to understand as much, Malek made a quick introduction of Ida, then requested for her and Cecilia to help him inside.

Eideard's horrific tale of unimaginable beasts, a flying balloon, a shark attack, prison, and agonizing memory-wiping treatments left Amalardh cold. He had been too eager to get out of Vitus and travel with Forbillian to the Croilar Tier Archives. If he'd muted his fervor, stayed a day or two longer, he would've been there when Eifa's beasts arrived. He should have paid more attention when Cecilia spoke of her concern for Analise and Noah. The two teenagers had lived far too sheltered a life to undertake such a long journey on their own. They hadn't deserved their heinous sacrifice to Eifa.

Amalardh lowered himself to the building's front stoop and gripped his balled fist. How could he have been so reckless with Cecilia and Alistair's lives? He was supposed to be a protector, and in every way, he'd failed. Not surprising the Goddess of Light had shown him a vision of another man raising his son. If not for Cecilia's competence, things would've been far worse. Because of her clear thinking in handing Alistair to Marion, she'd spared their son's life. Despite all else, Amalardh could at least rest easy knowing Alistair was safe from Eifa and her Terefellian horde.

How could the chest for the Croilar Tier knives be empty? The blades had been there. At least, four decades ago they had. "These are not toys," Wyndom's father had told ten-year-old Wyndom. "We must not open this again until the eighth and final knife arrives." No one could open the chest without the Terefellian ring. From age twenty, the silver band had decorated Wyndom's finger at all times, until Rudella had stolen it to become the Maddowshin. But she couldn't have taken the knives. She didn't know the combination. If the knives had not been taken during Wyndom's reign, then someone must have emptied the locked box during his father's rule. But who?

The temperature inside the temple dropped to freezing. Wyndom's breath turned to ice.

The building shook.

The queen's eight-foot-tall, humanistic form was gone. She must have returned to her central mass.

"We must go," said the Maddowshin. "The queen is in a rage."

Wyndom bolted to the exit. As he reached the opening, a force stronger than a hurricane sent him and the Maddowshin flying into a row of Wirador Wosrah.

Rolling onto his back, Wyndom gaped at a plume of black smoke rocketing up from the temple. "Why is our queen so angry? Why are these knives so important?"

The Maddowshin hauled itself to its feet, then, to Wyndom's surprise, offered him a hand. "On its own, a Croilar Tier knife's only use is to gut a fish or a man. All eight together unlock a powerful weapon capable of defeating our queen's army."

When Cecilia had escaped her Wirador Wosrah captors and fled across the Epona Ocean, Wyndom had not understood why the queen hadn't put forth resources into recapturing her. Now, he knew why. The Croilar Tier knives had always been the queen's key advantage. As long as Terefellia possessed even just one knife, the Treoir Solas would not be able to access the weapon the Maddowshin had spoken of. The empty chest, however, had changed things. If the person who stole the knives also acquired Amalardh's eighth knife, and if they held allegiance to the Goddess of Light, then the result could be disastrous. Wyndom had spent his life dreaming of his rightful place in the Sworn Province. He couldn't come this far and let his dream slip away.

"We should attack Vitus now," he said.

The Maddowshin craned its neck at the darkening sky. "The queen will never give her blessing to a battle she cannot attend. The knives are gone, and that is a problem, but the queen wouldn't be who she was if she didn't have a back-up plan."

The ground beneath Wyndom's feet dropped. As though he were a bird, high in the sky, he looked down upon himself and the Maddowshin standing with a sea of Wirador Wosrah.

"What is happening?" he asked.

"You, along with every Terefellian, have become the queen's eyes, viewing the vast lands below through her particles of smoke. She blackened the sun so we can see our enemy's light."

Possibly because Wyndom felt as though he was flying, his fear of heights didn't kick in. He smiled like a giddy child as he drifted north along the Terefellian Valley to the coastal flatlands where Cecilia had floated off in her balloon. Instead of drifting off to the right, he remained in a forward direction. "Why are we continuing north, when the one who holds this supposed light fled east, across the ocean?"

"We are not searching for the one they call Cecilia," the Maddowshin replied.

"What, then, are we looking for?"

"Her child."

Wyndom had all but forgotten the importance of this infant. When Brother Atlas had captured Cecilia, Wyndom—along with everyone else—had assumed the bundle in her arms was her baby. During Cecilia's escape from the Wirador Wosrah, a doll had fallen to the ground, advertising the deception. Wyndom's queen certainly was brilliant. Securing the child for leverage was the perfect back-up plan.

The great walled city of Vitus came into view and tingles shot through Wyndom's skin. Even under the cover of dark, the Sworn Province looked more magnificent than he'd imagined. Grain fields and paddocks stretched for miles. These were the fertile lands over which Wyndom deserved to rule, not some bland patch of dry sand and sunburnt rocks.

As he passed a dazzling waterway, his eyes widened at a vast pillow of tree canopies. A forest! Oh how he longed to experience such a place.

Look! Over there! the voice of a Terefellian compatriot echoed in Wyndom's mind.

In the distance, twinkled a tiny light. As the speck drew closer, a secluded valley appeared. Far below, a silhouetted woman scooped up a toddler, whose essence shone like a miniature star, and ran with him into a small cottage built into the cliff. The door closed, and the light disappeared.

Without the need to travel back south, the Terefellian campground returned under Wyndom's feet. The queen's smoke dissipated, and the sky above turned blue. Overcome from witnessing riches that would soon be his, Wyndom stood motionless.

Dust from a dozen Wirador Wosrah, carrying four Terefellian riders, plumed into Wyndom's face as they galloped by, pulling him from his stupor. Did the queen have to send that many to collect one little infant?

"No. I did not," said the queen. He spun to see the eight-foot-tall version of his goddess standing behind him. "But since I could, I did."

Wyndom bowed. "My Queen. You must believe me when I tell you, I did not know the knives were missing from the chest."

Her liquid skin swirled. "Many times, I have requested for the Maddowshin to dispatch you, and many times, the captain of my army has pleaded for your worth. You humans have emotions beyond my understanding, which is why I need the Maddowshin. I would've let Sister Darna do whatever she needed to give me my child. The Maddowshin knew better." She stepped closer, bringing a puff of ice-cold air with her. "I may punish failure, but I will praise success." She pressed her frozen hand to Wyndom's cheek and smiled. "You secured me my child. Because of this, your previous sins are forgiven. I release you of your obligation to kill your daughter."

Wyndom sucked in a lungful of air. "Thank you, my Queen. I do not deserve your love."

"In return for my forgiveness, I have one small request."

"Anything. Anything, my Queen."

"When the time comes, I will give Cecilia a choice. Her life for her child's. If she fails to comply, you will kill her son."

Kill a baby? Wyndom grew numb.

"You look displeased by my request. Is my Terefellian leader no longer willing to show his love for his queen?"

"I am your faithful servant, who loves you with all that I possess," Wyndom said. "It's just . . . why would you release me from killing my own flesh and blood, only to replace this sacrifice with a lesser life?"

A smirk formed on the queen's inky face. "I should think slaying the child of the man whose heart makes yours go thump would be a more"—she paused as if searching for the right word—"interesting way to show your love for me, don't you agree?"

Wyndom didn't. He didn't want to kill anyone, least of all Amalardh's son, but what choice did he have? The queen wanted what she wanted. Who was he to deny her? He swallowed past the lump in his throat. "Your wish is my command, my Queen."

Her frosty lips kissed his and she disappeared.

"How can our queen ask this of me?" he uttered.

The Maddowshin placed its hand on Wyndom's shoulder, and life flickered into its—Rudella's—eyes. "What this place forced you to become is a shadow of what you could be. If you come through this, you will be a better man for it. I will be sad that I won't be there to experience that."

The raw sadness in the Maddowshin's voice moved Wyndom. Rudella had given up life as a human to ensure victory for Terefellia, so that her people could finally be freed from their buhleycob existence. Her sacrifice would've been just as terrifying to face as what the queen asked of Wyndom, yet she had gone through with it, anyway.

Rudella was right. If Wyndom were to survive this, he would be a better person, because he would no longer be the spineless man he'd always been. If his loyal wife could find the strength to make a sacrifice that went beyond the pale, then so could Wyndom. He balled his fist. When the time came, he would obey his queen's command and kill Amalardh's son.

THE SMOKE FILLING the control room screens dispelled. The outside world, as captured by Rabbit Cove's external cameras, turned bright. The image of an older male with smooth, silver hair appeared on a screen, wanting to know what the hell just happened. *Colonel Adams* read the name under his image. Saffron recognized him as one of the official people who had joined them in the lab. More troubled expressions filled the screen.

After silencing the talking heads, Jensen paced the room, as though searching for the best way to explain an evil entity capable of not only spitting out murderous beasts, but converting itself into a plume of smoke powerful enough to block the sun. The faces on the screens remained passive as they listened to Jensen's seemingly far-fetched words. When he finished, questions flew: "What are we going to do?" "Do we stand a chance against these things?" "Should we go into lockdown?"

Lyrik shared a flat look with Zack.

"What does 'lockdown' mean?" Saffron whispered.

"No one in or out," Lyrik replied. "To make sure we don't break our own rule, the tunnel door will be time-locked. The last time this place locked itself in was two centuries ago during the Great War."

"You'll shut down for what? A month or two?"

Lyrik's lips compressed. "More like fifty years."

Saffron's eyes grew wide. "Fifty years!"

"Back then, that's how long they needed for the air to clear," said Zack. "Those who built this place didn't expect the lock being activated a second time, so it only has one setting."

Lyrik leaned close to him. "If these idiots put us in lockdown and Rabbie's sister ends up defeating this . . . Dark Goddess, I don't want to be trapped here. You need to get Yoyo started on cracking the code."

"Yoyo can do that?" Saffron said. "He can open this lock once it's closed?"

Lyrik didn't seem too confident as she shrugged. "I hope we don't have to find out."

Saffron turned to Rabbie to gauge his response to this "lockdown" talk. His distant expression suggested that his thoughts were a million miles away. While everyone else worried about their own safety, Rabbie lived the personal agony of knowing Eifa had most probably discovered his sister's whereabouts and would somehow figure a way to travel across the ocean to get her. "Cecilia will be okay," she whispered.

"I don't see a way out of this," Rabbie said. "If we stay here, we might at least stand a chance."

Stay here? What was he talking about? "They're discussing going into lockdown? Did you know that?"

Rabbie nodded.

"Did you hear the part about fifty years?"

He nodded again.

"You can't honestly suggest we stay here until we're old and gray!"

"At least we would live long enough to become old and gray."

How could Rabbie be suggesting such a thing? He was the one who taught Saffron life was for living, not just existing. He had planted a dream and made her believe it was real. "If I fight Eifa and die, so be it," she said. "But I cannot live underground. I want to be free. I want to see your forest; spend what days I have left surrounded by beauty. The more I learn about Eifa, the more I understand. For her to do what she just did, something must have gone wrong. Because she wants everything and more, she let her focus wonder. Somehow, somewhere, she messed up. We can't give up. Not now."

Rabbie's expression livened. He seemed as surprised as Saffron by her passion.

"Well then, I guess that's settled," said Colonel Adams, the silver-headed man on the screen.

Rabbie turned to Lyrik. "What's settled?" he asked.

Her complexion went gray. "They just voted. We're going into lockdown."

"Wait!" Rabbie said to the group. "Before you do this, can you give your science team a few more days? My people don't have the luxury of hiding. Eifa's army will massacre them. We don't have the technology to study the Wirador Wosrah's weakness. Your people do. If you give them a little more time, we can take whatever they learn back to our people. And maybe, we might stand half a chance."

"Your passion is admirable," said Colonel Adams. "When the former Senators ruled Vitus, we survived because we did not get involved. What happens outside our home is not our concern. Unfortunately, this time, because of the actions of two well-meaning, but thoughtless, young Rabbits, we have inadvertently become involved." Those sitting at the control room's desk side glanced at Lyrik and Zack. "We will do what we can to help you find a solution for your problem, but be warned. The moment we sense danger, we will cut ourselves off. Are we clear?"

"Yes. Thank you," Rabbie replied.

"Good. I suggest we all retire and let our scientists get on with things."

The faces disappeared from the screens and pictures of the outside world took their place.

Although disappointed, Saffron understood why these people would rather lock themselves in for a lifetime instead of facing a fight. Sticking with the norm was easy when you didn't know what you were missing. Her sheltered existence had boiled down to climbing ropes, living in caves, and keeping to herself. She would've continued her insular life, if not for her mother's impending Rite. After experiencing the outside world, and connecting with Rabbie, Cecilia, and Eideard, she could never go back to life in Terefellia. "If your people knew the beauty of what the outside world holds," she said to Jensen, "you would never want to lock yourselves in."

"We are very much aware of what we are missing," he replied. "We simply don't miss it." He turned to Lyrik and Zack. "I take it you haven't shown them the sensory room?"

"We'd planned to after lunch," said Lyrik. "But then, the sky turned dark and all."

Because of the lateness of the hour, Jensen suggested Lyrik and Zack set Saffron and Rabbie up in a room for the night. Tomorrow, he would schedule the sensory room for their use.

Saffron and Rabbie followed Lyrik and Zack down more corridors. "What's this sensory room?" Saffron asked.

"I guess you could say it brings the outside world in," Lyrik replied.

What was so special about that? Saffron had grown up in a cave, and more often than she cared for, outside wind and rain had entered.

The corridor ended with a hallway leading left and another right.

"This is where we say goodbye," Lyrik said. Hooking Saffron's elbow, she led her to the left, away from Zack and Rabbie.

"Wait. What's going on?" Saffron asked.

"Oh. I'm sorry," Lyrik replied. "I just assumed . . . I mean, you and Rabbie aren't married or anything, right?"

"What? No. Of course not." Caught off guard, Saffron hadn't meant to sound so offended.

"Ouch," Lyrik uttered with a playful smirk. "He's hardly that bad of a catch."

Heat from Saffron's neck radiated to her cheeks. "What? No.

That's not . . ." She cuddled her arms to her chest. Why the heck was Lyrik even talking about marriage?

Undaunted by Saffron's flustered state, Rabbie nodded to a sign on the wall that read *Female Dorm*. Across the ways, she noticed another sign read *Male Dorm*.

"Unless you're hitched, you need to go your separate ways," Lyrik said.

Separating males and females just because they weren't married? That was ridiculous. Saffron had spent every waking and sleeping moment with Rabbie since they'd met. "We're not separating," she said.

"But it's the rules," Lyrik replied.

Since when did someone like Lyrik care about rules? "I don't care. We're not separating."

"It's okay," said Rabbie. "We're their guests. It's just for the night."

Saffron's heart twinged. He wasn't fighting to stay with her. His response confirmed what she already knew. Rabbie thought of her as just a friend.

"I'll see you in the morning, okay?" he said.

"Whatever," she uttered and strode off. After a few steps, she stopped. Rabbie had enough to worry about with Eifa tracking his sister. He didn't need her drama. She turned to tell him sorry, but he had already disappeared behind a closing door.

"That went well," said Lyrik.

Saffron glared at her.

"Geez. So sensitive. Come on."

With a dash of resistance, Saffron followed Lyrik's tug.

Multiple doors lined each side of the hallway.

"Kids live with their parents in family units until age fifteen," Lyrik said. "Then, if there's one available, we get our own room. At the end of the hall is the female recreational space—no boys allowed. We also have co-mingle areas, like where we're taking you tomorrow."

She opened a door numbered "86" and led Saffron into a compact and unexpectedly pleasant room. A painted forest adorned one wall. On another, a fake window looked out at a green field dotted with yellow flowers. On the horizon, a red glow mimicked the setting sun. Daisies covered the single bed's quilt and featured sparingly on the bathroom's tiled walls. There was a plush blue resting seat with a matching foot cushion and a white desk and sturdy chair.

Pulling two bundles of clothing from a chest of drawers, Lyrik set them on the cabinet's top. "This is for tomorrow," she said, placing her hand on one set. She then motioned to the other pile. "And these are your pajamas."

"My what?"

"Pajamas. You know. Night clothes."

"You wear different clothes to bed?"

"Duh. Of course. I'm in room fifty-five if you need anything. I'll come grab you in the morning." Waving good night, she left.

The door clicked closed, and the room fell silent. As Saffron glanced around the small space, her emotions bubbled. She'd never spent a night alone. She'd either slept next to her mother or Rabbie. Annoyed with herself for becoming teary, she wiped her sniffly nose with the back of her arm. Baked-in grit scratched across her upper lip. During her hike north with Rabbie, they'd come across scant waterways to wash off with. She eyed the shower through the open bathroom door. Saffron had seen similar devices in run-down buildings surrounding Terefellia and in her hideout house, but they'd all been non-functional. If she could glean how to fire a shotgun, surely she could figure out the device.

She stepped into the compact space. A thin strip of red and another of blue curved halfway around a lever located in the shower wall's center. She rotated the lever into the blue section. Nothing happened. Turning it up into the red made no difference. She pulled the lever forward and sprung back as droplets rained down from the spout above. Pushing the lever closed, she smiled. This would be far better than splashing murky stream water over her face.

Goosebumps shot up her naked legs as she stepped into the square cubical. The cold tiles felt soothing on her aching feet. She pulled the lever, this time slowly to control the downpour, and quivered under the icy flow. Her eyes widened as the water warmed. *Oh wow! This is delicious.*

Her skin scorched. *Ouch. Too hot.* She smacked the lever closed, shutting off the flow. The handle sat halfway inside the red arc. Twisting it closer to the blue line, she turned the flow back on. A comforting warmth enveloped her skin. She would've stayed under the flowing stream forever if not for the sign reading: *Our resources have limits. Please keep showers to under three minutes.* Saffron had already brought Eifa's beasts to Rabbit Cove. She could hardly drain their precious supplies. After washing off a lifetime of muck with fragrant soaps, she dried herself off with a fluffy towel.

She studied her face in the mirror and slumped. Saffron didn't consider herself pretty. Not that she cared. Well, she kind of cared. She'd never had feelings for a boy, until now. She wanted Rabbie to like her, but what was to like about her widely-spaced eyes, narrow face, and thin lips?

White polka dots covered the shiny red clothing Lyrik had referred to as pajamas. Saffron pressed the soft cloth to her cheek. Wow. So luxurious. Slipping them on, she climbed into her snuggly bed and breathed in the quilt's fresh lemony scent. The willingness of Rabbit Cove's leaders to seal off their tunnel from the outside world was beginning to make sence. Would fifty years of this life really be so bad?

Mimicking sunrise, light shining through Saffron's fake window woke her. She'd never had such a deep, restful sleep. Her "clothes for tomorrow" were comprised of denim pants and a yellow T-shirt, both of which fitted a little too close for Saffron's comfort.

Her eyes rolled at the word *sunshine* written across the top's front. Lyrik was definitely poking fun with that. She lounged in the blue chair, waiting for Lyrik to arrive.

Opening the door to Lyrik's knock, Saffron received a hearty up and down look. "Someone cleans up well," Lyrik said. "Who knew you actually had some curves? Rabbie's sure to like your butt in those jeans."

Saffron glared at her.

"What? I'm just saying. You've got a cute figure. Nothing wrong with flaunting it."

Self-conscious, Saffron wanted to change, but into what? Her old clothes were too crusty to put back on.

"Come on," Lyrik said. "Jensen's booked the sensory room for nine, which means we've only got a few minutes for breakfast."

Saffron followed Lyrik to the dining hall, where the stale smell of overcooked oil and last night's dinner blended with the aromatic scent of fried eggs and potatoes. Her lips parted at Rabbie's freshly groomed hair and stubble-free face. His well-fitting jeans and blue shirt certainly agreed with his fit frame.

"What?" he asked in response to her stare.

"Nothing. It's just"—she touched the back of her knuckles to his smooth cheek and a tingle fluttered up her arm—"you shaved." He didn't seem to mind her overly familiar act, even after the bratty way she'd acted last night.

His eyes flitted up and down her body. "You look great," he said.

Heat rose from her cheeks. Her closely fitted garments made her feel far too exposed. "I'm sorry for how I acted last night," she said, to change the subject.

"It's fine. Seriously." Glancing at her chest, he smirked and added, ". . . Sunshine."

Saffron folded her arms across her front and groaned. *This stupid top.* Because of Rabbie's adorable grin, she couldn't hold back her own. Argh. Why did he have to be so charming?

After shoveling down their breakfast, Saffron and Rabbie followed Lyrik and Zack to the famed sensory room. Along the way, they passed a space filled with rows of pod-type beds.

"That's our UV room," Lyrik said. "It mimics the sun's rays. It's whatever. We go there 'cause we're told to." She waved them forward and into an empty room with a domed ceiling and bland walls. "This is the place we want you to see."

Saffron glanced around the space. What was so exciting about this place? The door snapped closed. The room fell dark and silent. "They said sensory, correct?" she whispered to Rabbie. "Not sensory deprivation."

Overhearing the jibe, Lyrik scoffed. "Hold your horses. I need a moment to set things up."

Stars appeared in the blackness above. An owl hooted. A cricket chirped. Saffron smiled. Okay, this was pretty cool. The light increased and a golden sun rose over an ocean. This sunrise looked equally as beautiful, equally as real as the one Saffron had witnessed the other morning.

Birds whistled. The rhythmic sound of waves hitting rocks matched visuals of an ocean swell lapping at a rocky outcropping. The smell of salt and seaweed tickled Saffron's nose. Just when she thought the moment couldn't seem more realistic, a sea lion snorted and dove into the water. Did a drop of liquid just land on her cheek? She wiped the area and gaped at her wet fingertip.

Lyrik turned a dial. A flock of seagulls on the sandy shore took flight. The sun rose into the blue sky and warmed Saffron's skin.

"This is unbelievable," said Rabbie.

"This is nothing," Lyrik said. "Take off your shoes."

Saffron and Rabbie slipped their foot coverings off and, under Lyrik's direction, stepped forward. Saffron's breath sucked in as her naked feet trod in sand and water.

"We can pretty much go anywhere we want," said Lyrik. "But we can't change the location until you step out of the touch zone."

She guided them onto a rubber mat, then pushed a button. The beach became a forest. Colorful birds sang in high-up branches. The scent of moss hung in the thick air. Saffron stepped into the touch zone and damp undergrowth squished between her toes. This place was fantastic. Even Rabbie, who knew the sights, sounds, and smells of a real forest, seemed impressed.

"I feel like I'm back in Plockton," he said.

Directing them back out of the touch zone, Lyrik pushed another button. Saffron shivered as the world around turned white. *Snow!* She'd seen the stuff in books and always wondered what it felt like. Her skin tickled as tiny crystals falling from above landed and instantly melted.

"We like this one the best," said Lyrik. She scooped a ball of snow from the touch zone and threw it at Zack.

Saffron did the same to Rabbie.

His retaliatory snowball exploded on her face.

Her belly ached from laughing so hard. This was what Jensen meant about Rabbit Cove folk knowing what they were missing and not caring. If something looked, smelled, sounded, and felt real, then the experience was reality.

Lyrik turned on the lights. "So, what do you think? It's pretty cool, right?"

"I could stay here all day," said Saffron.

"You think this is fun, wait until you try this," said Zack. Waving for them to follow him, he led them to a room, which he described as his "favorite place."

Red rope sectioned off areas to practice a range of activities, from shooting guns with no actual bullets to riding motorbikes and other vehicles on terrain projected onto a screen. Saffron studied the shooting range. No wonder the fighters had been so proficient in killing the Wirador Wosrah. They could practice daily without worrying about burning through their limited ammunition supply.

Bypassing this station, she stepped over to a trail bike. After riding on the back of Lyrik's, she had to know how it worked. Lyrik gave her a quick lesson, then turned off the engine. "Okay, your turn," she said.

Kicking over the engine was much harder than Lyrik had made

it seem, as was figuring out the clutch and accelerator. After several failed starts, Saffron took off along a virtual dirt track. The ride was as thrilling as the real thing—and better because no dust stung her eyes. For the rest of the morning, the four of them had a blast, racing each other and crashing their virtual vehicles on sand dunes and rocks.

After lunch, they spent the afternoon in a communal rec space playing fun games on green tables. One was called ping pong, which involved hitting a plastic ball back and forth over a little net. The other one, billiards, required the calculating use of a stick to direct a white ball into knocking a colored ball into a pocket. Losing to Saffron for the third time, Lyrik made a face and mockingly called her a hustler, whatever that meant. If not for Yoyo coming over and commenting that the Lab had no news to report on Eifa's substrate, Saffron wouldn't have given Terefellia, Wirador Wosrah, or the looming battle another thought.

"I get why Rabbit Cove doesn't want to get involved in anything outside these walls," she said to Rabbie as they played a game of billiards. "This place is its own world. After a while, you'd forget an *outside* even existed."

"You're not thinking of staying, are you?" Rabbie asked.

Leaning over the table, Saffron lined up her shot. If she sank this ball, she'd win. "Of course not," she replied. She glanced up. Was he staring at her butt? She arched her back the slightest bit. "While I'm here, though, I figure I may as well have some fun."

She sank her ball.

Rabbie smirked and shook his head. "Lyrik was right. You *are* a hustler."

Over the next couple of days, the scientists made slow progress with Eifa's substrate. Acids, super coolants, and X-ray blasts made no impact. While Saffron didn't know what these things were, the concern on Rabbie's face suggested he understood and if these extreme measures hadn't worked, then nothing would.

"Our parents won't give up," said Lyrik. "If there's a way to destroy that stuff, they'll find it."

While they waited for the Lab to discover answers, Saffron and Rabbie slotted into Rabbit Cove's comfortable life. To earn their keep, they helped in the kitchen. During their down time, they spent as many hours as they could in the simulator room. Saffron was practicing jumping the trail bike over a small ditch when her screen went blank.

"Yoyo, what the heck?" said Lyrik.

Anxiety poured from Yoyo as he dashed from the master power switch over to them. "I was calling out, but you all were making such a ruckus. Listen up. I just caught wind that we're going into lockdown in T-minus twenty minutes. Jensen's not happy, but he's been overruled."

Saffron's skin prickled. Their leaders had promised they wouldn't go into lockdown unless they sensed danger, but the battle couldn't possibly be starting. Saffron had done her calculations. Based on the rate Eifa birthed her warriors, she still had several more weeks before she finished. And the Terefellian queen wouldn't send her army to war unless she could be there to oversee the destruction. Something else must be going on. "What's happening?" she asked. "Why the sudden rush to lockdown?"

"Our drone spotted a dozen beasts heading north, with four human riders. The higher-ups fear they're coming our way."

"They're not," said Rabbie. "They're after my sister. The black smoke was searching for her. They know that. You need to tell your leaders not to panic. They don't need to start lockdown."

"Too late. That's why I rushed over. Once the clock starts ticking, there's no stopping it. You and Saffron need to decide if you're staying or going."

Rabbie sank back against the buggy he'd been practicing in. Saffron slumped next to him. Their plan had been to go, but that was when Saffron thought Lyrik and Zack's parents would discover a way to destroy Eifa's sludge. "The lock is set for fifty years, correct?" she asked.

Yoyo nodded.

"Can you override it?"

"I wouldn't be basing any decisions on my ability to do so."

"You're saying we've only got twenty minutes to decide what to do?" Rabbie asked.

Yoyo glanced at a small timepiece attached to his wrist. "Negative. You've got eighteen minutes and ten, nine, eight . . . well, you get the drift."

Lyrik and Zack exchanged looks. The prospect of locking down for fifty years seemed equally concerning to them. "What are you guys going to do?" Lyrik asked. "I mean, it's pretty cool here, right?" Was she trying to convince Saffron and Rabbie or herself?

Rabbie's worried eyes locked onto Saffron's. "Without a way to destroy the Wirador Wosrah, Vitus will fall. If we stay, at least we might stand a chance of survival. I'll do whatever you want to do."

Saffron took in Lyrik, Zack, and Yoyo's apprehensive expressions. If she and Rabbie stayed, it would validate their world—their existence, which, as Lyrik had pointed out, was pretty cool. In Rabbit Cove, Saffron had a possible future with Rabbie. The only possibility outside was death. "I think we should stay," she said.

CHAPTER

15

MALEK HAD CALLED the building on top of the mountain the Nian Temple, but based on the furnishings, Nian House would've seemed more fitting. Although Cecilia didn't know what this place should've looked like, because the word "temple" implied some kind of grand, open interior, she hadn't expected to step through the front doors and into a luxurious living room. She ran her fingers back and forth over the plush arm of the red velvet chair in which she sat. Focusing on the way the material darkened and lightened kept her eyes off the person seated directly opposite her—Amalardh. He was staring at her. She wished he wouldn't.

Ida set a pot of tea in the center of a low, ornately carved wooden table. The woolly man called Forbillian asked Cecilia if she would like a cup. She nodded. Maybe the warm liquid would thaw her icy insides. Even though the crackling fire heated the voluminous room, sitting four feet from a man she supposedly loved—had slept in the same bed with—sent shivers down her spine. As Forbillian handed her a steaming mug, she smiled a silent thank you. She liked the way the lines around his eyes made him seem permanently happy. Unlike Amalardh. What could she possibly have seen in the man who looked as though he'd never smiled a day in his life? Well . . . besides high cheekbones, a confident jaw, and oceanic eyes that bore into her soul.

Unusual artwork based on a white tubular flower adorned the room's walls. In one painting, a tiny vine twirled around the elongated flower. In another, dewdrops clung to its petals. Barbed wire strangled another version of the flower, and bugs covered another.

There had to be at least two hundred of these differently sized and shaped paintings. Cecilia sipped her tea and studied each in detail. Anything to keep her eyes off the man across from her.

She hadn't spoken with Amalardh yet. Part of her was thankful. More memories of her life in Plockton had trickled in, including ones of her other brother, Rabbie, and her mother. Cecilia recalled everything up until the night of Baby Jonah's joyous Hinge Celebration. According to Eideard, the next morning, Soldiers of Vitus raided their village, killed everyone, and kidnapped the young men. "Your memories have stopped at that night," Malek told her, "because your mind does not want to deal with all that has happened since then." Remembering Amalardh might expose all the trauma Cecilia had suffered. She didn't want to recall any deadly raids or gruesome battles. The images that had flashed through her mind while fighting the dark-skinned woman had been bad enough.

On the wall behind Cecilia hung the image of the white flower void of any further embellishments. Walking over, Ida removed it, exposing a metal box. She turned a dial back and forth, then opened a thick door. Inside sat a bundle of brown hessian, which she removed and placed on the low, round table in front of everyone. Seating herself on the sofa next to Malek, she smiled. "Welcome all," she said. "I have been expecting the Treoir Solas and last Croilar Tier's arrival."

Hearing these titles made Cecilia's skin crawl. She glanced at Amalardh to gauge his reaction. Her stomach knotted as his liquid blue eyes locked onto hers. Wriggling uncomfortably, she dropped her focus back to the chair's arm. Why did his facial features have to be so appealing?

Ida placed her hand on top of Cecilia's.

Cecilia stiffened at the old woman's thickened skin. Eideard had described the Terefellians—the evil Eifa worshippers—as having a similar touch.

As though sensing Cecilia's concern, Ida withdrew her hand and settled it in her lap. "Sometimes we are forced on journeys we don't understand and told to do things we don't want to do, and while trapped in these dark moments, we struggle to remember exactly who we are and what we are fighting for. I had many days where I struggled to know who I was. I had little left to remind me." She pulled up her loose blouse sleeve, revealing a grotesque scar on her upper arm. "I, like Malek, am a Shadow Croilar Tier; only, I had to burn off my tattoo to infiltrate the Terefellians."

Forbillian choked on his tea. "You lived amongst those murders? What insanity possessed you to do that?"

"I did what I had to do." She sipped her hot drink, then recounted her life story.

Forty years ago, when Ida was twenty-five, the Soldiers of Vitus raided her village. She managed to escape with her young daughter and fled south, where she came upon a pleasant young man, who took pity on them. He introduced himself as Brother Pernell. His strange haircut and bland, hessian tunic didn't register until Ida spotted his goat-skull ring. Fifteen years prior, she'd witnessed a similarly dressed man murder her Croilar Tier grandfather. The killer had worn the same ring.

When Brother Pernell asked if Ida believed in gods, she quivered. Pernell was a Terefellian. Their leader, no less. Ida's answer would determine whether she lived or died. Lifting her chin, she told him she didn't believe in *gods*. At the chilling clench of Pernell's fist, she added, "I only believe in one god, for there is only one. The good and the great, Eifa. I pray for her arrival every day, so she may deliver her believers to everlasting life." Although the words tasted like rot, Ida knew the Goddess of Light would understand that for good to fight evil, good must sometimes don a black coat. Smiling wide, Brother Pernell welcomed Ida and her daughter into the fold. From that day on, her life became a constant struggle to ensure her deception didn't cloud her heart from Siersha's light.

Remorse filled her red-rimmed eyes as she spoke of things she'd done in service of the greater good, such as burning off her tattoo, tuning out the Terefellian's callous social norms, and taking part in their depraved Rite of Quinquagenary. She studied her thickened hands and sighed. "Even though the climbing drained me, I welcomed the pain. It helped block the anguish of my betrayal."

Over time, Ida's body became what she needed it to be to survive. Her palms thickened. Her muscles hardened. Her mind grew wise to the cunning of seduction. She'd almost forgotten what she was fighting for, when the sickening years as one of Brother Pernell's mistresses paid off. "The great failure of men," she said, "is their desire to always prove themselves right."

Forbillian's lips pursed as he nodded. "You're not wrong about that."

Amalardh remained quiet. A man like him probably never felt the need to prove anything to anyone.

One drunken night, Brother Pernell told Ida about a chest containing seven Croilar Tier knives. Feigning disinterest, she told him she didn't believe him. To prove he'd spoken the truth, he stumbled with her to the Terefellians' temple.

As she gazed absentmindedly into her tea, Ida recited, "The first Terefellian takes three steps right. The second Terefellian is left with upside-down sight. The Third Terefellian goes right back home. And the fourth Terefellian stays alone."

The next time Brother Pernell placed himself in a mincelase trance, a near death state to communicate with Eifa, Ida removed his ring and broke into the chest. She hid the seven knives until the time came to flee. "Death comes to all Terefellians at age fifty," she said. "On the eve before my Rite, I grabbed the knives and left."

"What about your daughter?" Cecilia asked.

Ida's head lowered. "My sweet button was only five-years-old when we joined the Terefellians." She smiled as though reflecting on a memory. "She took to the ropes like a bird to air. I did my best to instill the teachings of Siersha. I taught her our family history and her true destiny as a Shadow Croilar Tier. I begged her to come with me, but she wouldn't." She swept a tear from under her eye. "I led my daughter into Eifa's lair and left her there, alone."

"I'm so sorry," said Cecilia. "No mother should ever be forced to leave their child behind."

Gazes dropped throughout the room.

"What is it?" Cecilia asked. "Is there something you're not telling me?"

Forbillian cleared his throat and stood. "Would you mind directing me to the little boy's room?" he asked Ida.

She pointed him to the external bathhouse, then picked up a silver bracelet from on top of the hessian bundle. The jewellery's central design featured the same tubular flower depicted throughout the room. Placing it around Cecilia's wrist, Ida said, "As much as you are the Treoir Solas, you are also the Caladium. The poison flower is our only hope to destroy Eifa. I made this, so that you will not forget who you are."

Cecilia's belly knotted. Keeping the gift implied she agreed with her role as the Caladium. But she couldn't hand it back. Ida would've put many hours into crafting the delicate piece. Rejecting it would make Cecilia seem rude and she didn't want to come across as ungrateful, especially in front of Amalardh. But why should she care what he thought? She glanced at him and her heart raced. Why was she responding this way? Was her body recollecting something that her mind didn't? Her cheeks burned at the idea of a prior intimacy with this man.

"Thank you," Cecilia said to Ida. "I shall treasure this."

Offering a pleased nod, Ida unwrapped the hessian bundle and laid seven Croilar Tier knives on the table. Amalardh pulled his blade from its sash and placed it with the others. All the knives were unique in patina and wear. Only two silver wolf heads kept both red-ruby eyes. Three had no eyes at all. None had the tree mask, except for Amalardh's, and his was the only knife missing its right eye.

Cecilia removed the mask and ran her fingers over its cool contours. According to Eideard, their great ancestor had found this mask lying on the ground during the Great War. Interpreting the image as a tree, he saw the symbol as a sign to flee west, where he set up a nature-loving society deep inside the Plockton Forest. The memory of discovering this item—which, because of an attached chain, had seemed like a pendant—inside her mother's charred wooden box flashed in Cecilia's mind. Her muscles tensed. The discovery had happened *after* the Soldiers of Vitus had destroyed her village. Not wanting to encourage any more memories of her people's massacre, she placed the mask on the table.

"After escaping Terefellia, I fled north," Ida said. "I had no plan, other than to get the knives as far away from Terefellia as possible. Somewhere across the ocean seemed a good idea, and since I needed a boat, Vitus was the most logical destination."

Back then, the Senators had Vitus locked down. Unable to scale the thirty-foot wall, Ida used her climbing prowess to track horizontally along the southern cliff face, upon which the wall sat. Of all places to end up, she landed in the military zone. Soldiers of Vitus were everywhere. As it turned out, she probably arrived in the safest place possible. The one area the Soldiers failed to patrol was their own.

Plentiful boats floated along a pier. The problem was, those big enough to make the journey would be impossible to manage alone, and the tiny ones with two oars looked like death traps, besides which, Ida had no sailing experience. She resigned herself to living the rest of her days in a sizable burrow in the rocky cliffs near the wall's southern end, scavenging leftover food scraps.

One dark night, while exploring near the northern wharf, she noticed shackled men loading bales of grain onto a large ship. With the opportunity to leave Vitus, Ida snuck aboard. Two weeks later, the ship docked on a small island where the shackled men swapped the bales of grain for what she later learned were parcels of spices from Bayton.

"My mother was the ship's captain," said Malek. "She discovered Ida hiding below deck and planned to hand her over to our ruling Count. You cannot imagine Mother's surprise when she saw Ida's treasure. She hid Ida and the knives up here in the Nian Temple."

"Why are those knives so important?" Oisin asked.

"In the right hands, they unlock the Forbidden Pool," Ida replied.

"Unlock it to do what?"

"The Terefellians believe that beyond life-giving waters, the pool holds a weapon strong enough to withstand Eifa's army."

"We need to get that weapon," Eideard said. "Because there's no way Vitus can fend off five thousand of the Dark Goddess's beasts."

"Unfortunately, I don't have any answers," Ida replied. She regarded Cecilia and Amalardh. "But since the Treoir Solas and last Croilar Tier seemed destined to meet here, I can only assume the solution lies with you both."

"I have no memories, so I am no help," Cecilia said.

From the doubtful look on Ida's face, Cecilia's attempt at distancing herself from all of this had fallen flat.

"Maybe we should start with how you both got here," Ida said.

After Eideard explained his and Cecilia's journey, Amalardh recounted how he, Oisin, and Forbillian had made their way to the Nian Temple. Eideard had spoken of Amalardh as though he were an enigma, and Cecilia was beginning to see why. He had a self-contained nature that, on the surface, made him seem cold, but underneath, she saw warmth. She only had to glance at Oisin to know the boy idolized him. And why wouldn't he? Amalardh was the type of person who, when he spoke, everyone listened, except Cecilia at this moment. Her intense focus on his commanding charm tuned out most of what he'd just said.

Returning from his extended bathroom break, Forbillian took a seat. "What did I miss?" he asked.

"Show Ida the scroll," Amalardh said.

Reaching into his shirt pocket, Forbillian handed Ida a rolled piece of parchment.

She unravelled the item and her brow furrowed. "There's nothing on here."

"Do you have any idea what message the Prophet intended to send with it?" Amalardh asked.

She shook her head and gave it back to Forbillian. "I cannot explain its meaning. All I can tell you is if it came from the Prophet, keep it close. Everything he does has a purpose."

Amalardh removed a leather-bound book from his bag and referred to it as the Prophet's diary. He opened it to a page with a foreign script. "Do you recognize this text?" he asked Ida.

Her lips parted. "It's written in Terefellian." She scanned the text. "You must forgive me. I'm a little rusty. Clearing her throat, she began reading. " 'I long for the day when I may rid myself of this claustrophobic shell called a body. A soul is not meant for eternity amongst flesh. The Great War is coming. My ice home awaits my arrival. There, I will be safe from the poison air. I pray the years will pass swiftly until the day when the wolf, bear, and lynx enter my home, so that the goat may release my soul from a mind ready to implode from the relentless agony of living yet another day.'"

Cecilia eyed the wolf, bear, and lynx capes hanging from a wooden stand by the front door. With every word uttered, the story she'd hoped was only a fairytale edged closer toward reality.

Ida examined the next page. "He writes that after revealing the Prophecy to the world, he became a marked man. Non-believers destroyed his lab and burned much of his writings. Because there would always be those who feared the truth, who would rather silence someone like the Prophet so they could control their own narrative (control the people), the Prophet went into hiding, living in one secluded place after the other. When the Great War started, he placed his diary in the Croilar Tier Archives and fled to his ice home to wait in seclusion for two centuries until he could finally meet with death."

Wetting her finger with her tongue, Ida turned the page. "The Prophet never had visions as to whether Eifa or Siersha would win. He does, however, postulate which side is best for humanity. He writes, 'Though eternal life on earth sounds wonderful, I have experienced the living hell of Eifa's promise. Fearing the location of the Forbidden Pool would fall into the wrong hands, I have left clues to its whereabouts that only those with a true belief in Siersha will understand. When the Treoir Solas was in her darkest days, she saw her ultimate power.'" Ida looked at Cecilia. "Do you know what the Prophet means?"

"I don't," Cecilia uttered. And she didn't want to. The last thing she wanted to remember was her "darkest days."

Ida continued reading. " 'In the front, we see what is possible. In the back, we find the way. But beware, for that which is not will bring death. You will find what you seek, the same way you found me.' " She closed the diary and once again directed her words to Cecilia. "The Prophet is saying that the map to the real Forbidden Pool lies with you. Whatever memories you have lost, you must find. If Eifa moves with her army of Wirador Wosrah, and we don't have what we need to confront her in battle, then the Dark Goddess will win."

As the room's focus turned to her, Cecilia curled into herself. What was she supposed to do? What was she supposed to say?

Standing, Amalardh walked her way.

Her eyes grew wide. What did he want?

CHAPTER

16

FROM THE MOMENT Amalardh had first met Cecilia, he'd sensed something about her. Unlike Ida and Malek, he hadn't grown up knowing his connection to the ancient Order of Croilar Tier. He didn't know he was Cecilia's protector. How could he? He'd been an assassin sent to kill her. He hadn't spared her life out of pity or a sense of loyalty to her for saving his. He'd stowed his weapon because an inexplicable sensation told him that killing her would be a crime beyond reproach. In the weeks that followed, Amalardh's role as protector for the Treoir Solas had come in many forms. He'd saved Cecilia from deadly swamp beasts, carried her for miles across a harsh salt lake, and pulled her from the torrents of a raging waterfall. Right now, Cecilia needed saving from the room's intense scrutiny. Ida had lumped an unfair demand on her: You must remember because the fate of the world depends on it.

The fearful widening of Cecilia's eyes as he walked to her crushed his heart. Although Forbillian, Oisin, and Ida were just as much a stranger to her, only Amalardh seemed to scare her. He would rather receive her disdain, which he deserved. But fear?

"Come with me," he asked, as softly and as friendly as he knew how.

Although her wariness remained, she stood.

He led her to where Ida had exited with the pot of tea, under the assumption the room had to be a kitchen. It was. Large, airy windows looked out over the surrounding mountain peaks. The kitchen connected to another expansive room. Adorned with

123

bright tiles and rows of bench seating, the space looked to represent the building's "temple" aspect. He poured water from a clay jug into a mug and handed it to Cecilia.

Her cautious eyes scanned from the offering to him. "I'm not thirsty," she said.

"Trust me. You are."

She took a reluctant sip, then chugged the rest of the contents. Her frown indicated she didn't like him knowing more about her than she knew about herself. During the many weeks they'd spent hiking from the outskirts of the Plockton Forest to the city of Vitus, Amalardh had learned that stress made Cecilia thirsty. And everything about the way she'd been sitting in the chair—her curled shoulders, sullen face, and fidgety hands—showed her stress.

"I don't remember you," she said.

Although her actions had told him as much, her verbal confirmation stung. "I know," he replied. "I'm not here to force you to recall anything."

"But if I don't, we won't find this map Ida seems to think lies with me."

"We will find what we need to find. We do not need your memories to do it." He topped up her mug with water. "Before you even knew Siersha, you and your people lived your lives according to her ways. When you learned you were the Treoir Solas, you told me the reason you could accept your role was because you felt the Goddess's light inside, guiding your every step."

Cecilia's jaw clenched as she banged her mug on the bench. "When will everyone get it through their heads that I don't know this Goddess, and I certainly don't feel her?"

Far from startled, comfort wrapped Amalardh like a warm blanket. Despite Cecilia's lack of memory, she remained the fiery young woman he knew and loved. He may have lost her, but she hadn't lost herself—which meant she retained the ability to achieve greatness.

His lack of response to her outburst seemed to throw her. She swept a lock of hair (that, because of her shaved head, wasn't there) behind her ear. A nervous habit he loved.

"You will remember Siersha in time," he said. "You just need to stop worrying about what is going on in here." He placed his hand on the side of her soft, spiky temple. "And focus on what you feel here." He moved his hand to her upper chest. The thumping of her heart reverberated into his throat, creating a lump he couldn't swallow past.

Her wide eyes connected with his. He wanted to kiss her. Desperately. But beyond his betrayal ruining his right to embrace Cecilia again, he was a stranger who had no business invading her space more than he just had. Withdrawing his touch, he led her back to the sitting room and waved Forbillian over. When it came to puzzles, his uncle's mind ticked to an alternate beat.

"Look around this room," he said to Forbillian. "What do you see?"

"A shyte-ton of flower paintings that I don't mind admitting are creeping me out," Forbillian replied.

"Since these paintings are all of a caladium flower and Cecilia is the Caladium, would you agree they hold the key to the Prophet's latest riddle?"

Forbillian nodded. "It would be all that makes sense to me."

Turning to Ida, Amalardh requested she read out the first line of the Prophet's clue.

Ida flipped to the page. " 'In your darkest days, you saw your true power.' "

"You have seen one of these images before, and we are going to figure out which one," he said to Cecilia.

Tension marred her face.

"Remember, listen to your heart, not your head."

She breathed deep.

"Read out the next line," he said to Ida.

" 'In the front, we see what is possible. In the back, we find the way.' "

"What do you make of that?" he asked his uncle.

Forbillian scratched his beard and studied a version of the white flower wrapped in a spiderweb. "The front would mean the actual picture. Here, what is possible is a spiderweb suffocating a flower."

"So, the back of the correct painting would have the third piece of the map?" Amalardh asked.

"Aye. That would be my take."

Oisin plucked a painting of the flower covered in bugs from the wall. "Why don't we just open all of them?" he asked.

"Read out the next line," Amalardh asked Ida.

" 'Beware, for that which is not, will bring death,' " she said.

A cockroach scuttled along the floorboard. Amalardh scooped it up. "Did you know these bugs are one of the few creatures able to survive the poison fallout from the Great War?"

Taking his knife from the table, he sliced a small hole into the bottom of the painting's firm paper backing. He dropped the roach in and swirled the canvas around, making sure the bug received plenty of whatever poison Amalardh suspected was inside.

Using the tip of his knife, he pried out a dead bug covered in white dust. "As you can see, we cannot risk opening a painting unless we are certain it is the correct one."

Oisin's wide eyes blinked from the dead bug to Amalardh. Although their relationship had been strained, at least Amalardh could still awe him. He washed the poison dust from his knife with water from the kitchen's jug and set it back on the coffee table.

"Walk around the room," he said to Cecilia. "Let me know if any images seem familiar."

Taking her time, she made a full circle, then returned to the painting of the white flower that had hidden the wall box Ida had earlier opened.

"What is it about this one?" he asked.

"I'm not sure. Out of all of them, I enjoy looking at it the most. It makes me feel at peace."

In the note Ida had read out, the Prophet had written, "When the Treoir Solas was in her darkest days, she saw her true power." This power represented Cecilia's new role as the Caladium. Cecilia describing a painting as evoking "peace" would be the end product of the Caladium's success, not the role's actuality. Bringing down Eifa would push Cecilia to her limits. Maybe an image inciting the opposite emotion might provide more answers. "Which one is the most terrifying?" he asked.

"That's easy." She strode to a painting in the far corner depicting two tiny snakes wrapped around the flower, their open mouths ready to pierce the delicate petal with their fangs.

As she stared at the picture, her head tilted. "That's strange. When I first looked at this, I felt unsettled because the flower seemed so defenseless against those awful fangs. But now, I see that's not the case. The snakes are trying to bite the flower, but they can't. The flower won't let them."

Interesting. Eideard had described Eifa's black warriors as almost indestructible. Slicing off their heads did little more than create a ball of death gunk capable of consuming a human and turning them into a replica warrior. Eideard had also spoken of Cecilia's ability to repel these globs. Her description of the flower not letting the snakes bite it seemed very much in line with the Caladium's possible power over Eifa. "Is this the painting you would choose?" Amalardh asked.

"I think so."

"Not good enough."

"Yes. This is the one I choose."

As Amalardh pulled it from the wall, Cecilia snatched it from him.

He took it back. "You cannot risk your life opening this. As the Treoir Solas's protector, it is my responsibility."

She held his stare. "That may have been so when I was the

Treoir Solas. Maybe the Caladium no longer needs the Croilar Tier's protection."

Reality jolted Amalardh. Cecilia's tree pendant and his wolf knife had brought them together. But now, the same knife and its mask no longer belonged to him. It sat on the coffee table with the seven others. In the Caladium's life, Amalardh held no more value than Ida and Malek. Cecilia no longer needed him. As he processed this painful conclusion, Malek snatched the painting from him and dug his fingers into the backing. If the insides held poison, his death would be imminent.

"Neither of you can afford to die," Malek said.

"But if that's not the right painting, dust will go everywhere. You could kill all of us," said Cecilia.

Malek ripped the paper open, exposing a dust-free inside. "When you pointed out this painting, the image felt familiar. And then I remembered, in your cell at Bayton, I recall seeing a similar sketch on the wall. You almost died recovering from your infection. I can't imagine you would've had darker days than those."

Malek's words further confirmed Cecilia's standing as the Caladium. From her pursed lips, Amalardh doubted this brought her much joy. He tore the remaining backing free and frowned at the blank canvas. "There's no map."

"Give it here," said Forbillian. He laid the frame face down on the low table. With the tip of a Croilar Tier knife, he pried the staples from the wooden frame, revealing a second layer to the artwork. Drawn on this layer's underside was a map, the top edge of which clearly looked as though it would've lined up with the bottom of the one the Prophet had given Amalardh.

A dotted red line dropped from the map's top center. Forbillian placed his finger on the table just above the line's start. "This is about where we are now." He traced the red line in its easterly direction through *Lava Fields* to where it stopped just before a solitary crater. "Well that's strange. An obvious place for a forbidden pool would be in that crater, not in the middle of nowhere."

Based on his prior experience with the Prophet's clues, Amalardh was certain the map's directions were incomplete. "The end of the line marks the location of the pool's entrance, not the pool itself," he said.

"How do you figure?" Forbillian asked.

" 'You will find what you seek, the same way you found me,' " Amalardh said, repeating the last phrase of the Prophet's riddle. "We found the Prophet by going through a tunnel. And that's the same way we'll find the pool."

Straightening his spine, Forbillian clapped his hands together. "Alrighty then," he said. "Saddle up, everyone. We've got some hiking to do."

CHAPTER

17

Saffron's heart pounded as the heavy door ahead steadily closed. What the heck had she been thinking? Of course she couldn't spend fifty years locked underground. She'd never taken the safe route in the past, and she certainly wasn't about to now. And neither was Rabbie. If they'd come to their senses five minutes earlier, they would've already departed Rabbit Cove, not racing against a shrinking exit. She floored her bike's throttle, chasing Rabbie's wheel. At this speed, only two outcomes were likely: escape past the closing door or slam into it.

ZROOM! The sound of Rabbie's bike rushing through the tightening enclosure reverberated in her ears. Would she make it, too?

ZROOM! Sunlight blinded Saffron's eyes. Hitting the brake, she skidded to a stop beside Rabbie. Her hands trembled as she cut off her engine. The virtual training in the simulator room had not prepared her for the actuality of the bike's awesome power. "That was insane," she said.

Rabbie's round eyes remained focused on Rabbit Cove's shutting door.

Inside the tunnel sped Zack and Lyrik on their bikes. Were they insane? They couldn't possibly make it through in time.

The door creeped closed.

Saffron's breath stilled. *Come on, Zack! Come on, Lyrik! Faster!* She gripped her handlebars. *They're not going to make it.*

Zack jetted out, followed by Lyrik.

The mighty door clamped shut.

Pulling up by Saffron and Rabbie's side, the two young Rabbits cut their engines.

"Are you both crazy?" Saffron said. "What are you doing?"

Lyrik lifted her goggles. "The idiots who think that virtual reality stuff is real life haven't stepped a foot in the outside world. When I ride, I want real wind on my face, real dust in my eyes, and real bugs choking my throat. Before Zack dies, he wants to swim in a real ocean, not just dip his toes in a bucket of sandy water."

"Actually, I was just hoping to get out so I wouldn't be stuck another fifty years inside with her," Zack replied.

Lyrik jabbed his shoulder. "Baby brother, you'd be completely lost without your big sister." She handed Saffron and Rabbie a set of goggles and a tube-shaped scarf to cover their nose and mouth. "I don't really care for the real dust and bug thing." She stared at Rabbit Cove's massive closed door for a moment, then slammed her foot on the kick starter. "Follow me," she said, revving her engine.

Several minutes later, Saffron felt as though she sat on rocks and insisted they take a break. During the stop, Zack explained how Vitus sat about one hundred and twenty-five miles northeast of Rabbit Cove. At a comfortable cruising pace, he expected their arrival in about five hours, give or take. Although the bikes' tanks only held about an hour's fuel, he wasn't worried. With their scouting trips taking them closer and closer to Vitus, he and Lyrik had discovered fuel storage spots along the way.

Dusting herself off, Lyrik ordered everyone onto their bikes and told them from now on, the only breaks would be at fuel stops, so everyone's butts were going to have to suck it up.

Nothing Saffron had heard in Terefellia came close to conveying the size of Vitus. The surrounding farmland with acres of abundant grain and vegetables surpassed her expectations. Waking up every morning knowing food lay readily at hand would be a dream come true. During some lean winters, if not for the Rite of Quinquagenary, the Terefellians would've starved.

Her neck craned at the thirty-foot-high wall arching over the city's periphery. She'd heard about the tall barrier encasing the Sworn Province, but never imagined anything this impressive. The city had more protection from Eifa's army than she'd expected. While Wirador Wosrah possessed exceptional climbing skills, the warriors still needed foot and hand holds, and this smooth, massive structure had none.

As Saffron, Rabbie, Lyrik, and Zack rolled through the enormous wooden gates, locals going about their daily activity cowered back from the bikes' harsh sounds. Removing his goggles and face-scarf, Rabbie waved to ease his people's concern. Kids appeared from nowhere shouting, "It's Rabbie!" and ran excitedly behind the bikes. Saffron hadn't expected him to have such notoriety. Then again, a certain level of fame would come to the brother of the young woman who had dethroned the oppressive Senators. Her fingers numbed as a group of bold, young women flashed flirtatious smiles his way. Was she in competition for Rabbie's affection? Her hard muscles, prickly edge, and bark-rough grip could never rival their soft curves, silky skin, and brazen confidence.

She followed Rabbie's bike around a corner and a chill shot up her spine. The Tower. Her father's obsession. Did he somehow think reigning from this monstrosity would nullify his fear of heights? The audacity of her father to tell Saffron that other kids would tease her because of Glimglob—her toy tin can—when he was her primary source of embarrassment. She could've lived with her father's condition, been his ruthless supporter if he'd just been honest. If he'd confessed his fear of heights and hammered home to his people how, in spite of all, he still persevered and asked for no lenience, their respect would've skyrocketed. The openness would've made the difference between his people gaining strength from his climbs, as opposed to snickering behind his back. Her father held the misguided belief that because no one challenged his leadership, he had everyone's respect. No one challenged his rule because no one wanted his role. Those who cared to read the scriptures understood that the person in possession of the Terefellian ring became the Maddowshin. Why take up the reins to spend eternal life as a beast, when they could stay a follower and keep their bodily form forever?

As Rabbie pulled to a stop at the Tower's grand steps, a man with blond hair, graying beard, and anxious eyes rushed from a doorway next to the Tower's main entrance and down the outside stairs. Hugging Rabbie tight, he told him how he'd been worried sick. He'd heard unsettling news about how Rabbie and Eideard—alongside Parlan and Feltor—had fled because some people who claimed to be allies of Vitus had kidnapped Cecilia and Alistair? Because the pitch of his voice rose, his statement sounded like a question. As did his comments about, these "allies" being the same people they'd unwittingly sent with Finn to go after Amalardh and Forbillian? And now Marion and Tomkin were gone?

After confirming the man's broad-stroke understanding of what had happened, Rabbie asked, "I take it there's been no word from Amalardh?"

As the man's head shook, Rabbie's expression fell. The worry dragging on him from knowing Terefellian hunters stalked his good friend must be immense. Although he had described Amalardh as possessing exceptional skills, could the Croilar Tier fend off two Wrethun Lof?

Describing Saffron, Lyrik, and Zack as trusted allies, who'd saved his life, Rabbie made introductions to the man, named Danmar, and asked him to gather the council as they had much to discuss. He then led the way through the same doors Danmar had earlier exited and into the Council Chambers.

Saffron and the others slid onto high-backed chairs surrounding a grand, round table and waited for the members to arrive. With the meeting called to order, Rabbie made further introductions and explained for Saffron, Lyrik, and Zack's benefit that to ensure all the formerly segregated Vitus groups felt heard, a representative of each made up the council membership. He then updated his people with all he'd been through and finished with, "The Dark Goddess is back and plans to attack Vitus with a horde of near-indestructible beasts."

Drawn faces exchanged looks of fear and disbelief.

One question grew into a cacophony.

In a firm yet measured tone, Danmar demanded silence and level heads. The room quieted. "Good," he said. "Now I suggest we start a battle preparedness plan."

"Our wall will protect us," said Lyzol, a spindly woman with thin lips who represented the former Tower Folk.

"She's right," Saffron whispered to Rabbie.

As she quietly explained about the smooth wall, Danmar interrupted. "In times like this, secrets are either important enough to share with the room or left for a private discussion."

Although Danmar's tone had remained non-judgmental, Saffron's cheeks still burned. Rabbie had yet to inform the group of her standing as a Terefellian. He'd no doubt avoided the topic for fear they'd blame her (and rightly so) for their city's impending threat. With an encouraging nod, he signaled for her to tell the room what she knew. If anything went awry, he would support her.

Facing the group, she swallowed past a nervous lump in her throat. "While the Wirador Wosrah are expert climbers, your wall lacks hand and footholds. That being said, if the enemy can't climb it, they will find another way in. Our advantage is that their flooding attack will be reduced to a trickle."

The attentive looks surprised her, and she realized just how much she liked sharing her expertise. Although she was next in line to lead Terefellia, never once had her father offered her a "seat at the table" to hear her counsel. How could he? Those who seated themselves on a throne, metaphorical or otherwise, had no table for others to sit at.

"My first concern is the city's main gates," she said. "They seem strong with their reinforced metal brackets, but a horde of Wirador Wosrah will be stronger." She turned to Rabbie. "The tunnel you told me about, the one Amalardh used to smuggle in Cecilia—that, too, is a weak spot. And then there are the north and south headlands where the wall ends. The cliffs below offer perfect entry points for a warrior's climbing expertise."

Lyzol's narrow eyes filled with distrust. "How do you know all this?" she asked.

"I grew up in Terefellia. My father, Brother Wyndom, is the leader."

As feared, the room fired heated questions at Rabbie, admonishing him for leading a spy into their home. Helderic, a beefy former Ground Man whose face seemed locked in perpetual concern, slammed his fist to the table, bringing instant silence. "I was there the day a man, a leader no less, scolded his young son for leading the enemy to our doorstep. This leader was Winston of the Ground People, who gave his life during the Battle for Freedom. His young son is Oisin, and the enemy let in was Amalardh, a trained assassin for the Senators of Vitus. Now I ask you, was Oisin wrong for doing what he did? Should Winston have slain the Dark Shadow of the Senators when he'd had the chance?"

Heads hung as Helderic's point hit home.

"Rabbie is brother to our Treoir Solas, the purest soul I have ever met. I fought by this young man's side during the Battle for Freedom. You will give him the respect he deserves. If he's brought someone here who he thinks can help, then we will let the young woman tell her story." He motioned for Saffron to continue.

Taking a calming breath, she offered Helderic a thankful nod and told the group about her life in Terefellia. When she spoke of Eifa's black muck consuming her mother, she tried not to cry, but disobedient tears escaped.

Brassal, an elderly, silver-headed former Blind Prisoner, who wore strange black discs over his eyes, found Saffron's forearm with his searching hand. His surprisingly soft, yet prune-like fingers moved to her palm. Perhaps he wanted to feel her hardened skin for himself? When his fingers got to her callouses, they didn't linger with curiosity. Instead, he entwined his bony fingers in hers and gently squeezed her hand. A lump caught in her throat. Her people had not dignified life enough to allow anyone to reach this man's age. Was this what elders did? Care for the pain of the young? Because if that were the case, Saffron wanted elders. Desperately.

The discussion progressed to the Wirador Wosrah's weaknesses and ways to reinforce the Great Gates and northern tunnel. With everyone clear about their next steps, Danmar ended the meeting. As the council members dispersed, Zack motioned for Saffron, Rabbie, and Lyrik to stay behind, then pulled a tube of paper from his backpack and unrolled it on the table.

"That looks like a map of Vitus," Rabbie said.

Pointing to an area on the map, Zack ran his finger to the south end. "We're here, and we need to get here."

"That's the old military zone," Rabbie said. He scanned from Lyrik to Zack. "If you know something, why didn't you bring it up during the meeting?"

"We're only following that other guy's order," said Lyrik. In response to Rabbie's flat look, she added, "You know, the stuff about secrets being important enough to share with the room or left for a private discussion. This is the private discussion. Now, can you get us to where Zack needs to go?"

"I can. Are you going to tell me why?"

Rolling up the map, Lyrik handed it to Zack. "If we find what we're looking for, we will. There's no point getting everyone's hopes up and wasting time talking about something that doesn't exist."

The late afternoon sun cast long shadows down Vitus's main thoroughfare. With vines snaking up buildings and trees sprouting from potholes, the overgrown city looked like a strange, angular forest. Rabbie stopped his trail bike on a cemented stretch of land. The obstacle course, target boards, and hanging practice dummies ran true to his reference of this place being an old military zone. Beyond this area stretched a beach and a high, rocky cliff, atop which sat the Great Wall.

"This is the place," Rabbie said.

Following his lead, the group killed their engines and dismounted.

Zack unrolled the map and studied it. His expression crumpled as he scanned the area. "That stupid wall is not supposed to be there. They probably built the darn thing right on top of it."

"On top of what?" Rabbie asked.

"There should be an entrance somewhere around here."

Over by the cliff face, a slab of square concrete protruded from the hard ground. Squatting at the slab's side, Rabbie eyed a set of rusted studs in each corner. He pointed to a section of the rock wall covered in vines. "I'd say your entrance is up there."

"That's a ridiculous place for an entrance," said Lyrik. "How's anyone supposed to get to it?"

"Using the stairs that used to be here," Rabbie said. "Your sensory room may have been able to replicate the feel of sun, wind, and salt, but unless you've lived those elements, you probably wouldn't know what they do to metal over time."

Lyrik smirked at Zack. "Looks like you've met your smarty-pants match."

Saffron regarded both Zack and Rabbie. "Since neither of you can risk falling and cracking open your smarty-pants skulls, I'll go check it out." She reached through the vine curtain to the wall's rough surface. The hand and footholds seemed generous enough.

Up she went with ease until her hand slapped flat ground. She pushed the vines aside and sunlight lit up a constructed hollow about ten feet high, six feet wide, and just as deep. An old blanket and scraps of dried food suggested someone had used this place as a hide-out many years ago. What fool would've hidden so close to where the former Soldiers of Vitus lived and trained?

At the back of the opening stood a gray, metallic door. This had to be the entrance Zack sought. "Come on up," she called to the others.

CHAPTER

18

MALEK ESCORTED CECILIA, Eideard, Oisin, Amalardh, and Forbillian to the Nian Temple's side yard and handed each a rifle and a belt of bullets. Beyond the possibility of running into Bayton Fighters, the journey ahead could expose the team to unknown dangers.

Oisin happily snatched his weapon. Cecilia hesitated.

"If good is to prevail, the virtuous must meet their attackers with equal force," Malek said.

His correct statement didn't lessen Cecilia's apprehension. She took hold of the cold, weighty object and lined up with the others.

Using various clay pots as targets, Malek instructed his students on how to point, aim, and shoot. The lesson left Cecilia with a sore shoulder and a surprising rush. Hitting a small object many feet away offered more satisfaction than she'd expected.

Since the risk of encountering Bayton Fighters on the narrow trail Cecilia and Eideard had already hiked was too great, Malek led everyone to where Amalardh, Forbillian, and Oisin had climbed up. With his wound preventing travel, he bid the team good bye. Cecilia had imagined she would also want to stay, but she didn't. Trekking into the unknown with her brother and three unfamiliar men felt right. She hugged Malek and Ida goodbye, thanked them for everything, and began the mountainous descent.

At the bottom, they stopped for a quick lunch break. As she massaged her aching thigh, she caught Amalardh watching. If the two of them had supposedly had such a close relationship, why did he make her feel so . . . ill at ease? Did the idea of physically embracing a man as complex as him cause her inner turmoil, or did she remain on high alert for other reasons?

With the rest break over, Forbillian led the way through a lush green valley, where they camped for the night by a pristine stream. As Cecilia collected firewood, Eideard caught her glancing Amalardh's way. "You need to talk to him," he said. "He's afraid to come to you because he doesn't want to overwhelm you."

She wanted to talk to him, but she didn't know where to start. Needing to fill her canister, she wandered over to the water's edge, choosing a spot deliberately close to Amalardh. Maybe if the opportunity arose, she could strike up a conversation. He removed his woolen robe and placed it neatly on a rock. The way his white undershirt draped from his broad shoulders and the beige trousers clung to his tight hips made her belly flutter. Not wanting to get caught staring, she averted her attention to Forbillian, who sat on a nearby rock, mopping mud spots from his bear cloak with a damp cloth.

"You didn't bring your wolf coat," she said to Amalardh.

"It was extra baggage I didn't need," he replied.

He pulled off his shirt. Rippled muscles covered his torso. He would be the perfect specimen if not for the abundance of scars. Thickened, crisscross marks across his back looked as though they'd been a part of his skin for a while. Asking about them when he had probably already told her of their origin would only cause him—and possibly her—discomfort. Faded grazes across his upper chest and arms appeared recent. Inquiring about them might help start this much needed conversation Eideard felt she and Amalardh should have. "What happened?" she asked, motioning to the scrapes.

His brow furrowed, as though unsure what she meant, then glanced down. A glimmer of fear shot through his eyes. "I had an unfortunate encounter," he said, and reached for the shirt he'd just placed on top of his robe.

How could such insignificant wounds unsettle someone as composed as Amalardh? "An encounter with what?" Cecilia asked.

Stepping over, Forbillian seemed surprised to see the marks. He sized Amalardh up and an understanding of where the marks had come from registered on his face. "I wouldn't worry about it," he said to Cecilia. "I'm sure this *encounter*"—he emphasized the word—"involved more baggage that thankfully is no longer needed."

What did that mean?

From the look Amalardh exchanged with his uncle, he, at least, seemed to understand the cryptic comment. He flung his shirt back on and strode off.

Squatting next to Cecilia, Eideard dipped his water canister into the stream. "What was that all about?"

She shook her head. "I have no idea. So much for trying to talk to him. He's way too complicated."

"Well, yeah. But that's what you always said you liked about him."

She blinked at her brother. She did?

The dense greenery gave way to pale green hills interspersed with shallow valleys. A black, jagged expanse that stretched for several hundreds of feet cut through their path ahead. Where the previous lands had transitioned slowly, this new black mass was as sudden as a river cutting through a paddock.

Cecilia stepped up to the transition mark. "What is this stuff?" she asked to no one in particular.

"Lava fields," Amalardh replied.

Not expecting his close presence, she turned and met with his overwhelming stare. Forcing a swallow down her tight throat, she jabbed a rocky protrusion with her boot. The top broke off. The substance seemed hard yet fragile. Not too dissimilar to the man standing next to her. In the uncertain terrain ahead, green pockets of seedling bushes offered hope. Despite the brutal layer suffocating the soil, life persevered. Whatever harsh truth elicited her fear of remembering Amalardh, Cecilia needed to be just like the plants and burst through her crusty wall. She stepped onto the bumpy terrain. "So, other than that I'm thirsty when I get stressed, what can you tell me about myself?"

A soft smile crept on his face.

Oh, my. He has dimples.

"You really want to know?" he asked.

"Well . . . yes."

"You're stubborn, willful, and sometimes, painfully obstinate."

She glowered at him. If she hadn't needed to stay focused on the uneven ground, she would've punched him.

"You're also kind, generous, and the most amazing woman I've ever met."

Her foot twisted on the irregular surface.

His hand shot out, steadying her. Everything about him, his robust grip, uncompromising honesty, and woolen scent, felt familiar.

With the tension broken, they chatted with the comfort of close friends. Unlike Eideard, with his "do you remember this?" and "do you remember that?" barrage, Amalardh let Cecilia ask the questions, of which she had many.

Eideard had only revealed bullet points of Cecilia's journey after her village's raid. Amalardh painted a detailed picture. He spoke about her saving his life after he fell into a massive pit with death spikes at the bottom. In return, he took her prisoner, making her walk behind him while tethered to a fifteen-foot length of rope. Pain etched his face as he admitted his regret for doing that to her. After surviving swamp beasts, which he clarified was her name for crocodiles, her conviction to bury one of her own, who'd fallen in the unforgiving desert, left to die by the Soldiers who'd captured him, convinced him she wasn't the enemy the Senators had suggested, so he let her go. "You refused to leave," he said.

He held her stare and she could tell her refusal had actually made him glad.

Her belly fluttered. Eideard was right. Amalardh's complexities attracted her beyond the superficial desire to fix what was broken. Amalardh didn't need fixing. He needed saving. Mostly from himself.

Dusty soil and pockets of small shrubs marked the end of the lava field. As the group made camp on the compact ground, an unsettling energy hung in the air. Terse looks flashed between Forbillian and Amalardh, a continuation of the edginess that had started when Cecilia had asked about the markings on Amalardh's chest. Meanwhile, Eideard and Oisin huddled close. The skittish way their eyes flickered at Cecilia suggested their conspiratorial whisper involved her. She was willing to leave them be until she overheard Eideard say, "Malek said it's safer not to bring it up. She needs to remember on her own."

"What do I need to remember on my own?" she asked.

Their cheeks reddened.

In response to her demanding glare, their heads dropped. Whatever secret they held, their compressed lips confirmed their intent to keep it.

Pushing herself into standing, Cecilia marched over to Amalardh and told him they needed to talk. He'd answered all of her prior questions and now she had new ones.

The powdery ground squeaked under the weight of her uncertain step.

Shielding behind a cluster of bushes, she turned to Amalardh. "Everyone seems to know something that I don't. I have a sense it involves you. I'm not scared of you, yet for some reason, the idea of you as someone who used to be in my life terrifies me. Why would that be? Why do I not want to remember you?"

Her rigid muscles faltered at his flinching expression. She

hadn't meant to hurt him. Or . . . maybe she had. Deep down, was some part of her angry at Amalardh? If so, why?

He lowered himself onto a log. "I imagine whatever block you have is for your own protection. I brought you nothing but pain."

He had? How could someone who seemed so protective of her possibly hurt her? She settled herself next to him. "My brother said I loved you. Did you not love me?"

His shattered look bordered on horror at the suggestion. "I've loved you from the moment I saw you. And I've never stopped."

As centered as Amalardh seemed with his emotions, the feelings he had for Cecilia seemed to consume him. If her feelings for him were as far-reaching, and if they'd somehow gone awry, could this explain her reluctance to remember him?

"Did I stop loving you?" she uttered.

A film of water covered his eyes. "I don't know."

Her chest tightened. How rotten had her behavior become toward this man, who she'd supposedly shared so much with, that he no longer knew if she still loved him? "Were we happy?" she asked.

He rubbed his palm with the pad of his thumb. "We were happy once. And then . . . we weren't."

"What happened?"

"I happened. I drove you away." From his robe's pocket, he pulled out a small, red teddy bear.

Her breath hitched at the familiar toy.

"When I left with Forbillian, you hid this in my bag."

"Why?"

"I imagine you were worried that I planned to never return." Shame etched his face. "Part of me was . . . wanting to leave. For good. You wanted me to remember where home was."

Their relationship had been that bad that he'd contemplated leaving? She took the bear from him. "Why would this remind you of home?"

"Because it belongs to our son, Alistair."

Every inch of her body grew numb. *I have a son?*

As she ran her trembling finger along the bear's mangled ear, the image of a delightful baby chomping on the spot with his gums flashed into her mind. She pressed the soft toy to her aching chest. The deep void in her heart suddenly made sense.

She had a son. And she'd left him.

As Malek had predicted, Cecilia's memory dam broke. Tears dripped on to the bear's belly as her lost life flooded back. Amalardh had been right. They had been happy. Against all odds, they had won the Battle for Freedom. Peace reigned. She and Amalardh made love. Many times. With these memories came a fresh perspective. She began to see that Amalardh had never been as joyous after the battle as she. He had tried to reach out, tell her that something didn't feel right, but she shut him down, forbade further talk of the Prophecy. She had happily forgotten her role as the Treoir Solas and wanted Amalardh to do the same.

Because he couldn't let go of whatever troubled him, instead of becoming the father she had expected him to be, he remained a detached protector. Her annoyance grew. Nothing he did for Alistair was good enough. The more she complained, the further he pulled away. Her insides folded as image after image of his growing torment pounded her brain. What she'd labeled as disinterest . . . was fear. Amalardh had been struggling to understand his role as a father, and instead of helping him cross the bridge, Cecilia had tossed him over the railing.

Her desperate desire for the Prophecy to have ended didn't automatically make it so. Her attempts to smother the Light of Siersha that burned inside had suffocated her relationship with Amalardh. She had accused him of being selfish when she was just as guilty. In the Temple Cave, a porcelain sculpture of Amalardh's wolf knife and her tree-pendant-mask had a plaque with the words: *The Croilar Tier protects the Treoir Solas. The Treoir Solas is the Croilar Tier's savior.* Cecilia had failed as Amalardh's anchor. He had been there to catch her when she fell, but the second he needed her, she had folded her arms and watched with utter disregard as he plummeted.

She wiped her sniffly nose. "I'm so sorry. I expected that what came so naturally to me would also come to you. And when it didn't, instead of offering you my understanding, I buried you in resentment."

Because of who he was, Amalardh had shouldered all the blame for their failed relationship. Hopefully, her proclamation would allow him to share the burden. He took the red bear from her and caressed its tattered ear. "The moment I laid eyes on our son, I froze. He was so tiny and perfect and pure. I didn't want to ruin him. But from day one, I did. I couldn't even hold him."

The memory of presenting Alistair to Amalardh rushed back. Rather than acknowledging that Amalardh's hesitance to hold his son reflected his terror, Cecilia became embittered. Old Vitus had a hideous rule that deemed a baby's life not valid until a father held it in his arms. How could she have been so stupid to believe that Amalardh, the man who had fought to secure freedom from such oppressive laws, was invoking such a twisted act on his own son? She knew of Amalardh's horrendous upbringing. She should've understood that he needed time. Instead of offering him compassion, she thrusted their baby into his arms and forced fatherhood upon him.

Cecilia's fear of remembering Amalardh hadn't stemmed from the pain he'd caused her, but rather, the agony she had inflicted on him.

"Maybe our love wasn't meant to be," she uttered.

Although the statement was a horrendous conclusion, someone had to say it. If the thought had rattled her brain for many months, then Amalardh, with his analytical approach to life, must have surely entertained the idea. She blinked through her teary eyes at him. "The Prophecy doesn't say the Treoir Solas and last Croilar Tier live happily ever after. It says, 'together they form the Ceannaire Fis.' Maybe our only purpose was to create Alistair. And direct our love at him, not each other."

Her throat closed at his gaunt expression. Amalardh, it would seem, had never once entertained the idea that his love for her was not meant to be.

"Is that what you believe?" he asked.

Cecilia didn't want to believe it, but too much had happened to convince her otherwise.

After Alistair's birth, she'd encouraged Gildas's interaction with her son. She'd hoped Amalardh seeing another man becoming more of a father to Alistair than himself would inspire him to step up. When her plan resulted in Amalardh pulling further away, she continued to involve Gildas out of spite. She'd wanted to get a rise out of Amalardh, a sign that he didn't want another man in Alistair's life. She'd taken his acceptance as disinterest, when really, her thoughtless actions had confirmed a belief that had been eating Amalardh alive—a former assassin could never be a role model for their son. A few days after Gildas's departure, Amalardh's lack of support finally pushed Cecilia over the edge. "I should've gone back to Plockton with Gildas," she'd blurted. The pained look that had etched Amalardh's face came gushing back.

"I don't know if I believe our love was meant to be or not," Cecilia said. "What I do know is that if you love someone, you should never intentionally hurt them. I said and did some horrible things to you."

His warm fingers intertwined with hers and her heart fluttered. "I made you do and say those things. I knew my distance was hurting you, yet I continued to cause grief. What kind of man would do that to someone they love?"

Cecilia squeezed his hand. "Let's promise to forget everything that's happened. We can pretend we just met a couple of days ago. You were simply a handsome stranger who saved my life."

His grip withdrew from hers, confirming her impossible request. Amalardh never made a promise that he knew he couldn't keep. "I wish I could forget everything that has happened," he said. "Everything I have done. You deserve a fresh start. But I cannot give you one."

Cecilia's head hung. She'd suggested the forgetting of their past because she'd been hopeful for a reprieve from her own act of betrayal. On the night Gildas had left, she'd kissed him. Passionately. The guilt had consumed her, compounded the wedge between her and Amalardh. "When I first met you, you treated me harshly because you wanted me to hate you," she said. "You ask what kind of man knows their distance is hurting, yet does nothing to stop the pain? The kind of man who wants his loved ones to stop loving him."

His lowered head confirmed she'd hit upon his truth.

If the child in the Prophecy represented Alistair, then Amalardh wouldn't live to see his son's second birth year. "You thought that by pushing me away sooner, you'd spare me the pain of losing you later." Her voice cracked. "Surely you know there is *nothing* you could do that would make me stop loving you." She flung her arms around him and squeezed him tight.

"You say that now," he whispered. "But you don't know. There could be something I've done—"

She pressed her lips to his and in this moment, nothing else mattered but their love.

But this love couldn't stop the Prophecy's prediction of Amalardh's death. Breaking from the kiss, Cecilia buried her face in his shoulder and sobbed. The true reason why her memories of Amalardh had remained blocked had become painfully clear. Cecilia's mind hadn't wanted to remember him, because her heart didn't want to live the rest of its life without him.

MORE THAN ANYTHING, Amalardh wanted to give Cecilia her fresh start. He would give the world to forget his interaction with Sister Darna had ever happened. But it had. And from Forbillian's stony looks, his uncle knew it had, too. Waking from his restless sleep, Amalardh sucked in the cold morning air. With the golden sunrise outlining a lonely crater less than a mile away, the entrance to the tunnel that the Prophet's riddle had referred to must be close.

Several yards away away stood a large rock cluster about the size of a small house. Curiously, three hand-carved pillars that the previous night's fog had obscured sat perched at the top. Stepping up beside Amalardh, Forbillian nodded at the rocky expanse. "I'd say that there marks the end of our red dotted line."

At the landmark's base, Amalardh sent everyone in different directions to hunt for an opening. Several minutes later, they reconvened. No one seemed to have found the entrance.

Forbillian tossed his arms in the air. "How hard could a gaping hole be to find?"

"What exactly have you been looking for?" Amalardh asked.

"A big, round opening for a tunnel. Why? What has everyone else been looking for?"

"Pretty much anything wide enough to crawl into," Eideard said.

"Same here," replied Oisin. "I found a narrow crack, which I thought might be it. But after crawling on my belly for a few feet, it dead-ended."

Forbillian squirmed. "Well, if we're getting on our bellies and crawling . . . I might have found it up over here."

He led the group to a narrow fissure, which sat about four feet from the ground. A few feet in, what looked like a shadow-cast rocky floor was actually a drop.

"F-o-r-b-s!" Oisin said, drawing out the name. "How could you miss this?"

"It's an honest mistake," Forbillian replied.

Lantern in hand, Amalardh lay on his belly and scooted halfway into the hole. The yellow light illuminated a rocky climb down to a lava tube that looked to run under the desolate flats ahead in the crater's direction. "This is it," he said, and waved for the others to follow him.

Shiny black crystals adorned the round ceiling and sparkled like stars under the lantern's light. A musty odor laced with a hint of sulfur floated in the dense, cool air. The last time Amalardh had walked a tunnel with Cecilia, they'd entered the Temple Cave and learned of the Prophecy. What fate would await them at this tunnel's end? What weapon could a pool of water provide? The water itself? If it gave eternal life, might it also cause death to that which is not alive—Eifa's monsters?

The tube ended at a grand, white chamber roughly twenty feet wide and high. Crystalline stalactites up to six feet long hung from the arched alabaster ceiling, which blended seamlessly with the walls and shimmery stone ground. In the floor's center sat a perfectly round pool, about eight feet in diameter. Its still surface gleamed like glass.

"The Forbidden Pool," whispered Oisin.

"I caution you all against filling up your canisters with this stuff," Forbillian said, "unless you like the idea of roaming these lands for eternity. What do you suppose we do next?"

Amalardh didn't know. If the Croilar Tier knives were supposedly some sort of key, maybe they would provide a clue. "Hand me the knives," he said to Forbillian.

Dropping his bear cape and gear onto the ground, Forbillian

retrieved the hessian-wrapped knives from his pack. As he turned to hand them to Amalardh, his foot slipped on the pool's edge. The loud splash as he fell into the water reverberated loudly in the empty chamber. His arms flapped wildly as his horror-stricken face came up for air. "I didn't swallow! I didn't swallow!"

Hauling his sopping uncle out of the pool, Amalardh handed him a dry cloth to wipe his face. "Spit out whatever's in your mouth," he ordered.

Forbillian made a bunch of "Pth-pth" sounds and wiped his tongue with the cloth. "Blasted Terefellians and their eternal life."

"Oh no! Look!" said Oisin, pointing at the pool.

At the bottom lay the open hessian wrap and the eight Croilar Tier knives.

"This can't be good," Forbillian said.

Amalardh restrained his annoyance. What were they going to do now?

Cecilia began removing her outer garments.

"What do you think you're doing?" Amalardh said. "I'm not letting you dive in there. I can't let you become what that water makes you." Pulling her aside, he kept his voice low. "You know my destiny. If anyone should go in there, it's me." For most of Amalardh's existence, he'd been bereft of life's essence. A few more months of living as the actual dead before he met with his prophesied end would hardly make a difference.

"Amalardh. Look," said Oisin. He and Eideard had been helping wring out Forbillian's wet clothes. In Oisin's hand lay the scroll the Prophet had given Forbillian, and it was no longer blank. The water had revealed a circular marking with eight evenly spaced dashes around the circumference.

"Well bowl me over with a six-legged donkey," said Forbillian. "That's what I call a happy accident."

"Or maybe the Prophet had told you to keep it with you at all times because he'd already seen you falling into the pool," Oisin replied.

SPLASH! Amalardh spun to see Cecilia diving into the pool. That girl was far too willful.

His brow furrowed. What was she doing? Instead of scooping the knives up and carrying them to the surface, she swam to the pool's perimeter and stuck a blade into a barely perceptible groove. Seconds ticked by as she slotted the remaining knives into their respective grooves.

"Surely, she'll come up for air," said Forbillian.

"Nope. Cecilia's part fish," Eideard replied. "She can hold her breath longer than anyone I know."

Based on the time needed for Cecilia to reach the deep bottom, Amalardh would never have been able to complete the task. Exhaustion from resurfacing multiple times for air would've led to him no doubt swallowing a lung full of water.

"Do you think Cecilia can hold her breath for as long as she can because she needed the skill for this very moment?" Oisin asked.

With all the other "coincidences" surrounding the Prophecy, Amalardh supposed so.

At the three-minute mark, she burst through the surface, inhaling air. Offering his hand, Amalardh pulled her out. Her thin undergarments stuck to her like a second skin, revealing her curves. His gaze halted at a cruel scar on her right thigh. He should have been there to protect her.

Taking the wet parchment from Oisin, Forbillian studied it. His brow knotted as he glanced into the pool. "So, that's it? That's all we have to do? Where's our darn weapon?"

SAFFRON, RABBIE, LYRIK, and Zack stood outside the small man-made cave's locked door. Removing a key from her pocket, Lyrik pushed it into the lock's hole. So far, so good. She tried to turn the key, but it didn't budge. Frustrated, she kicked the door.

"Let me try," said Zack. When the key proved just as stubborn, he accused Lyrik of grabbing the wrong one.

"Maybe someone didn't do their research properly," Lyrik said.

"You're pinning this on me?"

"Well it's not my fault."

Inching past the bickering siblings, Rabbie took hold of the door's looped handle, pulled upward, and twisted the key.

CLUNK.

Lyrik and Zack immediately quieted.

"The skewed frame placed too much weight on the lock, making the key hard to turn," said Rabbie. "Again, mostly a problem the outside world faces."

Lyrik smirked at Saffron. "You better keep your eye on this one. He's too cute for his own good."

Hopefully the cave's shadows covered the burn radiating from Saffron's cheeks. Even if Lyrik was correct (which she was), she needed to stop with the suggestive comments hinting at Saffron having a "thing" for Rabbie.

Seemingly unaffected by Lyrik's quip, Rabbie pulled the door open, and all four stepped into a dank hallway. To the immediate right, a red metal lever labeled *Auxiliary Power* poked from the wall. Zack pulled it down. Tiny lights flickered on, illuminating a fifteen-foot concrete hallway.

"Electricity in Vitus? This is impossible," said Rabbie. "What is this place?"

Lyrik closed the door and locked it. "Come on, we'll show you."

At the end of the hallway, a metal stairwell directed the journey back downwards to an antechamber with four unlocked doors. One opened into a room with metal bunk beds to sleep six—another into a recreational space, complete with couches, magazines, a dining area, a kitchen, and two green tables. *Ping pong and billiards!* Two of Saffron's favorite games. The third door opened into a bathroom and the fourth into a control room, similar to the one in Rabbit Cove, only much smaller.

Zack laid out the paperwork he'd brought with him from Rabbit Cove and peeled away the sheet he'd used to find this place. A series of line drawings covered the next page. "According to these schematics, this place is Rabbit Cove's satellite office," he said. "All comm lines, auxiliary power, and water connect directly to the Cove's central systems. During times of war, this office acted as a strategic outpost for the head command at Rabbit Cove."

He flicked a bunch of switches on the bench in front and the room lit up. He pressed a white button. "Red Dog, this is Alpha and Omega coming at you from the world beyond. Do you read?" Nothing but static followed. He repeated the phrase.

"Dude!" came Yoyo's voice. "It works! This is Red Dog reading you loud and clear. Switching to visuals." Zack flicked another switch. The screen in front filled with Yoyo's face and curly red hair. "This is insane! I can see you," Yoyo said. "Where have you been? I was expecting to hear from you hours ago."

Lyrik updated him about the long council meeting, then turned to Rabbie and Saffron. "Zack and I didn't want to discuss this place earlier because, in the event it no longer existed or was non-functional, we didn't want to get everyone's hopes up. Yoyo came across the paperwork for this place a few months back. Zack and I had always wanted to come and check it out." Her expression grew genuine as she leaned back against the room's bench-like table. "I know Zack and I can fool around, but we were serious about wanting to live in the real world. We figured if you guys were leaving, we needed to at least give you a fighting chance. Now, anything our Lab learns, we learn, too."

Rabbie's head shook as he looked around the compact space. "Never in a million years would I have thought a place like this possible. This is brilliant. Thank you!"

Lyrik turned back to Yoyo. "How's the time lock coming along?"

Yoyo exhaled through pursed lips. "Slowly. But, I think I'm making headway."

"What about our parents? Have they made any progress?"

"To be honest, I don't know," Yoyo replied. "This evening's update was cancelled. I ran into Jensen and he seemed . . . I'm not sure. Like something was up. He said to let him know when I got in contact with you guys. I'll dial him in."

Saffron's belly squirmed. Had the Lab failed? Were Lyrik and Zack's parents giving up?

The screen split, and Jensen's face appeared. His drawn look confirmed the news he had wasn't good.

"What's going on?" Lyrik asked. "Please don't tell me Colonel Adams shut the research down."

"No," Jensen said. "We always had his full support. Zack, Lyrik, you have to know, your parents . . . they are amazing. They did it. They discovered a way to beat these things. Your mom will fill you in on everything you need to build the weapon."

Lyrik, Zack, Saffron, and Rabbie high-fived each other. With this news, they might actually stand a fighting chance.

Yoyo pumped his fist in the air. "Dudes! I knew they could do it!"

Although Jensen joined in with the delight, a level of apprehension dulled his sheen.

Was he regretting not stopping the other leaders from initiating lockdown? Had Rabbit Cove closed itself in for another fifty years prematurely?

Something beeped. "Your mom is ready," Jensen said.

His and Yoyo's image dropped to the screen's bottom right as Dr. Margaret—Lyrik and Zack's mom—filled the space. Her smile, while genuine, oozed with a tension similar to Jensen's. Although hidden behind dark-rimmed glasses, her eyes held the puffiness of someone who had recently shed tears. Was she heartbroken that her children had run off? With the decision to flee happening at the last minute, Saffron doubted Lyrik and Zack would've said goodbye. Stuck behind a time-locked door, Margaret and Mike might never see their children again.

"We're sorry for running," Lyrik said. "We had no choice. But don't be sad. Yoyo will find a way to override the timelock. We'll win this thing and we'll see you and Dad soon."

"You did the right thing in leaving when you did," her mother replied. "We're proud of you for helping Rabbie's people."

"We heard you and Dad found a way to destroy that stuff," Zack said. "Tell us everything."

Dr. Margaret explained that she and Dr. Mike had thrown everything they had at Eifa's substance and nothing had made a dent. During their discussions, they always circled back to the one known fact—destroying a Wirador Wosrah's eyes rendered the substance unviable. With the expression of eyes being windows to the soul, they hypothesized that any destruction to that window (for example, blindness) would bring about a warrior's death. They debated the best way to damage the retina and came up with laser beams.

For Saffron's benefit, Zack described a laser as a concentrated beam of light, the effects of which were like forcing someone to stare at the sun.

Saffron's lips parted as she nodded. She'd experienced the dangers of looking at the sun. A few years back, she'd gazed up at a cloud. At the same moment, the sun's rays had broken through, stinging her eyes. For the next few seconds, her vision had failed.

"So, these laser beams, they burned that blob away?" she asked Dr. Margaret.

"Duh," Lyrik said. "Mom just explained they tried everything on it and nothing worked. That would've included lasers. She's saying that instead of firing bullets at those monsters' eyes, we can use ray guns instead." She draped her arm around Zack's shoulder. "With Mom and Dad's help, we're going to save the world."

"This actually makes sense," said Rabbie. "So where do we get these ray guns?"

"We make them," said Zack. "Don't worry. I've made stuff like this before." He turned to the screen. "Dad drew up some specs, right?"

His mother nodded. "I'll have Yoyo send them through. You should have plenty of supplies in the city. He's listed off the places to start looking for what you need."

"Wait," Saffron said. "All of this is hinging on a theory?" She turned to Rabbie. "Your people still have time to flee. When we present this weapon to the council, it's important they know, until we build this weapon and fire it at a warrior, we can't give any guarantees that these laser beams will do what we hope."

"Yes. You can," Dr. Margaret said.

Saffron blinked at her. Such certainty could only come from already testing their theory. But they didn't have a Wirador Wosrah. They only had the glob.

Her stomach dropped. Where was Dr. Mike? Why hadn't he joined this discussion?

"Zack. Lyrik," their mother said. "Your father loves you very much."

"Where is Daddy?" Lyrik asked.

Saffron's belly flip-flopped. Jensen's sullen demeanor and Dr. Margaret's teariness suddenly made sense. They weren't regretting a fifty-year lockdown or upset with the possibility of never seeing Lyrik and Zack again. Something far more untoward had happened.

From their slumped postures and stony expressions, Rabbie,

Yoyo, and Zack seemed to understand what Jensen, Dr. Margaret, and now Saffron knew. The only person not catching on was Lyrik. "Mom. Get Dad now. I want to show him—"

Zack grabbed her arm. Other than saying Lyrik's name, he seemed incapable of speaking.

Lyrik's brow crinkled as she looked around the room. "What?" she asked. "What is wrong with everyone?"

Lifting her glasses, Dr. Margaret dabbed her eyes. "Lyrik, sweetie. You remember your father's favorite saying..."

"Yeah. When there are no mice left, the scientist becomes the mouse. So?"

"There were no mice left."

Zack curled into himself.

Saffron gulped back her tears.

Lyrik's shoulder twitched. "What? I—I don't understand."

"If the need arose, your dad had always planned to do what Grandpa Huxley had done. The need did come. Just in a different way."

Grandpa Huxley? Who was he?

Agony gripped Dr. Margaret as she pressed her hand to the screen. "The look on your faces when you and Zack came back from exploring the outside brought us such joy. That's the world you belong in, not here. If there was a chance Rabbie's people could destroy this army and allow you and Zack to roam as the free spirits you deserve to be, then your dad was going to do everything he could to give you that chance."

Lyrik's expression turned ashen as she processed. "No. I don't want that. Tell him he can't do what Grandpa did. I want to come home. I want my father. Where is Daddy?"

Tears poured down Lyrik's cheeks. The reality of her father's sacrifice had sunk in. She pressed her hand to her mother's. "Mommy, please tell me it's not true. It would've worked. The ray guns would've worked. He didn't need to test them on himself. Please. Please tell me he didn't let that stuff turn him into one of those beasts."

Saffron's skin grew cold. It was one thing to have Eifa's muck accidentally glom onto you, but to willingly step inside that glass chamber? She quivered at the unfathomable act.

Shell-shocked, Zack stared at his feet.

Equally stunned, Rabbie pressed his hand to his mouth.

Yoyo wiped his wet eyes. "I'm going to get your mom out, okay, Lyrik? You and Zack, you guys just make sure you make those weapons. You be ready for that battle, because I'm going to crack this lock. We're coming to you, okay?"

"Just stay where you are!" Lyrik yelled. "I never want to see any of you ever again."

Guilt tore through Saffron as Lyrik bolted from the room. She could've put a stop to all of this pain and suffering long ago.

CHAPTER
21

STEAM ROSE FROM the Forbidden Pool's surface.

The water bubbled.

The walls rumbled.

"We should go before this whole place caves in," Eideard said.

Deep within Cecilia's chest, Siersha's warmth pulsed. "It's okay. Nothing bad will happen to us."

Too curious for his own good, Forbillian leaned over the pool's edge. Snatching him by the collar, Amalardh yanked him back as a funnel of water shot into the air. It stretched to the ceiling and swallowed a long stalactite, forming a column of ice. The column's inside must have remained fluid, because the stalactite broke free from the ceiling and the cone-shaped mass slowly moved down the center. As it did, the top of the column melted, releasing a bright light.

When the piercing brightness faded, Cecilia opened her eyes. In the center of the frozen pool stood the Goddess of Light. Her skin and woven-ribbon gown glistened like the chamber's crystal walls. While Cecilia hadn't specifically imagined what weapon the pool might bring forth, she certainly hadn't expected Siersha. Relief flooded her. With the Goddess's power, good would certainly prevail.

Siersha's glowing light pulsed as she spoke with an airy calmness. "Thank you, my forthright Forbillian; my dutiful Oisin; my endearing Eideard; and my steadfast Amalardh, for keeping my resilient Cecilia safe in the face of such unimaginable adversity. I am sorry for all that I have put you through because of my failings. My father—the Great Creator—had warned me not to go near the Forbidden Pool. I should never have given into temptation. But I did. And here we are."

Forbillian motioned to the frozen water under the Goddess's unshod feet. "Is this *the* Forbidden Pool from your story?"

"While this pool and the one in which I swam exist in different spheres, they are a gateway of energy connecting the two realms," Siersha said. "As long as the earthly pool remains intact, I can ferry souls into the Pass-Over World." She stepped off the frozen surface, and the ice turned liquid. "Eifa planned to use the Croilar Tier knives to break the portal. Snapping off the handle of just one inserted blade would've not only prevented my arrival but severed the two realms forever. With the link broken, she could remain down here, and all souls in this realm would be hers for eternity."

"I'll be damned if I let the Dark Goddess keep my spirit floating down here," said Forbillian. "I've got friends in the Pass-Over World I plan to visit. So, what now? You'll use a blast of light or something to send her into oblivion?"

"Something like that," Siersha said.

With loving wistfulness, she stared at Cecilia and Amalardh and placed her warm hands on each of their cheeks. Horror engulfed her. Retracting her touch, she pressed her clenched hands to her chest.

Everyone shared a concerned look. What just happened?

As the Goddess spoke directly into Cecilia's mind, the slight parting of Amalardh's lips suggested he, too, could hear Siersha's words. *I am so sorry for what I have done. In my realm, I cannot feel beyond love, happiness, and peace. I knew that what was happening was testing your resolve, but I had no idea of the pain—the damage to your love—my actions have caused to you. When this is over, I hope you can understand and can forgive me for all that I have done and all that I still need to do in order to right my wrong.*

The tears Cecilia had seen Siersha shed in the Gods' realm had been beads of shiny crystal. The drop rolling down the Goddess's cheek was liquid. Touching the drop, Siersha rubbed the tips of her wet fingers together. "This heaviness I feel in my heart . . . I do not like this sensation." She closed her eyes and a ring of light dropped from her head to her toes. Opening her eyes, she smiled. The act seemed to have wiped her emotional slate clean—reset her only known experiences back to positive ones. "Come," she said to the group. "We have a long journey ahead of us."

Several feet into the lava tube, Oisin piped up about forgetting his backpack. With the Goddess's glow providing enough light for the group, Amalardh handed Oisin the lantern.

"Don't you go falling in that pool," Forbillian said.

"I won't," Oisin replied, and dashed off.

When he returned, the quick glance between him and the Goddess evoked intrigue. Although Cecilia itched to dig further, Amalardh's cool look her way reminded her that secrets were for the holder to keep, not for the overly curious to expose.

As Siersha led the way southwest, across another lava field, toward Bayton, Forbillian sidled up beside her. "I hear the Dark Goddess is building an army five thousand strong. Will we have a force just as powerful?"

The crystalline speckles embodying Siersha sparkled. "We will."

Forbillian clapped his hands together and rubbed them. "So, when do you get to work? Do we need to find a spot for you to, you know, birth our army or something?"

"The weapon to fight Eifa's army is already built."

"Even better!"

"That weapon is you, correct?" Cecilia asked.

Siersha glanced at the gun slung over Cecilia's shoulder. "You could say, if I am the rifle, then the Caladium is the bullet."

Cecilia's knees went weak. Not that word again. "I don't know what I'm meant to do."

"You are the Poison Flower. As with most poisons, you kill from within."

Amalardh's boots kicked up dust as he stopped in unison with Cecilia. He seemed just as affronted as her by the only possible interpretation of Siersha's statement.

"You can't be serious," Cecilia said. "You expect me to let Eifa eat me?"

"I am always serious," the Goddess replied. "I am incapable of telling a lie. I do not expect Eifa to eat you, but you must get inside her. Infiltrating her is as simple as jumping into her like one would a pool. I must caution, only those wearing the Ring of Terefellia can enter her *and* maintain control of their soul. If you get close to her without wearing this ring, she will consume you, your soul, and the portion of my light that you carry within. Instead of killing her, this light will be enough to keep her alive for eternity."

As Brassal had once explained: in the absence of good, there can be no evil, for there can be nothing at all. He likened Eifa and Siersha's relationship to a shadow. Light can exist without a shadow, but for a shadow to endure, it needs light. If Eifa were to kill Siersha, then Eifa would also die. But if Eifa consumed a speck of Siersha's light before eliminating her, she could live on forever.

"How do we get hold of this ring?" Cecilia asked.

"We have a friend inside Terefellia who will help us," the Goddess replied.

The Terefellians hosted a spy? How was that possible? "Who is this . . . friend?" Cecilia asked.

"Ida's daughter. Rudella."

Cecilia gaped at the Goddess. "Ida thought she'd lost her daughter to Eifa's darkness long ago."

"Rudella is a descendant of the Croilar Tier. As you well know, protection of the Prophecy is their nature—at any cost."

The truth of the Goddess's words stung. Amalardh's stoic adherence to placing the Prophecy before all else had cost his and Cecilia's relationship a great deal.

*

By sundown, dusty brown soil and grassy lumps replaced the lava field's onyx surface. Trees about fifteen feet tall, with bulbous clusters of long thorns capping the tips of their branches, dotted the landscape. Since embarking on this unwanted journey, very little had tickled Cecilia's imagination. These bizarre-looking trees did. As she collected wood for the campfire, she imagined Eifa's dark monsters barreling toward her. She held no fear because her army of trees stood by her side. The surrounding land turned into a pool of black as warrior eyeballs succumbed to the deadly force of her trees' spiked fists.

The glow of Siersha's light appearing by her side pulled Cecilia from her fantasy. She got back to gathering her kindling, which she'd absentmindedly stopped. Mirroring the activity, Siersha picked up a stick and smiled as though pleased with herself for completing the menial task.

"You said earlier that you cannot lie," Cecilia said.

"And that was the truth."

"But you can conveniently disappear when asked a question you do not want to answer."

When Saffron's mother had passed, Cecilia had witnessed the tug of Eifa's smoky essence attempting to prevent Siersha from ferrying Esme's soul away. With Cecilia's help, Siersha had won. As Eifa dissipated, she told Cecilia, "Ask Siersha to tell you the truth about who I am." In the moment of Cecilia's question, the Goddess of Light floated away.

"My disappearance was not a convenience I had planned," Siersha said. "I was ferrying a soul back to the Pass-Over World. I could not linger beyond the time needed to perform my duty."

"Since you are currently not ferrying a soul, I will ask again, who is Eifa?"

"Eifa is me. And I am her."

The hairs on Cecilia's arms stood on end. "What do you mean?"

"My father, the Great Creator, held a singular focus—constructing a world that would birth the perfect soul. A perfect soul meant one that could build things as magnificently on earth as he could in the universe. All he wanted was miniature replicas of himself. Early versions of his worlds failed. Although souls growing under one hundred percent pure light lived in pure harmony, they lacked the curiosity and tenacity needed to explore their own capabilities. To counter my perfect goodness, he planted a seed inside me. A tiny speck of black to dull my light the smallest amount, enough to make the pure soul question their world, investigate their environment."

"Eifa," Cecilia said.

"What my father didn't realize was that dropping this seed inside me was like placing a toddler on a bucking stallion and expecting it would know how to control the wild steed. I had no idea how to handle this darkness, how to resist its pull."

Buckling to Eifa's call, Siersha swam in the Forbidden Pool. Angered, her father pulled her from the black waters. "Now you shall see the results of your inability to control your dark side," he bellowed. Dripping from her, the pool's black waters clustered together, forming Siersha's shadowy mirror image. As Eifa's blackness crept into humanity's hearts, the desire to consume, to build bigger and have better things, created a rot so deep that the thin veneer of goodness holding everything together could no longer withstand the strain. The world fell to a mighty war, so powerful that the few who survived should've perished in the decades of poison air that followed. Exhausted from ferrying the millions of souls belonging to those who'd died during the Great War into the Pass-Over World, Siersha collapsed to the ground, her light almost depleted. "Come," her father said. "Let us try again. Maybe next time, you will get it right."

But Siersha couldn't leave the handful of people who had survived the Great War. Without someone to guide them into the Pass-Over World, their souls would linger in an endless abyss of nothingness. "Then I shall send a plague, end their suffering right now," her father had said.

Picking up a stick, Siersha placed it on Cecilia's bundle. "His callous comment broke my heart. Not all the surviving souls suffered."

From the Goddess's expression, Cecilia knew Siersha was referring to Cecilia's ancestors, who'd fled the Great War to the Plockton Forest, where they built a life based on peace, love, and oneness with nature.

"They do not produce enough goodness to keep you alive," the Great Creator had said about Cecilia's ancestors. But Siersha didn't care. As long as goodness glowed within Cecilia's people, Siersha would stay, even if doing so led to her death. Unwilling to waste further time, the Great Creator left.

"My father no longer cared if I lived or died," Siersha said. "Driven by his purpose as a creator, all he cared about was developing his perfect soul."

Cecilia's breath shallowed. The Goddess had risked death to give Cecilia's ancestors a chance at life?

"My inability to control my inner darkness has caused far too much pain," Siersha said. "I need to fix what I broke."

A maimed beetle with a snapped wing fluttered on the dusty ground. Its attempts to fly alerted a team of ants to its presence.

"You wish to help this beetle, don't you?" Siersha said.

"I don't want to watch it die," Cecilia replied.

"Then we will walk away."

"But I've already seen the poor thing. I'll still know of its awful death."

"Then what are you going to do?"

Cecilia weighed her options. She could walk away and let the ants eat the beetle alive, or she could place the beetle out of harm's way, where its death would be just as horrendous. Unable to fly, it would dry out under the sun's rays. Biting her lower lip, she stomped the beetle with her foot. A quick end to its suffering meant a win for both the beetle and the ants.

"When faced with a choice that could ease your soul, you chose to do what was hardest: the right thing," Siersha said. "This is why you are my Caladium. I, too, have chosen to do the right thing. Eifa gave me a choice. And when I say Eifa, I mean, I gave myself a choice. I could either let Eifa remain down here and take possession of the earthly souls for eternity, while I remain in the Pass-Over World existing in the company of the millions of souls I have ferried over the centuries, or I could risk all and destroy Eifa forever. The problem I faced was that the only place Eifa could die was in the human realm." Her light dulled as she placed another twig on Cecilia's bundle. "I needed to set things up so she had the power to cross over."

When Cecilia had first learned of Eifa's arrival, a moment of unconsciousness allowed her to meet with Siersha in the Pass-Over World. During the visit, Siersha had explained that after the Battle for Freedom, when Amalardh had lain dying in Cecilia's arms, the life-giving light the Goddess had sent to save him had caused a void through which Eifa had slipped. The explanation had made Eifa's arrival seem accidental. But the Goddess's comment of needing to "set things up" for Eifa to cross over cast a different light.

"Are you saying the only reason you saved Amalardh was because you needed an excuse to form a hole between the two realms? You did what you did because you wanted Eifa down here?" Cecilia asked.

"Yes. But what you must also understand is that Amalardh's near death was also part of my design," Siersha replied.

The sticks in Cecilia's arms crackled as her muscles tensed. "My people, my friends, those I love are not some chess pieces you can move around so that one day you can say checkmate to Eifa."

"Your analogy for my actions is correct. All the things I have done and plan to do are well-thought-out moves. Sadly, the board I have created is far from a game. If we fail—if you fail—I cannot reset the pieces and ask for a rematch."

Marching back to camp, Cecilia dumped her sticks on the firepit. "Why involve me? Why can't you destroy Eifa on your own?"

The glint in Siersha's eyes dulled. Her ongoing battle with her dark self seemed to drain her. "Imagine a game where you must abide by all the rules while your opponent has the freedom to break them. I do not have the ability to destroy even that which seeks to destroy me. All I have is you and the power to protect those who fight with you. I cannot force humans to choose a side, only the human spirit has that power. The time will come when you will face the hardest choice you'll ever have to make in your entire life. Your decision will determine which side prevails. The Prophet could not predict your answer, because neither can I. My only hope is that you will choose to do the right thing, knowing full well that this will also be the hardest thing."

Siersha placing humanity's existence on some solitary choice that Cecilia would have to make was too much to ask. Attempting to light the fire, Cecilia struck a match. Its delicate head crumbled. She tried again, but because of her anxiety, this match also broke. She threw the box to the ground.

Holding up her hand, the Goddess directed a beam of light at the kindling. "All Eifa needs is the tiniest speck of my light to remain viable in the human realm. If she consumes you, she will possess of a piece of me. *The end for all*, as written in the Prophecy, will not be a destruction of the world as you know it, but a living nightmare for the human spirits trapped in Eifa's version of a Pass-Over World." Smoke rose from the kindling. "If you do not prevail as my Caladium, you will condemn the souls on earth to an eternity of darkness."

The smoking stack of twigs burst into flames.

Forbillian, Amalardh, Eideard, and Oisin strode into camp carrying a bighorn sheep.

"I dare say, Lady Goddess, you bring good fortunes," said Forbillian. "We are going to feast tonight."

Cecilia folded her arms across her chest. As far as she was concerned, Siersha's arrival was far from fortuitous.

SAFFRON WOKE TO the annoying pop-clunk sound of a wooden paddle hitting a ping pong ball. She frowned at the empty bunk room. What time was it? Why hadn't anyone woken her? She followed the pop-clunk to the recreation room. One half of the ping pong table sat upright. Paddle in hand, Lyrik batted the small ball against the vertical end over and over. Although irritated by the noise, Saffron bit back her urge to say anything. After last night's horrific news about Lyrik's father giving his life to test his and Dr. Margaret's ray gun theory, Saffron would give Lyrik free rein to do whatever she needed to deal with her grief.

Rabbie and Zack stood hunched over the billiard table, going over a bunch of paperwork. Her head tilted as she took in Rabbie's new outfit of a mottled beige canvas top and matching pants tucked into black boots. He looked so . . . hot. "Where did you get those clothes?" she asked. She wanted some as well. Her *Sunshine* T-shirt and denim jeans didn't feel appropriate for battling Wirador Wosrah.

"Fifty-watt laser diode banks," said Zack into a foam ball sitting in front of his mouth. A strip of metal connected the ball to another metallic band hugging his head. "Yeah, yeah, I've got it."

While jotting down some notes, Rabbie whispered for Saffron to give him a minute. He, Zack, and Yoyo were refining the inventory list for the weapons. He directed her attention to a screen on the wall displaying a detailed sketch of a strange-looking gun with a short, snub-nosed muzzle and a mass of wiring. *That must be the ray gun. What a crazy-looking device.*

The annoying pop-clunk stopped. "Are we about done yet with the shopping list?" said Lyrik. "I need to get out of this place."

"I'll chat with you later," said Zack into the mouthpiece. Removing the thin headset, he addressed the room. "All right. We have our list. Time to start our scavenger hunt." Where Lyrik had converted her pain into anger, Zack seemed to bottle his away.

Helderic's hulking silhouette arrived in the rec room doorway. Rabbie greeted him and explained that last night, while gathering their dinner, he'd run into Helderic and updated him with everything. "The former Ground People have some brilliant minds," Rabbie said. "Later today, we'll join up with their science team, so we can figure out how to build this weapon."

"Whatever," said Lyrik, "just so long as everyone knows: my brother is running the show. He's got more smarts in his little finger than the lot of you combined."

Helderic glanced at the paperwork on the table. "I don't claim to know a scant thing about"—his nose scrunched as he read—"constant current drivers and laser diodes. I'm here to build stairs so that getting in and out of this place will be easier. If you all stay out of my carpentry, then I'll keep out of whatever you have going on in here."

Lyrik huffed and stormed off. Saffron followed. They wound up down at the beach.

"I don't need your pity," Lyrik said.

"That's good, because I don't have any to give," Saffron replied. She hadn't intended for her honest comment to make Lyrik grin, but she was glad that it had. "Who is Grandpa Huxley?" she asked. In response to Lyrik's creased brow, she added, "Last night, your mom said that if the need arose, your dad had always planned to do what Grandpa Huxley had done. What did she mean?"

Lyrik scuffed the sandy ground with her boot. "If you haven't figured it out, Zack and I are twins. In Rabbit Cove, a family planning pass offers permission for a couple to have *a* child, not multiple. When tests revealed Mom carried two fetuses, the law required she abort one. There is a loophole. A community member can trade their life to another in need of a planning pass." Burying her face in her hands, she sobbed. "My grandfather gave his life so Zack and I could have ours, and now, my Dad's gone and done the same. I should've just stayed home. What was I thinking? We're probably going to die, anyway. I'm so scared."

Saffron was too. But she had to stay strong, for Lyrik's sake. She put her arm around her. "We'll figure this out, okay?" Thankfully, Lyrik didn't ask her "how" because Saffron had no answers.

Over the next few days, where Saffron had once spent every waking moment with Rabbie, she barely saw him. Day after day, he and Zack huddled in the satellite bunker's rec room with Vitus's leading minds, trying to create a ray gun that seemed more theory than possibility.

Since spearheading the weapons build with Zack, Rabbie had become infinitely sexier. Saffron's attraction to him had grown to frustrating levels. Out in the field, she could compete head-to-head with his physical skills. In this new world, the brilliance of his mind was completely out of her league. Her one consolation was their matching outfits. He'd found her a set of mottled beige clothing, similar to his, inside the bunk room's lockers.

Breaking from his huddled conversation with Zack, he turned to the group of council members who, along with Saffron and Lyrik, had arrived in the rec room. "Thank you for coming, everyone. Let's get started."

The group pulled a set of dark goggles over their eyes. The first ray gun was ready for testing.

A half-dozen freshly severed sheep heads lined the back of the room. Handing the gun to Zack to do the honors, Rabbie secured his eye covers and stepped back. Zack aimed the gun and flicked a switch. A beam of light shot forth. Smoke rose from the sheep's face. The smell of roast lamb filled the air. Zack flicked the switch the other way, and the light disappeared.

"If these animals were alive, we can safely assume their retinas would be toast," Rabbie said.

The room cheered.

Saffron's joy vaporized as Hanna, a young woman with brown hair pulled into a high ponytail, hugged Rabbie and kissed his cheek. Although he'd stiffened in response to Hanna's act, he'd probably done so because of the open display of affection, not because he held no feelings for her. How could he not develop an attraction? Look at her. She was everything Saffron wasn't: smart, confident, bubbly. And she spoke the same "technical" language as him. As part of the development team, Hanna had been working closely with Rabbie. Saffron had thought nothing of their relationship, until now. Her chest tightened, making it hard for her to breathe. She steadied herself against the wall. What did she expect? Of course Rabbie would fall for someone who was his intellectual equal.

"Zack burned the sheep's head purely for effect," Rabbie said. "During the battle, the moment a gun's light hits a Wirador Wosrah's retina, immediate blinding should kill it. For safety, all fighters will be issued goggles to prevent accidental damage from stray rays. The brilliance of this weapon is that minimal skill is required. Unlike an archer's need for pinpoint precision, if aimed centrally, the ray gun's beam is wide enough to span both eyes."

From the way Hanna hung on Rabbie's words, she clearly found his authority as impressive as Saffron did.

"How many can we make?" Danmar asked.

"One hundred? Maybe," Rabbie replied.

The supply of electricity presented their biggest hurdle. Guns situated on the south wall could receive power directly from the building they were in. While Vitus had yet to connect to a reliable power source, the city's newly formed science and engineering lab had made substantial progress in developing salt water batteries.

Rabbie's team were looking into using this technology to provide power to the distantly located ray guns.

One hundred guns might seem like a lot, but when stationed along the battlement's long arc, this meant only one weapon for about every two hundred feet. "The longer we can make our power cables from the battery pack to the light blasters, the greater our shooters' lateral reach," Rabbie said.

"How far can the beam travel?" Danmar asked.

"Effective range is about forty feet, give or take, based on electric current variables."

How did Rabbie know all this stuff? More than ever Saffron wanted to grab him, pull his lips to hers, and show everyone: "He's mine. I found him first."

Danmar clapped his hands together and praised the team for a job well done.

As Rabbie disappeared behind a wave of shoulder-slapping council members, Saffron turned and walked off. She was about to climb the stairs when Rabbie called to her. Her heart leaped and she immediately felt bad for sneaking away.

"Great work," she said. "I'm sorry I couldn't stay. I have to go check on something." A complete and utter lie. The only thing Saffron needed to check was her bruised heart.

"We barely see each other anymore," he said.

"We've both got things to do."

"Maybe we can catch up later tonight?"

A ball of hope lodged in her throat. She desperately wanted to hang out, just him and her, like they had been since they'd met. She was about to tell him, absolutely, when Hanna's head poked out from the rec room, interrupting the moment.

"Rabbie, we need you. Some of the council members have some questions."

Saffron's jaw tensed. The combatant inside her wanted to fight for Rabbie, but she cared too much about him to come between him and another girl. "I'm not sure about tonight," she said to him. "I've got a thing with . . . uhm." She sucked at coming up with on-the-spot lies. "The gate needs my help."

Did disappointment flash through Rabbie's eyes? Or was this just Saffron's wishful thinking? He waved as Hanna dragged him away.

Lyrik strode over. "The gates don't need your help."

No kidding. Turning from the playful dig, Saffron marched up the metal stairs.

Lyrik followed. "Looks to me like someone's in love."

"That someone isn't me. I don't have time for such nonsense."

"Okay. Fine. Looks to me like someone's jealous."

Saffron's face scrunched at Lyrik's correct assessment. She was jealous and she hated herself for it. Needing a distraction, she strode down the external wooden steps Helderic had constructed and over to the nearby weapons training area. Previously established for the Soldiers of Vitus to hone their skills, plentiful straw-and-sand-filled training dummies hung in the open space.

She and Lyrik walked a line of boys and men practicing jabbing Wirador Wosrah with dual-pronged spears of Saffron's design. One well-placed stab would skewer both of a warrior's eyes. Saffron might not have the smarts to build a laser gun, but at least the city could easily mass-produce her weapon, giving every Vitian a fighting chance against Eifa's beasts.

A group of women stood watching from the sidelines. Surely they weren't doing the polite thing and waiting their turn. Saffron stepped over to Margot, a weathered woman of about forty years of age with curves for days, and the council representative for the former Night Wives forced to service the Soldiers.

"How is your training coming along?" Saffron asked.

"It's not," Margot replied.

A girl of about thirteen folded her arms and huffed. "The stupid council voted for all the women and children to hide during the battle with the blind and elderly."

"What? When? No one told me this," Saffron said. Granted, she'd not attended the recent meetings. Her time was better spent building spears, not listening to ray gun and gate reinforcement updates.

"They passed the vote just last night," Margot said.

Saffron turned to the girl. "What is your name?"

"Bethany."

"Well, Bethany, if you want to fight, then you will. Come with me." Handing the young girl a weapon, Saffron walked to the nearest practicing fighter and politely asked the man to step aside. When he refused, she disarmed him, tossed him to the ground, and held the dual-headed spikes to his throat. "You will let the women train. Am I clear?"

Wide-eyed, he nodded.

Helderic and Gregore, who were returning from the laser reveal meeting, strode over. Gregore, a muscular man with cropped, bright red hair and haunting blue eyes was the council delegate for the former Soldiers. Because of their respective skills as an archer and a swordsman, Helderic and Gregore were in charge of weapons training.

"I thought we were fighting the enemy, not each other," Helderic said.

Saffron removed the spikes from the man's throat. "Where I come from, women are not reliant on men for protection. These women and girls want to train, and they will."

Gregore folded his thick arms across his meaty chest. "The council decided it would be safer for the women and children—"

"To be sent to their deaths," Saffron said. "Yes. I heard. And when the Wirador Wosrah find them, which they will, what then? Even in hiding, you will leave them defenseless?" She turned to Helderic. "You fought next to Rabbie in the Battle for Freedom. He told me about your people and their years spent hiding from the Soldiers. You were integral in convincing your leader to take up arms. You more than anyone know the frustration of being forced to hide, when all you want to do is fight for what is right."

She held Helderic's glare.

Nodding, he turned to the practicing men and halted them with a piercing finger whistle. "Step back," he said, "and let these women have their turn."

Even though Gregore stood taller and broader, he didn't seem willing to go up against Helderic. He waved his arms at the men and, with a firm tone, reiterated the order.

Stepping up next to Bethany, Saffron motioned to the hanging pell. "That monster is all yours. All you have to do is jam your spear through its eyes."

"You mean like this?" Her expression turned scary as she drove her weapon into the target's painted eyeballs.

Saffron smiled. "Exactly."

She and Lyrik spent the next few hours training the female squad, refining their stances and core stability. Saffron recognized a trainee as one of the bold young women who'd tried to dazzle Rabbie with her provocative smile when Saffron and Rabbie had rolled into Vitus on their bikes.

"Thank you for supporting us," she said.

The comment threw Saffron. She had expected someone as well-preened as this girl, with her silky-smooth hair and flowing skirt, to be the first to want to run and hide.

"My name is Brie," the girl said. "My mother died during the Battle for Freedom. She went to war with nothing but a pitch fork to fight against men like that"—she nodded at Gregore—"wielding four-foot-long blades so my sisters and I could have a chance at a better life. If I don't fight, what does that say about the value I placed on my mom's life?"

When Saffron had arrived in Vitus, she'd feared judgement from others before they'd taken the time to get to know her. Now, here she was, making the wrong assumption about another. She motioned to the spear in Brie's hand. "Would you like some lessons?"

Brie smiled and nodded. After some practice drills, she wiped the sweat from her brow. "I have a confession. When you arrived with Rabbie and we saw how close you two were, some of us were a little jealous. I mean, let's face it, Rabbie and his brother are a bit of a catch. Eideard is the biggest flirt. Rabbie, though, keeps to himself. We've never seen him with a girl. For a while, we thought maybe, you know, he preferred a different type of company." She thrust her spear at the hanging target and groaned when she skewered its upper chest. "Well, now I get it."

"Get what?"

"What Rabbie sees in you. You're amazing. I can't even spear that stupid thing."

Brie certainly had her signals mixed up. If she'd witnessed the kiss Hanna had just given Rabbie, she certainly wouldn't hold the misguided notion that he "saw" something in Saffron. "Trust me. Rabbie and I are just good friends."

Brie gave her a look. "So you say." Lunging forward, she speared her weapon through the dummy's eyes. "I did it," she said, jumping up and down.

Good. Saffron's job was done. She'd visited the weapons training to take her mind off Rabbie, not have him be the center of discussion. She gave Lyrik an "I'm cutting out" signal.

Nodding, Lyrik motioned to give her a minute.

"Thank you," said Margot. "When the council gave me a seat at the table, I assumed they would listen to what I had to say. When they didn't, I gave up. I see now that if I want to be heard, I need to rise above the noise."

"In Terefellia, we learn early that if someone pushes you, you push back harder. It's all a test to weed out the weak from the strong."

"So young. And yet so wise. I'll be sure to push back from now on."

Although she remained poised, Saffron wanted to scream. She hated always having to push back, always needing to be strong. She wanted to throw her arms around Margot and be the scared child her father had not let her be.

*

Golden sunlight danced along the Epona Ocean's rippling surface. Could Brie have been right? Had Rabbie "seen" something in Saffron? A quick tap to her arm pulled Saffron from her thoughts. She followed Lyrik's pointing finger from where they stood on the battlement's southernmost end. A dust ball approached from the southwest. Not the right direction for Eifa's Army. Also, the Tower's warning bell remained silent. If the approaching mass had been a horde of Wirador Wosrah, the watch guard's powerful scope would've certainly detected as much.

"They're coming from the direction of Rabbit Cove," said Lyrik. "They look like two of our vehicles. Come on."

Saffron and Lyrik sprinted around the battlement's long arc and arrived above the closed Great Gates just as two hefty, dark green Rabbit Cove machines pulled to a stop. One had a wide base and chunky wheels; the other was tall and long, with a canvas wrap covering a boxy trailer. From the wide vehicle stepped Jensen. Kayla, his daughter, exited the other.

Lyrik's eyes went wide. "Yoyo did it! He cracked the time lock." Calling out to Kayla and Jensen, she waved madly.

"Open the gate," Saffron yelled to those below.

Not an easy feat after her reinforcement suggestion. The engineering team's first attempt had involved adding thick beams across the central opening. "That won't be enough to stop the pushing force of five thousand Wirador Wosrah," Saffron had said. She pointed to two massive train hoppers filled with stone. "It's a shame we can't block the gates with something heavy like that." Taking her suggestion to heart, the team laid new tracks parallel to the Great Gates, and used a restored steam engine to roll the massive door stoppers in place. Thankfully, Jensen and his crew were not in a rush to get inside because the process to open the gates took a good twenty minutes. By then, Saffron and Lyrik had trotted down the battlement stairs and were waiting just inside the wall's grand entrance.

The two vehicles rolled in and pulled to a stop. Dozens of Rabbit Cove fighters filed out from the taller vehicle's canvas-covered back, carrying armfuls of guns and ammunition.

Lyrik's tears flowed as her mother stepped from Jensen's machine. Flinging their arms around each other, they hugged tight.

Following Dr. Margaret came Yoyo, his red hair bouncing wildly.

Saffron dashed up to him. "I can't believe it! You're here! You did it!"

He shrugged, nonchalant. "It's all just ones and zeros. Move a decimal point here and another one there and *ka-pow*. Fifty years becomes fifty hours, give or take."

After the welcome hugs, Lyrik updated everyone. "You have to come and see the laser gun," she said. Hooking her mother's arm, she led her in the direction of the satellite bunker.

Yoyo shoved his hands in his pockets as he watched Lyrik walk off. He seemed as love-struck with her as Saffron was with Rabbie.

"So . . . are you ever going to tell her?" Saffron asked.

"Tell who what?"

She motioned Lyrik's way. "You like her, right?"

Yoyo scuffed his boot on the ground. "Maybe."

In response to her cocked brow, he sighed. "She's so darn amazing and completely out of my league."

That was exactly how Saffron felt about Rabbie. Maybe if Yoyo would be brave enough to talk with Lyrik about his feelings, Saffron could find the courage to do the same with Rabbie. "So, you're not going to say anything?"

"Heck, no."

"Why not?"

"You're honestly asking why I'm not willing to get my heart smashed into a million pieces when she rejects me?"

Good point. Nothing good could come out of Saffron telling Rabbie how she felt. With confirmation that suffering in silence was the right thing to do, she patted Yoyo's shoulder. "Come on," she said. "I'll show you around."

CHAPTER

23

A RAGING INFERNO filled Wyndom's dreams. He jumped awake, but the blaze remained. Acres of corn fields dancing with crackling golden flames lit up the night sky. Wyndom viewed the disaster from a Wirador Wosrah watching the destruction from a distant hill. He pressed his hands to his head. His Promised Land was on fire. Had the enemy realized they would lose and burned their fields to spite his pending victory? His brow furrowed as Vitus's great gates swung open. Buckets of water in hand, dozens of people rushed out and began dousing the flames. If the enemy had deliberately ignited their field, why were they attempting to settle the flames?

Because they didn't start it, said the Maddowshin, reading his thought.

You ordered this? he asked.

The queen did.

Why would she destroy such a vast amount of our food supply?

That field holds already harvested maize. The ash will be good for the soil. As for why she ordered the burning? I do not question her will.

Apparently, the group of Wirador Wosrah sent to collect Alistair received a secondary assignment: on their way back, they were to burn the field. But why? Was his queen sending a message? Or had she simply wanted Wyndom and his people to have the richest soil possible when they entered the Sworn Province?

*

The endless rows of Wirador Wosrah, all carbon copies of each other save for their human eyes, shimmered under the sunlight. The end, or rather, the beginning, was near. The warriors carrying Amalardh's son were due to arrive within the hour. Once the queen had her bargaining chip, her army would march. Vitus would fall, and supreme reign over the Sworn Province would be Wyndom's for eternity. He would soon have everything he wanted. Why, then, did he feel so . . . unsettled?

"Great glory comes at great cost," said the Maddowshin.

From the distant look in the beast's eyes, Wyndom knew the words came from Rudella. The effort required to secure a win for their queen seemed to drain her as much as it did him. He sighed as he breathed in the warm, dry air. Wyndom would have his glory, but at what cost? The sum of his tragic life amounted to a wife he hadn't appreciated until she became a beast, a daughter who despised him, and a lover—Amalardh—who didn't know he existed. He rolled out his stiff shoulders. Wyndom might not be able to secure Saffron's love, but he could demand her loyalty. "When the battle begins," he said to the Maddowshin, "I do not wish harm to come to my daughter. Have your warriors find her and bring her home."

Once Saffron was back in the fold, the Maddowshin could connect her to the Terefellian consciousness. All her thoughts would be known, her actions seen. Wyndom could mitigate any chance of escape the moment the idea crossed Saffron's mind. Over time, she would see the fruitlessness of trying to fight. Shaping her into the daughter Wyndom needed her to be might take months, or even years. Whatever the case, he didn't care. One way or another, he would not enter eternity alone. He would bring Saffron with him, kicking and screaming if necessary.

The Wirador Wosrah sent to capture Alistair galloped into camp. Wide-eyed, Wyndom stood from his resting mat and dusted himself off, more as a nervous response than anything else. The Maddowshin's orders to the raiding warriors had been simple. Get in and get out with minimal bloodshed. Until their queen could be certain she'd destroyed the false goddess, she wanted as many souls as possible to remain with her on earth. Obeying their orders, the warriors stole Alistair in the dead of night while his protectors slept.

Sister Leona, who'd gone with the pack to act as a carer, slid off her beast's back and carried the bundled infant over. Alistair's striking blue eyes mirrored Amalardh's. He smiled and guilt ripped through Wyndom. The innocent child had no idea of Wyndom's role as executioner.

"So this is the supposed Ceannaire Fis," said the queen as she walked up from behind.

She stroked the back of her black, rubbery finger against Alistair's rosy cheek.

He burst out crying.

Surprising himself, Wyndom grabbed Alistair from Sister Leona and bounced him gently up and down. "There, there," he said. "It's okay."

Alistair immediately settled.

In response to the queen's thin lips, Wyndom quit his bouncing.

"Do not get too attached," she said. "You will soon have my daughter in your care."

The daughter she referred to was the baby growing in Sister Darna's belly. The queen was right. Wyndom could not risk getting too close to Alistair. Amalardh's son or not, if she sent her order to dispatch of him, Wyndom's heart would need to be as icy as possible to complete the task. He thrust Alistair back into Sister Leona's arms and told her to take the child from his sight.

Smirking approvingly, the queen turned to her grand army. Lined up perfectly, the Wirador Wosrah glistened like statues of polished onyx. After months of birthing the rugged beasts, she was finally done. She stretched her arms out wide. "Tonight, we march."

The warriors stomped their feet.

The Terefellians cheered.

"My people, prepare the Repithaf!" said the queen.

Wyndom's face crumpled. *Repithaf?*

"The fire path," the Maddowshin replied.

Although Wyndom nodded, he had no idea what the "fire path" meant. The rest of Terefellia seemed to (either that, or the Maddowshin had fed orders directly into their minds) because they all got started on various tasks. Some collected the resting mats and dumped them in a central pile, others uprooted bushes and clumps of weed grass, adding them to the stack. Anything that could burn, his people tossed onto the growing heap.

"What is going on?" Wyndom asked.

"The queen is preparing to march on Vitus," said the Maddowshin.

"But how is building a bonfire aiding that plan?"

"An explanation will not do the Repithaf justice. Only by seeing will you understand."

As the last of the sun's rays disappeared in the western sky, a group of Terefellians arrived with planks of wood scavenged from the decayed, pre-Great War structures skirting the nearby lands and dumped them on the massive mound.

"It is time," said the queen.

Stepping up to the stack, she lifted her hands. Bolts of fire shot from her palms, igniting the pile. Orange flames lit up the night sky as the burning mass crackled and popped.

She turned to her Wirador Wosrah army and waved them forward. The closest warrior bolted toward the flames. Bounding high into the air, it dropped into the fire and disappeared. One after the other, the warriors repeated the act.

Wyndom's mouth went round. "What is happening to our army?" When the Maddowshin didn't respond, he turned to the beast. Was that a tear rolling down its cheek? Impossible. According to Rudella, the Maddowshin only felt calm and rage. Any other emotion it experienced through others. No other Terefellian was crying.

"Rudella," Wyndom said, to get her attention.

The beast's brow furrowed at him. "What?" it replied.

"Your cheek."

It pressed its gnarled fingers to the wet spot and terror gripped its face.

"You can feel?" Wyndom asked.

He flinched as a rubbery length of rope shot from the queen and ensnared the Maddowshin's waist. Another thread burst into the remaining mass of Wirador Wosrah, capturing a warrior. Like the recoiling of a spring, the black strands retracted, pulling both parties into the queen's pliant flesh.

Rudella. What is happening? Wyndom asked.

Goodbye, came her somber voice.

Protruding lumps and bumps—reflective of arms, legs, and other bodily parts—rose and fell within the queen's expanded belly. Why had she consumed the Maddowshin and a warrior? Was she planning to rebirth a hideous combination of them both?

The Maddowshin's beastly head protruded from the queen's rubbery form. As its snout broke free, it let out a rumbling roar. Its bulging arms wrestled out, followed by its powerful torso and hoofed legs. Everything about its disdainful posture made Wyndom wary. In the past couple of weeks, his relationship with Rudella had mellowed to where they were more compatible, more respectful of each other as man and beast, than they'd ever been as husband and wife. He caught sight of the Maddowshin's eyes and stiffened. The dark irises weren't his wife's golden amber. "Where is Rudella?" he asked the Maddowshin.

"In the eternity where she belongs. She played you for a fool, a far greater fool than you played me."

Wyndom stiffened. If Rudella no longer controlled the Maddowshin, then who did? From the way the beast spoke, its inner soul seemed to know Wyndom.

"I guess I should be thankful for what you did to me," the Maddowshin said. "Because of your lack of lenience to my plight, I am now where I belong as the queen's right hand. Rudella may have caused damage, but none that is beyond repair. Do as our queen has ordered, and the Sworn Province will be yours. Fail and the wrath will be mine."

Wyndom squinted at the Maddowshin's eyes. "Brother Lasair?"

On the eve of the queen's arrival, Brother Lasair had begged Wyndom to stay his Rite of Quinquagenary, but Wyndom had ordered the ritual to continue. Lasair was burned; his soul was collected in a Tenococill Olus basket and stored in the temple with the other five thousand captured souls, which the queen birthed into her Wirador Wosrah army. The warrior the queen had sucked into her belly must have harbored Lasair's spirit.

The captured Wirador Wosrah's hulking body lumbered out from the queen's black mass.

Rudella? Wyndom said. *Can you hear me?* But of course, the beast couldn't. Wirador Wosrah were nothing but killing machines incapable of communication. Rudella's golden amber eyes didn't even acknowledge him as the beast marched to the rear of the queue waiting to jump into the fire.

What had Rudella done to warrant a demotion to a foot soldier?

One by one, the Wirador Wosrah disappeared into the awaiting fire. The line dwindled until only Rudella's beast remained. It sprinted for the flames, leaped into the air, and dropped into the fiery portal. Wyndom rubbed his achy chest. *Goodbye, Rudella.* He truly had developed a soft spot for his former wife.

"My faithful servants," the queen said to the Terefellians. "Your loyalty has served you. You are the chosen ones. At daybreak, our army will march and the infidel city of Vitus will be yours."

Everyone cheered, except Wyndom. With Rudella's soul rendered to nothingness and Saffron's abandonment, he had no one to spend eternity with.

CHAPTER

24

WITH CECILIA'S CONNECTION to the Goddess of Light, Amalardh had expected the two of them to behave like a pair of celestial best friends, not like a despondent mother and rebellious child. It was as though Siersha had placed a plate of bitter greens in front of Cecilia and told her, "You must eat these for your own good." In response, Cecilia had made a point of showing the Goddess just how foul the role of the Caladium tasted in her mouth. As the group followed Siersha toward the city of Bayton, Cecilia trudged along with a facial expression that warned everyone, Amalardh included, to leave her alone.

The grasslands gave way to a long, narrow valley cutting through the southern portion of the Korfkahn Mountains. The narrow divide opened into an abundance of green that thickened into a dense forest. While trekking over the sharp lava fields, hard savannah soil, and rocky valley floor, Amalardh had paid little mind to Siersha's unshod feet. He assumed a layer of thickened crystals on her soles provided protection from the unforgiving surfaces. The soft forest ground made him reconsider this theory. As she walked next to him, Siersha's feet made no imprint at all, for they didn't touch the ground. Instead, she trod on a thin pillow of light.

She nodded at Cecilia, who walked ahead of them. "She still loves you."

Amalardh wanted to believe the Goddess. "You ask too much of her," he said.

"Do you think your resentment toward Cecilia for saving you

after the Battle for Freedom was an accident? Do you believe your confusion about whether you were supposed to live or die was arbitrary? Had you not withdrawn from Cecilia, would you have done what you did with the Terefellian?"

A chill settled in the small of Amalardh's back.

"I have asked too much of everyone. Especially you."

They walked in silence for a long moment.

"I know what you are thinking," the Goddess said. "For as good and pure and kind as I am, I am also calculating."

She was not wrong in her assessment of Amalardh's thoughts.

"You, more than anyone, understand that manipulating a situation for a desired outcome is not in and of itself evil. I ask a lot because the stakes are great."

Siersha's soft light radiated outward and touched his skin, creating crystalline speckles that engulfed his body. He exhaled and all his pain, anguish, and guilt dissipated. His racing mind slowed, and the shards of glass encasing his heart melted like snowflakes under the sun's warm rays. For the first time ever, Amalardh understood the meaning of inner peace.

The light extinguished. His breath sucked back in. With it returned his pain.

"I cannot make you feel something that isn't possible," Siersha said. "What you just experienced came from within. While I do not know how all this will end, because of what you just felt, I know that one way or another you will find peace."

Of course, Amalardh would find peace. This much, he knew. All who entered the Pass-Over World did so with an airy heart and spotless conscience. If Cecilia's conversation with the Goddess had been this inane, then no wonder she stropped along with such a maddened gait.

His pulse spiked at a yelp from up ahead. He raced to a small clearing, where Oisin hung in a net. At the sound of guns locking and loading, Amalardh pulled his weapon. With their backs to each other, he, Forbillian, Eideard, and Cecilia fanned into a circle.

"Drop your weapons," came a voice from a clump of foliage.

Amalardh aimed his gun at the spot.

"Drop your weapons, or we drop the boy."

Although standing on the wrong side of a negotiation riled Amalardh, he couldn't let Oisin fall. He placed his gun on the ground. "Do as they say," he said to the others.

Cecilia, Eideard, and Forbillian obeyed.

A dark-skinned man, dressed similar to the Bayton fighters, stepped into the clearing. A dozen other fighters revealed themselves around the periphery. The man's eyes flickered from Eideard to Cecilia. "The Countess is highly disappointed in your lack of gratitude for her hospitality. I see you have collected new travel companions."

"The Countess's hospitality was as warm as a block of ice," Cecilia replied.

"Cut the boy down," the man said to his men.

As Amalardh calculated various plans of attack, Siersha's voice echoed in his head. *Calm your soul. These people are misguided. They are not our enemy.* He glanced around, but the Goddess was nowhere in sight.

The netting lowered to the ground, and a fighter pulled Oisin to his feet. Clutched to Oisin's chest was a crystal the size of a man's head.

Amalardh narrowed in on the object. Where did that come from?

"What do you have there?" the fighter asked.

Oisin handed it to him.

As the other fighters crowded around, Oisin stepped back and motioned for Cecilia, Eideard, Forbillian, and Amalardh to cover their eyes.

Pained squeals from the Bayton fighters echoed in the air. In between their cries came the thud of what sounded like the crystal ball dropping to the grassy ground. The man holding it must have released his grip in order to protect his sight from a presumably bright light.

The cries settled and Amalardh removed his face from the crook of his arm. Where the crystal ball should have been stood Siersha.

Cowering back, the fighters blinked wildly at her.

Panic-stricken, the dark-skinned man released a trail of ear-biting bullets.

Amalardh stiffened. The Goddess had no sooner arrived on earth and he was letting her die? As the spray of bullets dropped to the ground, his tension eased. Her protective light seemed impenetrable.

Aiming their weapons, the other fighters pulled their triggers. Thankfully, their bullets met the same ineffective fate.

As the ammunition ran dry, the clamor ceased.

The ashen-faced men stood rock still, their wide eyes locked on Siersha.

"I mean you no harm," she said. "Your Countess knows who I am. Take me to her."

Amalardh shared a confused look with Cecilia. This Countess knew the Goddess of Light existed? Wasn't the whole point of wiping Cecilia and Eideard's memory a tactic to make them forget about an entity that wasn't real?

CECILIA, SIERSHA, AND Amalardh, along with Eideard, Oisin, and Forbillian, marched into Bayton's courtyard. Behind them strode the fighters who had attempted to capture them. Baytonites in their vibrant attire stopped in their tracks, their eyes locked onto the Goddess.

A swarm of fighters rushed from the Countess's grand residence and stood guard, their guns clutched across their chests. With her chin held high, the Countess stepped outside and motioned for her fighters to open a path. As she drew close, her stunned eyes bounced from Cecilia to the glowing Goddess.

Confidence bloomed on her face as she took in the Bayton fighters standing behind Cecilia's group. She seemed under the impression that Cecilia, along with the Goddess and the others, stood in her courtyard as prisoners.

Cecilia glowered at the poised Countess. This woman's "treatments" had caused unnecessary pain and suffering.

Clutching her fist, Cecilia stepped forward.

The wall of fighters flanking the Countess readied their guns.

Maintaining her composure, the Countess motioned for them to stand down. "We've been worried for you and your—"

Cecilia punched the regal woman in the face. "That's for stealing the memories of my son."

The Countess pressed her fingers to her bloodied lip and studied the red liquid. As she looked up, her self-assurance wavered. The fighters behind Cecilia's rebel group aimed their rifles at her.

"Are you still convinced my stories of the Goddess of Light

and my battles with her Dark Shadow are a fantasy I made up to cope with the destruction of my village?" Cecilia said.

From her stunned look, the Countess didn't seem to know what to believe.

Siersha joined Cecilia's side. "You hold anger toward me," she said to the Countess, "when it should be directed at those who let my Dark Shadow into their heart. They took from you what I could not give back."

The Countess wavered as though dizzy.

A young, dark-skinned woman ran from the crowd and steadied her. "Mother, please. This has to stop. When you asked me whether I believed their stories, I lied and told you no, because I knew what you would do. I'm telling you now, I believe their every word."

The Countess's stunned eyes locked onto her. "Nina. How could you betray me this way?"

"I am not betraying you," Nina replied. She pressed her hand to the Countess's cheek. "You have been betraying yourself—and my father's memory. It must stop."

The myriad of expressions bouncing across the Countess's face reflected her heart's internal struggle. Eifa's spikes clawed deeply. Fighting her need for vengeance took great inner strength.

Nina's loving eye searched the Countess's face. "Mother, please. I miss Father, too. But you must stop this madness."

As the Countess's head lowered, she waved for her fighters to stow their guns.

Cecilia did the same with those on her side.

"When your husband was dying," Siersha said to the Countess, "you prayed to me, and I wept for you. You asked to see him one more time. I brought him to you in your dreams. He told you he loved you, and that he was happy and safe. He asked you to let go of your anger. When you woke, you hated me even more."

The Countess mopped her eyes. "I just wanted him back. Why couldn't you let me have him back?"

"If Eifa wins, you will never see your husband again," Cecilia said. "Our souls will be trapped here while those who have already left their earthly bodies will be forever without us in the Pass-Over World. We must get to Vitus. Will you help us?"

Straightening her spine, the Countess nodded. "I will give you my fastest ship."

CHAPTER

26

THE MOON'S SILVER rays danced over the ocean's black waves. Although the sea spray filled the air with a crisp saltiness, the stench of soot from where acres of corn fields had mysteriously caught fire a few days ago still hung heavily. Eifa, no doubt, was behind the destruction—her way of sending a warning that she had finished birthing her army and that Vitus would be best served forgoing any foolish notion of trying to fight her and instead, preparing for their surrender.

Far from affected by the Dark Goddess's attempt to instill fear, Saffron sat on the southern pier and dangled her legs over the edge. From her pocket, she pulled out a small, wooden carving of Glimglob. While the real Glimglob had been nothing but a tin can with stones for eyes and goat fur stuck to its hinged head, to four-year-old Saffron, he'd been her everything. Until the day her father threw him into a Quinquagenary fire. "Future leaders of Terefellia don't play with toys," he'd told her.

During her trek to Vitus, Saffron had opened up to Rabbie about the pain her father had caused. A few days later, she woke to find a three-inch-tall version of Glimglob whittled out of wood, sitting on her stomach. Although she'd tried not to read anything into the sweet, thoroughly unexpected gesture (wood-carving was Rabbie's thing; he'd probably made it just to pass some time) she couldn't stop her heart from falling in love. She ran her finger over the delicate object and sighed. Life wasn't fair. Saffron should be with Rabbie. Not Hanna.

Intermingled with the gentle slapping of waves against the

pier's support columns came the sound of Rabbie's easy-going plod along the wooden planks. During their long hike, Saffron had learned his every nuance, even the patterning of his step. She glanced up and bit back her smile at his approaching silhouette. Tucking the precious gift into her pocket, she gripped the pier's edge with her clammy palms.

Her heart raced. Her toes wiggled. She was nervous. Why was she nervous? *It's just Rabbie.*

"This is a nice surprise," he said. "I'd been wondering where you were."

A rush of heat burst to Saffron's cheeks. Her being there was hardly coincidental. When they'd first arrived in Vitus, Rabbie had pointed out this pier as his favorite place to relax at night. On several occasions, she'd come there hoping to find him, but his work had kept his evenings long.

He sat down next to her and her anguish dissipated. His comforting presence reminded her that he really was just Rabbie. Her good friend.

The poor guy looked exhausted. He'd just finished walking the battlement and inspecting the installed guns, and he lamented that each station only had four hours of power.

"That should be enough, shouldn't it?" Saffron asked.

He lay on his back, his lower legs still dangling off the edge. "I hope so," he said. "Realistically though? I'm not sure." He explained that the Battle for Freedom had stretched for eight hours and his side had only been fighting a thousand Soldiers. If Saffron's estimate of five thousand Wirador Wosrah was correct, the fight could drag out. "I'd feel more comfortable if we could have the guns powered for at least twelve hours."

While Saffron didn't fully understand how the batteries worked, knowing that Vitus had an entire ocean of salt water that they couldn't tap into was frustrating. From what she'd picked up during status meetings, zinc, the metal needed to generate energy from the salt water, was in short supply. The team had grappled with whether they should build fewer weapons that would last longer or as many as possible to maximize battlement coverage. The council had opted for the latter.

"I just don't know if we made the right decision," Rabbie said.

Saffron didn't know either. She lay down next to him. Worry aside, lying under the stars with Rabbie was nice. During their road trip, they'd passed time at night by joining the dots in the speckled sky and pointing out the picture. Saffron motioned to a collection of bright stars. "I can see a big letter S over there."

Rabbie didn't respond. Beyond his concern for the ray guns, he surely fretted for Cecilia, Eideard, and his other friends, who'd left and were yet to return. He probably worked as hard as he did to help stem his worry. Saffron wanted to say something comforting, but she was far from practiced in the art. When she'd been heartbroken about her mother's death, Rabbie had hugged her and she'd felt reassured. Maybe doing the same for him would help. Not knowing how else to replicate the act while lying down, she cuddled into his chest.

Her eyes widened as his arms closed around her. His pumping heart remained steady. Hers raced. Worried that he might "feel" her intense attraction, she inched back. His arms tightened.

Okay. He either didn't mind or couldn't tell that in this moment she felt way more toward him than "just friends."

He gently stroked her forearm with his thumb. A tingle shot to her toes. Her internal insecurity questioned everything: What did this mean? What about Hanna? Wasn't he with her?

A lump formed in her throat. Now what was she going to do? She'd never be able to swallow past the wretched thing without making a horrid noise. When Yoyo had given his reason for not telling Lyrik how he felt as protecting his heart from being smashed into a million pieces, his fear had made sense. But in this moment, the harder Saffron tried to shield her heart by not saying anything, the more her mind felt ready to explode.

"Rabbie," she said, keeping her cheek to his chest. "There's something I need to tell you."

"Okay," he replied.

She bit her lip, unsure if she should say what she probably should've said long ago. "I really like you."

His thumb stopped stroking.

Her breath froze. Shoot. She shouldn't have said anything.

"I really like you, too," he said.

The lack of surprise in his voice threw her. He must have assumed she'd been referring to liking him as a friend. "I don't think you understand. I really, really like you. A lot."

"That's good," he said. "Because I really, really like you, too."

She pressed up onto her elbow. "You do? What about Hanna?"

His brow furrowed. "What about her?"

"I thought you and her were, you know . . . together."

"Why would you think that?"

"You're always with each other."

"Because we're both on the build team. We're just friends." His drained expression held sincerity. "The only person I want is you."

His confession stunned her. "Really?"

"Since the moment I met you."

Her cheeks flushed as she remembered how Rabbie had been naked. "But I wasn't exactly nice to you."

He smiled. "I guess I'm a glutton for punishment."

In Terefellia, attraction rarely went beyond the physical. And since Saffron had little in the way of physical assets, what could Rabbie possibly have liked about her from the very start? When she asked him as much, his brow knotted.

"Are you serious? First of all, you're a fiend with a bow and arrow."

Her mouth twisted. She could accept that compliment.

"Second of all, you're not a pushover."

Certainly not.

"And third of all, I think you're beautiful."

Her heart skipped. *Rabbie thinks I'm beautiful?*

Leaning forward, she inched her lips close to his, lingering just short of touching. For Saffron—and Rabbie, too, it seemed—the anticipation added to the thrill. Who would break first, give in to their lust?

Saffron. She couldn't hold back any longer.

She pressed her lips to his and a jolt shot through her. Her pulse raced. Her breath quivered. Her body ached for more.

Placing his hand to the small of her back, Rabbie forced her hips to his. All those nights she'd spent alone with him and they could've been doing this? Why hadn't she made a move sooner? His hand slipped under her shirt and slowly ran up her spine, sending tingles to her toes.

Her breath sucked in as he gently cupped her breast. The arousing sensation was unlike anything she'd felt.

Desire gripped her. She wanted to touch him, but how? Her fingers wavered at the base of his shirt. If she caressed him, would her hideous palms hurt him? Riddled with self-doubt, she pulled back and immediately stiffened at the sight of a horned shadow dashing along the pier.

Crashing sounds echoed within the city.

The bell atop the Tower rang. A warning that the enemy had arrived. How had they breached the wall?

Grabbing her knife, Saffron leaped up.

The warrior tackled her to the ground, pinning her with its mighty grip.

As Rabbie sprang on its back and attempted to spear its eyes with his knife, the warrior bucked and flung its head. Like a rider atop a wild bull, Rabbie steadied himself with the beast's horns. Angered, it plucked him from its back and flicked him away.

With the act requiring the beast to use both hands, Saffron's arms were now free. Snatching up Rabbie's fallen knife, she stared the warrior in the eye, hoping her father was watching. "You should've killed me when you had the chance," she said and rammed her and Rabbie's blades into its eyes. Black liquid splashed on her as the beast liquified.

Springing to her feet, she rushed to Rabbie's side.

"I'm okay," he assured her.

She scoured him anyway, noting only a smear of blood on his cheek from where he'd grazed it on the pier's rough wood.

They bolted to the battlement's southern stairs and raced to the top. Saffron leaned over the edge, expecting a crowd of warriors below, but the shadow-cast ground lay empty.

"No! No! No!" yelled Rabbie.

The southernmost laser gun and battery pack were destroyed. As he sped to the next one, Saffron followed. It, too, had been smashed to oblivion.

And the next. And the next.

Her heart broke as Rabbie dropped to his knees. All his hard work. Hours and hours of toiling away. Gone. What were they going to do now? Without the laser guns, they were virtually defenseless. She placed her hand on Rabbie's shoulder and stared into the blackness. Lingering above the smell of soot came the stench of death. A chill settled into the small of her back. Eifa was out there. Somewhere. And she was closer than they realized.

The council convened to assess the damage. Other than Saffron and Rabbie, no one else had been harmed. Saffron's father had probably planned her kidnapping. He wouldn't want her dead, not when he could cause her more pain by forcing her to watch those she loved die during battle. Destruction, not death, seemed the goal of the raid.

Walter, the spotter who'd failed to alert the city of the encroaching raiders, paced up and down, apologizing profusely. He'd been looking for a vast sea of black raiders in the dark. A crash coming from the battlement's southernmost periphery had drawn his attention to what looked like a shadow gliding across the surface. Another shadow did the same at the northern end. By the time he'd figured out what was going on, they'd converged above the gate, where three more shadows sped from within the city and joined them. "I've never seen anything like it," he said. "Those things leaped from the battlement to the ground with the ease of a cat jumping from a cupboard, and then, they ran toward the burned fields and disappeared into the night."

Helderic and Gregore arrived and confirmed what everyone suspected: every single battlement gun station was destroyed. On the bright side, the four portable laser guns powered by special battery packs Jensen had brought from Rabbit Cove remained untouched. As did the shotguns and spears.

The raiders had to have entered through the wall's northern and southern end points. Although Saffron had been aware enough to insist on a weapons team to cover these areas for when the fighting started, no one—Saffron included—had thought to monitor these weak spots on a day-to-day basis. Why would they? Given the Tower's height and visual scope, and the sheer size of Eifa's army, everyone expected plentiful forewarning of the attack.

"Are any of the laser guns salvageable?" Danmar asked.

"Actually, quite a few," said Zack.

Downcast heads popped up.

From Zack's assessment, the beasts had gone for large-scale annihilation as opposed to targeted destruction. He held the original prototype and described how most of the guns had snapped nozzles—an easy enough problem to fix. He pointed to the wired area on the gun's body. "Had they smashed this, we would've been screwed."

"What about the battery towers?" Danmar asked.

"We can rebuild them," Zack replied. "It's just . . . a lot of work."

"Then let's get to it," said Saffron.

"Now?" asked Danmar.

"Yes. Now."

Mumbled protests sparked amongst the group. Teams had been preparing twenty-four seven and needed to rest. The argument spiraled as the tired, over-worked leaders looked for someone to blame. Helderic and Gregore copped the brunt of the group's frustration. As the military leads, they should've had guards posted at the wall's northern and southern end points.

"Stop it," Rabbie said.

The arguments continued.

He tried again, slightly louder. No one listened.

Standing, he lifted his chair and pounded it to the ground.

The ear-ringing sound brought instant silence.

"This is what she wants!" he said.

As his powerful voice boomed in the enclosed space, Saffron rubbed the chill from her arms. She'd never seen Rabbie so enraged.

"This is how Eifa wins," he continued. "She feeds off fear and chaos. She didn't destroy our weapons because she's worried she'll lose. She did it because she derives more pleasure from watching us implode from within. We rebuild what we can, now. Because we don't have time to do it later. We need to assume she's out there, somewhere close."

"If she's as close as you say, surely our spotter would've seen them marching from the south," said Gregore. "You can't hide an army that big, day or night."

"Eifa turned the sky black," said Rabbie. "Her powers are beyond our comprehension."

"I agree with Rabbie," said Saffron. "Don't ask me why, but I get the sense Eifa is closer than we think."

The group exchanged worried looks.

"All right, everyone," said Danmar. "You have sixty seconds to yell and scream and get whatever frustrations you have off your chest. Then, we're going out there and getting this done."

Margot picked up her chair and threw it at the wall. Helderic did the same, as did Lyzol and Gregore. The room became a cacophony of excruciating noise. Rabbie handed Saffron a chair. She shook her head. She understood the concept of releasing her aggression to think more clearly. She just didn't need to.

"Come on," he insisted.

Fine. She smashed the chair to the ground. The wood splintered. Oh wow. That felt good. She crashed it down again and again, each time with more power than the last. Her anger for her father, for her people, for her mother's death, for everything, came rushing out.

"Time's up," said Danmar.

Everyone stopped, except Saffron. With a wild yell, she pulverized the last of her chair against the wall, then turned to find everyone staring at her. Breathing heavily, she swiped a clump of stray hair from her sweaty brow. Okay. She was done.

Danmar surveyed the mess and looked impressed. "Good. Now let's get on with it."

As the room cleared, Rabbie lingered. He seemed to need a moment to regroup.

Saffron hung back with him. "That was crazy," she said.

"Yeah." He sounded distant.

"I feel responsible," she said. "They came here to get me. They couldn't have known about the guns. Destroying them was a bonus."

"It's not your fault."

With her heart still thumping from the chair-smashing, Saffron's desire to kiss Rabbie flipped into overdrive. She stretched onto her toes. Her lips were millimeters from his when he gently pressed his hand to her chest, stopping her. A deadening chill flickered across her skin. This was the part where he was about to tell her he liked her, but . . .

"I don't want all this craziness to define our relationship," he said.

Beyond the immediate mess, Saffron understood Rabbie meant all the insanity that had happened since they'd met. Disaster had thrown them together, chased them across the lands, and waited for them on the other side of the wall.

Leaning back against the table, he lowered his gaze. "I always imagined that if I found a love as deep and rich as my sister's, my world would be complete. Cecilia and Amalardh had the kind of bond I expected would last forever."

Rabbie had told Saffron a lot about Cecilia and Amalardh individually, but not so much about their relationship. "What happened to them?" she asked.

He shrugged. "The battle. Life." He'd overheard Cecilia talking with her friend, Analise—the young woman who, along with her boyfriend, Noah, had been sacrificed to Eifa. Through sobbing tears, Cecilia had confessed to regretting falling in love during such turmoil. Looking back on everything, she wasn't sure which feelings were real and which were only the excitement, thrill, and terror of the moment.

"You're worried that after the battle, you'll wake up and no longer really, really like me," said Saffron.

"No. I'm terrified we'll both feel that way."

"That's not going to happen with me."

"You might think what you're feeling is real, but you can't know for sure. You kissed me once, then went completely cold. We've been together for weeks and you wait until now, hours before the battle, to say anything?"

Saffron's eyes heated up. Rabbie was being so unfair. He had no idea the agony she'd been going through thinking he just wanted to be her friend. How could she have been so stupid to let her guard down? Nothing good ever came from being vulnerable. She folded her arms across her chest. "Fine. Whatever," she said.

He reached for her. "I didn't mean to—"

She pulled away.

"Rabbie," came Hanna's voice from the doorway. As the awkward timing of her arrival registered on her face, a thick tension hung in the air. "Hi. Uhm. Sorry. Rabbie, they need you in the lab."

"Looks like we've both got places to be," said Saffron.

She stormed from the building and her chest tightened. The outside air felt just as thick and regretful as the room she'd come from. Hiding in the shadows, she waited for Rabbie and Hanna to leave, then pulled the miniature Glimglob from her pocket. Her father had been right. Only stupid little girls cared about stupid little toys. With utter disregard, she threw it to the ground and stomped on it. Destroying the shitty little sculpture was the revenge her soul craved.

At least, in the moment, it was.

As the rush subsided, grief took hold. What had she done? Picking up the splayed mess, she set it on her palm as though it were the most fragile baby animal and sobbed. Yoyo had been right. She should've kept her feelings to herself, protected her heart from being smashed into a million pieces.

The sound of footsteps milling around woke Saffron. Did she even get any sleep? She must have gotten a little because the sky had hung dark when she'd lain down, and now the first rays of sunlight poked over the horizon. She'd made camp on the battlement, atop the gates, ready to face Eifa's army. Hundreds of other Vitian fighters lining the wall's grand arc had done the same.

Lyrik, who'd bunked beside Saffron, looked formidable with her powered backpack, dark goggles resting on her forehead, and laser gun strapped across her chest. She, along with Zack, Rabbie, and Jensen, were chosen to fight with the cordless guns. A belt loaded with shotgun slugs lay across Saffron's chest, ready to feed the weapon lying at her side.

During the night, the armament team rebuilt fifty percent of the laser guns. On the plus side, many stations had additional battery cells, allowing them to last longer. Along with the shotguns, Rabbit Cove had provided weapons called assault rifles that fired long, pointy bullets at high speeds. Unlike a shotgun, where the mass of pellets destroyed both eyes at once, the high-speed rifles relied on a spray of bullets to hit one eye after the other. With each shot causing a chunk of material to blow out the back of a test dummy's head, Saffron feared that the bits of Eifa's muck flying off a Wirador Wosrah in the milliseconds between complete blinding might not liquify, leaving small globules of intact muck capable of latching onto a human. Shotguns were so effective because they destroyed both eyes at once. Every beast that received a direct facial hit during the Rabbit Cove skirmish had liquified, bits and all.

"Last night's rush to rebuild the gun stations was a waste of time," said Lyrik. "The Tower spotter is yet to see anything out there." Her face scrunched as she waved her hand in front of her nose. "What is that stench? It's getting worse."

Standing, Saffron sucked back her gag. The stink had started last night and had grown so thick, it stung her eyes. She stepped up to the battlement's railing and scanned the emptiness beyond. This didn't make sense. Where was Eifa's army?

The burned field's blackened surface shimmered the way moonlight did on the nighttime ocean. But how could that be possible? The field wasn't wet. Or was it?

The hair at the back of Saffron's neck bristled as thousands of black columns sprouted.

"What's happening?" said Lyrik.

"Fighters of Vitus! Ready yourselves," Saffron called.

Lyrik's eyes grew wide. "What's going on?"

"Eifa didn't set fire to the crop as a warning. She did it to make a portal for her army."

The ground shook as the multitude of pillars vibrated upward from the base, revealing the mighty Wirador Wosrah. The raiders that Walter had seen run into the field last night had not merely disappeared into the shadows, but rather, had literally dropped into the black soil.

Saffron's breath quivered. How were they ever to win against such a massive force?

To her right stood Rabbie. She hadn't acknowledged him yet. And now, saying something as simple as "hey" seemed too late.

The Maddowshin—a grand beast, taller and broader than the Wirador Wosrah—stepped forward. Although the Terefellian leader was meant for this role, Saffron knew for certain her father did not inhabit this beast. When she'd first escaped Terefellia, she'd monitored her valley from atop a watch tower many miles away and had seen her father standing next to the grand Shadow Mind. Because he would've been too fearful to take on the role, he would've tricked some other poor soul into giving up their life to spare his. But who?

"People of Vitus," said the Maddowshin. Its guttural voice grated like two rocks rubbing together in an echo chamber. "Lay down your weapons, release these gates, and allow your queen's entrance."

Standing tall, Rabbie stepped forward. "Eifa is no queen of ours," he said.

"Your souls are the property of the one true goddess," said the Maddowshin. "If you freely give them to her, renounce your false god, and accept your queen into your hearts, she will take mercy. You may live out your existence in your miserable flesh. If you choose to resist, she will free your souls immediately. One way or another, she will have what is hers."

Rabbie stood firm. "We will not submit to her darkness."

Gaining strength from his forthright demeanour, Saffron's tension settled. Although the Wirador Wosrah army seemed insurmountable, Vitus still stood a chance. With the city's defensive wall preventing an all-at-once attack, so long as the battlement fighters maintained their stamina, good stood a reasonable chance at defeating evil.

Smoke rose from the mass of warriors, forming an enormous plume. Now what was happening?

The massive stack solidified from the ground up, forming a towering goddess made from the same slick, black substance as the beasts. *Eifa.* The mighty deity stood at least one hundred feet tall.

Discord rumbled through Vitus.

"Settle," said Rabbie to his people. "She feeds off your fear. Do not show any."

"I do not wish for bloodshed," said Eifa. "You must see that you cannot win."

Although her honey-sweet tone sounded fortified with compassion, Saffron had grown up with a manipulator—her father—and wasn't falling for Eifa's fake sincerity.

Neither was Rabbie. "I see nothing but an enemy who I am sworn to fight," he replied.

Like a strange, rubbery snake, Eifa stretched forward until her face stopped directly in front of Saffron. "The one that fled the flock." Eifa presented her hand. "Come, my child. Join us."

Within Eifa's pitted eyes, Saffron saw her father and herself laughing happily. This wasn't a memory, for she'd never lived this moment. Her skin tingled as Rabbie joined their fun.

This is what you really want, whispered Eifa inside Saffron's mind. *And you shall have it. I can make it so.*

Saffron's breath sucked in. The Terefellian queen was right. All Saffron truly wanted was a relationship with her father and to spend the rest of her life with Rabbie.

You will live with no regrets, Eifa said. *Take my hand and your deepest wants will be yours.*

With her silky-smooth voice permeating through to Saffron's heart, Eifa began feeling like a long-lost loved one calling Saffron home. Drawn like a wondrous child to a magical kingdom, she stretched her hand to the Dark Goddess's.

"Saffron! What are you doing?" Rabbie said.

"She wants to take me home. I think I should go."

"No! It's a trick."

"Come with me," Saffron said. "We'll be happy."

"She's inside your head. You cannot believe her lies. You must block her out."

Do not listen to him. He is the enemy, said Eifa. *He was toying with your heart this entire time. Using you for his own gain.*

A flurry of anger swarmed Saffron as Rabbie's rejection came rushing back. Eifa was right. Rabbie had never cared for Saffron. He'd dangled the idea of a friendship in front of her so he could bleed her for information. She cocked her gun at him.

His eyes grew wide as he held up his hands.

"Saffron! Stop it!" "What are you doing?" "Put your gun down!" came a flurry of panicked voices from behind.

You know I have the power to give you everything, Eifa said. *Come, my child. These people have nothing to offer you.*

"Saffron, focus on my voice and nothing else," said Rabbie.

With her gun still trained on him, she directed her words to the Dark Goddess. "If I come with you, you will give me everything I want?"

"And more," Eifa replied.

As Rabbie's trustful eyes burned through Saffron's fog, clarity hit. Eifa offered something that wasn't hers to give. Rabbie's love. She turned her gun on the Terefellian queen. Her father's image remained clear in the goddess's eye. "Until you can offer me something real, this is what I want." She fired.

Eifa's head puffed into smoke.

Saffron stiffened. Killing the black queen couldn't have been that easy, could it?

Of course not.

The smoke morphed into a vicious serpent with long, dangerous fangs. Hissing, the snake rose high.

The Vitian fighters gasped.

"Run!" someone yelled.

"Stand your ground," said Rabbie.

"Your false god has failed you," hissed the Eifa serpent. "Your Treoir Solas and Croilar Tier have abandoned you. This city is mine!"

"She's right," said a Vitian fighter. "Where are Cecilia and Amalardh? They saved themselves and left us for dead."

Chaos ensued as terrified fighters fled.

"Stop!" said Saffron. "You must fight."

The snake retracted into the one-hundred-foot version of Eifa.

A half-dozen Wirador Wosrah galloped forward and piled a bundle of short, thin cylindrical tubes at the base of the Great Gates.

Rabbie's expression turned ashen. "Run!" he yelled. "Get away from here! They're blowing the gates."

The primary goal of last night's raid had not been Saffron's capture. The Wirador Wosrah had been intent on stealing Vitus's store of dynamite. Rabbie's two young friends, Analise and Noah, must have known about the death sticks. The moment Eifa absorbed their souls, anything they knew, she knew, too.

Panic poured through the city like blood gushing from a wound.

Saffron fled along the battlement, away from the gates.

BOOM! Her world silenced as a powerful shock wave sent her tumbling.

Disoriented, she lay on her back, blinking bits of dirt and dust from her eyes. Her ears rang. Her head throbbed. Rabbie stood above her, his eyes wide with fear. His mouth moved, but no sound came out.

"Saffron! Are you okay?" His words finally bled through.

She nodded and took hold of his outstretched hand.

Outside, Eifa's black horde raced to the splintered gates.

"Mobile gunners! Get to the ground level," Saffron yelled.

The Wirador Wosrah may have secured a way in, but with the heavy train carriages unaffected by the blast, Vitus still stood a chance against the enemy's stemmed flow.

Rabbie, Lyrik, Zack, and Jensen fled down the nearest stairs and stood with their portable guns aimed at the splintered gates.

The first handful of warriors climbed over the rock-laden hoppers and within seconds, four white laser rays sent the beasts splashing to the ground.

A spotter from the battlement warned of warriors running the wall's perimeters toward the northern and southern cliffs.

Jumping onto her trail bike, Saffron sped to the southern end. Her plan to install laser gun units at these entry points had better be working. Silhouettes of distant warriors dissolving suggested it was. With the southern gunners keeping the beasts at bay, she turned north. Her spirits soared at the sight of disappearing Wirador Wosrah.

Confident that the gunners stationed at the wall's end points would continue to hold off the enemy, she sped back through the city and slid to a stop in front of a group of fleeing Vitians. "Running will not save you," she said. "Grab your weapons and fight!"

"Cecilia and Amalardh knew this unwinnable battle loomed, so they fled," said one of them. "We have the right to flee, too."

"They did not flee," said Saffron.

"Then where are they?"

She didn't know. "You must listen to me. Run, hide, or give up, your souls will still be lost. If you fight, you stand a chance."

Alongside the four mobile gunners, a group of Vitians armed only with dual-headed spears were holding their ground. The weapon worked just as Saffron had hoped. One well-placed jab sent a warrior to mush.

"Look," she said to the deserters. "Your people are fighting and they are winning."

The group turned just as the two massive hoppers toppled over. The beasts had overcome the resistance.

"Run!" yelled a defector. The group shrieked and fled.

So much for Saffron's inspiration. With no time to waste, she floored it to the gates, primed her shot gun, let go of the handle bars, and fired.

Splash. Splash. Splash.

Three beasts down. Thousands more to go.

"Get to ground level!" she yelled to the laser gunners on the battlement. The cables connecting their weapons to the power banks were plenty long enough.

As the gunners made their way down, she corralled several foot fighters and ordered them to secure their goggles. "You're going to run directly toward our gunners, okay? As long as your eyes remain covered, the rays won't harm you."

Nodding, the group dashed off. As the Wirador Wosrah gave

chase, the newly positioned ray guns blasted the enemies' eyes. Puddles of black liquid littered the ground.

If only the council had discovered the missing dynamite, they could've figured out Eifa's plan to blow the gates. The military team could've loaded all the laser guns front and center. The black army would've been annihilated in minutes. But this was the hand dealt to Saffron's side. She needed to quit her complaining and get on with it.

"Everyone, goggles on!" she yelled. "Run to the wall! Draw the enemy to our light rays!"

The assault rifles—the ones that blew bits out the back of a warrior's head—caused less collateral damage than Saffron had expected. As long as another beast stood directly behind the intended target, the flying globules were immediately absorbed.

Needing to reload, Saffron ditched her bike and ran behind Lyrik for cover. "I don't suppose you want to trade weapons," she quipped as she fed slugs into her gun's chamber.

"Never," Lyrik replied. And why would she? This moment was like Rabbit Cove's virtual training room coming to life. Lyrik seemed to have far too much fun with her weapon, telling warriors, "Take that," "Too slow, sucker," "You want a piece of me?"

As always, Rabbie remained calm and focused with his aim. Did nothing rattle him?

Closing one of its eyes, a warrior sped at him. "They're learning to protect themselves!" he yelled.

Light from his gun hit the warrior's open eye. Although it squealed in agony, the beast remained intact. It barreled into him, sending Rabbie to the ground.

Skidding to a stop, the beast turned around and sped back. With the need to see its target, its solitary eye remained open as it leaped. Holding his ray gun at the beast's face, Rabbie squeezed the trigger. Nothing happened. His power pack was broken.

Saffron's blood drained. If she fired at the beast from where she stood, the sideways blast might not kill it. The act could cause a headless body to collapse on Rabbie, devouring him.

As she bolted to the beast, its horns straightened into deadly spikes. Seconds before it skewered Rabbie's belly, she barrelled into it, deflecting its trajectory. Winded, she lay on the ground. The impact had hit with the force of running into a wall at full speed.

A spray of rapid fire blasted her ears. A well-meaning fighter with a high-powered rifle was shredding the beast's head. Although the Wirador Wosrah liquified, the bits of Eifa muck that spewed from the back of its skull before the fighter's bullet destroyed its remaining eye splattered against a nearby wall.

"Saffron! Quick! Get up!" Rabbie yelled.

But her head still swam from the impact, leaving her unable to move.

Dropping from the wall, the muck formed into a clump and raced her way. As Rabbie hauled her to her feet, her leg jolted from the force of the black ball latching onto her boot.

Slicing through the stiff footwear with his knife, Rabbie pulled her foot free and tossed the tainted object at a distant beast. The intent had been for the muck on the boot to blend with the target upon impact, but as with the warriors learning how to protect their eyes from the ray guns, Eifa's substance seemed to also grow smarter. Separating itself from the flying boot, it dropped to the ground. As though bent on revenge, it sped back at Saffron and latched to her boot-free leg.

She cried out in pain as the tiny teeth she'd seen magnified at Rabbit Cove's lab ate through her canvas pants and sank their fangs into her skin.

"We have to get this off!" Rabbie said regarding her trouser leg. Using his knife, he cut the material at knee height. "I'm going to pull down hard, okay."

Saffron nodded. If all went well, the process would rip the small hair-like fibers from her flesh like wax does with hair.

As he yanked down, her body jerked from the miniature teeth holding firm.

"Pull harder," she said.

Throwing his weight into it, Rabbie tried again.

A tearing sound stung her heart.

His horror-struck look at the chunk of material in his grasp confirmed Saffron's fear—the muck had burrowed so deep; the pant leg had torn around it.

Tears welled in her eyes. "You know what you have to do. Okay?"

"No!" he said. "You're not leaving me. I won't let you."

"There's nothing that can be done." He'd seen Eifa's muck latch onto enough people to know she was right. "I love you, Rabbie," she said. "I always have. I'm so sorry for everything."

"I love you, too. I should have told you earlier."

He pressed his satiny lips to hers and in that blissful moment, the pain ravaging her leg dissipated. Rabbie's passion, his tender love, pulled Saffron into another world, another place, one where she no longer felt alone, no longer had to remain brave or wear a hard outer shell. In this safe place, Saffron was free to let go and join her mother in Siersha's Pass-Over World, where one day, she would see Rabbie again.

"This is not the end," she whispered to him. "This is only the beginning."

CECILIA STEPPED ABOARD the Countess's *Bayton II* and craned her neck at the enormous ship's four tall masts. Where Amalardh could manage *Vitus I's* singular boom on his own, this vessel would need at least ten deck hands to get moving. Because this ship also possessed a motorized engine, the captain estimated the trip to Vitus to take only four days.

While several brave Baytonites had volunteered to join the fight against Eifa, most had stayed behind. The Countess couldn't force her people to fight, and Cecilia didn't have time to convince them to join a battle that wasn't on their doorstep. Even Siersha's presence failed to convey the severity of doom unfolding on the other side of the ocean. As one Baytonite put it, "If in the end, there are such things as gods, then so be it. Any battle is theirs, and theirs alone to fight." Cecilia couldn't have agreed more. Unfortunately for her, the gods had seen fit to drag her into the middle of their mess. Leaning on the stern's railing, she watched as Bayton's colorful buildings drifted away. Next to her stood Eideard, his eyes locked on Nina, the Countess's daughter.

"You like her, don't you?" Cecilia said to him.

"Even if I did, what does it matter? The sprouting of love during the time of war has about as much chance of success as planting a seed and pouring acid on it."

Although he didn't say it, the look on his face suggested that Cecilia, of all people, should know this. Shoving his hands in his pockets, he walked off. While her heart broke at the awful timing of a potential love interest finally entering his life, Eideard was right. Better for him to let whatever seed had formed between him and Nina die now than to sprout roots that would only end up strangling his heart.

The early morning fog hung thick and low. According to the ship's captain, Vitus should be a few miles ahead. Cecilia cuddled her arms to her chest. Had Rabbie and Saffron made it home safely? And what of Tomkin and Marion? She'd given strict instructions for them to take Alistair somewhere secure and not to return until Vitus sent a sign—a red flare shot from the Tower's roof.

Cecilia stiffened as a distant boom echoed through the air. The rumble sounded very much like the Ground People's death sticks. Had the battle already started? Surely not. Rabbie and Saffron would've warned the council against the use of dynamite on Wirador Wosrah. The force would blow death globs everywhere. Unless . . . the warning had never reached her people. Her knuckles blanched as she gripped the railing. Had something happened to Rabbie and Saffron? They should've reached Vitus by now.

The city's grand silhouette broke through the fog. Looming high above the Great Gates stood Eifa. The fight *had* started.

"Get this thing moving faster!" Cecilia yelled.

Anxious bodies spilled out from below deck, their faces fraught with despair. They'd come to fight, not watch a massacre play out from a distance.

Standing at the back of the boat with her eyes closed, Siersha stretched out her arms. Like a pillar of salt, she dissipated into the air, creating a cloud of shimmering crystals.

The particles shot forward, filling the sails. At the sudden lurch, Cecilia gripped the rail. Wind bit her cheeks as the ship raced through the water.

The southern end of the wall drew near. Just as Ida had described doing, Wirador Wosrah used their climbing prowess to shuffle sideways along the cliff face, bypassing the wall's end. For the first time since its inception, the Great Wall of Vitus was doing its job of keeping the enemy out, as opposed to its ulterior purpose of locking the former Citizens in. Cecilia's rattled nerves settled. With the flow of five thousand warriors stemmed to a trickle, her people stood a chance against the attack.

As a beast surfaced inside Vitus's southernmost corner, a blast of white light from a strange-looking gun connected with its face.

Cecilia startled at the warrior's instant liquifaction. "What is going on?"

Amalardh's expression turned calculating. "From your own words, stabbing a Wirador Wosrah's eyes renders them dead. Our people must have discovered that any damage to a beast's sight does the same. I can only assume the light from those guns is blinding them."

Similar light rays blasted from the base of the northern wall. This weapon offered hope.

Calling her fighters together, Cecilia directed their attention to the ray guns. "Listen up, everyone. Our people have new weapons. Keep your eyes away from that light. Those beams are powerful enough to burn your sight. The only way to kill Wirador Wosrah is to damage their vision. Without their sight, they will drop into a pool of black. Once this happens, their liquid cannot harm you." Knuckles turned white as apprehensive fighters gripped their guns.

A ship the size of *Bayton II* would normally need to dock in the northern Port of Vitus, where the waters were deeper and the jetty longer.

The vessel suddenly veered left.

"Captain!" Cecilia yelled. "The water is too shallow in the southern dock. We'll run ashore."

"It's not me." His face strained as he tried to right their course. "The wheel is locked."

What did the Goddess think she was doing? While the southern beach was certainly closer to the battlefront, the time gained would be lost trying to disembark.

As the enormous ship ran ashore, the crystals filling the sails dove into the water. A massive wave splashed up and immediately froze, forming an ice-slide from the ship's deck to the beach.

Cecilia thrust her gun into the air. "Fight hard, everyone! May the Light of Siersha keep us safe." Waving her fighters to follow, she slid down the ice to the sandy shore. From there, she and her team had a straight shot to the Great Gates—or what was left of them. The blast she'd heard had destroyed the wooden entry point. The sight of Wirador Wosrah pouring through the splintered mess sent her legs racing.

The cacophony of screams, roars, and gunfire hit like a brick wall. Arriving in the middle of a battle was disorienting. Cecilia had no plan. With no time to think, she cocked her gun and fired at an approaching warrior. The slightly off-center shot blew off the right side of its face, destroying only one eye. Not only had she not killed the beast, she'd foolishly sent bits of Eifa muck everywhere. With its mouth wide open, the beast sprang into the air—

BANG!

Black liquid rained down as Amalardh's well-placed shot finished the job.

The clump of material that had blown from the beast's head formed a fist-sized ball and bounced toward a fighter. As Cecilia ran to intercept, the ball flew away, as if hit by an invisible bat, before she could reach it.

Up ahead, a warrior running at a fighter flew backward. The same thing happened to another, and another. Wirador Wosrah jetted through the air as if blown away by a selective wind. Only, instead of wind, light flowed across the ground like water rushing in from a massive wave. Down on the beach, towering as tall as Eifa, stood Siersha, her radiant white beam repelling the Dark Goddess's spawn.

Through the crowd, Cecilia spotted Rabbie behind an abandoned car. She bolted to him.

As she rounded the vehicle's corner, her stomach dropped. Eifa's darkness had enveloped Saffron's entire right leg.

"Cecilia!" said Rabbie as he collapsed into her arms.

The joy they should've felt for their reunion drowned under the terror of the situation. Although Cecilia had used her inner light to repel Eifa's muck in the past, they both knew she couldn't force this much gunk from Saffron's leg. Cecilia had tried to do so with Esme—Saffron's mother—and had failed.

Sweat poured from Saffron's brow as she cried out in pain. Cecilia had to try something to save her, but what? She narrowed in on Siersha's light dome. "Help me get her up," she said to Rabbie. "I have an idea."

Slinging Saffron's arms over their shoulders, Cecilia and Rabbie rushed her to Siersha's light. At the glowing dome's perimeter, Cecilia directed Saffron to sit with her back to the light. "You have too much on you for me to drive away with my hands, but if Rabbie and I pull you into the light, our combined strength might be enough to force that stuff to roll back on itself. Okay?"

Saffron nodded.

Hooking their arms under hers, Cecilia and Rabbie slowly dragged Saffron into the light. As expected, when the black substance drew close to the bright border, it resisted in the same way the like poles of a magnet repelled each other.

Saffron tightened like a rope.

"Keep pulling," Cecilia said.

Saffron cried out in pain. The poor girl must have felt as though her leg was ready to rip from its socket.

Under the intense strain, Cecilia's grip faltered. Saffron was going to need a greater force than what she and Rabbie could provide. "I need some help over here!" she said.

Amalardh and Forbillian rushed over.

"You need to pull her, but slowly," Cecilia said.

The two powerful men took hold of Saffron and eased her backward.

Although Rabbie did his best to comfort her, no amount of knuckle kisses and hair swipes could ease Saffron's torment.

Unable to fight the force, the muck began folding down on

itself as though it were a thick black sock rolled by a pair of invisible hands.

"It's working!" said Cecilia.

As the blackness neared Saffron's ankle, Amalardh and Forbillian gave a final yank, freeing the gunk from Saffron's foot.

Cecilia's joy was short-lived. If she didn't stem the blood pooling in the muck's wake, Saffron could bleed to death. "Get me some cloth," she said. "We need something to bandage her leg."

With the towering version of Siersha maintaining its glow down on the beach, life-sized Siersha appeared by Cecilia's side. Rubbing her hands together, she created a fine dust which she rained down onto Saffron's wounds. As the blood droplets congealed and faded away, Saffron's heavy breath settled.

While those witnessing the miracle expressed awe, Cecilia tensed. Siersha's light no longer covered Saffron's feet. The giant Goddess on the beach had shrunk, decreasing the glowing dome's radius. When Siersha had described the amount of light needed to save Amalardh after the Battle for Freedom as being immense, Cecilia had not fully grasped the issue. Now she understood. Saving lives diminished Siersha's power. Unlike Saffron, Amalardh had actually died. If helping Saffron depleted this much light, bringing Amalardh back would've drained Siersha to the nub.

"Thank you," Cecilia said to the Goddess.

"It is not Saffron's time," Siersha replied. She glanced at the frightened fighters huddled under her light. "It is not most of these people's time. Unfortunately, I do not have enough light to save everyone."

"Can't you destroy Eifa's beasts by shooting beams into their eyes?" Cecilia asked.

"I have no powers to fight, only to protect."

Smoke from Eifa poured into Vitus, blocking out Siersha's rays.

The Wirador Wosrah rushed at the exposed fighters.

The towering version of Siersha thrust her hands forward, releasing a rain of crystal dust. As the particles showered down,

Eifa's smoke dissipated, and the warriors bounced off the protective light wall. The act, however, led to the tower and light dome's circumference shrinking. In order to maintain a reasonable bubble of light, the Siersha tower moved closer inland.

"I am stronger than you," hissed Eifa. "I always have been." She billowed more smoke at the protective dome.

As the Siersha tower rained more crystals, life-sized Siersha turned to Cecilia. "She is right. The loss of my light adds to her strength." She placed her hand on Cecilia's shoulder. "Only the ultimate sacrifice can kill her. I will protect our people for as long as I can. The rest is up to you." Crystalizing into dust, she merged in with her larger self.

The ultimate sacrifice had to mean Cecilia giving her life for the sake of her people, which she was prepared to do. She just didn't know how. All she knew was that she needed to get hold of the Terefellian ring, and soon. Although her people's ray guns, bullets, and spears had been effective in destroying Wirador Wosrah, they'd barely made a dent in Eifa's vast horde. At the rate the Dark Goddess's smoke drained Siersha's light, the protective dome would soon fail. Without it, the end would come swiftly to Cecilia and her people.

As Saffron lay on her back, catching her breath from her close brush with Eifa's muck, her eyes drifted to the man wearing a hooded robe who'd helped drag her under Siersha's protective dome. So, this was Amalardh. The man who had broken Cecilia's heart. She understood Cecilia's attraction. Beyond his good looks, he possessed a steely confidence that made Saffron fear him, while at the same time, craving his approval. He tied two dual-headed spears together, creating one spear with pointy ends. Clever. Why hadn't Saffron thought of that?

She hauled herself to her feet. "What did Siersha mean when she said the rest is up to you?" she asked Cecilia.

"I need to get inside Eifa and somehow poison her with Siersha's light."

"You need to do what?" Rabbie said. "That's crazy."

"I have to agree," said Saffron. "All who enter Eifa lose their souls."

"Not if they're wearing the Ring of Terefellia," Cecilia replied.

Although Saffron didn't understand the full extent of the ring's power, she knew the wearer became the Maddowshin, a beast capable of communicating with Wirador Wosrah and humans. The ability to do this would suggest the wearer's soul would remain intact. "The Terefellian ring resides on the finger of the most fearsome beast in Eifa's army," she said. "Getting a hold of it will be near to impossible."

"Wait. You're not seriously suggesting that Cecilia does this?" said Rabbie.

"Saffron isn't suggesting anything," Cecilia said. "Siersha is. According to the Goddess, this is the only way."

Saffron's heart knotted at Rabbie's crestfallen look. At every turn, he was forced to stand back and watch his little sister face insurmountable danger.

"Apparently, there's a Terefellian on our side who can help us get the ring," Cecilia said. "A woman called Ida is a Shadow Croilar Tier and so is her daughter, Rudella. Do you have any idea how we can find her?"

The air escaped Saffron's lungs. Rudella? A Shadow Croilar Tier? Pressing her hand to her mouth, she took a moment to process. Rudella's union with Saffron's father had always struck Saffron as strange. She'd understood what her father got out of the relationship—a strong workhorse who could haul him up a cliff—but she'd never quite figured what Rudella received in return, until now. Access to information. Rudella had eagerly learned everything about Terefellian lore to defy Saffron's father, not help him.

When Saffron had first left Terefellia and spied on her old home from the distant watch tower, she'd occasionally spotted Rudella going about her business. Rudella's absence since the Terefellian queen's arrival had not struck Saffron as curious until this moment. All this time, she'd assumed her father had duped a random Terefellian into wearing the ring in order to transform them into the Maddowshin. But if Cecilia needed the ring and Rudella was helping the Goddess of Light . . .

"Oh my gosh," she uttered. *The Maddowshin has to be Rudella!*

Beyond the black sea of Wirador Wosrah, which stretched outside and beyond the crumpled gates, loomed Eifa. At her feet stood the Maddowshin. Even if Saffron could corral a group of fighters willing to form a protective bubble around Cecilia, they could never fight off the warriors as they attempted to make their way to Rudella. She needed another plan.

The beasts seemed to understand that a direct hit in the eyes from a portable ray gun could kill them, because rather than face Siersha's light dome, they stood perpendicular to it.

"Hey you," Saffron said to one of them. "Look at me."

The snarling beast complied.

Staring directly into its eyes, she spoke, intending Eifa to hear. "Why are we bothering with this battle? The fight you have is with the Treoir Solas. So let's stop this posturing and end this now."

Her skin prickled as the sea of Wirador Wosrah parted, creating a direct path to Eifa. She motioned to the Maddowshin. "I have reason to believe Rudella inhabits that beast," she said to Cecilia. "On its finger is the Ring of Terefellia."

"What if that creature isn't who you think it is?" Cecilia asked.

"Then I will be there to help."

"No. Coming with me means certain death. Just tell me what I need to do. Tell me how I get into Eifa."

"My death is inconsequential to your success," Saffron said. "I can't let you go out there alone."

"Neither can we," said Rabbie. With him stood Eideard, Lyrik, Zack, Jensen, Forbillian, and a dozen other fighters, armed and ready to perform the death march with Saffron and Cecilia.

Since Amalardh's stance was a given—where Cecilia went, he went, too—he remained silent. Removing his gun and ammunition belt, he handed them to Rabbie. Since Rabbie's ray gun was beyond repair, Amalardh would use the spear that he'd earlier fashioned. His selflessness in giving up his superior weapon for the sake of her brother seemed to throw Cecilia. As they stood staring at each other, the tension between them hung thick. This was the intense relationship Rabbie held his and Saffron's up to? No wonder he'd run scared.

Breaking from her rigid stance, Cecilia threw her arms around Amalardh. Their tight embrace oozed regret. Everyone knew what this moment represented: goodbye. As the Caladium, Cecilia was heading into a darkness where no mortal soul could escape.

*

Exiting Siersha's protective light, Saffron, Cecilia, and their armed guards walked with caution along the Wirador Wosrah path to the awaiting Maddowshin. At any moment, the beasts could converge on Saffron's meager group and kill them all. But Eifa was more cat than ravenous dog. Given the choice between a quick kill or prolonged torture, the Dark Goddess gleaned greater pleasure from toying with her prey. The fear pulsing from Saffron and her group's collective hearts as they edged ever closer to darkness would be as tantalizing to Eifa as the smell of fresh fish was to a famished feline.

Saffron's neck craned as she neared the Dark Goddess's towering form. Although Cecilia seemed miniscule in size compared to Eifa's mass, she was, after all, the Caladium. The Poison Flower. If a drop of venom from the ground-dwelling spiders found near Terefellia could kill a man a thousand times its size, then if delivered correctly, the speck of light within Cecilia could reasonably destroy Eifa. The caveat being "delivered correctly." Without the Terefellian ring, Cecilia would fail.

With its chin held high, the Maddowshin stood with regal poise at Eifa's feet. Saffron's breath quavered as she stepped up to the grand beast. "Rudella? Is that you?"

The Maddowshin's right arm shot forward and grabbed Saffron's throat. "Rudella isn't here anymore," it said.

Saffron's pulse raced. The beast's gray eyes weren't Rudella's.

"Fool child," said the Maddowshin. "You should've returned to the fold when our gracious queen offered her welcoming hand. Now your father will watch you die."

Bedlam rang out as Wirador Wosrah lunged at Saffron's group.

As Cecilia spun and fired at an approaching warrior, the handle of the sword strapped to her back came within Saffron's reach. She grabbed it. "Or maybe, he'll watch this," she said.

The Maddowshin's confused gaze trailed to its left hand as Saffron's blade sliced through its wrist. The resulting black glob dropped to the ground along with the Terefellian ring. Without the ring's power, the Maddowshin shrank to the size of a Wirador Wosrah, its right hand losing grip on Saffron's throat in the process.

Pulling her knife, Saffron stabbed its left eye while a bullet from Rabbie's gun destroyed the other.

Out from the pool of black liquid rolled the Maddowshin's severed hand.

"Cecilia! Watch out!" Saffron yelled.

As Cecilia kicked the blob into a nearby warrior, Lyrik liquified the beast with her laser gun.

Where the Maddowshin had once stood sat the Terefellian ring. Snatching it up, Saffron turned to Cecilia. Her blood drained at the sight of a Wirador Wosrah holding Cecilia over its head. The beast was about to throw the Caladium into Eifa's mass. Without the Terefellian ring, Eifa could consume Cecilia and her light. Birthed as a Wirador Wosrah, the famed Caladium would become an eternal servant to the Dark Goddess.

As the only fighter with a direct line of sight to the beast's eyes, Saffron aimed her shotgun.

Her finger quavered. Fighting directly behind the creature were Amalardh and Rabbie. Pellets from her shotgun could kill them.

"Amalardh! Rabbie!" she called. "Get out of the way."

Amalardh spun. His stoic eyes didn't flinch as he looked down the barrel of her gun.

Why wasn't he moving?

Saffron startled as the spikes from Amalardh's spear shot out from the warrior's eyes. The skillful Croilar Tier, with his impeccable aim, had rammed his weapon into the back of the beast's skull, skewering its eyeballs from behind.

As the warrior dropped, so did Cecilia.

Threading the Terefellian ring onto Cecilia's finger, Saffron then hauled her to her feet.

"What do I do now?" Cecilia asked.

"You jump inside her," Saffron said, motioning to Eifa.

Cecilia's complexion turned white. Possessing the power to kill Eifa didn't automatically provide the strength to deliberately leap into the Dark Goddess's black abyss.

Saffron had promised she'd be there for Cecilia, no matter what. "I believe in you," she said. "Please forgive me." Planting her boot in the small of Cecilia's back, she shoved the Caladium into Eifa's writhing mass.

Turning, she came face-to-face with Amalardh's desperate stare. Although he knew Cecilia had to enter Eifa's oblivion, watching the abrupt way Saffron had made it happen would've torn like shards of broken glass through his heart. Would he ever forgive her? "I'm so sorry," she said.

Although Rabbie looked equally horrified, the clutching of his hand to hers suggested his terror was for her immediate safety. "We've done all we can," he said. "We must go."

The grieving of Cecilia's loss would have to wait. Right now, they had to get back to the safety of Siersha's light.

As the sloshing sound filling Cecilia's ears rang out, her world went black and silent. The air felt thick and smelled of rot. A tiny glow emanating from her belly revealed she floated in a cavernous space made of a smooth, black substance. Saffron had described the process of Eifa building the Wirador Wosrah army as "giving birth." The idea of being inside the Dark Goddess's womb sent a shudder down Cecilia's spine.

Black buds sprouted from the walls and grew into long tendrils that writhed toward her.

One darted at her face.

THWACK! It hit Cecilia's light and bounced back. The vibration of its attempt to penetrate her bubble rumbled across her skin.

Angered by the shield, the worm's end split open, exposing long, spiked teeth. The serpent hissed.

THWACK! THWACK! THWACK! More snakes smashed into Cecilia's light.

A serpent slithered to the Terefellian ring on Cecilia's finger and hissed. Not only did Cecilia's light seem to anger them, so did the golden jewel.

Unlike Analise and Noah, whose souls were immediately stripped and packaged with Eifa's substrate into a Wirador Wosrah, those who wore the Ring of Terefellia transformed into the Maddowshin through a different process. With the ring's power preventing the soul's separation from the human form, the ring wearer did not immediately die. Instead, as the hundreds of serpents in Eifa's womb bit into the wearer's flesh, the Maddowshin would slowly transform from the outside in, effectively cocooning the human soul within its core. Rudella had undergone this process, and so would've Cecilia, if not for Siersha's light preventing the serpents' attack. As though accepting of the roadblock, the black snakes settled and began writhing hypnotically around her.

"Did your false goddess tell you who I was?" said Eifa from a snake's mouth.

"You are the dark part of all our souls," Cecilia replied.

"Then, truly, I am only as bad as you want me to be."

"You are wrong. You are as bad as our weakness allows you to be. You are a virus, a parasite. Once you get inside, you eat us alive."

Eifa laughed. "You are too kind with your compliments."

Wrapping their long, inky bodies around Cecilia's bubble of light, the serpents squeezed.

Like the tightening of a corset, the pressure of Siersha's glow constricting against Cecilia's chest forced her breath to shallow.

"This is a dangerous game we play, my good self and I," Eifa said. "We know each other's moves. I suspected she would have you use my ring. And you call me cruel? Death for a ringless body would've happened by now. But here you are, lingering inside me with no chance of escape. Siersha is forcing my hand in a way that will cause you more pain than you can imagine. Of course, I am happy to oblige."

Cecilia's ribs crushed inward as the serpents' coiled bodies tightened.

"This torment can stop," Eifa said. "Submit to me and peace will be yours."

"Peace? You don't know the meaning of the word."

"Are you sure about that?"

Cecilia's lungs sucked in air as the pressure on her chest suddenly stopped. Her brow furrowed as she looked around. Gone was Eifa's blackness. Birds chirped, the sun shone, and on Cecilia's lap sat Alistair, looking, smelling, feeling as real as ever. Joy poured from her heart. Her little boy, who she'd missed so dearly, was with her. She kissed his chubby fist and the hairs on her arms stood on end. Something about her son didn't feel right. She lifted the right leg of his trousers, expecting to find a brown, butterfly-shaped birthmark on his inner thigh, similar to one Amalardh had, which, according to Forbillian, Amalardh's father had also possessed. Her stomach churned at the flawless skin. This infant was nothing but a copy, a projection of the parts of Alistair that Eifa had seen. With the Dark Goddess's deception exposed, the constricting pain on Cecilia's chest returned. Hissing replaced the chirping birds and the smell of rot once again filled the air.

"Where is my boy?" Cecilia said between gasping breaths. "You leave him alone!"

Uncoiling themselves, the serpents returned to their hypnotic writhing.

"I do not intend to harm him," Eifa said. "This was all Siersha's doing. She placed her light inside him, turning him into a bright beacon, so I could find him. As I said earlier, you think I'm cruel. Your goddess is crueler. She used your son as a pawn. She wanted me to find him. I have no other choice than to play along."

Cecilia's skin chilled. The day she'd climbed the dangerous mountain with Malek and Eideard, Eifa's dark cloud had not been searching for her. She'd been hunting for Alistair. Although Cecilia wanted to believe Eifa was lying about Siersha's plan for the Dark Goddess to find Alistair, too much had happened for Cecilia to conclude otherwise. Had Cecilia been wrong to trust the Goddess of Light? Had everything just become one big celestial game? Was Siersha so focused on "the win" that she didn't care about the cost? Or maybe . . . had Siersha lived too long with Eifa that she no longer knew where her dark self began and ended? Was Siersha's darkness more in control than Siersha realized?

"Your son is quite safe and in the protection of my loyal followers," Eifa said. "You can see for yourself."

In the emptiness in front of Cecilia, Alistair's image appeared. He sat upon a hessian-covered lap, similar in tone to the tunics worn by Terefellians. Her chest ached at the sound of Alistair's soft cooing. "How do I know this is not another one of your fabrications?"

"You tell me."

"Show me the inside of his right thigh."

A pair of thick, hairy hands attached to equally hairy forearms unbundled Alistair and pulled up his right trouser leg.

Cecilia's breath sucked in at the small, butterfly-shaped birthmark.

Smoothing out Alistair's trousers, the hairy hands cradled him safely as the knees upon which Alistair sat began bouncing gently up and down. Tears welled in Cecilia's eyes as Alistair squealed with delight.

"This can be his life," said Eifa. "He can be happy and safe and loved. But that comes with a cost. If you choose to fight me, I will kill your son. If you give in and accept your fate, Alistair will live a long and happy life. The choice is yours."

As despair gripped Cecilia, the light within her diminished. Seizing the opportunity, a serpent sprung forward and broke through Cecilia's protective barrier. Although she winced at the sting of its fangs, its venom felt strangely relaxing.

"Are you willing to let your son die?" Eifa whispered.

Alistair was Cecilia's everything. She couldn't sacrifice his life.

Eifa was right. The Goddess of Light was cruel.

The waning of Cecilia's faith further dimmed her light. More serpents broke through, impaling their sharp fangs into her flesh.

"I'm not as bad as everyone thinks," Eifa whispered. "If you stay with me, you can stay with your son."

As the venom coursed through Cecilia's blood, her mind grew foggy. Would giving into Eifa really be so bad? At least Cecilia would no longer need to fight. Living under the Goddess of Light was draining. Being on the side of good was too hard. Eifa truly was more powerful. If Cecilia couldn't beat her, then the smart thing to do would be to join her.

"All you need do is proclaim your love for me, and your son and the world will be yours."

"I can have it all?" Cecilia asked.

"Yes. You can have it all. Amalardh included."

Cecilia's heart skipped. Alistair and Amalardh. No more choosing between the two of them? No more fighting for Amalardh's love? No more exhaustion of trying to keep her splintered family together? For all her faults, Eifa at least possessed enough heart to offer Cecilia everything.

"The Prophecy you follow, this supposed path to freedom, is a lie," Eifa said. "Surely by now you've figured that out."

Tears rolled down Cecilia's cheeks. Once again, although she wanted to, she couldn't deny the truth of Eifa's words. With everything that still needed to happen, how could the final image of the Prophecy—Cecilia sitting under the Freedom Tree reading to a group of children—possibly come about? If Cecilia fought Eifa, the Terefellians would kill Alistair. And if by some miracle Alistair and Cecilia didn't die, then according to the signs in the Prophecy, Cecilia would still lose Amalardh six months from now. Where Eifa's offer was simplistic and straightforward, holes and uncertainty riddled Siersha's path to peace.

Like the dwindling of a candle's flame, Cecilia's inner glow fluttered. Siersha should have never placed Cecilia in this position. Her choice to do so had been wrong. And if the Goddess of Light was wrong, then by default, her Dark Shadow was right. Focusing in on the image of Alistair's radiant face as he continued to bounce up and down on the man's knee, Cecilia readied herself to seal her fate and proclaim her love for Eifa.

A flickering light from her wrist drew her attention. The silver bracelet Ida had given her reflected Cecilia's dying glow. As she ran her thumb across the embossed flower, Ida's words rang in her head. "Sometimes we are forced on journeys we don't understand and told to do things we don't want to do, and while trapped in these dark moments, we struggle to remember exactly who we are and what we are fighting for."

In that moment, Cecilia knew who she was—the Caladium. And she was fighting for the lives of thousands, not just her son's.

Beyond Eifa's dark walls came the muffled sounds of gunfire. Why were Cecilia's people still fighting when they could huddle safely under Siersha's protective light?

How could Cecilia give up on her people when they refused to give up on her?

She shook her foggy head. Siersha wasn't the one playing tricks. Eifa was. The Dark Goddess's venom had induced confusion, heightened Cecilia's trust in Eifa's empty promises.

Empowered by her people's love, Cecilia's inner glow pulsed back to life.

A serpent bit her. *Ouch!* Cecilia grabbed the spot. Blood dripped from the bite mark.

Angry red welts from the previous bites appeared.

"I see through your lies. And reject your poison," Cecilia said.

Spitting and hissing, the serpents reeled back from her bright glow.

"You dare to turn against me?" Eifa said.

"I dare very much."

"Then you have sealed your son's fate."

The serpents writhed wildly as the knee upon which Alistair sat stopped bouncing. Setting him on the dusty ground, the hairy hands held the blade of a shiny knife to Alistair's rosy cheeks.

"No mother who loves her child would let him die," Eifa said.

Siersha's discussion with Cecilia about the maimed beetle flooded back. Cecilia's choice had been to either save the beetle from the approaching ants only to let it slowly die because of its broken wing, or end its suffering, giving the hungry ants food for their survival. Right now, Alistair was the beetle. Cecilia could save his life, but to what end? Living under Eifa's rule? His soul trapped on earth for eternity? If she let him die, thousands of innocent lives would be spared, and Alistair would at least be at peace, his spirit enjoying its happy self in the Pass-Over World.

"When faced with a choice that could ease your soul, you chose to do what was hardest: the right thing. This is why you are my Caladium," Siersha had said. "Only the ultimate sacrifice can kill Eifa."

The ultimate sacrifice was Alistair's life, not Cecilia's. "You can take my son," she said, "but you will never have him."

"You have no right to call yourself a mother," hissed Eifa.

The thick fingers lifted the shiny blade up over Alistair.

"This is your last chance to submit to me," said Eifa.

"I would kill him with my own hands if that meant saving him from you," Cecilia yelled.

Screaming with rage, the serpents shot forward.

As the knife plunged down, Cecilia closed her eyes and thrust her arms in the air. "I love you, Alistair. May Siersha's light be with you always!"

Intense love for her son poured from her heart.

Pained squeals assaulted her ears.

Smoky rot suffocated her nostrils.

Shock waves pummeled her body.

Everything went black.

CHAPTER

30

AMALARDH WATCHED AS Rabbie pulled Saffron into the gunners' safety bubble. Under the protection of the ray guns, they would make it back to Siersha's light. The two young lovers deserved their life and their happiness. But not Amalardh. He'd had his chance with Cecilia and had thrown it away. He had abandoned her once and would never do so again. He would stay where he was meant to be—by her side. And if that meant his death, so be it. Spinning from Saffron and Rabbie, he rammed his forked spear into a warrior's beady eyes. Eifa had ruined Amalardh's life. He would destroy as many of her beasts as he could before the Dark Goddess took him.

A slight miscalculation pierced only one eye of a galloping beast. The squealing warrior pummeled into Amalardh, sending him to the ground. It sprang on top of him and was about to smash its balled fist into Amalardh's face when Forbillian barreled into it. Readying his spear, he jammed a spike into the beast's remaining eye.

"You shouldn't be here," said Amalardh.

"What? And let you take all the glory?" Forbillian had made himself a dual-headed weapon, too, and proved just as competent, if not better, with its use. "If you think I'm going to stand back and watch my only nephew die at the feet of the Dark Goddess, you're a bigger fool than I."

A beast lunged at Forbillian.

"Hey, ugly! Over here," came Eideard's voice.

The beast turned and its eyes met with the skewers of Eideard's spear.

"This thing works like a charm," he said, hefting his own dual-headed weapon.

More beasts collapsed at the hands of Rabbie, Saffron, Danmar, Helderic, and a host of other fighters.

"If Cecilia continues to fight, then so must we," Saffron said.

Seeing all these people risking their lives to fight by his side tore at Amalardh's tough edge. All his life, he'd remained solitary because he'd never known how to ask for help. Mostly, he'd never needed to. More than ever, he needed these people. Not for the sake of his own life, but for Cecilia's. She was willing to give her life for them. Knowing they were willing to do the same filled him with the strength and tenacity to keep fighting until he dropped.

From inside Eifa, an ear-piercing squeal rang out.

Her wide eyes glowed bright as light from her open mouth shot out.

Her midsection split. More light beams burst forth.

From the gash, serpent heads emerged, flopping side to side, hissing wildly.

The Wirador Wosrah's eyes blanched.

Hands pressed to ears as Eifa let out a piercing scream.

Her towering column of slime collapsed and splashed down like a massive fountain losing power.

As the surrounding Wirador Wosrah horde liquified, Amalardh stood motionless. Throughout his life, he'd experienced many forms of torture: whippings with barbed spikes, beatings from Soldiers of Vitus, the burn of alcohol poured onto open wounds. With all that he'd experienced, nothing compared to the agony he felt at that moment.

His spear dropped from his grasp as he fell to his knees.

Cecilia was nowhere to be seen.

SAFFRON GAPED AT the gigantic black lake that had been Eifa. The Dark Queen's annihilation was not the joyous moment she had imagined. How could anyone celebrate Cecilia's great sacrifice? Heads lowered as heartache rippled through the crowd. Many shed tears. Rabbie seemed locked in disbelief. Would he forgive Saffron for throwing Cecilia to her doom? And Amalardh—she couldn't bear seeing such a powerful, fearless man broken to his knees. Cecilia's terrified expression as Saffron shoved her into Eifa's black abyss would haunt her until her dying days.

The black liquid dissipated, uncovering Cecilia's crumpled body. Hopeful whispers ricocheted through the crowd. Might Cecilia still be alive?

Amalardh bolted to her. Rabbie and Eideard followed.

"She's alive!" Rabbie called.

Saffron exhaled her relief.

"Help! Someone!" called Margot. "Something's wrong with the Goddess."

Saffron spun to the city and a chill rippled through her. The towering version of Siersha that had stretched above the wall's height was no longer in sight.

Speeding through the smashed gates, Saffron dashed down the main street. Where Siersha had once stood lay the life-sized Goddess, her skin crystalizing. Saffron dropped to her side. Huffing and puffing, Forbillian kneeled next to her.

"What's happening to you?" Saffron asked the Goddess.

"In the Gods' realm, the Rule of Equity governs all," Siersha said. "Now that Eifa is gone, there is no more wrong for me to right." Her jaw creaked as her flesh hardened.

"What do we do?"

"You must get me back to my rea—" Her mouth seized.

Saffron spun to Forbillian. "How do we get her back to the Gods' realm?"

"I venture to say, the same way she got here. The Forbidden Pool. According to the Goddess, it acts like a portal connecting the two realms."

"How do we get there?"

"The safest way is back through Bayton, where we can take the valley path through the Korfkahn Mountains. We end up going a little further south than our intended destination but the time saved sailing directly east from here would be lost hiking up and over the range."

"You can lead the way? You can get us there?"

"Aye. I'll get you to the Forbidden Pool. You just focus on keeping the Goddess safe."

His calm confidence soothed Saffron's worry. "Please don't die," she whispered to the Goddess. "We'll get you home. You just need to hold on."

Springing to action, Forbillian set about organizing the life-saving trip. Thankfully, high tide had helped free *Bayton II* from its beaching, allowing the captain to moor the vessel at the appropriately sized northern jetty.

Rabbie and Eideard insisted on coming. With their sister's life linked with Siersha's, any effort on their part to save the Goddess would offer more help to Cecilia than sitting by her side.

With the Goddess's joints too stiff to move, Saffron, Rabbie, Eideard, and Forbillian carried her onto *Bayton II* and the grand ship set sail. Day and night, Saffron sat by Siersha's side as the Goddess creaked and cracked and steadily shrank. By the time they entered the Bay of Bayton, Siersha's arms had fused to her body. Her two legs had become one.

An elegant, dark-skinned woman, who Eideard introduced as the Countess of Bayton, greeted the arriving ship. Confusion stole over her as she glanced at the three-foot-high crystalline statue carried by Forbillian and Rabbie. "Where is the Goddess?" she asked.

"You're looking at her," Forbillian said.

Her expression glazed as he brought her up to speed.

"Countess," he said, snapping his fingers. "Did you hear me? We need to get the Goddess back to the Forbidden Pool. We need your help."

A poised young woman with high cheekbones and arched eyebrows stepped forward and introduced herself as Nina, the Countess's daughter. "Come," she said, "you will have our fastest horses." She led the group around the city's main building to a row of stables. The unique smell reminded Saffron of goat droppings.

Brightly dressed helpers made short time of saddling up a group of steeds and loading them with food, water, and sleeping blankets.

The door of a changing hut opened and out stepped Nina dressed in figure-hugging trousers, knee-high boots, and a white blouse tucked into her trim waist. Compared to Saffron's oversized pants and thick, heavy footwear, Nina looked mighty stylish. From the look on Eideard's face, he seemed to think so, too.

Because of Saffron's standing as an incapable rider, she rode with Rabbie. The joy of wrapping her arms around his muscular body quickly wore thin. Within twenty minutes of their steady trot, her rump ached more than riding five hours on the motor bike.

Other than the heart-wrenching creak of Siersha's crystals as she slowly shrank, silence shrouded the journey. How could anyone feel chatty under such circumstances? Even wrapped in a blanket and secured to her own horse, the sounds of the Goddess's gradual death battered the group's ears. The worst moments were at night. On *Bayton II*, the wind, cranking engine, and the slapping of sea spray against the boat's hull had helped drown the Goddess's nighttime noise. East of the Korfkahn Mountains, the lack of bubbling streams, chirping birds, and still air heightened Siersha's desperate cries.

The sky darkened as the glowing red sun sank behind the silhouetted mountains. Ahead lay a lava field. With the jagged rocks too dangerous for horse hooves, the group would have to traverse the final leg of their journey on foot.

"All right, folks," Forbillian said, "we have a decision to make." He pointed to a shadowed outline of a crater about two miles northeast. "The Forbidden Pool is below that dormant volcano." Several hundred yards ahead, a darkened rock formation with three stone columns on its top rose up from the otherwise flat land. "The entrance to the tunnel that gets us to our destiny is within those rocks. Do we risk hiking across this lava field in the dark or wait until morning?"

Negotiating the lava field's jagged rock in the moonless night would be near impossible. One slip and the Goddess could smash into a million pieces. "I think the best option is to wait until daybreak," Saffron said.

Everyone agreed.

Lying on her blanket, Saffron cuddled the football-sized Goddess to her chest. The vibrating of the reshaping crystals offered comfort. So long as they moved, the Goddess remained alive. "You need to hold on just a little longer," Saffron whispered. "In a few more hours, you'll be home."

Saffron woke with a start. The bundle she'd been cuddling had shrunk to the size of an ostrich egg. Was the Goddess still alive? She seemed awfully quiet. Closing her eyes, she placed the weighty object to her ear and listened. *Creak. Crack.* The Goddess was still holding on. She studied the egg and sure enough, tiny, almost imperceptible crystals realigned inside.

As Saffron marvelled at the sight, the ground suddenly shook, knocking Siersha from her grip.

Quick with his reflexes, Rabbie caught the precious globe before it smashed on the stony ground.

The wind picked up. Dark storm clouds cloaked the rising sun's golden rays.

The earth shook again. Whinnying loudly, the horses reared onto their hind legs and bolted. Rabbie and Eideard shared a worried look.

"This is it," Rabbie said.

"This is what?" said Saffron.

"The end of the world," he replied. He explained that during Cecilia and Amalardh's first journey to Vitus, Cecilia had almost drowned after falling over a waterfall. While unconscious, she saw what would happen if the Goddess of Light died: complete and utter destruction of the world, beyond that of the Great War. "If Siersha dies, so will all life. We have to get to the pool. And fast!"

Although Saffron regretted wasting time by resting for the night, in the light of day, the lava field's jagged surface confirmed how dangerous it would've been to negotiate in the dark. "You're not going to die," she said to the Goddess. "I'm not going to let you." Tightening her trouser belt to secure her tucked-in top, she slipped her precious cargo inside her shirt.

The earth rumbled. Drops of hard rain poured from the sky.

For the sake of pace, Forbillian and the Bayton riders stayed behind, while Eideard, Rabbie, Saffron, and Nina raced across the lava field.

Between the sleet and the shaky ground, staying surefooted on the rugged surface proved difficult. Saffron slipped and grazed her forearm. Her hand slapped to her belly. The hard lump confirmed the Goddess remained intact. Breathing a sigh of relief, she pushed herself to her feet. Because no one had seen her stumble, the others had continued on and were now a good fifty feet ahead.

An enormous cracking sound rumbled from within the ground. Like the tearing open of an old cloth, the lava field split open, separating Saffron from the others. With the fifteen-foot-wide crack running hundreds of yards to her left and right, there was no going around this barrier. This couldn't be happening. The rock cluster destination was on the other side of the chasm, and so were Rabbie, Eideard, and Nina.

Without thinking about the craziness of what she was about to do, Saffron sped to the crevasse's edge and leaped. Her skin seared as she flew through a wall of intense heat. By less than an inch, her fingers missed the far edge. Because the newly formed wall's rough surface provided plentiful hand and footholds, after slipping about ten feet, she steadied herself against the cliff face.

Her chest stiffened as she looked down. Like the fast rising of a tide came a flow of bubbling lava. Steam created from the rain sizzling against the red glow scorched her skin. If she didn't get moving—and fast—she'd cook faster than a barbequed bug. Stealing her nerves, she scrambled to the top, where Rabbie and Eideard hauled her to her feet. "We've got to keep moving," she said.

As they sped toward the rocky mound, lava flowed from the crevasse like water breaching the banks of a river.

Pockets of steam burst from random places.

The entire flatlands looked ready to implode.

The unforgiving lava field ended, giving way to sporadic pockets of green bushes and compact soil. While the smooth surface made for an easier run, the slightly downward slope added to the lava's flowing speed.

The closeness of the rock formation with the three columns gave Saffron the boost she needed to fight the exhaustion tearing at her lungs. Death by burning alive in fire had been the Terefellian way. After everything she'd been through to escape such a hideous end, she couldn't allow herself or the Goddess to succumb to the molten lava's lust.

Seconds before the sweltering flow scorched their feet, the group climbed the rocky formation to safety. Steam rising from rain pummeling the scorched earth created a threatening sight. The world really was coming to an end.

Saffron pressed her hand to her lower belly and gasped. Siersha! Had the Goddess fallen out? Frantic, she patted the area down and hit upon a small, hard object. Reaching down her shirt, she pulled out a delicate crystal the size of a hen egg.

Please be alive. She pressed the cold crystal to her ear. Between the wind, rain, and steam sizzling from the lava field, she could barely hear herself think.

Creak. Crack. Saffron exhaled. Siersha continued to hold on.

"Come on," said Eideard. "This way."

He led the way to a narrow hollow where they climbed down several feet into a tunnel. "This runs directly under that field above to the Forbidden Pool," he said. "The last time we came here, there wasn't a lava lake sitting above. Let's hope none of that stuff seeps through."

Light filtering from the entrance provided scant illumination. The path ahead remained pitch black.

Rabbie wiped the rain water from his face. "I don't suppose anyone thought to bring a lantern."

In their haste, no one had.

Nina's head tilted at Saffron's clasped hand. "I'm not sure we need one," she said.

A soft light radiated between Saffron's closed fingers. Holding her palm in front, she spread open her hand. Light from the crystal brightened the dark space.

Hope filled Saffron as the group set off down the dark hollow. "We're nearly there," she whispered to the Goddess.

Several feet into the tunnel, a loud crash from behind made the group turn. A portion of ceiling had collapsed. Molten lava from the lake poured in. Elsewhere, dollops of liquid rock dripped from above. The area looked ready to cave in.

"Run!" Eideard yelled.

The group sped forward.

From Saffron's understanding, the only way in and out of the Forbidden Pool's chamber was this tube. With flowing lava corking the imploded section, the group would never exit this underground. The best Saffron could hope for was to ensure everyone's soul made it into the Pass-Over World. The only way to do that was to get the Goddess back to her realm.

Her muscles burned. Her chest heaved as she sucked in the thick, stagnant air.

The long, dark tunnel felt endless.

Like a flower wilting under a hot summer's day, Siersha's crystal steadily shrank to the size of a stone. The diminished light made dodging droplets of lava and crumbling ceiling even more challenging.

Saffron tripped. The Goddess's bright stone bounced out of her hand.

Siersha! No!

Glowing like a tiny bud on the ground sat the Goddess. Molten rock from the ceiling dropped in searing clumps around the fragile light. As Nina reached for the tiny crystal, a chunk of lava the size of a plum scorched the back of her lower leg. She screamed in agony.

Magma pouring from the earlier cave-in continued to make chase.

Nina could barely walk, let alone run. She handed the small crystal to Saffron. "Go," she said.

"I'm not leaving you," Saffron replied.

"Yes, you are," said Rabbie. "We've got this." He and Eideard flung Nina's arms around their necks. "Get the Goddess to the pool. Don't worry about us."

Saffron stood a frozen moment, staring at the encroaching lava. Would they be able to outrun it?

"Go. Now!" ordered Rabbie.

His terse tone was enough to get her legs running.

The tube led her to a magnificent white chamber. In the center, the shaking ground sent water sloshing from a circular hollow. The Forbidden Pool.

Siersha's light pulsed as if knowing home was near.

Saffron spun at a loud crashing sound. A section of the tunnel's ceiling had collapsed.

"Rabbie!" she screamed. He, Eideard, and Nina were trapped on the other side with the flowing lava. While every ounce of her wanted to dig her friends out, she couldn't waste any more time. Siersha had shrunk to the size of a pea. "Look after our souls," she said to the Goddess. "When our time comes, may we see you once again in the Pass-Over World." Tears poured down her cheeks as she tossed the tiny crystal into the sloshing water.

Siersha's light dropped.

As it neared the bottom, beams shot from the silver wolves perched on the handles of the eight knives and converged with the crystal.

A luminous ray shot up, leaving a hole the same diameter as the pool in the chamber's ceiling. In the sky above, departing storm clouds exposed a welcoming blue sky.

Saffron's breath escaped. Siersha had left an opening, a way to escape.

She darted to the rubble wall. "Rabbie! Can you hear me?"

A rock tumbled from the top.

"We're okay," Rabbie said.

Climbing the barrier, Saffron heaved the rubble away.

Rabbie's dusty face appeared.

"I was so worried," Saffron said.

"You and me both. The lava was coming for us, then light flickered through this debris and the flow instantly stopped. If you'd waited a second longer, we'd be toast. Literally."

After several minutes of digging, Rabbie, Eideard, and Nina climbed over the blockage and into the bright chamber.

Although Nina remained composed, her compressed lips suggested she bit back an extreme amount of pain.

Eideard studied the hole in the ceiling. "That wasn't here the last time I came. Thank you, Siersha, for giving us a way out." His attention dropped to the ground. "What happened to the pool?"

Saffron blinked at the chamber's pristine floor. In the commotion, she hadn't noticed the pool's disappearance.

The group shared a concerned look. After all their efforts, had Eifa somehow still won? Without a portal connecting the two realms, how would Siersha ferry souls to the Pass-Over World?

Cecilia's throat closed as she took in a vast, empty nothingness that stretched for miles. Where was she? The last thing she remembered was releasing Siersha's light to destroy Eifa. Was she still near Vitus? She couldn't be. Where were her city and her people? Where was the ocean? The headlands? The distant mountains? Was this day or night? The gray sky, which blended with the ashen ground, lacked any shadow or contrast. The thin, dry air felt devoid of oxygen. If everything in this place seemed dead, could she be dead, too?

Agonized cries and desperate moans folded in and around her. Something flew by. What was that? Another whoosh came, and another. Cecilia spun frantically, attempting to spot whatever taunted her.

"Show yourselves!" she yelled.

The moans and cries grew louder, the whooshing more frenetic. There had to be thousands of these things jetting around. She pressed her hands to her ears, but no amount of pressure seemed capable of drowning the tortured cacophony.

"Leave me alone!" she yelled.

She startled as an entity flew to her. Stopping inches from her face, a faded young woman with flowing hair hovered, as though floating in water. Her ghostly complexion and threadbare clothing matched stories Cecilia had heard of the spirit world. This person was dead. As were the thousands of others darting around her.

"Save us," the spirit whispered.

Her face contorted as it let out an ear-piercing shriek and flew off.

"They are trapped," came a voice from behind.

Cecilia turned.

Completely devoid of her glow, the Goddess looked as gray and transparent as the swarming spirits.

"Where are we?" Cecilia asked.

"Eifa's perverse afterlife. A dark desolation within the human realm."

"Are we dead?"

"Almost."

Cecilia's blood chilled as she studied the faded texture of her own hands. "Why aren't we in your Pass-Over World?"

"I am not there to ferry you. I'm trapped here. On earth. If I die, this is where we stay. Forever, in this agony. If that happens, even though she is gone, Eifa still wins."

Another spirit flew down to the Goddess and hissed wildly. It calmed as she stroked its cheek. Then, like an unpredictable cat, its expression turned demonic. Letting out a shrill cry, it sped off.

"They want to show love, but they've forgotten how," Siersha said.

The tortured mass flying above included thousands of harvested Terefellians who Eifa had birthed into warriors, hundreds of fighters from Cecilia's army who had died during the bloody battle, and any other soul who had passed on since Siersha's arrival on earth.

"You have to save these souls," Cecilia said. "We cannot leave them here."

"I cannot do anything until I'm back in my realm. By rights, both of us should already be dead. But just as Saffron's love and determination to get me back to the Forbidden Pool is keeping my light alive, someone else's love, who you've doubted for many months, is giving you the will not to pass over."

Cecilia cuddled her arms to her chest. Amalardh.

Why had her journey with him been so painful? Back when

she'd had the chance to love him, comfort him, she hadn't. The thought of their spirits spending an eternity in this place, never knowing love again, tore at her.

Swooning, the Goddess collapsed to the ground.

Cecilia dropped to her side and took hold of her ever-fading hand. "I know Saffron. If she has her mind set on something, she'll finish it. Just keep letting her know you're with her."

Siersha squeezed Cecilia's hand and a creaking sound vibrated into Cecilia's palm. "Do you think she will understand that?" Siersha asked.

Swallowing back her tears, Cecilia nodded. "Yes. That's perfect. Just keep making that noise. Saffron will know you're still with her."

For what seemed like hours, but could've been days—time was nebulous in this place—Cecilia stayed strong for Siersha, holding her hand.

The Goddess's breath rasped as she struggled to breathe.

"Stay with me," Cecilia said.

"I am so tired," Siersha replied.

"You can't give up. You must let Saffron know you're still holding on."

Siersha's fingers quavered. Although the movement was small, a vibration fluttered against Cecilia's skin. If Saffron concentrated hard enough, she would hopefully hear the tiny creak.

Like crazed crows in a flock, the desperate spirits swirled above.

Suddenly, they silenced. Gray faces with flat expressions stared down at Cecilia and Siersha.

Had the Goddess died?

A warm glow pulsed in Siersha's belly and radiated out. Like a paintbrush, the light rays brought color to everything they touched. The ground sprang to life with vivid green. The sky turned a radiant blue. Siersha's transparent body brightened, and the color returned to Cecilia's skin.

Cheerful chatter filled the air as thousands of people filed by and into Siersha's Pass-Over World. From their bright smiles and relaxed dispositions, memories of their time spent as a tortured soul trapped in Eifa's dark eternity seemed erased. Breaking away from the congregation, a tall, broad woman wearing a Terefellian tunic walked over.

"This is Rudella," Siersha said. "Ida's daughter."

Cecilia pressed her hands to her chest. This amazing woman had sacrificed everything for the Goddess's success.

"I'm sorry I wasn't there to help you at the end," Rudella said. "I tried to keep my emotions in check, but when Eifa's army made its final push to Vitus, my walls crumbled and my tears fell. I had intended to be at the battlefront to ensure you did not enter Eifa without the Ring of Terefellia, but you managed without me. You truly are special."

"The only special person standing here is you." Cecilia flung her arms around her. "Your mother will be very proud. I will tell her of your selfless bravery."

When they broke from their hug, Rudella wiped her wet eyes. "There is a man from Terefellia who you will meet. Go easy on him. His living soul is far more tortured than those you just saw. He is the reason a particular soul is not among us." Offering a warm goodbye, she walked off.

The last of the happy travelers disappeared into the Pass-Over World.

"Where is Alistair?" Cecilia asked.

"It is not his time," Siersha replied.

"But I saw the knife."

"Did you see it spear your son?"

Well, no. Cecilia had closed her eyes. She couldn't bear to witness it. "Am I staying here, in the Pass-Over World?" she asked.

"Do you want to stay?"

"In this place, I don't feel any heartache."

The Goddess's head lowered. "Your pain was all my doing. Everything Eifa said was true. My dark self knew all my moves. While neither of us knew which decision you would make, her failure was assuming your choice was the only one at play. But another soul also had a choice. Eifa arrogantly believed her followers possessed love only for her. Love comes in many shapes and sizes. It makes us do things we never thought we'd do, like a Terefellian saving the life of his enemy's child, in direct contradiction to his queen."

Out of nowhere, a slew of daisies popped up. Snapping one off, Siersha spun it. In the still air, it should've dropped. Instead, it floated up and away.

"By setting all the pieces in such a way that led you to choose between your people and your son, I put you in a horrendous place. I needed Eifa to believe she maintained control. In the human realm, she is ten times stronger than me. With the flick of her wrist, she could've wiped out humanity in an instant. But what pleasure is there for evil if there is no prolonged suffering? By letting her have Alistair, she thought she also had you. Eifa does not understand love. She only knows it by what she sees in others. She had come to the conclusion—a generally correct conclusion—that no stronger love exists than a parent's love for a child. She believed you would give your life for Alistair. I knew, as painful as it might be, you would make the sacrifice for the good of humankind because you trusted I would take care of Alistair until your souls could once again reunite. I knew Eifa's threat to kill your son had a flaw. Because of an alternative move Rudella had helped me set up, I trusted that Brother Wyndom, the man Eifa ordered to kill your son, would not be able to."

The Goddess handed Cecilia a daisy. "I am sorry I made you and your loved ones pawns on my chess board. I derived no pleasure from this game. In the two centuries it took for me to regain my strength after the Great War, I used the time to devise a way to make things right. Of all the scenarios I played out in my mind, the only one that showed promise of success was this one. I hope you trust me when I tell you, if I could've done it another way, spared you, Amalardh, everyone from all your pain, I would've."

She placed her warm hand on Cecilia's cheek. "Now that the

battle is over, I hope you and Amalardh can overcome your wounds."

The world flashed white.

Cecilia woke.

Amalardh's soulful blue eyes stared down at her. He had one hand on her cheek and the other she squeezed.

CHAPTER

33

AFTER CARRYING CECILIA'S unconscious body to their bed-room, Amalardh cleaned and wrapped an alarming number of bites on her arms and legs. He pressed her knuckles to his lips. *Come back to me. Please. You cannot leave me,* he said to her in his mind. She squeezed his hand and his tension eased. Wherever she was, she was still with him. He stroked her short, silken hair. "I will be with you day and night," he whispered. "My hand will not separate from yours until you come home."

By his side sat Oisin. "She's going to make it," he said. "Saffron will save the Goddess and when that happens, Cecilia will wake. I know she will."

Although Amalardh tried to take comfort in Oisin's words, because of the wrongs he'd committed, his penance meant never knowing the tranquility of hope.

Over the next three weeks, they slept in shifts, one of them always by Cecilia's side, squeezing her hand, letting her know she wasn't alone.

Waking up from a restless sleep, Amalardh rolled the stiffness from his shoulders. Saffron and the others had to be close to the Forbidden Pool. What if they'd already been and gone? What if Siersha was already back in the Gods' realm? What if Oisin's hope had been wrong? What if Cecilia never woke up?

Dark clouds rolled in, bringing with them a violent storm. As sleet turned to ice, Amalardh paid little mind to the outside weather. Although coastal storms at this time of year were uncommon, they weren't entirely unheard of. Only when Oisin rushed in, wide-eyed, talking about waves as tall as houses flooding the coastal streets, did Amalardh connect the signs to the end of the world Cecilia had once spoken of.

The earth shook, sending a bookcase in the living room crashing to the floor. Amalardh leaned over Cecilia to shelter her. The Goddess remained alive, but barely. If Saffron didn't save Siersha, and soon, Amalardh wouldn't need to worry about Cecilia waking up. She, along with the entire world, would be thrust into an eternal sleep.

Amalardh had never prayed a day in his life. He'd never needed to. But now . . . the urge gripped him. *Stay strong, Siersha,* he said to the Goddess in his mind. *I've finally woken up from my years of tortured sleep, finally know who I am. You have to survive, not for my sake, but for Cecilia, Alistair, and Oisin's. They're my family, and I've put them through hell. In the few months I have left—before this death that I know is coming takes me to your realm—give me the opportunity to show them the love I've denied them. They deserve to know that they are the most special people in the world to me.*

A bright light lit up the sky.

The winds stilled. The clouds broke.

Gasping, Cecilia squeezed Amalardh's hand.

His chest heaved. Was this the moment of her death?

Her eyes opened and relief tore through him.

"I knew you wouldn't leave us," said Oisin. His eyes suddenly popped wide. "There's something I have to do."

Amalardh watched as Oisin dashed off. What could be so important at a time like this? His focus dropped to Cecilia.

She smiled weakly at him. "We did it. We stopped Eifa and saved all those souls."

Amalardh kissed her knuckles. "You did it," he replied.

Her body swayed as she eased herself onto the edge of the bed.

"You need to rest," Amalardh said.

"No. I need to get Alistair." Looking deep into his eyes, she softened her defiant plea. "We need to get *our* son."

Because of their deteriorating relationship, Cecilia had stopped using the inclusive "our." On too many occasions, she had referred to Alistair as "my" son. And on just as many occasions, Amalardh had failed to correct her. "Where is he?" he asked.

"Terefellia."

The Terefellians had Alistair? He was supposed to be hiding somewhere safe with Marion and Tomkin. Cecilia was justified in her rush to leave.

Taking hold of her hand, Amalardh helped her to her feet. "Let's go get our son," he said.

Packed and ready to go, Cecilia and Amalardh exited the front door, where Oisin waited with two saddled steeds.

"Where's your horse?" Amalardh asked.

"I need to stay here," Oisin replied. "There's something I need to keep my eye on."

Amalardh studied the kid. What was Oisin up to? Why had he run off earlier? Before he could inquire further, the two hefty vehicles from Rabbit Cove pulled up. From the smaller one stepped Danmar and Jensen. Remaining seated at the wheel of the truck with the canvas-covered back was Kayla, Jensen's daughter.

Danmar grinned and shook his head at Cecilia. "After everything you've been through, you should be resting."

"I cannot rest until I have my son."

"And that is precisely why we are here."

"Our technicians at Rabbit Cove have narrowed down the Terefellian's location," said Jensen. He motioned to the vehicles. "Seeing as time is of the essence, we thought you'd like to get there sooner rather than later."

The relief pouring from Cecilia matched Amalardh's own. With the limited time Amalardh had left in this world, he didn't want to waste a second without his son.

CHAPTER

34

WYNDOM'S STOMACH CHURNED as he paced up and down. He'd done it now. He'd totally and utterly messed up. Why couldn't he have done as he was told? He nibbled his fingernail. Maybe things weren't as bad as they seemed. Stomping his foot, he flung his arms in the air. Who was he kidding? Things were way worse than he'd allowed himself to believe. He'd angered the queen so much that she'd cast him from the fray. That must have been what had happened, because he no longer felt her connection. She'd given him one last chance to prove his loyalty, and he'd failed.

He nodded to himself. Yes. That was what had happened. The queen had not sent word about her win because she didn't feel Wyndom deserved to share the news. Any other explanation for her silence—like that she had lost—couldn't possibly be true. Could it?

The mighty Wirador Wosrah had left close to three weeks ago. How long could a battle take? The clean-up would require a few days, not to mention the journey back. Right now, a horde of Wirador Wosrah was probably on their way to collect the Terefellians and gallop them back to the Promised Land.

The queen had not shared all this with Wyndom because she'd kicked him out of the fray. He exhaled a calming breath. He'd fallen out of her good graces before and had wended his way back in. When she calmed down, she'd forgive him. He just needed to remind her of his importance to the tribe.

Leaping onto his preaching rock, he called his people to

prayer. Sweat poured from his temples as he pranced up and down, praising their queen for her magnificent win. As always, at the conclusion of his sermon, he lifted his arms and yelled, "My Queen, we are forever yours."

"Our Queen, you are forever ours," echoed his people.

He waited for his queen's smoke to shoot through his chest, but no smoke came. Instead, black clouds rolled in. Thunder rumbled as lightning split open the sky.

"My Terefellians, do not fear," Wyndom said. "This is a sign from our glorious queen to let us know the Promised Land is ours."

The ground shook.

The wind howled.

Rocks of ice pelted down.

Worry twirled in Wyndom's belly. His queen certainly had a strange way of demonstrating her victory. "My people!" he yelled. "Our glorious queen is showing the non-believers her might. We will be safe in our temple. Come. Follow me."

As he rushed to the vast structure, its facade split open, sending the outer pillars crumbling to the ground. Wyndom slid to a stop. From deep within, a loud cracking sound rumbled. His precious temple was about to implode.

"Run! Everyone!" he yelled.

As he bolted away, the force of the massive structure's collapse sent him face first into the sloshy ground. His heart thumped. Why was his queen doing this?

In the far east, a bright light shot into the sky.

The rain stopped. The clouds broke.

What just happened?

Pushing himself to his feet, Wyndom wrung out his muddy tunic. "Settle all," he said. "Our queen has not forsaken us. Quite the contrary. She has just shown us we no longer need our temple, for soon we will walk through the gates into our Sworn Province."

Although Wyndom didn't believe his own words, until he could figure out what was going on, he needed to ensure his people kept their faith. Doubt created dissent, and Wyndom was not equipped for this. A leader did not become great because of heroic actions. A successful leader led with impunity because he was skillful enough to find a simple-minded flock willing to offer up blind loyalty.

Gathering his people around the prayer rock, he stepped onto his platform. "The storm has passed. Let us conclude our praise." He thrust his arms into the air. "My Queen," he yelled, "we are forever yours!"

His jaw clenched at his people's half-hearted response.

"Our queen went to battle for us," he said. "And this is how you repay her?" He again thrust his arms in the air and repeated his praise.

This time, the response came with vigor.

With his arms frozen to the sky, Wyndom waited for the queen to send her euphoric smoke. She was far away in Vitus, so maybe it needed extra time to arrive.

When no rush came, he had no other choice than to fake it. He cuddled his chest and quivered. "Thank you, my Queen. You fill me with such joy. I am but your humble servant."

His people side-glanced at each other.

"You feel your queen, don't you?" he said to them. "Because I do, and it's glorious. Only those who feel her love will be delivered to the Sworn Province. All others shall be forsaken."

Brother Angus pressed his hand to his chest. "I feel her," he said.

Sister Odette admitted the same.

Like a virus sweeping across the lands, one by one, his people caught the bug.

"We feel her!" they said. "Give praise to the queen."

Taking his leave, Wyndom walked to the water's edge and buried his face in his hands. As hard as he tried to convince himself that he'd felt something, he hadn't.

Alistair's cry burned in his ears as Sister Leona stepped up with the infant.

"I told you to keep him away from me," Wyndom said.

"But I can't settle him," she replied.

And Wyndom could?

Staring at the wailing infant, he sighed. Of course, he could. For some reason, Alistair had taken to him. And against his better judgement, Wyndom had taken to Alistair. How could he not? The precious child was the perfect likeness to Amalardh. The only difference was Alistair's smile. In the short time Wyndom had spent watching Amalardh through Sister Darna's view point, he hadn't seen the enigmatic man crack so much as a grin.

Hooking Alistair on his hip, Wyndom walked the stony shoreline with a gentle bounce in his step. In a matter of seconds, the ear-throbbing wail settled. Wyndom studied Alistair's wet eyelashes and his heart wrenched. Why hadn't he been capable of showing this level of affection to Saffron?

Until meeting Amalardh, Wyndom's life had been a daily exhaustion. Every minute of every day had required an ongoing series of pre-meditated thoughts ensuring he stood, talked, and walked the precise way a leader of his stature should. He'd been so caught up with protecting his image that he'd not given his heart the opportunity to take center stage. Because of Amalardh, Wyndom had experienced what could be possible if he just let go of his insecurities and let himself be.

He stroked Alistair's soft cheek with the back of his knuckle. "You have a very special daddy," he said.

Sighing, he cuddled Alistair to his chest. Surely the queen would understand why he couldn't do as she had ordered. He'd been laying on his prayer rock when her voice had entered his conscious, telling him to collect Alistair and a knife. "Be at the ready to complete your duty," she had said.

Until that point, Wyndom had convinced himself that he could obey his order. But when the actual moment came, when he held the shiny blade high, the trust in Alistair's big blue eyes tore through him. He swung the knife down, jamming it into the ground. After that, the inexplicable bond he'd felt with his queen disappeared. He assumed she was mad. Of course, she was mad.

"We've gone and done a bad thing," he said to Alistair in an exaggerated baby voice. "Our queen will get over it." She had to.

A chill rolled across his skin. Although cuddling Alistair's warm bundle helped, Wyndom still shivered. The iciness came from within. Deep down, Wyndom knew why his queen hadn't reached out. He just wasn't ready to admit it.

"Come on," he said to Alistair. "Let's go collect some shells."

The menial activity had fast become Wyndom's favorite pastime. He'd never appreciated the look of a shell's unique color and shape until studying one through the eyes of an innocent child. The simple things in life truly did offer the most pleasure.

Sweating and out of breath, Brother Stilton sprinted over. "Brother Wyndom, people are coming."

"People? What people?"

"I don't know. They're in two machines moving faster than a horse galloping at top speed. They'll be here within minutes."

Rushing over, Sister Leona went to pick up Alistair.

"Leave him be," Wyndom said, brushing her away. He understood Leona's intent. She had assumed the burden of a child would interfere with Wyndom's ability to govern. But during a moment such as this, Alistair was far from a burden. An innocent infant offered protection from these strangers. Women and children (and men holding babies) were the general rule as to whom shouldn't be harmed. While this wasn't Terefellia's belief, those who fought on the side of the false goddess would surely hold this view, and everything about Wyndom's unsettled belly told him that was who these people were. His queen wasn't giving him the silent treatment because of her displeasure.

Wyndom's queen was dead.

Scooping Alistair up, he marched to the center of camp and called for his people to gather around. "My dear Terefellians, I have some heart-aching news. Our queen lied to us."

Confused murmurs rumbled through the crowd.

"She had never planned to deliver us to the Sworn Province or bless us with eternal life. She was merely using us for her own gain. The enemy is coming. They will be at our doorstep shortly. In order to protect ourselves, we must disavow our queen and present ourselves as the innocent, non-threatening people we are."

He compressed his lips as he waited for their response. Would they take his word at face value? He hoped so. The last thing he needed was angry, disappointed voices shouting, "How could the queen do this to us?" His people needed to accept the situation and put on their merry faces fast. One way or another, Wyndom was getting into Vitus. If not by force, then by the "grace and peace for all" attitude the enemy supposedly held.

When no questions came, Wyndom relaxed. His people truly were sheep. "This is what we are going to do," he said to them.

Facing the valley's southern exit, everyone lined up in rows as though readying themselves for a group portrait: small children sitting in front; tall adults in the back. Flanked on either side by young women, Wyndom stood in the middle. A man holding a toddler, and surrounded by youthful faces, would surely come across as non-threatening.

"They're coming," said Brother Stilton. Dashing from his spying spot, he jumped cross-legged into an open space in the second row.

"Places, everybody," Wyndom said. "And remember, smile. We are just one big, innocent family, oblivious as to anything that may have gone on."

CHAPTER
35

As Cecilia's Rabbit Cove vehicle bounced along an open field, Wirador Wosrah tracks confirmed the team was headed in the right direction. The hoof prints disappeared into a narrow path, which presumedly led down to the valley Cecilia had seen from Saffron's watch tower.

"Okay, folks," Jensen said, as he pulled to a stop. "Looks like we're on foot from here."

From the back of Kayla's vehicle jumped six armed Rabbit Cove fighters.

Jensen handed Cecilia and Amalardh each a gun. Although Cecilia doubted the Terefellians possessed dangerous armory, she welcomed the offer. Alistair was all that mattered. The more threatening her team looked, the more likely the Terefellians would be to hand her son over without a fuss.

With their guns at the ready, Cecilia, Amalardh, Danmar, Jensen, Kayla, and the armed fighters trekked down the narrow path and along the dusty valley floor.

This place felt cold. Not just in temperature. The rows and rows of empty caves looked like open mouths in a perpetual state of shock, as though in disbelief that this desolate place had become their prison. As though reflecting the caves' moans, the wind funneling through the narrow divide added to the eeriness.

Pity crept into Cecilia's heart as she studied the highest hole. Unlike the former Senators of Vitus who had embraced Eifa's darkness for their own self-indulgent pleasures, she couldn't fault the Terefellians' desire to secure themselves a better life. If they'd simply abandoned Eifa's madness and turned up at Vitus's gates, Cecilia would've welcomed them with open arms. But the whole point of Eifa's influence was to turn the sane irrational and make crazy seem like the norm. While cloaked in the Dark Goddess's veil, the Terefellians' ability to see her corruption was as likely as a blind man seeing his own hand in front of his face.

Goosebumps rippled across Cecilia's skin as she neared the valley's end. What would these people be like? Sure, she'd met Saffron and her mother, but they'd had the good sense to flee. What about the remaining tribe? Would they be as cold-blooded as Brother Atlas, the Terefellian who'd come to Cecilia's home and threatened to slice her brothers' bellies if she made a sound?

A bright-eyed, earth-toned group, huddled just outside the valley's exit, caused her pause. Their overly enthusiastic smiles were unexpected. Brushing aside the oddity, Cecilia scanned the group for Alistair. Six long months had passed. Would she recognize him?

She hit upon a bearded man in the center, holding a toddler with dark hair. The child turned to her, and Cecilia's breath hitched. *Alistair*. Although his cheeks had lost their rosy puffiness, she knew those piercing eyes. The ache lingering in her chest fanned out, consuming her entire being. Just as lungs needed air, Cecilia needed her son.

Mouths of the children seated in the front rows opened as she marched forward. Those in the center scooted out of her way, allowing direct passage to the man.

"Give me my son," Cecilia said.

Looking over her shoulder, the man's wide eyes stared at someone. Amalardh, probably. Terror and bewilderment engulfed his face. These people hunted Croilar Tier. They surely knew who Amalardh was. Perhaps seeing that the last Croilar Tier remained alive shocked him? Her eyes narrowed at his hairy arms. This was the same man who'd held a knife to Alistair's throat. For whatever reason, he'd chosen not to kill him.

"I will not ask twice," she said in a calmer tone.

"What? Oh, yes," the man said. "He's safe. And healthy. We caused him no harm."

He handed Alistair over, and the hole in Cecilia's heart finally closed.

The grumble from being moved from one person to another quickly settled as Cecilia held Alistair close. She remembered his sweet baby scent, and he seemed to know hers. Although she tried to remain strong, her tears fell as she strode back to her group.

Joy and relief fluttered through her as Amalardh stroked Alistair's cheek with a tenderness she'd never seen. She should never have doubted his love for their son. With no reason or desire to linger a moment longer, Cecilia requested they leave.

Danmar motioned at the Terefellians. "What do we do with them?"

"We can deal with them later, when my son is safely away from this place," Cecilia said.

As they all turned to leave, the man called out. "Wait! What about us?"

Cecilia spun to him. "You dare to ask 'what about us?' as though we should care what becomes of you all?"

Danmar kept his voice low. "While I agree their wellbeing sits low on our priority list, we should consider the dangers this group might pose with no oversight."

Too emotionally drained to deal with these people, Cecilia glanced at Amalardh. His nod told her he understood her silent plea for him to take over and decide what was best for Vitus. He scanned the ramshackle campground. "We can't leave them here," he said to Danmar.

With Danmar agreeing, Amalardh turned to the man. "We will take what children we can with us in the vehicles. Everyone else walks."

"Just one moment!" the man said. Shoving his way out from behind the children, he scurried over. As though suddenly lost for words, he fidgeted like a nervous mouse desperate to get the cheese, but at the same time, terrified the cat might get him.

Amalardh, for some strange reason, appeared to represent both the cheese and the cat.

"My name is Brother Wyndom," he finally said to Cecilia. "I believe you know my daughter, Saffron?"

Only now did Cecilia realize his dark, curly hair and diminutive stature matched the person Saffron had pointed out as her father when they had viewed Terefellia from the watch tower. "I know your daughter," she said. "What of it?"

"It's just . . . please believe me. Your son was never in danger."

Although the blatant lie made Cecilia's blood boil, Amalardh's rage seemed to burn hotter. She touched his balled fist and his guarded posture eased.

In the same way Gildas's expression had fallen the first time he saw tenderness between Cecilia and Amalardh, curiously, so did Wyndom's. Rudella's spirit had told Cecilia she would meet a man with a soul far more tortured than those in Eifa's afterlife, and to go easy on him. Could Wyndom be who Rudella had spoken of? His strange mannerisms certainly reflected a person suffering from much inner turmoil. Although Wyndom seemed to match Rudella's description, Cecilia wasn't ready to go easy. "Your daughter wants your death," she said to him. "Be thankful I'm not bowing to her wishes."

As she and Amalardh walked off, Alistair's little hand waved goodbye. Cecilia's heart ached at the innocent gesture. Eifa had seemed confident in her ability to control her people's will. She'd clearly ordered Wyndom to kill Alistair. Yet, he hadn't. After years of loyalty to Eifa, something—maybe Alistair's innocence—had made Wyndom defy her. She glanced back at him. His small frame seemed to shrink as his nubbly fingers returned Alistair's wave. He seemed aware of the damage he'd caused and, from the desperate look in his eyes, he craved redemption. Cecilia's heart caved. As much as she wanted to stay cold toward these people, she couldn't.

"The hike to Vitus is long," she said to Wyndom. "Have your

people wait here. We will use our vehicles to shuttle your people to our city."

His spine straightened as though a massive weight had lifted from his shoulders. "Thank you," he replied.

With Alistair cuddled on her lap, Cecilia leaned her head against the vehicle's closed window. In the past two years, she'd witnessed too much death, too much destruction. As they drove by the southern headlands, the sight of the Freedom Tree reminded her of the agony that still lay ahead. The stick-thin plant was far from the broad-canopied tree depicted in the Prophecy. This suggested that at some point, Cecilia and Alistair would return to Plockton, where a fully grown Freedom Tree bloomed, allowing the final moment of the Prophecy to play out. The only reason Cecilia would move back home would be as Amalardh had suggested—upon his death, which, according to Alistair's size and the toddler depicted in the Prophecy, couldn't be more than a few weeks away.

Amalardh, too, focused on the spindly plant. Was the same thought running through his head? Perhaps so, because he bent down and kissed Alistair's tiny foot.

Pressing her knuckles to her lips, Cecilia sucked back her tears.

Amalardh placed his hand on her thigh and a jolt of electricity ripped through her heart. "It's going to be okay," he said.

For him, maybe. He'd be in the Pass-Over World where pain and suffering didn't exist.

Cecilia would feel every ounce of her soul's agony for the rest of her life.

Eideard's troubled expression shifted from the pristine ground, where the Forbidden Pool once was, to Rabbie. "The Croilar Tier knives. They're gone," he said.

"What does it matter?" asked Saffron. As far as she knew, the knives had done their job: opened the portal. What further use were they?

"The Prophecy doesn't end until Cecilia stands under the Freedom Tree reading to a group of children, one of whom is Alistair," said Eideard. "According to the painting of that moment, Alistair is wearing Amalardh's knife around his waist. But if the knife is gone, how can this event still happen?"

Rabbie's eyes went wide. "Oh, my gosh! Of course. That's it. He doesn't have to die."

"What are you talking about?" Saffron asked.

"Amalardh. He doesn't have to die."

Rabbie may have understood his own words, but no one else did. Even Eideard seemed confused. His palm-up hands indicated Rabbie needed to explain what he was babbling on about.

"This entire time, we've assumed that Amalardh must face death because Croilar Tier knives are only passed down to the next in line upon a Croilar Tier's death," Rabbie said. "The moment in the Prophecy can still happen because the knife isn't Amalardh's. I carved an exact replica for Alistair's Hinge Celebration. That's what's around Alistair's waist in the Prophecy painting. Not Amalardh's knife."

Eideard's expression lit up. "Brother. You are amazing. I can't wait to tell Cecilia this news." Seconds later, his joy stagnated.

"What's wrong?" Rabbie asked.

"Maybe we shouldn't get too excited. We still have the confusion about the Freedom Tree's location. The only fully grown tree is back in Plockton. Cecilia told me of a vision Siersha had shown her of the man who would raise Alistair. This man wore the clothing of our people. If Amalardh is not destined to raise Alistair, then only one person makes sense. Gildas. I have spoken at length with Cecilia about this and she's adamant the only reason she'd return home would be because of Amalardh's death."

Rabbie's joyous expression morphed into confusion. Saffron understood. The final image signifying the Prophecy's end perplexed her, too. How could this moment take place in a forest when the tree in the painting was backdropped by water? And how could the sapling growing on the southern headland represent the Prophecy's Freedom Tree when it would need another decade to mature? That being said, where gods were involved, anything seemed possible.

"Eifa birthed beasts and could turn herself into smoke," she said. "Siersha brought Amalardh back to life and healed my wounds. Who knows, maybe the tree on the southern headlands will sprout overnight. Whatever the case, we need to go. Forbillian and the others will be worried. And not to mention poor Nina." Although the temperature in the white chamber was cool, sweat dripped from Nina's temples, showing just how much pain her leg burn caused. Hopefully, she had enough strength to negotiate the plentiful handholds protruding from the chamber's knobby wall surface.

"Follow me," Saffron said to her.

To ensure a suitable path for her injured climber, Saffron scaled the wall using only her arms and left leg. "That's it," she said, as she watched Nina's fingers search for the hold Saffron had just used. "Two more inches to your right."

At the top, she hauled Nina to the surface and praised her impressive work.

"A student is only as good as their teacher," Nina replied. She let go of Saffron's hand. "That's quite the grip you've got there."

Saffron frowned at her callouses. Every time she started to feel normal, these ugly things reminded her of her defects.

"Our scars make us who we are," Nina said. She studied her nasty burn. "My first war wound. It will fade, but I never want it to go away. It's a reminder of what I've been through. My mother has spent her life searching for ways to erase memories. I am everything that has happened to me. The good and the bad. I don't want my past erased because if I do that, who would I be?"

Saffron pondered Nina's words. "Without my callouses, I'd still be me . . . just a shittier climber."

They shared a smile.

Seated on the crater's rim, Saffron, Rabbie, Nina, and Eideard took in the vast view. Smoke and steam rose from the smoldering lava lake surrounding the lonely crater, its surface blackening as it cooled.

Eideard shook his head at the sight. "It's kind of strange how we're sitting on a volcano, yet instead of spouting from this, the lava flowed from cracks in the ground."

The notion didn't seem strange to Saffron. "The Forbidden Pool used to sit below this crater," she said. "It clearly had its own power. It makes sense that the lava would have to find another way out."

"Ahoy up there!" came Forbillian's voice.

Everyone turned in his direction. What the heck was he doing walking on the smoldering lava field?

"Forbillian! Are you crazy?" Rabbie said. "You're going to burn alive down there."

Forbillian made a scoffing motion. "Fiddlesticks. Molten rock cools quicker than you'd think. In as little as fifteen minutes, you can get a crust thick enough to walk on. Just like an ice lake, you have to keep away from the thin stuff." He hooked his hands to his hips and beamed at them. "Well, I'd call this a job well done."

So would Saffron.

Waiting at the edge of the original lava field were the four Bayton riders who had come with them. Thankfully, they'd managed to corral the runaway horses. The group rested while Yumi, a dark-skinned Baytonite with a focused stare and caring touch, cleaned and dressed Nina's wound. As Nina's face scrunched with pain, Eideard offered his hand for her to squeeze. Saffron's head tilted. When she'd first met Eideard, he'd lobbied for Saffron's attention constantly. Around Nina, he remained measured and polite, the very picture of a gentleman. If goofy flirtation meant Eideard was not attracted to someone, then did reserved politeness suggest he was?

The exhausted group clomped into Bayton and cheers rang out. Streamers flew through the air and colorful scraps of paper rained upon them. Saffron sank into herself. She hated being the object of praise. In that regard, she was not her father's daughter. Sitting high on their stallions, smiling and waving, Eideard and Nina soaked up the attention. Rabbie, as usual, took the whole thing in stride.

Determined to rebuild Bayton's relationship with Vitus, the Countess loaded *Bayton II* with sacks of aromatic spices and medical supplies.

Relieved of caring for a dying goddess, Saffron enjoyed the ride back to Vitus, a place she was happy to call her new home. She sat on the ship's pulpit and took in the vast blue expanse as sea spray doused her dangling toes. Rabbie plonked himself next to her, and for a long while, they sat in silence. They hadn't yet spoken about the kiss they'd shared before the battle and their resulting fight. Maybe with time, she would revisit their feelings. For now, though, she wasn't about to ruin anything by discussing what had happened. She'd rather keep Rabbie as a friend than risk pushing him away.

"I have a confession," Rabbie said.

Her stomach flip-flopped at his serious tone. "What?" she asked tentatively.

His intoxicating hazel eyes bore into hers and her anxiety grew. Whatever he was about to say couldn't be good, because he was taking too long to say it.

"I really like you," he finally said.

Her heart skipped. He did? "I really like you, too."

"I don't think you understand. I really, really like you. A lot."

She bit back her grin. She liked how they were reliving their previous encounter on Vitus's southern pier, but with the script flipped. "That's good," she said, "because I really, really like you, too."

"Really?"

"Since the moment I met you."

He eyed her suspiciously. "I was naked when you met me."

She smiled wide. "Exactly."

He swooped in and kissed her.

Tingles shot through to her toes.

Rabbie insisting that they wait until after the battle to pursue a relationship was the right thing to do. How else could they figure out which emotions were real and which ones were hijacking their fear, scurrying along for the ride, only to end up scooting away in the calm?

"I have a confession, too," she said. She gingerly pulled the smashed mini-Glimglob from her pocket.

"Oh no," Rabbie said. "Did he get damaged during the battle?"

His genuine concern heightened Saffron's guilt. "Not exactly."

He took hold of the crushed artifact and studied it. "Looks like the poor thing found himself on the receiving end of an angry stomp." His understanding smirk suggested he knew exactly when the damaging blow had happened. "I'm not making you another one."

"I don't want you to," Saffron said. "He'll always be precious to me." She went to take her toy back.

Playfully, Rabbie closed his fist and pulled his hand away. "Uh-uh. I don't think so."

"He's mine. Give him to me," Saffron said as she pried his fingers open.

During their scuffle, her treasure plopped into the ocean.

"Glimglob! Noooo!" Although he was just a toy, Saffron's heart felt genuine pain. Crestfallen, she turned to Rabbie. "He's gone."

Grinning, he put his arm around her. "It's all right. I'll make you another one."

W AKING WITH A start, Amalardh ran his hand down his face. The nightmare that had started while hiking the Esjan Range with Forbillian and Oisin continued to haunt him. In it, he fought another man dressed in a brown, hooded robe, similar to his own. What had made him jump awake each time was his inability to swing his sword down on his unseen attacker. Amalardh had never met an adversary he couldn't kill. Because of the hood's shadow, he hadn't seen his attacker's face until now. The man Amalardh had been unable to kill was himself.

He looked around. Why was the house so quiet?

On the nightstand lay a note: *Oisin is with Brassal. Alistair and I are down on the beach. I didn't want to wake you as I know you've been having trouble sleeping. Good news—Bayton II has been spotted and is expected to dock tomorrow afternoon. Love Cecilia.*

Amalardh rarely napped during the day. Between the journey across the eastern lands, the battle, and his restless nights, he must have been more exhausted than he'd realized. He walked into the bathroom and splashed water on his face. Leaning on the sink, he stared at the man from his nightmare. He avoided looking at himself in the mirror because he couldn't stand the sight of the person looking back at him.

The Goddess of Light had shown him a vision of the man who would raise Alistair. "Who is this man?" Amalardh had asked. "Deep in your heart, you know his name," Siersha had replied. "Only when you accept what is best for Alistair will you be free from your torment, and the man who was supposed to die today will finally face his death."

The man with the cold blue eyes, messy beard, and disheveled hair staring back at Amalardh was not the man destined to raise Alistair. And neither was Gildas. As he studied his empty reflection, he finally understood Siersha's words. Amalardh was Alistair's true guiding light, but he could never be that person until the man in the mirror died. In order for Amalardh to move forward, he needed to let go of his past. Let go of the assassin.

SINCE RETURNING HOME, Alistair had developed an obsession with collecting seashells. The fascination must have started during his time in Terefellia. If so, could that mean Wyndom had treated Alistair with a kinder heart than Cecilia had given him credit for? Although the Rabbit Cove vehicles had transported all the Terefellians to Vitus, Cecilia had kept out of Wyndom's way. Something about him—mainly the way he looked at Amalardh—unsettled her. With the Prophecy hinting at Amalardh's death, the leader of the group whose very purpose was to kill Croilar Tier, showing curiosity about the last remaining one, kept her on high alert.

The afternoon drew late. Holding her hand out, Cecilia called to Alistair. As his delicate grip intertwined with hers, she turned toward home and froze. Ahead stood a stylish man holding a single red sunflower. With his tightly cropped dark hair, clean-shaven face, loose-fitting Plocktonian toggle-button white shirt, and beige linen pants, he resembled the man from her Pass-Over Zone vision.

The handsome stranger smiled. Cecilia glanced over her shoulder. Surely, he was staring at someone else, but besides her and Alistair, the beach was empty.

He must have confused Cecilia with someone he knew.

Breaking from her grasp, Alistair trotted to the man. "Dadda," he said.

Cecilia's mouth fell open. *Amalardh?*

Her breath faltered as Amalardh bent down and performed

the exact same lift with Alistair as the man from her vision had. When Cecilia had asked Siersha to show her the man's face, the Goddess had replied, "I cannot show you what you yourself are not ready to accept. You question whether Vitus or Plockton is the best place for your son. I know what I want for Alistair, but only you can decide."

Cecilia's eyes misted over. Amalardh truly was the one destined to raise Alistair.

Stepping up to him, she bit back her smile. He looked so young. So handsome. Since she'd known him, a stubbled beard and shaggy, shoulder-length hair had hidden his face. With his fringe no longer veiling his brow, his eyes looked brighter and more . . . alive. The way the cuffs of his trouser legs gently bunched on his sandals made her skin tingle. How could such a small thing look so sexy? Maybe because the exposure of his normally booted toes made him seem vulnerable.

Cecilia had given Amalardh the Plocktonian outfit over a year ago. He'd offered the clothing a cursory glance and tucked them in the back of his closet. While the act had stung, Cecilia understood. When Amalardh had emerged from the Tower dungeons as the Dark Shadow of the Senators, his robe had defined him, its hood hiding him. A year ago, he hadn't been ready to let go of his past and become the man he didn't believe existed.

"You're wearing sandals," she said.

"The weather's getting warmer," he replied.

She stroked his smooth cheek. "Siersha showed me a vision of the man who would lead Alistair to be the Ceannaire Fis. And you're him."

"She showed me the same thing."

"Does this mean you don't die?"

"I'm tired of trying to figure the Prophecy meanings." His earnest eyes bore into hers. "You once asked if we could leave our past behind. I said I couldn't. But I want to. There is something I've done that you don't know—"

She pressed her fingers to his lips. "And I don't want to."

"But what if you knowing the truth changed the way you thought of me?"

What if Amalardh knowing Cecilia's truth of kissing Gildas changed the way he thought of her? "There's only one thing I need to know. Can you leave your past in the past?" she asked.

He nodded. "I can."

Pulling her close, he pressed his silken lips to hers. Her stomach fluttered as though kissing him for the first time. Which, in a way, she was. She wasn't kissing Amalardh the assassin, Amalardh the last Croilar Tier, or Amalardh her protector. She was kissing just him. And he was kissing just her.

Because of their promise to leave bygone days behind, Cecilia could sleep well without the fear of her past coming back to haunt her.

The next day, *Bayton II* docked on the northern pier, reuniting Cecilia with her brothers, and the day after, Tomkin and Marion (who'd fled Vitus with Alistair) arrived back from their hiding spot deep in the Wynn Forest. Siersha's light truly was shining bright. Not only was Cecilia and Amalardh's relationship the strongest it had ever been, Eideard had found love, Rabbie and Saffron remained close, and Forbillian rekindled the long-lost flame he'd once shared with Marion. Although tidings of the Forbidden Pool's disappearance made Cecilia's stomach twinge, just as Amalardh had grown tired of trying to figure the Prophecy meanings, Cecilia would no longer spend energy fretting over things outside her control. If the portal was broken, then so be it. This was Siersha's problem, not hers. Cecilia had enough to deal with, like helping the council integrate the newly arrived Rabbit Cove folk and Terefellians.

While Cecilia wholeheartedly remained open-minded about the former Eifa worshippers, Wyndom—Saffron's strange little father—continued to perplex her. His desperation to join the council as the Terefellian representative didn't reconcile with the boredom plastered on his face during meetings. Or maybe Cecilia saw sadness? On occasion, she'd witnessed him watch Saffron as if trying to will the courage to talk to her. Understandably, Saffron kept her distance, refusing to even acknowledge her father's existence. Thankfully, Tomkin and his partner Omerod took a liking to Wyndom and offered valuable friendship.

"Do you think he will revert to praising Eifa?" Cecilia asked.

"I don't believe so," replied Tomkin. "All he talks about is Siersha this and Siersha that. He seems to have become a true convert."

A few days later, Cecilia spotted Wyndom standing on a wooden crate, calling for others to gather around and join him in a celebration of love for the Goddess of Light. Her jaw grit as she marched over. Restraining the desire to kick the crate out from under him, she excused herself and told the crowd, "Siersha loves you. If you feel the need, offer up a quiet prayer in private. Go now and continue to live in the goodness of her light."

Wyndom glowered at her. "What are you doing? We must give praise to our Goddess."

"No, we must not," Cecilia replied.

"You forbid your people to show their love for their Goddess?"

"The request is not mine. It is Siersha's."

"The worst thing you can do to a god is praise them," Siersha had told Cecilia. "A quiet thank you is nice. Boisterous adoration is addictive. I am not supposed to be the center of anyone's universe. Humanity's love is meant for each other, not me."

While Siersha wasn't designed to accept praise, Eifa was. Like water to a seed, the Dark Goddess absorbed the devotion and germinated. The bigger the worship centers grew, the bolder Eifa became, until the day she tempted the Goddess of Light to swim in the Forbidden Pool. During the Final Battle, Cecilia's light had not destroyed the Dark Goddess, but returned her to the seed she'd once been. Cecilia couldn't risk Eifa once again sprouting and tempting Siersha to do something the goddess shouldn't do. Since she didn't trust Wyndom's loyalty, she kept the reason Siersha forbade group praise to herself. If the former Terefellian leader knew that mass displays of devotion had the potential to reawaken his queen, he might attempt to re-establish his people's old beliefs.

Using the encounter as an opportunity to get to know Wyndom, Cecilia requested he come for a walk with her. "I won't bite," she said, in response to his surprised look.

He smiled and the lines on his face softened. Her congeniality seemed to lift a weight from his shoulders. "I find it strange that Siersha does not want our praise," he said, as they strolled the bustling street. "How will she know we love her?"

"Her light is fed through goodness, kindness, and forgiveness. If we treat each other this way, she will know our love for her."

"But preaching is what I do. It is what I know. It is who I am."

She tilted her head at him. "Is it, though?"

His eyes narrowed as his chin lifted. "You may not have agreed with whom I praised, but don't dare cast aspersions on my ability to preach. I was the best. I am the best."

In that moment, Cecilia saw the man Saffron despised. Wyndom was an empty shell, a ship with no sails . . . a life with no purpose. She'd once told Amalardh, "I know Vitus dispatches those who have no purpose. The Plockton way is to find purpose in everything." Just because Cecilia didn't see Wyndom's societal benefit didn't mean he lacked one. Crossing to the other side of the street, she led him into the library, newly established from the wealth of books recently discovered in the Tower. If Cecilia didn't feed Wyndom's need for recognition, she'd find him right back on a podium getting his fix from his attentive crowd.

"Do you read?" she said.

"I know how to, if that's what you're asking."

She pulled from a shelf a hardcover book with a golden title, *The Complete Works of Eugene Cummings*, and handed it to him. "This book contains plays written by a famous playwright from before the time of the Great War. You say you're a preacher. I say you're a performer."

Wyndom's spine straightened as his wide eyes scoured the cover. "I'm not sure what you mean," he said. "What is a play?"

As she led him from the library to an ornate building called the *Grand Majestic Theater*, she explained the concepts of character, plot, and story.

Pushing open a set of double doors, she walked with him along a red hallway into a massive, golden, domed room with three seating levels arched around a glorious stage. "That, up there," she said, motioning to the stage, "is where you perform the words in this book."

Wyndom gulped. "Up there is where I would stand? On that great platform?"

She directed his attention to the seats. "And here your audience will hang on your every word."

Wyndom's eyes grew glassy as he cuddled the hardcover book to his chest. He seemed so overcome, he looked ready to collapse in a sobbing heap.

CHAPTER

39

ON THE NIGHT Saffron and her team had arrived at Bayton, after returning the Goddess of Light to the Forbidden Pool, the Countess had thrown a party. At the celebration, Eideard had introduced to everyone an elderly lady called Ida, who, to Saffron's surprise,was Rudella's mother, and the closest person Saffron had to a grandmother. After a night of bonding over Rudella's fearless exploits, Saffron asked Ida if she would come back to Vitus with her. "Nothing would make me happier," Ida had said.

They both moved into a quaint cottage not too far from Cecilia and Amalardh's residence. Annoyingly, Tomkin and Omerod, who also lived close by, had taken Saffron's father under their wing and were letting him stay in one of their spare rooms. Since returning from saving the Goddess of Light, Saffron had inadvertently crossed paths with her father more times than she'd cared. She'd yet to speak to him, and as far as she was concerned, she never would.

Nina—who had convinced her mother that the re-opened trade route needed a Bayton liaison stationed in Vitus—moved in with Eideard and Rabbie. As an adult, she was old enough to decide her sleeping arrangement. While Saffron's eighteenth birthday had come and gone without fuss, she and Rabbie didn't want to rush living together.

They did, however, spend an intimate night. The encounter had somewhat been planned. Eideard had taken Nina on a sight-seeing trip through the Wynn Forest, leaving Rabbie with the place to himself. The evening started off nicely. Saffron and Rabbie cooked dinner and after a sunset stroll along the headlands, returned to his place, where (probably because of unspoken expectations) things suddenly became awkward and weird.

"I don't want you doing anything you don't want to do?" Rabbie said.

Talking made things worse.

"Just shut up and kiss me," Saffron said.

Pulling him to her, she pressed her lips to his. Passion shot through her.

Every inch of her skin tingled at his soft, sensual touch.

Overcome with desire, she ran her hands down his back and immediately tensed at his flinch.

"What's wrong?" he asked.

"Nothing. I'm fine."

"Are you sure? We can stop."

"No. Keep going." She felt awful and didn't want him having a horrible time because of her.

As she tried to reconnect with the moment, the image of Rabbie's flinching continued to pierce her mind. The intimate act ended and all Saffron wanted to do was cry. The magical night she'd dreamed of had fallen worse than flat. Rabbie, at least, seemed to enjoy himself.

The next morning, the sound of knocking on the front door crept into her waking mind. Too miserable from last night's failed encounter, Saffron feigned being asleep while Rabbie climbed out of bed and answered the door.

"Hey, sis," he said.

"I've decided to start a tradition at my place," Cecilia said. "Keep this Sunday night fr—"

Her voice clipped. "Rabbie, what on earth happened to your back? It's all grazed."

Wide-eyed, Saffron flung the blanket back. Blood smears covered the white sheets.

In the dark of night, she hadn't noticed how badly she'd harmed Rabbie.

Shirtless, he walked into the bedroom and studied the marks in the mirror. "It's nothing," he said to Cecilia, who'd followed him to the open doorway.

Water welled in Saffron's eyes as she cowered under the covers. It might be nothing to him, but the scrapes marring his flesh mortified her.

"Good morning, beautiful," Rabbie said and kissed the top of her head.

She didn't move. She couldn't. She was too embarrassed.

He stroked her hair. "Saffron? Are you okay?"

"I'm fine," she said, without looking up. "I'm just tired."

Her silent tears soaked into the pillow. *Please, just leave,* she told him in her mind. She was about to start blubbering and she didn't want him to hear her cry.

He kissed the back of her head. "I love you," he whispered and walked off.

As the bedroom door clicked closed, Saffron burst into tears.

The side of the bed dipped down from the weight of someone sitting on the edge. Saffron blinked at Cecilia's blurry image and was eternally grateful that she'd stayed.

"I hate my hands," Saffron said in between sobs.

"It's okay. We can fix them."

She blinked at Cecilia through wet lashes. *We can?*

Back at Cecilia's house, Cecilia dipped Saffron's hands into a pot of deliciously warm, waxy liquid. After letting them soak a few minutes, she pulled a hand out and rubbed the thickened skin with a rough stone. She'd learned about hot wax therapy from Omerod, a former Tower Folk, who'd used the treatment to smooth Cecilia's battle-hardened hands. Apparently, the Senators and their kin had indulged in many alluring delights.

"Starting this Sunday, I'm hosting family dinner," Cecilia said. "I'd like for you and Ida to come."

Saffron bit back her excitement. Being invited to such an event meant she had a family. "You're not inviting my father, are you?"

"Not if you don't want him."

Saffron didn't.

The boisterous night arrived and the evening was perfect. Cecilia was a gracious hostess and Amalardh . . . the man was like night and day with his new look and disarming charm.

For the next two months, Sunday nights at Cecilia and Amalardh's became a thing. Because of the wax treatments, Saffron's palms softened and Rabbie no longer flinched at her touch. Life was perfect. Almost.

"Don't get mad at me for asking," Cecilia said, as they cleaned up after dinner, "but Tomkin and Omerod want to know if they could bring your dad next week."

Saffron tensed. Her instinct was to tell her no, but time, and the fact he'd supposedly changed because of some play he was putting on, had mellowed her. "Tell them they can bring him if they want, but that doesn't mean I'm going to talk to him."

At the next dinner, Saffron had expected her father's attendance. "So, is he coming?" she asked. A twang shot through her belly at Cecilia's shaking head. Had Saffron reached the point where she desired to make peace with her father? Or was she simply disappointed in a lost opportunity to ignore him?

After dinner, Tomkin brought Saffron a cup of tea and sat with her in the side courtyard. She liked Tomkin and Omerod and appreciated their civility toward her father. Tomkin had five daughters. Maybe by watching how a real father interacted with his girls—like hugging them and treating them as actual human beings capable of their own thoughts, feelings, and opinions— Saffron's father would understand what being a parent to a child meant.

"Your father's play is tomorrow night," said Tomkin.

"I know," she replied.

"He would like very much if you came."

Saffron gave him the side-eye.

"He's quite good, you know."

"I don't doubt that." As far as Saffron was concerned, her father's entire existence had been one big performance.

Needing some space, she excused herself and followed the moon-lit trail to the beach. With her focus on the immediate path in front, she accidentally brushed a passerby. "Sorry—"

Recognizing her father, she tensed.

He froze mid-step. "Saffron. Hi . . . hello."

They stood in silence.

Could this moment get any more uncomfortable?

"How are you?" he asked.

Like he cared. "Fine," she replied.

He scratched his temple. "I'm not sure if you've heard . . . I've mounted a play. It opens tomorrow night."

They hadn't spoken in months, and his first words were about him? Typical. She made a point of not answering. Her way of telling him, if that was all, then she would be on her way. She went to walk off.

"Wait, I, ah . . ." he said.

She'd never known her father to be stuck for words. Part of his manipulation, no doubt. Make her think his nerves were coming from an earnest place. She knew all his tricks and wasn't about to fall for any of them.

"I never wanted things to turn out the way they did between us," he said.

The pent-up anger Saffron had been holding on to exploded. "Then maybe you shouldn't have ignored me, destroyed my favorite toy, and made it painfully clear that I was nothing but a disappointment because I wasn't born a boy."

His eyes widened at the "born a boy" statement.

"Don't act so surprised. You may not have outright said it, but

I'm not stupid. 'Little girls don't throw stones. They learn how to bake,' I believe your words were."

Memory of the moment must have returned because he lowered his head. Six-year-old Saffron had been helping her mother knead bread while watching a group of young Wrethun Lof hopefuls throw stones at a small rabbit skull on a stump thirty feet away. Those with exceptional precision would progress onto the Siddachet—the spiked disk used to kill Croilar Tier. No one came close to hitting the distant target.

Bitterness stung Saffron's eyes. "You crowed to those kids about how you had endured months of training before you could hit a small target at such substantial distance. 'Persistence and fortitude' were your words. Even though you'd broken my heart, I still looked up to you."

His expression collapsed.

Was he feeling pain? Good. She would pain him more. "Funny how you never threw that stone you bounced in your hand to prove your skill. Back then, I didn't discern your lies. All I wanted was to be as brilliant and as competent as I thought you were. I ran over to you and asked if I could try. And that's when you prattled your 'little girl' spiel."

"You snatched the stone from my hand and flung it," he said. "I remember that rabbit skull flying off the stump."

Her eyes narrowed at his distant-sounding voice. Did the memory truly impress him, or was he weaving one of his pretend sympathy webs? "When Brother Atlas said I had quite an arm, your only response was that my technique lacked finesse."

He stubbed the sandy ground with the toe of his sandal.

"I had the makings of a Wrethun Lof. If I'd been a boy, you would've stood proud. Instead, you said that before any young Terefellian learns a new skill, they must first learn their place and sent me back to the women making bread. After that, I figured you out. Your pathetic lies. Your grand pretense of being something you're clearly not. You may not have wanted things to turn out the way they did between us, but you certainly did everything in your power to make sure they would."

His already small stature seemed to shrink.

"Is everything okay?" Tomkin asked. "I heard yelling."

"Everything's just dandy," said Saffron. Turning on her heels, she stormed off.

Confronting her father had not offered the satisfaction she'd hoped. Instead, it drudged up all the pain, anger, and hate she no longer wanted. As vast as Vitus was, the city was far too small for them both.

Although Saffron one thousand percent did not want to attend her father's play, Lyrik, Zack, and Eideard had parts, and Tomkin and Omerod had put such effort into the costumes. Arriving at the packed theater, she sat in an aisle seat for a quick escape. From the moment the curtain rose, she was drawn in. The man on stage couldn't be her father, could he? She had expected the over-the-top Terefellian preacher bouncing around, spouting words like a raven squawking over fresh meat. What she got was vulnerability so raw, it felt like a knife cutting through her soul. She wriggled in her seat. Just when she thought she'd slammed the door on her father, he showed he could be an actual human being. Where was this man when Saffron needed him? She folded her arms across her chest. *It's just a performance*, she told herself. Like everything else in her father's life.

But was it, though? Just an act? Tomkin didn't seem to think so. He sat next to Saffron, wide-eyed, and whispered about attending every rehearsal and never seeing her father break down to this level of devastation. Glancing at her with a mix of sadness and empathy, he placed his hand on her knee. His unspoken words suggested her father's heartfelt performance stemmed from last night's confrontation. She slumped on her armrest. Her entire life, her father had caused her nothing but pain, and now, she was feeling guilty? How was this fair?

After the show, her father walked out of the theater and the crowd swarmed him. Even if a tiny nugget inside Saffron wanted to mend fences, why would he need her now? He had regained everything he lived for: praise, adoration, notoriety.

He'd be fine.

She'd be fine.

No, she probably wouldn't be fine, but she'd have to be.

WOW! WHAT A rush. Wyndom's heart soared as he bounced back on stage for his encore bow. What a misguided fool he'd been. Until this moment, everything in his life had been fake. Even his belief in his queen. He'd gone along with the Terefellian faith because that was all he knew. He didn't dare challenge what the idea of eternal life would be like because accepting the possibility that existing forever would be a living nightmare meant facing the reality that he was wrong. If he was wrong, then his people weren't special. And if the Terefellians weren't special, then they—he—were nobodies. Nothing.

Other than hiding his fear of heights, Wyndom had never really had to work at anything. By virtue of his birth, he received the title of leader, and due to years of societal brainwashing, his people followed him faithfully. Because of his disingenuous existence, Wyndom had never felt comfortable in his own skin. He'd wanted to be someone else, like Amalardh, the great Croilar Tier. Back in Terefellia, when he'd seen Amalardh for the first time in real life, he'd felt like a teenager experiencing his first crush. While Wyndom would always have a soft spot for the man who had taught him how to love, just like everything else in his life, his bond with Amalardh wasn't genuine. He'd become infatuated with a blue-eyed enigma. But then, Amalardh shed his robe, cut his hair, tidied his face, and while he remained stunningly handsome, the mystery shrouding him vanished. Underneath Amalardh's dangerous shell lived an ordinary man (who accomplished extraordinary things).

In Amalardh, Wyndom had been drawn to what he thought he should be—a six-foot-tall, fearless, killing machine. Instead, he was a five-foot-two fraud, who by age fifty, had no concept of his own identity. His disappointment in himself had trickled down and negatively impacted his treatment of Rudella and Saffron. He had foolishly believed that his wife and daughter should love him, whether or not he deserved their love.

He had recognized his failure as a father two days before Saffron confirmed it. Tomkin and Omerod had stepped out of their house, leaving Wyndom sitting in the living room, studying his lines. When Tomkin arrived back, his youngest daughter ran to the front door, shouting, "Daddy's home!" and hugged her father with the fervor of a child who hadn't seen a parent for ten years. Tomkin, who had been gone less than two hours, seemed just as thrilled to see his little girl. Stunned, Wyndom laid his book on his lap. Was that how fathers and daughters were supposed to act toward each other?

Eifa's tenets of looking out for number one, indulging in your pleasures, and having others do for you that which you don't care to do for yourself were fine in the short term. But in the long term, selfishness and gluttony could not be sustained. Wyndom had thought he could let his problems with Saffron and Rudella slide. After he got eternal life, he'd have all the time in the world to fix whatever might need fixing. The problem with his approach was that before eternity had even arrived, Rudella had already given her life to ensure the victory of the other side and Saffron no longer wanted anything to do with him.

Wyndom no longer had an eternity to fix things with Saffron. All he had were the ticking seconds of the beating minutes of the passing days that, once spent, would never come back. He stepped out of the theater and fans swarmed him. Everything he'd thought he'd wanted was happening. He'd finally become the man he'd dreamed of, yet his heart still ached. All the adoration in the world was meaningless without the respect of one person—Saffron.

His heart leaped as he spotted her beyond the crowd. *She came!*

Linking arms with Rabbie, she began walking away. He couldn't let her leave. "Saffron!" he called.

She turned.

Ignoring her detached expression, he maneuvered his way through the crowd to her. "Everything you said last night was true. I was a miserable father. You deserved much, much better. I'm sorry."

His toes wiggled as he waited for her response.

She shrugged. "Fine."

Fine? Oh. Okay. Wyndom had fantasized about this apology all day. In his version, Saffron had thrown her arms around him, squeezed him tight, and told him she was sorry, too. He hadn't anticipated "fine." What did that mean?

As she stared blankly at him, he ran his hands through his hair. What should he do? What should he say? He glanced up at the starry sky. "It's a nice night for a walk," he said. "I'm thinking of heading down to the water."

"Don't you have some kind of celebration or party to go to?" she asked.

Although Saffron's tone remained cold, her progression from a one-word response to an entire sentence offered hope. "Yes, actually I do. But it's meaningless if I don't have someone to share it with. So, I'm going to walk to the beach, and I would dearly like it if you came with me."

The silence dragged.

Wyndom's chest tightened.

The limb he'd put himself out on was about to snap.

Conceding the loss, he nodded. "Okay. Maybe next time."

As he walked away, an ache more excruciating than anything he'd experienced ripped through his chest. He rubbed the smarting spot. As crippling as the pain was, he'd face it again. He would do whatever it took to win Saffron's trust.

"Wait," she called.

His heart skipped as she walked to him.

As they stood in silence, the dark hand of doubt once again choked him. Was he supposed to say something?

"So . . . are we going to walk or what?" she asked.

"Oh. Yes. Of course."

With his chin held high, Wyndom strolled the moonlit street with his daughter. He might only stand five-foot-two, but inside, he felt like a giant.

CHAPTER
41

AMALARDH STOOD IN his backyard, staring at a massive silver moon. Its intense glow lit up the nighttime lands.

"It's called a supermoon," said Oisin, who walked up beside him. Tucked under his arm was an astronomy book. "It means that tomorrow, the Prophecy will end."

Amalardh furrowed his brow at him. How could that be possible? Of the two Freedom Trees that could possibly mark the Prophecy's end, the one growing on the southern headland was still far too small, and the trip to get to the tree in Plockton, even if they drove with Jensen's vehicles, would take a week, if not two.

"Beyond telling you to steal my knife, what else did the Prophet say to you?" Amalardh asked.

Oisin sucked on his lower lip. "He said the first supermoon after Siersha's departure will mark eternal peace. To me that sounds like the Prophecy's end."

"Did he say anything else?"

Oisin was quiet for a moment, then shook his head.

Nodding to himself, Amalardh backed off. Oisin had a secret and Amalardh had always told Cecilia: secrets were for the holder to keep, not for the overly curious to expose.

Oisin seemed itching to say something.

"What?" Amalardh asked.

"Well . . . it's just . . . I like how things are with our Sunday night dinners and everything. I like seeing you and Cecilia happy."

"I like the way everything is, too."

Oisin's expression turned serious. "Promise me you won't do anything to mess that up."

Although Oisin's words stung, he had every right to maintain a healthy distrust for Amalardh. In betraying his love for Cecilia with the Terefellian, Amalardh had already committed the worst crime possible. He'd tried to confess his sin, but Cecilia had told him she didn't want to hear it. They had both agreed to put the past where it belonged—behind them—and build a new life together. With Amalardh committed to keeping "the assassin" dead, he had every confidence in maintaining this new life. He placed his hand on Oisin's shoulder. "You, Cecilia, and Alistair are my world. I promise I won't do anything to mess this up."

Oisin flung his arms around Amalardh's waist. "I love you."

Without hesitation, Amalardh held Oisin close. "I love you, too."

"All right, all right," said Forbillian as he lumbered over. "Why are all these hugs happening when I'm not here?" Wrapping his bulky arms around both of them, he squeezed tight.

Flush-faced and out of breath, Oisin burst through the front door. "Amalardh. Cecilia. Quick. You have to come and see this." He beamed at Amalardh. "I told you. Today's the day."

"Today's the day for what?" Cecilia asked.

"You didn't tell her?" Oisin said.

"Tell me what?"

Knowing how much the closure of the Prophecy meant to Cecilia, Amalardh couldn't bring himself to even hint at the idea. What if Oisin had heard the Prophet's words wrong? What if last night's moon wasn't the sign Oisin had thought it was? "According to our young man over there"—he motioned to Oisin—"the Prophecy ends today."

Cecilia's face pulled. "That's not possible."

"Would you two just grab Alistair and come?" Oisin said.

Amalardh stepped outside and stopped short at the sea of people flooding out the newly repaired Great Gates.

"What is going on?" Cecilia asked.

"I told you," Oisin said. He grabbed her hand. "Quick, let's go."

Lifting Alistair onto his shoulders, Amalardh walked with Cecilia and Oisin to the Great Gates. When they exited the city and turned south, he and Cecilia froze. In the middle of the southern headlands stood a fully grown Freedom Tree, its broad canopy blooming with red blossoms, just as in the Prophecy.

"How is this possible?" Cecilia asked. "How did it grow so fast?"

Amalardh side-glanced at Oisin. Certain behaviors were now making sense. During the hike from the Nian Temple to the Forbidden Pool, Oisin had asked to borrow Forbillian's empty liquor pouch (the one Amalardh had drained while cleaning Malek's gunshot wound), proclaiming his had sprung a leak. "When we were in the lava tube with Siersha and you'd run back to get your pack, that wasn't all you got, was it?" he whispered.

"I don't know what you're talking about," Oisin replied.

Amalardh cocked his brow at him. *Of course, Oisin didn't.* The Prophet had entrusted Oisin with this task because he knew the kid's capacity to keep a tightly bound secret. The day of the storm, when the Goddess had returned to her realm and Cecilia had woken up, Oisin had sped off, presumably to pour the Forbidden Pool's life-altering water onto the Freedom Tree sapling. Because of the many people who had learned of the pool's location, Siersha had probably sealed the portal. He studied the Freedom Tree. Could that mean this magnificent plant represented the new link between the two realms?

A bunch of eager children sat cross-legged at the tree's base. As Amalardh lowered Alistair to the ground, Eideard and Rabbie walked over.

"Oisin came banging on our door at the crack of dawn, telling us we had to meet him here and to bring Alistair's Hinge present," Rabbie said. He presented Amalardh with an immaculately carved Croilar Tier knife, painted to perfection. Since the Croilar Tier knives had disappeared with the Forbidden Pool, this replica, which Rabbie had made months ago for Alistair's Hinge Celebration, had to be the one featured in the Prophecy.

"I made this also," Rabbie said, handing over a child-sized sash.

Dropping to one knee, Amalardh wrapped the sash around Alistair's tiny waist and told him to go sit with the other kids.

Eideard pulled Cecilia's copy of *The Flower Princess and the Wolf* from behind his back and presented it to her. "The rest is up to you, sis," he said.

Cecilia's wide eyes trailed from the crowd to the grand tree. "Do you really think this is it? That this moment marks the end?" she whispered to Amalardh.

Her apprehension was justified. Their interpretation of the Prophecy had failed in the past. "The best we can do is follow the signs," he replied.

She squeezed his hand, then took her place under the tree. As she read the story of the Flower Princess and the Wolf to the eager children, Oisin retrieved *Exploring the Gaussian Tuetin Cave* from his backpack and flipped the pages to the photo of the Freedom Tree mural. The painting matched perfectly to this real-life moment of Cecilia reading to the children, all the way down to where Alistair had plonked his small self.

When Siersha had first arrived and touched Amalardh's forearm with her light, he'd felt an inner peace like he'd never known. As he watched Cecilia read to the children, that feeling came rushing back. The Prophecy and all its madness truly was over.

THWACK! Forbillian's freight train of a body sent Amalardh tumbling to the ground. A mixture of "boos" and "yays" rung out. With the fully grown Freedom Tree signaling the end of the

Prophecy, an impromptu party had broken out on the southern headlands and Amalardh had foolishly agreed to take part in a game of football. He grimaced as he rubbed his aching ribs. Having fun certainly came with a lot of pain. "What are you trying to do?" he said to his uncle. "Kill me?"

Grinning, Forbillian pulled him to his feet. "Come on, now. That was just a friendly tap."

"Dadda," called Alistair, as he trotted over.

Amalardh motioned that he was cutting out, then scooped Alistair into his arms.

"You don't have to stop playing. I can take him," Cecilia said.

Amalardh rolled his throbbing shoulder. "Trust me. I'm not stopping because of Alistair."

She smiled. Her glowing beauty entranced him.

"What?" she asked.

He placed his hand to her cheek and in a rare, unguarded moment, kissed her. He wanted the entire world to know how much he loved the mother of his son.

A slender woman with dark, shoulder-length hair walked his way. Her beige tunic made the hairs on his arms bristle. The Terefellians had retired their old clothing. Why did this woman still wear hers? And why did she seem familiar?

"Sister Darna? Oh my gosh! Where have you been?" Saffron said.

Amalardh froze. Sister Darna? The Terefellian assassin? The one he'd—

His eyes dropped to her round belly, that had not been immediately obvious under her loose clothing. His insides tightened as his worst fears were confirmed. Sister Darna had used Amalardh for his seed. Just as Siersha had chosen Cecilia as a vessel to pass her light through to Alistair, Eifa had done the same with Sister Darna. From the look on Forbillian's face as he stepped over, he understood the implications as well.

The Prophecy might be over, but Eifa lived on. And so did Amalardh's infidelity.

His weakened arms lowered Alistair to the ground. He should have insisted on telling Cecilia the truth when he'd had the chance. Now, she'd learn of his painful act in front of family, friends, and half the city.

The Prophecy's final imagery of the Treoir Solas reading to the children under the Freedom Tree flooded his brain. If Cecilia and Amalardh were meant to live happily ever after, why was the last Croilar Tier missing from the painting? As cruel as the Prophecy was in forcing Amalardh and Cecilia together to a point where they couldn't help but fall in love, the signs within the tale had always been clear: *The Croilar Tier protects the Treoir Solas. The Treoir Solas is the Croilar Tier's savior. Together they form the Ceannaire Fis (Visionary Leader).* Amalardh had lived up to his duty—he had protected Cecilia—and Cecilia had fulfilled hers—she'd saved Amalardh, rescued him from his former assassin self. The only purpose of their union was to create Alistair.

His blood drained as reality sank in. Today truly was the Prophecy's end. Cecilia would never forgive his betrayal. From this moment on, the Treoir Solas and last Croilar Tier would forever go their separate ways.

CHAPTER

42

WITH THE FREEDOM Tree miraculously sprouting overnight, the moment Cecilia ached for—the end of the Prophecy—had arrived. On top of which, Amalardh was playing football. He was actually letting others tackle him to the ground. Cecilia had not imagined the day could get any better when he kissed her, open-mouthed and passionately in front of everyone.

Breaking from the embrace, Amalardh immediately tensed at a leggy woman with dark hair and strong features walking their way. Why was this Terefellian woman wearing a tunic? Hadn't they abandoned their old clothing? And why had Amalardh stiffened like a guard dog?

When Saffron referred to the stranger as Sister Darna, Cecilia did a double take. The woman's rosy complexion and shoulder-length locks didn't align with the short-haired, sullen-faced Wrethun Lof Cecilia had unwittingly sent after Amalardh. The sudden arrival of a Croilar Tier hunter would explain Amalardh's apprehension.

Her gaze dropped to Sister Darna's belly. Goodness. The woman looked quite pregnant.

Stepping up beside Amalardh, Forbillian folded his arms across his chest. "You've got nerve showing up here," he said to Darna.

Why was he being so harsh? From what Cecilia had learned, all Darna had done was steal a false map to the Forbidden Pool and Oisin's pretend Croilar Tier knife.

She eyed Forbillian and Amalardh. Had something else happened that Cecilia didn't know about?

Clutching the football, Oisin ran over. He gaped at Darna's belly, then flung the ball at Amalardh's feet. "You're a liar. You promised you wouldn't mess things up," he yelled and sped off.

What was going on? Why was Oisin mad? How had Amalardh messed up?

Instead of being confused by Oisin's overt display, Amalardh hung his head.

Cecilia caught sight of Sister Darna's thickened palms and her belly flip-flopped. Her world slowed as images of Rabbie's grazed upper torso melted with similar marks she'd seen on Amalardh. Was an intimate encounter with Sister Darna the "past act" Amalardh had wanted to confess? She glared at him. "Tell me it's not true."

His expression crumbled. "Cecilia—"

His inability to deny her supposition provided her answer.

Her blood chilled as her breath shortened. When Cecilia had suggested they leave their past behind, she hadn't expected Amalardh's history included infidelity. How could the man she loved betray her in such a hurtful way? And with a Terefellian, no less. The same people who'd brought horrific destruction to humanity and danger to their son.

Amalardh reached for her.

She batted his hand away. "Don't touch me."

In his eyes, she saw his world die.

Her heart broke for the love they would never have again.

Fighting back tears, she grabbed Alistair and ran.

Marion and Saffron quickly caught up.

Not wanting to go home, Cecilia went to Tomkin's house. He'd been a trusted confidant from the moment they'd met and would know not to hound her with a bunch of questions until she was ready to talk. Handing Alistair to him, she dashed into his bedroom, flopped on his bed, and cried. The ache in her heart hurt worse than anything she'd felt before. How could this be happening? After everything she'd been through, how could her world go from perfect to an absolute mess? She would never recover from this. Ever.

A knock came at the door and Saffron's head poked in. "Can I come in?"

Cecilia nodded.

Swinging the door open, Saffron revealed Wyndom standing at her side.

What was he doing here?

"My dad has something to tell you that I think you need to hear."

What could Wyndom possibly have to say at a time like this?

"It involves Sister Darna," Saffron added.

Sister Darna? Trusting Saffron's judgement, Cecilia wiped her wet cheeks, pulled herself into a seated position, and nodded her approval.

Wyndom's hands wrung nervously as he took a seat on a wooden chair by the bed.

Stepping back into the hallway, Saffron started to close the door.

"You're not staying?" Cecilia asked.

"It's better if you have privacy. I'll be out here if you need me."

Cecilia tensed at the odd secrecy. What had these Terefellians been up to?

Wyndom cleared his throat. "First of all, I'd like to say that I am saddened and devastated for you. I can't imagine the shock Sister Darna's arrival must have caused."

He rubbed the back of his neck. "So, where do I start? You know that all Terefellians were connected, bonded together, correct?"

"I only know a little about that," Cecilia replied.

He nodded and explained a crazy notion of this "connectivity" allowing him not only to see, hear, and smell what other Terefellians or Wirador Wosrah sensed, but also to control them.

"What do you mean 'control?'" Cecilia asked.

"Imagine, if you will, a body—yours, mine . . . Sister Darna's—as one of those vehicles that drove you to Terefellia. Instead of you sitting at the controlling seat of your own vehicle, someone else was."

Cecilia didn't like where this conversation headed.

"You must know that our queen—" Catching himself, Wyndom apologized and confessed to needing a little more time to get used to referring to the Terefellian queen by her appropriate names of Eifa or the Dark Goddess. "Eifa was a jealous goddess," he said, "and quite resentful of Siersha passing her light onto a child, your child, so she set her mind to mothering a baby of her own. Sadly, for you, she chose Amalardh as her baby's father."

Cecilia rubbed her crawling skin. Of course Eifa would be behind this mess.

"Sister Darna is . . . was Terefellia's best assassin. She'd never failed an order until Rudella, in the role of the Maddowshin, assigned her as the vessel for Eifa's child.

"If Darna's job was to bear Amalardh's child, how exactly did she fail?" Cecilia asked. "Because the belly I saw screams success."

Wyndom scratched the back of his head. "Sister Darna didn't possess the necessary attraction or finesse to complete her order. Because of this, Rudella—the Maddowshin—relegated Darna to the backseat, so to speak, while someone else drove."

"Are you saying another individual was in control of Sister Darna when she was with Amalardh?"

"Yes. Pretty much."

"Who?"

Her jaw slackened at his drawn expression. Wyndom couldn't possibly be suggesting that he . . . and Amalardh . . .? The moment literally rendered her speechless.

"Please, you must not hold this against Amalardh," Wyndom said. "I've seen you together. You belong with each other more than the sea and the sand, the sun and the moon, thunder and lightning. You can't blame Amalardh. What happened was not his fault."

Cecilia shook her head at him. The nerve of this guy. "You are asking me to absolve Amalardh because the spirit in the body he desired was a man? I don't think so. Either way, he was attracted to Darna's flesh. That's what he wanted, and that's what his weakness brought him to."

"You are wrong. I would've thought you of all people understood that the last thing Amalardh desires is flesh for the pure sake of pleasure."

Deep in her heart, Cecilia knew Wyndom was right, but since those recesses were plugged with hurt and betrayal, she couldn't get to them right at this moment.

"I have few talents in this world," Wyndom said, "but the ones I do have serve me well. I can spot people's weaknesses and strengths, and I can work either to my advantage. I painted a picture of a soul desperate for human contact." He turned his hands palm up. "The skin on these was once so thick and sharp it tore through Saffron's soft, baby skin. In Terefellia, we never understood how important these are"—he emphasized his hands—"to human connection. You look at someone like me through Amalardh's eyes and empathy is thin at best. But if you replace this image with a young woman, an assassin no less, weeping over the lost relationship with a child she became too afraid to touch because of these, then maybe you can start to understand. Amalardh didn't reach out to her flesh. He reached out to her soul. If he could offer this damaged assassin some hope, then maybe there was some hope for him. Maybe his own scars wouldn't define him for life. Now, combine all that with the fact that over the past year, the woman he truly loved had been growing further and further away . . ."

Cecilia's hands went clammy. How could Wyndom have such intimate knowledge about her and Amalardh's relationship?

"I know what you are thinking," he said. "Your friends, Analise and Noah, did not betray your trust. Eifa absorbed their knowledge."

Of all the despicable things Eifa could do, she'd used Analise and Noah's insight into Cecilia and Amalardh's relationship not only to get a child but to drive an emotional stake through Cecilia's heart.

"I manipulated Amalardh, in that I knew the best way to approach him. Beyond that, everything I told him was the truth. If you cannot find the strength or courage to forgive him, maybe this will help. I'm not ashamed to admit that I developed a love, or at the very least, a deep infatuation with him. He showed me a side of humanity I never knew existed. In Terefellia, we don't make intimate love, we—"

"Yes. I know the word," Cecilia said, cutting him off. She'd learned the harsh term when Senator Nuka had described a Soldier's interaction with his Night Wife.

"I was connected to over three hundred people, yet I'd never felt more alone in my life," Wyndom said. "The people who knew me best—Saffron and Rudella—despised me and they'd had every right to. I didn't know what it was to speak from the heart until I started talking to Amalardh about my daughter. He sat there and actively listened. He didn't judge. If anything, he seemed to understand my pain. Pain that I'd denied even existed. I have a relationship with my daughter because talking to Amalardh made me realize how much I loved her." He exhaled a resigned breath. "If Amalardh's sole interest was simply to bed Darna's body, he could've at any point. Most men don't care to listen to emotional ramblings."

As Cecilia imagined Amalardh trapped miles away from the woman he'd grown apart from, in the freezing snow, with a warm, curvy body belonging to a doe-eyed assassin, who tugged at his compassion, understanding as to how he could have faltered seeped in.

She beat her thigh with her fist. How dare her logical brain paint a rational excuse for Amalardh's betrayal. No matter what, he still should've resisted. He shouldn't have so much as even kissed—

Her thought cut short.

If she'd been trapped miles away with Gildas when she'd kissed him, would she have stopped at that kiss? She side-glanced at Wyndom. "Clearly, you were too irresistible," she said in jest.

He smirked at the comment. "I know you're hurt and angry, and you should be. But when you weigh up what Amalardh did, you need to consider this. I had devoted my entire life to pleasing Eifa. Had I not experienced what I had with Amalardh, I would never have defied her order to kill your son."

Cecilia flopped back against the headboard. She may have won the battle, but the Dark Goddess had won the war. The instant Cecilia and Amalardh found peace, Eifa's blackness tore them apart. Eifa had discovered Amalardh's weakness—his struggle to understand his own humanity—and used it against him.

In time, maybe Cecilia could forgive Amalardh. But right now, a more pressing matter had arisen. If Eifa truly had passed her darkness on to Darna's child, then mother and baby would be in danger. Some members of the council might suggest killing the seedling before the poisonous vine had time to grow. Cecilia couldn't let that happen. Flinging herself out of bed, she opened the bedroom door, where she found Rabbie standing with Saffron.

"Where's Darna?" she asked.

"She's gone," Rabbie replied.

"Gone where?"

He shrugged. "When you ran off, she left."

"And you let her go?"

"Under the circumstances, I didn't imagine you wanted her to stay."

"Take me to that motor bike of yours."

Cecilia clung to Rabbie's waist as he and Saffron zipped through the streets of Vitus on their trail bikes. Exiting the Great Gates, they turned south. In the distance, Sister Darna's lonely figure marched in the direction of Terefellia.

The bikes pulled to a stop and Cecilia climbed off. "Darna. We need to—"

Side-stepping her, Darna kept walking.

Cecilia followed. "Darna, wait."

"This was a mistake," Darna said, maintaining her brisk pace. "I shouldn't have come."

"Why did you?"

She stopped and wiped wisps of hair from her sweaty brow. "Because of you. And Amalardh. But not him for the reasons you think." Her tough veneer crumbled. "I know what grows inside me. I have stood on edges of cliffs, held knives to my wrists, but I couldn't do it. Or maybe Eifa wouldn't let me. I don't know. I felt her connection until a couple of months ago, when she disappeared. A fiery storm came, like the world was about to end. I hoped it would. And then, a bright light filled the sky, and the world righted itself. In that moment, I knew the one we'd called the false goddess had triumphed. Amalardh had fought for that goddess. And all I could think was, if Amalardh was a good man, his people must be good, too. The safest place for my baby would be among people filled with Siersha's light. I thought you, the Treoir Solas, could protect her. But it was a silly dream. So now, I go where I belong. If I have to, I will lock my baby and myself in our temple, but I will not let anyone kill her."

Eifa had played her cards well. As much as Cecilia preferred to keep the woman who'd been intimate with Amalardh far from Vitus, sending Darna away would be exactly what the Dark Goddess had planned. Growing up in a desolate place like Terefellia, alone, embittered, and without a father, Darna's child would be certain to evolve into a dark figure bent on revenge.

"I will keep your baby safe, but I will not take her from you," Cecilia said. "You are coming back to Vitus with me."

Darna's expression held relief as she nodded her acceptance of Cecilia's request.

Thanking Rabbie and Saffron for their help, Cecilia waved them off. She would return on foot with Darna. As they strolled the grassy headland, Cecilia eased into a conversation about growing up in Plockton and revealed all she'd gone through, from meeting Amalardh through to her role as the Caladium—the Poison Flower that killed Eifa.

Much like Amalardh, Darna was less forthcoming about her life. With enough prodding, Cecilia learned that unlike Brothers Atlas and Skylark, who actively sought the role of a Croilar Tier hunter, Darna trained as an elite Wrethun Lof simply because her society told her that was what she was good at. "I've always had impeccable aim and excelled at hand-to-hand combat," she said. "From the day of my birth, my path was set, and I didn't question it. Wrethun Lof are revered in Terefellia. I became what I'd always thought I should be." From the regret on her face, the reality of what she'd become seemed to have sunk in.

"Wyndom said you didn't feel attracted to Amalardh. What did he mean?" Cecilia asked.

The corner of Darna's mouth pulled into a small smirk. "I believe what Brother Wyndom was trying to convey was that I do not care for the company of men. I prefer a curvier body."

Oh. Okay. Cecilia understood.

"When Brother Wyndom told me I couldn't just take what I needed, that I had to connect emotionally with my target, I got angry. Terefellians don't do emotion, especially Wrethun Lof. Why not the fat one? I asked. He was an uncle. Blood is blood, and he already despised me, which was perfect. We could've had wild, angry sex, after which I could've slit his throat." In response to Cecilia's concerned look, Darna whiffled her hands. "But that was the old me. I don't—I won't slit any more throats."

Her expression grew reflective. "Our queen—I mean, Eifa— was adamant that only Amalardh could be her child's father. At the time, I didn't understand why, but now, I see . . . she chose him to hurt you."

And Eifa had succeeded.

"What I don't understand is why Sister Rudella, in her role as the Maddowshin, sent me," Darna said. "We had three female

Wrethun Lof in Terefellia. Sisters Glynis and Eveline love men, love seduction. Why not send them?"

Cecilia knew why. Rudella had intentionally sent Darna on the mission because she knew Darna would struggle with her orders, giving the Maddowshin reason to let Wyndom take control. Rudella needed Wyndom to bond with Amalardh so when the time came, the Terefellian leader would have doubts when ordered to kill the Croilar Tier's son. She rubbed her brow with the heel of her hand. How could she possibly stay mad at Amalardh for his involvement in an act which, however indirectly, had prevented Alistair's death?

If Rudella was working with Siersha, then the Goddess had known that Amalardh (the last Croilar Tier) would have to betray Cecilia (the Treoir Solas) in order to ensure Alistair's (the Ceannaire Fis's) survival. Cecilia could deal with all the death, lies, and betrayal if it meant the madness with Eifa would be over. Forever. But the Dark Goddess was slowly brewing in Darna's belly. Everything Cecilia, Amalardh, and her people had gone through had been for nothing.

Their journey ended at the footsteps of Ida and Saffron's house. "This is where you'll be staying," Cecilia said. Who better to keep a close eye on the bearer of Eifa's darkness than a Shadow Croilar Tier and a young Terefellian who, in her own right, was as skilled as any Croilar Tier or Wrethun Lof?

Drained from her talk with Darna, Cecilia lumbered home. Her world was worse now than it had ever been. Through his slightly ajar bedroom door, she spotted Oisin lying face down on his bed. "Can I come in?" she asked. Taking his silence as a yes, she stepped over to him.

"I'm sick of this," he said.

"So am I," she replied.

"I want this day to go away and never happen. I want things to go back to how they were."

More than anything, so did Cecilia.

"I hate him for what he did."

Cecilia's heart panged. If Oisin was old enough to figure out what had happened between Amalardh and Darna, he was old enough to know that the Goddess of Light had not only known their union would happen, but had set the puzzle pieces in such a way that Amalardh's betrayal would be assured. After explaining everything to Oisin, his saddened expression tore through her.

"She won, didn't she?" he said. He was talking about Eifa.

The Dark Goddess most certainly had. Not only did her essence continue to live on earth, she'd succeeded in ripping Cecilia's world apart.

"Will you ever forgive Amalardh?" Oisin asked.

Cecilia didn't know. All she knew was that she was tired of fighting. She lay down next to him. "Darna seems to think her baby will be safest here, growing up under the protection of the last Croilar Tier and Treoir Solas. What life could we possibly offer that child if we can't even figure out our own?"

"But you will figure it out, right? I mean, you have to."

She stared at the faint lines mottling the high ceiling above and a deep resolve brewed from within. Oisin was right. Cecilia *had* to figure things out, and not just for her and Amalardh's sake. She couldn't let Eifa have everything and more. While she might not be able to do anything about the Dark Goddess's continued existence in the human realm, Cecilia could fight back against Eifa's attempt to destroy her and Amalardh's love.

After checking his workroom, Cecilia found Amalardh in the second place she expected—standing at the southern end of the battlement, staring out at the distant horizon. As she walked up next to him, his head lowered. Her intent had been to talk to him, but now that she was here, she didn't know what to say.

Although the silence was awkward, the cool sea breeze offered comfort.

"If you had to do it all again, would you have left with him?" Amalardh asked.

Cecilia sucked on her lower lip. He didn't seem willing—or maybe capable—of saying Gildas's name, and neither did she. "I'd only said I should've left with him to hurt you," she uttered.

"It worked," he said, keeping his focus forward.

It had? Amalardh had seemed impervious to her harsh words.

He glanced at her and his eyes held sorrow. "The night he left, I saw you kiss him."

Cecilia's eyes went wide. Amalardh had seen the kiss? Heat from her neck rose to her cheeks. The encounter had not been a simple peck. It had been open-mouthed and filled with regret.

"I am not telling you this to make you feel guilty or to lessen my betrayal," Amalardh said. "No matter what I do, I will always ruin you and Alistair. Maybe the best place for you both is away from this city. Away from me. And with someone who would never falter in his loyalty to you."

Cecilia's mouth went dry. After everything that had happened, the thought of leaving Vitus—leaving Amalardh—left her cold. She could forgive him for what he'd done, but they'd never be able to move forward if he couldn't forgive himself. "Remember when we left the Ground People and Brassal handed you a black and a white chess piece? You told me that Brassal had said, 'Regardless of your beliefs, a *game* has begun.'" She emphasized the word "game." "That's what all this has been. One big, painful, celestial competition. We've all been pawns, pieces on a board, our moves either predetermined or set up in such a way that we had no choice other than to slide in a particular direction."

His confusion morphed to intrigue. If there was one thing Amalardh understood, and even appreciated, it was a challenging mental match. Beyond all the pain, anger, and hurt Siersha's "plan" had caused, the one person who wouldn't be mad at her attempt to do what she'd done would be Amalardh. If anything, the Goddess's endeavor to outmaneuver the Dark Goddess would impress him.

Leaning up against the battlement wall, Cecilia told him everything. If hearing that Wyndom, and not Darna, was the broken soul who'd tantalized his flesh had any effect on him, Amalardh didn't show it. "I want to be mad at you," she said, "but how can I? If you hadn't faltered in your loyalty, Alistair would be dead." She cuddled her arms across her chest. "Besides, I'm not exactly blameless for pushing you away."

He hugged her tight, as though his life depended upon it. "I'm sorry that I hurt you," he whispered.

Her cheek felt wet.

Was the water from Amalardh's tears or her own?

"I'm sorry, too," she said.

CHAPTER

43

CECILIA LOUNGED UNDER the Freedom Tree, her head resting on Amalardh's lap as she watched Alistair play catch with Darna and Oisin. Although the sound of Alistair's happy squeals filled her with joy, her belly swirled. Because Eifa's child grew inside Darna, the future remained uncertain.

Sitting cross-legged next to her was Brassal. "Alistair's light burns stronger every day," he said.

After Cecilia had woken from her battle with Eifa, Brassal had whispered with concern that he could no longer see Siersha's light within her. Cecilia had suspected as much. The warmth she'd felt from the moment she'd met the Goddess was gone. Cecilia's job was officially over. Now, Alistair bore the responsibility of carrying Siersha's light.

Brassal's spine straightened. "Alistair? Where is he?"

Cecilia tilted her head at him. "He's fine. He's just over there with Darna. He's being adorable and placing his little hands on her belly."

"His light. It's gone," Brassal said.

The hairs on Cecilia's arms stood on end.

Just as when Siersha ferried Esme's soul away, the world stilled.

"Amalardh? Brassal?" Cecilia said, to rouse a response. But along with Oisin, Darna, and Alistair, they remained in a frozen moment.

The sky darkened. What was happening?

The Freedom Tree's red blossoms glowed white. Like tiny butterflies, the lights fluttered into a cluster, forming . . . *Siersha!*

"What are you doing here?" Cecilia asked.

The Goddess's light glowed. "You doubted my gameplay, and after all that I put you through, you have every right to do so. I am here to show you my last move."

Siersha's celestial game wasn't over?

"Eifa's greatest weakness was insisting the souls she possessed loved her blindly. She thought she knew my game. She believed she was always one step ahead. But what she couldn't plan for was the one thing she will never understand: the human spirit. To her, a person is nothing but a possession. To me, humans are the joy that make life worth creating."

She sat down next to Cecilia.

"With her child securely implanted in Sister Darna's belly, Eifa thought her bases were covered. If she won, she would have the glory of a child. If she lost, her child's birth would return her foothold on earth. Her arrogance led her to believe that Wyndom would do his job. When he disobeyed his order to kill Alistair, which would've destroyed the last of my light, she still believed she had another move. She knew you would protect her child, even at the cost of allowing her darkness back on earth. She knew you wouldn't allow the slaying of an innocent."

"And Eifa was right," Cecilia said. "Her darkness remains and there's nothing I can do about it. No matter the love we pour on Eifa's child, we can never remove her essence. We are not talking about a case like Amalardh, where I lightened his blackened heart. Eifa is inside Darna's child. And there she will stay. If your 'final move' involves harming an unborn baby, I will not let that happen."

"Surely by now you know and trust I only have the power— and desire—to create life, not take it," Siersha said. "The original Croilar Tier who painted the cave where you and Amalardh first came upon the Prophecy inscribed the words with an ancient text, the straight lines of which were easier to carve in stone. A misinterpretation of a stroke can change an entire meaning of a word. Although Alistair will become a great leader, the Ceannaire Fis is not the Visionary Leader, but the Visionary Light. You thought I'd placed my glow in him to help his ancestral line resist Eifa's dark pull for generations to come, but your children and your children's children already possess the means to rebuff Eifa's darkness. Your people have been doing so for centuries."

"Then why is Alistair carrying your light?" Cecilia asked.

"For my final move."

Cecilia followed the Goddess's nod to Alistair, whose darkened outline remained in the frozen moment of placing his hands on Darna's belly. Within his silhouetted frame shone a bright light. Was that the same glow Brassal had seen?

She focused in on Darna's belly and the hairs on her arms stood on end. A blackened splotch in the center had to represent Eifa's darkness.

The glow inside Alistair pulsed and floated out from his chest, along his arms, and into Darna's belly, where it blended with the dark splotch and disappeared.

Cecilia blinked at Siersha. "This entire time, the purpose of Alistair's light was to nullify Eifa's darkness?"

The Goddess nodded. "Eifa is gone from the human realm and she will never return. Because of what I put you and Amalardh through, I was able to solve my conflict with my own inner darkness. I now realize, the balance of power between good and evil is fluid. A soul can call on its dark side to summon the strength to drive a sword through an evil heart, but doing so does not hand over absolute power to Eifa. By watching you and Amalardh, I learned no matter how much you both called on your dark sides to help you survive the awful situations I put you in, you both always came out better, stronger, and more in love than before."

Siersha—a goddess no less—considered Cecilia a role model? "I am only the way I am because I choose to live in your light. My actions are only a reflection of yours."

Siersha smiled. "You are too modest. I cannot take praise for what you've taught me. Without you, I wouldn't have learned my full potential. Had I known earlier what I know now, this game I forced you to play wouldn't have needed to happen."

Cecilia tilted her head at the Goddess. "What do you mean, 'full potential?' Are you saying you have more power than you realized?"

"Much, much more. The relationship I have with my dark self explains the very nature of my strength. In the absence of good, there can be no evil, for there can be nothing at all."

Cecilia first heard this phrase two years ago from Brassal. He explained that goodness is life and when all goodness is gone, there is only death.

"I can exist without Eifa, but she cannot exist without me," Siersha said. "Her inability to survive on her own can only mean one thing—I am stronger than her."

Tingles shot across Cecilia's skin as the reality of Siersha's words sank in. Being good was hard. Being bad was easy. By its very nature, goodness had to be a more powerful force.

"I am sorry it took so much pain and suffering for me to understand my own strength," Siersha said. "I will see you again, but not for many years."

A bright flash forced Cecilia to bury her face in the crook of her arm. When the light settled, she looked around. The sky was blue, and the world had returned to its normal pace.

"Is everything okay?" Amalardh asked.

She stared at him and her love flowed. "Everything is better than okay," she said. Her mouth twisted. "There is one problem, though."

Concern gripped him. "What is it?"

Smiling wryly, she smacked his knee. "Tag. You're it." She sprang to her feet and bolted. "Quick!" she called to the others. "We've got to run!"

Alistair squealed as his little legs got moving.

Oisin dashed off with him.

Laughing, Darna stepped aside and gestured that she wanted no part of the madness.

Cecilia had covered less than twenty feet before Amalardh scooped her up in his arms.

"You can run, but you can never escape," he said.

"I don't want to escape," she replied.

Lowering her, Amalardh went to kiss her when Oisin and Alistair barreled into him, knocking him to the ground. Cecilia doubled over with laughter. Although she trusted Siersha could keep Eifa under control, in the event the Dark Goddess found a crack to slither her scaley self through, Cecilia held no fear. If she and Amalardh could get through what they just had, they could get through anything.

ACKNOWLEDGEMENTS

329

This journey would not have been possible without the tireless love, support, and encouragement of my wonderful husband, Kurt Oldman. Thank you to my editor, Jennifer Arena, for helping me make my story the best it could possibly be. Thank you to Rosemary Lawton for your keen, grammatical eye. Thank you to my design team: Matthew R. Hinshaw for your creativity with the map, Ivan Cakic for your brilliant cover design, and Phillip Gessert for your patience and attention to detail with the interior. Thank you to my readers. Your requests for more inspired my jumping back into Cecilia's world and creating her new adventure. And to all my friends and family who stood with me, supporting this epic exploit—Thank You!

Sandra is an Award-Winning author, who grew up in Sydney, Australia. She graduated from the University of Sydney with a BA in Applied Science and has an MBA from La Sierra University, Los Angeles. She enjoys skiing in winter, snorkeling in summer, and hiking whenever she can.